THE QUESTING ROAD

BOOKS BY LYN McCONCHIE

Beast Master Novels (with Andre Norton)
Beast Master's Ark
Beast Master's Circus
Beast Master's Quest

Witch World Novels (with Andre Norton)
The Duke's Ballad
The Key of the Keplian
Ciara's Song
Silver May Tarnish
Secrets of the Witch World (omnibus)

South of Rio Chama
Summer of Dreaming

Writing as Elizabeth Underwood/Lyn McConchie
Farming Daze
Daze on the Land
Tiger Daze
Daze in the Country
Rural Daze and (K)nights

THE
QUESTING
ROAD

Lyn McConchie

A TOM DOHERTY ASSOCIATES BOOK
NEW YORK

THE QUESTING ROAD

Copyright © 2010 by Lyn McConchie

Edited by James Frenkel

Book design by Ellen Cipriano

A Tor Book
Published by Tom Doherty Associates, LLC
175 Fifth Avenue
New York, NY 10010

www.tor-forge.com

Tor® is a registered trademark of Tom Doherty Associates, LLC.

ISBN 978-0-7653-2211-1

First Edition: August 2010

Printed in the United States of America

0 9 8 7 6 5 4 3 2 1

To Charles Brown, who always encouraged me and who said I should do this—now I have. I'm just really sad that it was a little too late for you to see it.

To all the *Locus* gang, whose magazine told me where to sell my first stories twenty years ago and who keep all of us in the business up to date—there's no one like you guys.

And to my agent, Jack Byrne, a gentleman and a scholar.

ACKNOWLEDGMENTS

Thanks to Jim Frenkel, who takes a chunk of mineral and polishes it until it shines. And to Terry McGarry, who had the job of chasing my typos, etc., thanks, you did a great job.

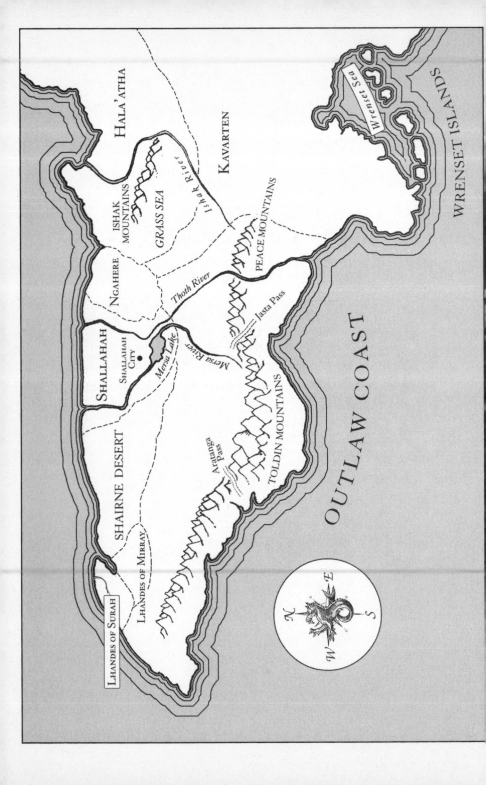

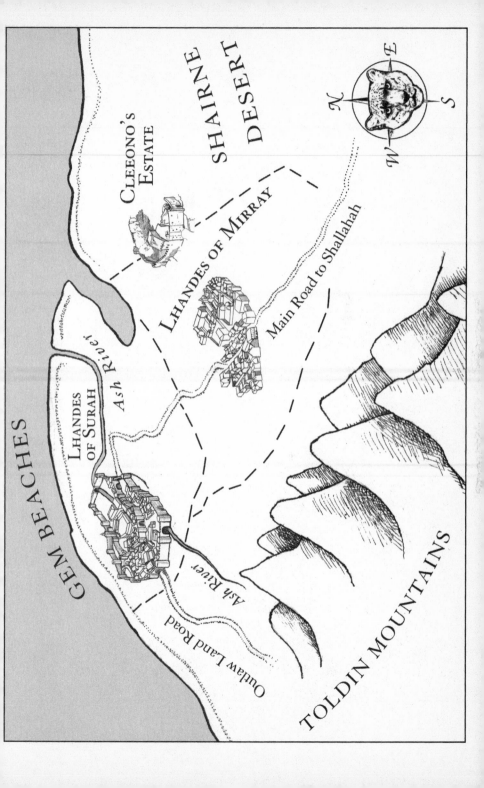

THE QUESTING ROAD

IN THE BEGINNING

On a world that was one of a number in an alternate time stream, in a country known to its people as Khaddishar, there was a sudden shimmering in the air. It was late morning at the end of spring when a portal opened between two worlds. Two men came through, dressed in clothing that was oddly hard to look at directly, riding nondescript bay horses. Neither of the riders was memorable; a watcher might have thought that all four had been chosen to be unnoticeable—as they had been. One of the men began to mutter in a rhythmic cadence. The shimmer of the portal vanished. It was still there, but no longer to be seen. Nor—surprisingly—were the men and their mounts.

The four, men and horses, headed at a steady walk toward a distant grazing area in silence and invisible, save for hoofprints that briefly showed in the flattened grass before it regained position. Everything had fallen silent on their arrival, small birds and the ubiquitous, chirruping feden, the singing locusts of the area. Birds and insects may have lesser intelligence, but more than those who consider themselves to be intelligent beings, they know when to be silent, when to fear what comes among them. Not until long after the grass had stood upright again did the first feden begin to sing once more.

On that grazing area to which two men rode, the felinoid Tarians gossiped, checked the beasts of their herds, and Chylo and Razaia, the Tarian leader and his mate, considered a forthcoming party with friends to celebrate the end of spring and the start of summer.

"Kyrryl says that it should be a good year. The weather looks as if it will clear for summer-born."

Chylo, the Tarian addressed, grinned, showing the long eyeteeth with which they took blood from their herd beasts. "That's well. Winter was too wet for my liking." He preened, smoothing down silver-gold fur and fluffing up the luxuriant mane that flowed over his shoulders, while he admired his mate, whose fur was wholly golden, something of a rarity among their people.

On the flat ground some distance away their tarilings played. Tayio, the younger, his emotions an uncontrolled aura about him, was male. His teeth had not yet developed and he drank only milk, but his sire regarded him with pride. Tela, the girl, was four seasons older and already drank the blood that was her birthright. Then too, precocious for her seven seasons, she also mind-sent with surprising range and clarity and a focus that she was learning to control so that only the one she spoke to heard her sending. Their silver-gold fur shone with health and good food.

Her sire relaxed, watching them play. He was, he considered, the most fortunate of his people: he had a beautiful mate, he had healthy, intelligent, and talented children, and his family had friends, good friends, among the humans. The lands of his clan abutted those of the human lord and lady, Yoros and Kyrryl. In a tenday's time, the Tarians would celebrate the summer-born with them.

Below, Tayio wandered off toward the stream. He could not have said what drew him, but there seemed to be flashes of color, and a faint sound of trilling on the wind. He reached out with his mind and touched nothing, but the flashes and trilling continued. He fell to all fours now and again to negotiate the rougher ground as he followed them, then remembered and walked upright.

"Tarians are people, not beasts," his sire always told him. "It is the mark of a Tarian to walk erect once he is past his second year."

Tayio climbed a bank and tumbled down the other side, giggling as he slid on the taller grass, and walked off down the winding gully, treading carefully beside the small trickle of water. The colored lights now seemed clearer, more intriguing. Twice he slowed, looking back. Perhaps he should return? But the lights came brighter, flickering and enchanting, the trilling sound enticed, and he followed.

He rounded a bend where the gully had dropped until the bank was above head height. Even standing upright, three-year-old Tayio was only two and a half feet in height, and where an adult Tarian might have been more cautious, for the tariling, being out of sight of the surrounding ground was not alarming. Something pricked his neck sharply and he slapped at it. He felt—he felt—blurred! Everything about him seemed to be fading, yet he felt no fear, only a spreading warmth that . . . Blackness enfolded him and he slipped into it.

*T*he voice that spoke was toneless. His companion dismounted and scooped up the small tariling as he listened.

"Keep him unconscious. The master said that his kind communicates by mind and that this young one has no control over the ability. If he wakes, he calls for help and his cries will be mind-heard over many miles."

"Too much of the yasin may be dangerous," his companion remarked as he remounted, passing the unconscious tariling to his leader.

"Only to his sanity." The comment was casual. "He'll have no need of that anyhow. And once we get him back to the master he will spell this creature into silence and compliance until we have need of his . . . gifts."

His companion laughed, a short, harsh, savage bark that held no real amusement. "Aye, power and blood, and from another world. That will force open the portal and we'll be avenged."

The voice that answered was no longer toneless; it held a crooning satisfaction. "Yes, vengeance! We shall repay them in blood and death for all that we lost twenty years ago to that king who thought that the law should not apply to him. Let he and his lose and weep the way that we did. Let them die, knowing who sent death, and I shall dance with joy on that day. So long it has taken us to learn all we needed to know. But the master learned, found and taught us, and our time is now, finally, at hand."

At first they walked downstream, the water rippling, slowly smoothing over the marks of hooves so that in an hour or two they would not show, even to a skilled tracker. When the stream turned away from their intended direction they allowed their mounts to climb up from the gully to the grasslands.

In the arms of the leader Tayio was curled in a padded bag with shoulder straps. In that position he was no larger than a good armful, and asleep as he was, he would cause them no trouble. He was beautiful in his silver-gold fur, and a human would have called him "adorable," since he resembled a large cat with a stub of fluffy tail that curled like a chrysanthemum in pale fur. But those who had taken him saw him only as the key to their desire, and no more than any other key would they consider Tayio to be something with rights or a mind of his own.

The tall spring grass was pressed down under two sets of hooves and sprang up again slowly behind them, The ridden mounts returned in silence and near invisibility the way they had come. Some hours later a shimmer in the air showed briefly where a portal opened; then it was gone, as were the riders—and a small, sleeping, tariling.

*N*o one noticed that Tayio had disappeared until a quarter of a day had passed. It was midafternoon when Razaia looked about her.

She called, not anxious at first, "Tela, where's your brother?"

"I don't know. He was playing near the stream."

Two Tarians strolled that way to find—no tariling. At first they were unworried. Tarilings wandered, it was a fact of life, and one who was three years old and curious could wander far in a quarter day. But there were no predators here, and even had there been, Tayio would have projected his fear the moment he saw danger. That he had not done so indicated he was safe. If he was lost he'd begin projecting the moment he was hungry, and then they could guide him back.

That comfortable assumption was discarded hours later when by then he would have been ravenous, and no one had received the slightest mind-call from him. By evening Razaia and Chylo had arrived, distraught, at their friends' keep.

Razaia was weeping. "He must be dead, or why wouldn't he be calling us?"

Yoros shook his head. "No, how would he die so quickly that he wouldn't have time to send his fear or pain? And if he had been killed surely we'd have found the body."

"Then what? How?" Chylo's lips curled back in a snarl.

Kyrryl entered the room in time to hear that. "I don't know, but have you the bit of his fur that I asked for?"

"Yes." Chylo passed her the wisp of silver-gold fur. "What will you do with it?"

"Use a prism to make a guide, but it'll take time."

"And what can we do while you do that?" Razaia begged. "We need to search further. Tayio could just be hidden somewhere we haven't looked. He could be unconscious."

"Yes, he could be," Kyrryl agreed, "so have your people spread out and search. Start from where he was last seen. See if your best trackers and scent hunters can find anything."

"What will you do?"

"Work on a seeking prism. If I can tune it to Tayio using the fur you brought me I may be able to find him. But it takes time to do that, Razaia, maybe a full day. I'm not strong in the gift, and I have to lay on the prism the spells and power one layer at a time. I'll do my best to hurry but it could even take longer than I've said. Go and search. You may find Tayio before I can tune the prism. If not then what I can do may be of real use."

Kyrryl watched the Tarians leave her keep and sighed, turning to her husband. "I'm worried. It's possible that Tayio hurt himself in a fall, something that happened so fast he had no time to mind-call."

"But you don't think it likely?" Yoros said shrewdly.

"No, I have no idea what could have happened, but I have a feeling that it might be something else, something stranger." She shrugged. "We'll find out. I'll start tuning the prism while you pack for a ride. If this trail takes us any distance it's best that we be ready even if we end up not needing to go. Razaia and Chylo have been our friends since we were all young."

"I'll tell Ashara to come with us. She is strong and loves Razaia and Chylo. I know she'll want to help. And she can ride and fight."

"She's seventeen." Kyrryl was doubtful.

"She's sensible, she's ridden and fought at need this past year. Let her come."

Kyrryl nodded and went to find the prism. Tuning that was going to take time, hard work, and all her concentration. She could leave it to Yoros to pack. Their country, Khaddishar, was large, composed mainly of grassy plains, and with the sometimes-warring tribes of Tarian and humans—even if the latter were several days' ride away—she and her husband were used to traveling long distances on horseback to trade . . . or to fight if they had to.

A thought occurred to her then: Could it have been another clan that had stolen the tariling? Kyrryl shook her head; she didn't think it likely. Theft was not Tarian custom—although now and again it happened between humans—and to reach Razaia and Chylo and their clan unfamiliar humans would have had to pass through the lands of at least one other clan, and for what profit? Tarian clans had their own beasts (and any kidnapper trying to vanish with an entire herd of those would be really obvious).

The Tarians created beautiful crafts for themselves, but while a clan might contribute toward a large collection of horse gear, decorated tents, jewelry, and clothing items for a ransom, all of it would be known as having been created by that clan. Word of such a ransom would travel across the Khaddishar grasslands with the speed of a lightning strike. No human would be able to sell such a big collection of clan property without searching questions being asked by those who traded for them. No, she did not think that Tayio had been stolen for a ransom, but why else would he have been taken?

She chose her prism carefully and hooked it to a strong neck chain. If the tariling was not found, there would be a place for her and this glittering thing. Kyrryl set to work, while on the grazing lands, Tarian searchers circled out wider and wider from the clan camp. Most of them, including Razaia and Chylo, were far away when the prism was at last tuned and three riders set out to follow the guiding spot of light that circled and glowed within the facets.

1

At dawn they came through the portal, although as yet they did not realize what they had done. An onlooker would have seen three people materialize, not present one heartbeat, then there and riding steadily on down the slope. They were led by a man in his mid-thirties, lean and tall, with a swordsman's muscular arms and a well-worn sword hilt jutting across one hip. He had a shock of black hair, keen hazel eyes, and a long white scar down the left side of his face. His mount was a dun gelding, Roman-nosed and wicked of eye.

A pace behind came a woman, of similar age, with the same black hair, longer and confined by a ribbon. Her brown eyes held a twinkle, but the hilt of her slightly shorter, lighter sword was also well worn, and the unstrung bow she carried showed signs of long use. The mount she rode was also a dun, this one a mare, clean-legged and wiry, an animal that walked with ears pricked forward in interest.

The girl who followed the pair was, at seventeen, a little less than half their age, and paler in coloring. Her hair was a light brown, her eyes blue, and the bow she carried, while of very good quality, showed less wear. She handled it with skill, however, and her eyes showed that she was alert. Her horse was dark chestnut, a mare, wearing expensive gear. A nondescript bay packhorse ambled behind them.

Yoros kept his mount a pace ahead of Kyrryl's horse, while their niece followed. This was a section of the country he didn't know well, and sometimes bandits lurked in such places. Ashara, watching about them with her bow drawn and an arrow nocked ready for any surprises on the trail they followed, was leading their packhorse, its lead rope tied lightly to the back of her saddle. All three were keyed up to shivering, gazes flicking constantly from side to side in angry anticipation. After all, the stolen Tarian tariling that they hunted was the offspring of Chylo and Razaia. This particular clan of the feline Tarians had shared grazing lands for two generations now, and the golden Razaia was a particular favorite among them.

"Kyrryl? Do you have any idea where we are now?" Yoros asked, gazing down the long slope. His eyes widened until white showed around the rims as he stared, abruptly frozen in shock, at a nearby clump of trees, until the other noticed his fixed gaze.

Kyrryl followed his gaze, her hand closing on the small glittering prism that hung about her neck on its chain. She stared at the trees. Then she spun in her saddle to look behind them, her face startled and afraid. "Beloved, I have no idea, but I'm scared." She held up the prism and turned it slowly. Light flared within it, died, and flared again. Kyrryl winced.

Ashara crowded up. "What is it?"

"The direction that this shows us, the way Tayio was taken, has completely changed. I felt nothing, but I've heard that a portal may be sometimes passed without warning. It's very rare but it can happen."

It was Ashara's turn to stare in horrified understanding. "We just crossed a portal? We're in another world?"

Yoros looked at his wife, who nodded slowly. "I think so," she said, her hand closing about the prism where it swung on the finely wrought chain. "I was careless. I watched for enemies, I watched for the path to lead us to poor little Tayio; it never occurred to me to look out in case we passed through a portal with no warning."

Ashara spoke again. "Why do you think we've done so now? I didn't see or feel anything. Are you sure we've crossed?"

Yoros pointed. "Have you ever seen trees like those?"

It was a tall growth, the branches odd elongated whips rather than true branches. They reached upward, divided from the trunk but not from each other so that the tree looked like a huge kindling stick, the kind made to start a fire by shaving curls from a short branch. It was certainly like nothing any of them had ever seen before. They were less than a week's ride from home, but a tree like that had never grown in Khaddishar.

Kyrryl watched her niece as Ashara considered the tree before shaking her head. "I've never seen one like it, no. But why does that mean a portal?"

Yoros answered that, mastering his own shock. "There are no trees like it anywhere that I have seen, and I know all of the trees within our country. On a trail Kyrryl and I know well we went from our own lands to some place where there are trees that I have never seen before. How else do you think it happened?"

Ashara looked tense, fearing the answer to her next question. "What about a portal to another land? One that's far away?"

Kyrryl replied to that, still staring about. "Look." She held up the prism, which was alternately glowing with light and dimming again. "This says that we've left our world, and so does the sun above us."

"Why?" Ashara asked, still trying to believe nothing so dangerous had happened.

"The prism shows the way we must go to find Tayio, but before Yoros noticed the strangeness of the trees, we were riding south. In a few paces we went from riding south to traveling east while apparently still riding forward. And that," Kyrryl said, her voice trembling a little, "is something no one could do normally. The worlds beyond a portal often have an orientation different from our world's—or so say the records. The only other possibility is that the people who stole Tayio have changed course that way, and that's no more likely. No, we've crossed a portal without knowing it—and that's almost unheard of. If it were so common or easy, half our people would be falling into other places."

Yoros straightened in his saddle. Kyrryl wasn't panicking, not yet, but he could see the fear in her eyes. Ashara was quite simply terrified. He must be strong for them, appear calm and confident.

"We have two choices. We follow your prism to find Tayio, then look for a way home. Or we try to return home now, leaving the tariling to those who stole him and whatever mercy they may offer." He managed a small grin at the immediate outcry. "I thought that would be the way of it."

Kyrryl reached out to touch his hand. She was really upset about having Ashara with them on a strange world. There were far too many dangers. And she worried about how Ashara's parents would react if they knew. Although there was a good side to that, she thought. Her brother and his wife hadn't expected to hear from Kyrryl, Yoros, and Ashara for several weeks—or even months—depending on where their search for the stolen tariling led them. If they could return within those months, her brother and her sister-in-law need not know, until the return, that their daughter had ever been in far more danger than had been expected.

"Let's ride on. The prism is still showing a direction. We'll trust to that but move more slowly. I want us all to stay really alert," Yoros said sternly. "We have no idea of the dangers here."

Kyrryl raised the prism, chanted the incantation for seeking in a voice that trembled very slightly, and heeled her mount into a steady walk in the direction that the small glow of light suggested. Behind her rode the other two, both quiveringly alert. They rode in silence for almost four hours, not wanting to talk in case they missed some sign of danger or distracted Kyrryl. Kyrryl's mind was a whirl of ideas and speculation, but she too said nothing, riding in silence, watching the prism's rainbow light brighten and dim while she followed the light that showed which way Tayio was being taken.

Her world had portals both to other lands and in and out of that world. But most required a mighty effort of will by someone with the mind-gift—often by a number of people at the least. Nor did she know of any portal in the lands that she and Yoros ruled in the name of their clan-family. Could it be a portal newly appeared?

Yoros brought his mount up beside hers. "Do you think we may have passed this portal so easily because of our seeking?"

"What? Why do you ask that?"

"Think about it, beloved. Someone stole Tayio, and I think there must have been more than one involved in the theft. Tayio is only three, but he's strong and healthy. He wouldn't have gone willingly and his parents were nearby. To enter the grazing lands unseen, to subdue a tariling so quickly and cleverly that he had no time to call for help, and then to spirit him away with no one knowing what had happened is not the work of an idle moment's amusement by some practical joker."

Kyrryl thought about that and agreed. "True. So you think then that perhaps his kidnappers came from this world? That because we are hunting them the portal may have let us pass?" She sucked in a breath. "Or is it that this was the portal they used? Could there be something in the way they opened the portal that allowed us to go through too?"

"I wondered."

"It's possible." Her mouth drooped in sorrow. "But what worries me is why. Why would strangers go to all this trouble to steal the tariling of an intelligent people? What will they do with him? He has no control over what his mind broadcasts; he must be sending distress and fear so strongly that even we could hear him if we were nearby. They may kill him for that." Her hand reached out and gripped his fingers hard. "I don't think they're meaning any good to him and I'm afraid, Yoros. I'm afraid."

"Courage, love. We'll find him. A pity Razaia and Chylo couldn't come with us."

Kyrryl shivered. "Maybe not. An adult might be stronger than they wanted, but it's still possible that Tayio's kidnappers could prefer a Tarian adult instead of Tayio—or as well as. Bad enough we've lost Tayio, without losing his kin besides."

She looked up to gauge the time of day. "It will be dark in another two hours if this world keeps similar time. Let's watch for a suitable campsite and pray to Sekmet that in the morning the prism still shows the way."

Yoros nodded. "Watch for a stream. We'll need water soon. But don't forget to be on the lookout for dangerous beasts, and people too." He looked at Kyrryl. "That's odd now that I think about it. We've been riding half a day and we've seen no one."

He was studying her anxiously. She found a smile for him. "In how many places at home could you do that?"

"True enough. You think we may have arrived in an area where the land is thinly populated?"

"Or too dangerous to settle," Kyrryl said. "How would we know?" Her voice was wry, and as she continued she kept it low so Ashara would not hear her. "If nothing has attacked us in half a day, or comes sniffing around our campsite tonight, then perhaps we could consider that the land is thinly settled."

Yoros nodded, smiling at her. "I'd rather it was that. The main problem we will face, if we meet the inhabitants of this world, is that neither of us will understand the other."

His wife muttered irritably under her breath. "This is a huge mess. We're far from home with no certainty we can return. What will happen to us? How will we survive?"

"All we can do is do the best we can. We're alive, unhurt, we have several weeks' worth of supplies, we have weapons and good mounts, and we have each other."

Behind them Ashara squealed in fright, turned, and shot. A large black creature that had leaped, claws-out, for the pack-horse reeled sideways in midair as the arrow struck, then fell over, kicked briefly, and went limp. The packhorse leaped side-ways and bucked at the sight of the beast, then stood more placidly when he saw that the beast was no longer a threat. He was used to seeing arrows fly past him.

Kyrryl halted her mount and reined back, leaning over to consider her niece's quarry. She studied the odd blocky shape, the huge claws. She prodded it with the end of her bowstave, observed that it was certainly dead, and looked up at her husband.

"This animal looks like a cross between a mountain cat and a guard dog. It's like nothing I've ever heard of." Her gaze went to her niece. "Where did it come from?"

"From the taller grass upslope. I saw the movement in the grass and nocked an arrow. I shot at the last moment when it jumped for the packhorse."

Yoros dropped from his saddle to consider the dead animal more closely. "It looks likely it's an efficient predator, but it's rather thin. Maybe the hunting has been poor lately and it was desperate." He ran his fingers through the black fur. "The skin is poor; tanning the hide wouldn't be worth the trouble."

He jerked the arrow free, wiping it on the grass then returning it to his niece before swinging up on his mount again. Ashara rode in silence. She was pleased that she'd seen the beast in time to shoot. Deep in her thoughts as she was, with her keen eyesight she was still the one who noticed the smudge that showed a winding line of trees well off to their right.

"Yoros, Kyrryl. Look! Is that likely to be a stream or a river?"

Yoros nudged his horse in the direction she indicated, and the other two followed. It was closing on dusk, but so far they'd seen no campsite they'd find comfortable—or, more importantly, defensible. Kyrryl turned after him and moved to lead them downslope, as the land dipped slowly toward the trees. They stopped when they found they were crossing a wide beaten-earth road leading away at an angle.

"That's more than an animal track," Kyrryl observed.

"I know, it looks like a major trail, the sort made by people and wagons using it regularly. Let's keep a watch on it. If we can get a good look at anyone going by we may get valuable information about this place." Yoros agreed. "But let's find a campsite. Just now that's more important."

He noticed that up ahead the road looped by the stream in an area where the trees were farther apart and the streambed was shallower and wider. It gave better access to the water and looked as if it might be used by travelers to fill water flasks or barrels and to allow their animals to drink. Better to stay away from there. He reined his mount farther to the right into the trees.

In half an hour they had found a likely shelter. They changed course onto a narrow beaten-earth trail that showed small hoof-prints in spots where the ground was soft. There they found the bank of a shallow, meandering tributary to the larger stream, lying within patches of heavier brush.

Yoros dropped from his saddle, tossed the reins to his niece, and strode to the edge of the water. "Firewood. Look, when this stream floods, lighter driftwood must wash up at the bend here." He began to gather dry sticks from the top of the drift, dropping them by a large patch of brush.

Kyrryl gathered twists of dry grass while asking, "What do you think about camping right here, Yoros? We'd be sheltered from any wind; there's wood, water—and good grass over there for the horses. There might even be fish in the water?"

"It's a good site. Yes. If no one has any objections then we'll stay for the night. But I want someone on guard all the time. Ashara, take your horse and tie him inside the edge of the tree line where the land rises. Climb a tree and watch all around, including across the stream. If you see anything we should know about, come and tell us at once. Keep a watch particularly for any campfire. We need to know if anyone from this world is nearby, and you should see a fire even if it's a long way off. Kyrryl, you'll be on guard after her. I'll unsaddle the packhorse and set up camp."

Wordlessly Kyrryl dismounted and unsaddled her own mount. The mare possessed a sensible nature, good speed and stamina, the ability to climb like a cat, and a willingness to do anything that she understood was wanted of her. Kyrryl had

selected her for a riding mount four years ago, since they lived
in dangerous country at home. She couldn't have a better mount
here.

They were all experienced in what they did, although Ashara
had some trouble climbing her chosen tree. It seemed to be in-
habited by birds, large aggressive ones that protested her arrival
until she chose another tree some distance from their colony. She
must remember to tell her aunt when Kyrryl came to take her
place, she thought.

After dark when her watch was ended she came to the fire
with some information. "I did see a fire."

"A campfire?"

"That's what it looks like."

Ashara looked at her uncle hopefully. "Are we going over
there to see?"

He grinned, a flash of white teeth in the moonlight. "No.
What do we do if we do meet the locals? Almost certainly we
won't speak their language, they may be hostile to strangers,
and all we can do is give ourselves problems."

"What if they're the ones who stole Tayio?"

Yoros shrugged. "Kyrryl says that the prism indicates that
the tariling is still a long way from here and not in that direction.
It's possible that if those were the people who stole him they took
him somewhere and left him, but we can hardly rush a camp
of strangers whose language we don't speak and start asking if
they're kidnappers."

Ashara smiled wryly. "Not if we won't understand a word
they say and they can't understand the questions either."

"That's what I think, so we'll just keep watch. Maybe if
they come closer to the cover here after daybreak we can see
what they look like. They may not even be human."

Ashara considered the other race she knew at home and

nodded. "No, they may not. Is Kyrryl really thinking, though, that we can hunt Tayio through half a strange world, retrieve him safely, and get home again, all without meeting a single native?"

Yoros smiled. "Ask her," he suggested.

Ashara thought that she wouldn't. Kyrryl wouldn't know any more than the rest of them. She'd adapt to circumstances and hope for the best, but that was a far cry from knowing what to do at all times.

The night passed quietly. In the dawn hour Ashara managed to catch three fish by hand from the stream. Yoros surveyed them. They looked edible, but what was for the best? Try the native food now and risk poisoning themselves, be driven to trying it later when the supplies ran out, or hope they'd have found Tayio and a way home before that happened? He decided to risk the native foods when he had a clearer idea of what might be safe. The ancient records he'd seen, written by an occasional wise one who'd set foot on other worlds, suggested that if the air had the sweetness of the air in their own woods—as it did, witness to their initial unawareness that they had crossed a portal—it was likely that plants and animals on this world were not entirely dissimilar to those at home. Some edible and delicious, some not palatable, and some poisonous.

He'd studied what land he could see from cover. There was the well-worn trail along the other side of the stream where there was less brush and more grass. Apart from the loop down to the stream it didn't follow the meandering course of the water, which was southeast, but struck straight off to the east under a narrow ridge.

Kyrryl was wrapping the fish in the large green leaves of some plant by the waterside. She raked small embers over the neat parcels and sat back. Well, he wouldn't say anything until the fish were cooked. Then one of them should try a single bite. If whoever tried it was still unharmed in half a day they could risk eating a little of the fish at noon. It certainly emitted a delectable smell. They ate journey bread and berry spread, and drank water from their flasks. Unnoticed, Yoros topped off his own half-full water flask from the stream. If the water wasn't safe, the effects would be diluted, and he could warn his family before they drank any. They'd be out of water very soon anyway, the horses had drunk last night without obvious ill effects, and they had to have water; there was no real choice about that.

In due course Ashara, as the fisher, claimed the right to take the first bite. She moaned in pleasure, savoring the firm white flesh. "It's wonderful. The best fish I've ever tasted. Sekmet's teeth, but I hope it's safe to eat it. I could live on nothing else for weeks and be happy."

"You'd be sick of it in a few days," Kyrryl assured her dryly. "But we'll take note of your wish." She glanced around. "Are we all packed?"

Yoros had scaled a tree and was looking to where they'd seen the fire the previous night. He observed movement and started down, dropping quickly from the final branch to hiss.

"Quiet. There's a group coming. The wind's blowing from them to us so be sure that the horses don't make a sound." In their own place it could be necessary at times to ensure silence, so all of them had muzzle straps available. They flicked the straps about the horses' noses before the beasts could whinny and, leaving them tethered, crawled to the edge of the scrub and flattened out, raising their heads and parting the stems to see through the tall grass. Looking through cover rather than over it made you less likely to be seen. They had effective cover and on their side of the stream the land was higher, giving them a good view of what would appear.

In the silence they could hear the approaching riders. Hooves thumped rhythmically along the trail on the other side of the stream and one of the beasts whinnied. Definitely horses. There was a creaking and rumbling that sounded like wagon wheels. Voices were raised, some in song, others in discussion, and the shrill cries of children at play.

Yoros's gaze met Kyrryl's. The sounds answered several questions. There were people on this world and they couldn't be too different from Yoros, Kyrryl, and Ashara. They had children, they sang, argued, rode horses, drove wagons. The voices, while speaking a different language, sounded like just any voices. They had to be human.

The riders, surrounding four driven wagons, came into view through the screen of brush. Yoros's and Kyrryl's eyes widened. About three-quarters of the riders and walkers were human, all right. The others . . . were not! He heard Ashara's breath drawn in with a tiny gasp as she joined them.

Kyrryl was cataloguing the differences. Like the Tarians, these others were catlike, black-furred, lean of shape—little body fat, she noted. They had long tails just like ordinary Khaddisha-ran cats, and fanlike ears—that moved to catch sounds—set atop and to either side of a slightly triangular head. All of the cat people she could see had a smallish white patch of fur on the upper chest directly beneath the chin. The muscles showed ropy and powerful under sleek fur. Their laugh was either a sort of coughing, or a gurgling wheeze, but from the reactions of those with them it was definitely laughter and not threatening growls. They rode astride comfortably, their tails set high enough that they didn't interfere with their seat in a saddle, and they laughed and talked to the humans with them. Clearly, within this party at least, humans and another race lived together in reasonable friendship.

The cat people looked quite a lot like the Tarians of her world, but they were taller and sturdier, their tails were long, not the short, curled puff of tail that the Tarians had, and even those she presumed to be males had no mane at all.

The humans were dressed differently from any she had ever seen, but their clothing was attractively embroidered and also looked practical. What appeared to be both sexes wore light trousers tied, so far as she could see, with a drawstring, and a light shirtlike top. The riders wore a tunic to midthigh that was split to hip height on either side. Those who walked wore a slightly longer sleeveless robe over the shirt and trousers. The robes fastened with several clasps down the front from mid-chest to waist, and both robes and tunics were embroidered in bright colors. She saw, as they passed slowly under her gaze, that most of the embroidered symbols were variations on a theme and guessed them to indicate a clan or family.

The cat creatures too were dressed. The cubs wore little more than a belt holding up a loincloth, but the adults wore a similar sort of attractively embroidered clothing to that of the humans. It appeared to be of lighter cloth and looser cut, with an opening to make allowance for the tail, but those were the only major differences.

As the four wagons creaked on by, Yoros considered them, his voice a murmur in Kyrryl's ear. "They use four horses and their wagons are mostly like ours, but look there, those second and third in the line have a cross shaft halfway. Why would they have that?"

"Maybe so they can dismount the front section of the shaft?" Kyrryl offered. "That way only one pair of horses with little alteration to the shaft could draw those wagons when they're unloaded. I think these people might be traders and if so that could be a useful ability to have for their wagons."

"They could be nomads on the move," Ashara suggested.

"True, but look, one of the wagons is carrying big, flat-bottomed jars, and the one behind it is carrying cured hides in bundles that could be merchandise," Yoros told her. "That could still indicate nomads, but somehow they have the air of traders like the ones we see at home." He felt that it was at least likely this was what they were.

Ashara was noticing the children. Catlike cubs played with human children. There was no obvious tension; it appeared that the children were all old friends. Whoever or whatever this group was, it was clear they had been together for some time and were comfortable with each other.

The group was clearly led by two humans. If they aged at the same rate as people on her world did, Kyrryl thought, they could be in the fifties, and it could be seen that there was affection between them, but there was authority also. Their people obeyed when they looked at one and spoke. She wondered who they were and where they were going. Were they really traders as Yoros believed, or nomads, or perhaps migrants moving to settle in unoccupied lands?

Yoros signaled once the wagons had passed, and they withdrew. "Traders, or so I think, although it's only a guess," he said once they were back at the campsite and Ashara had shared her thoughts. He grinned. "And as we suspected, this is surely not our world but it tells me something else." Raised brows urged him to continue, although Kyrryl already wore a knowing look.

"Yes, beloved, you know, but for Ashara's information: If other humans can live here then so can we. We should be very careful what we eat, but I would think that most fast-flowing water is safe to drink. I'm going to leave you for a little later today and follow that group. I want to see if they go hunting, what they kill if they do, and what else they eat. It'll give us some idea of what may be safe for us too."

Kyrryl nodded slowly. "That may be a good idea. I'll use the prism to follow Tayio, but if our path starts to diverge too widely from the group you follow, then you should come back to us."

"Done, love." And to his niece he said, "Now, is the campsite clean?"

"All clear. No human will ever know we camped on this spot." She shook her head thoughtfully, adding, "I'd take no wager on others, though. If those cat people have similar abilities to the Tarians as well as similar looks then they will have keener noses than we do. We may hide the signs that we camped here, but our scent will be all over the site. We were very lucky, if that's so, that the wind was blowing from them to us and not the reverse."

The other two turned to stare at her. Kyrryl nodded. "That's something none of us thought of until now. We'll have to do what we can, but," she turned to Yoros, "think of that when you follow them. Make sure you approach with the wind in your face and watch that it doesn't change."

Again she hid her fear. They were in a strange world, so many things could kill them, so many actions that they might take could get them killed. But she had to stay calm for Ashara.

Yoros looked serious. "Yes, that was clever, Ashara. They may have better hearing too. Best I take as much care as if I hunted mountain cats. I'll stay further from that group than I'd planned, I think. But we should move on now. Kyrryl, does the prism give you a direction?"

His wife lifted the prism on its chain and turned it slowly. "It does, beloved."

"Then you two follow your path while I follow mine. I'll find you tonight. I'll leave now, if I must stay further from them. I can close in to watch what they do when they stop and once I've checked the wind direction."

He forced down a shiver of fear. He needed to do this. They had to have more information about this world and its people. Even if he couldn't understand a word that was said, he could observe what was done. The ancient records compiled by the wise ones of his world, a handful of whom had passed portals into two companion worlds and returned safely, reported that humans on one world were basically identical to those on others . . . in most respects. They could interbreed, much of what humans could eat in one world could be eaten in another, and they had the same emotions, but neither report had mentioned cat people in the other worlds. He wondered if they just hadn't been seen or if there were none in those worlds.

However, even in his own world customs could be very different between peoples, even between people who spoke the same language. But he had to take the risk; otherwise they could be stranded here, afraid to drink the water or eat the food, breaking customs and laws with no idea of what they'd done wrong. He had to learn what while he could. He hated to leave Kyrryl and Ashara, but if most locals stuck to the road they might be safer than he was—if they stayed away from that.

They hugged him; then he was gone, slipping through the brush in the direction that the wagons had taken. His evil-eyed mount could be very quiet when it wished, or when Yoros demanded. Kyrryl mounted her pony, bit down the desire to chatter nervously, studied the rainbow light that glowed in her prism, then led off at a slight angle. It wasn't much divergence so far, but by noon the groups could be several miles apart. She worried, but Yoros was a good hunter and tracker; he'd find her. The mind-gift ran in their families, and both had a touch of it—not a lot, but just sufficient that they usually knew in what direction the other was and how far away.

Four hours after dark she felt him nearing her and warned her niece so that neither of them jumped when he appeared from the darkness leading his horse.

"Well, love?"

He smiled at her. "Well, indeed, my love. For one thing we can eat the fish in safety. I saw some of the children catch them, wrap them to bake in the same leaves we used earlier, and everyone shared the meal. They also drank freely from the water. That doesn't mean all streams are safe," he cautioned. "But it appears this one is regarded so. I also saw one of the cat creatures set out hunting ahead of the wagons. He returned just before dusk with what looked like a small deer."

"It really looked like a deer?" Kyrryl asked.

"It looked just like one of our own hill deer. I think if we see one it would be safe to shoot and eat it," Yoros said slowly. "What about the prism? Is it still pointing us in this direction?"

Kyrryl nodded. "The direction hasn't altered since we came here and it settled to point east."

Neither of them spoke aloud the idea that came into their minds: that the tariling might be already dead and the prism could be indicating only the small corpse. They had to know; if he was alive he must be rescued and if he was dead—if he was dead, Kyrryl thought, they'd take vengeance on whoever had stolen and murdered an intelligent creature, son to comrades in their world. Her love and friendship for Razaia and Chylo demanded no less. She must be able to tell them that their tariling's death—if dead he was—had been paid for in the blood of his murderers.

They camped the night, feasted lightly on baked fish, and rode on at a steady walk all the next day, waiting nervously for any signs that they had eaten something dangerous—and feeling only pleasantly filled stomachs.

The countryside they passed was empty of people. There was no sign of any cultivated land or civilization, apart from the wagon trail below them. Four days later they came to a pass through the mountains along whose foothills they had been steadily riding.

They camped there in a small flat area well off the road and were talking around the fire pit while they ate. Their camp was almost the highest point, so that an enemy might find it difficult to approach unseen, and they were taking the opportunity to eat together. Shortly, Yoros, taking first turn at guard duty, would go to find a place where he could be closer to the road.

Kyrryl clenched her hand on the only thing they had that might guide them. The tariling's kidnappers had hidden at some stage in a patch of thorny scrub near her home. She had hunted through every inch of it and found a small medallion. The link atop it was broken, twisted to one side, suggesting that it had snagged on something and been lost, rather than planted to mislead them. The design was like nothing she had ever seen—a strange swirling pattern with a rising spiral. She had hung it on the chain beside her prism. Maybe it would lead her to Tayio, she thought.

It seemed, Yoros said between mouthfuls of baked fish, that the kidnappers had taken to the higher trails along the foothills to avoid being noticed—perhaps by groups like the one they had seen. Ashara wondered, with the land apparently so empty of people, why it was that the possible trader group took this path at all.

Kyrryl shrugged. "Maybe that they go from one city to another. It probably doesn't matter to us. What I would like to know is who took Tayio and why."

Ashara sighed. "Yes. And are they hurting him, how are they feeding him?" Her face screwed up in distress. "He's only a baby, he wasn't weaned. Is he starving? Will they be expecting him to drink horse milk? That sometimes makes Tarians sick."

Her aunt spoke gently. "I know. Don't worry. We'll find and rescue him. Just go and do your turn on guard. The prism is still pointing the way. While that's so, we have hope for Tayio."

From the edge of the circle of firelight a voice spoke. The voice was soft, a crystal chime of words that to their disbelief they all understood. They jerked around to stare at one of the catlike people, who stood looking at them, her eyes calm. This one was different from those in the group that they'd seen. Two of the humans about the fire had some small share of the gift, and even Ashara, who did not, felt the power that poured from the figure, outlining it in a nimbus of mind-light. It spoke again, the words freezing them in place.

"You hope for the life of the young one, but time runs out for him like water through a cracked pot. I choose to give you a boon to help your search. What it is you shall know, when the time comes that it is needed. I can do little more and still hold the balance level. But you have advantages my people do not, since the power that lives here does not run in your veins. That is both blessing and curse. You will find unexpected friends on the road, and you will find enemies. My blessings upon you, and I give you a promise. A portal shall open to send you home when your search is ended. That much also I can do without the balance of my world is being shifted."

She was gone. Kyrryl, Yoros, and Ashara stared at one another a long time in silence before Kyrryl spoke.

"That was either an adept of this world or a goddess—the latter, I think. I have never seen such power, and she spoke of the balance of her world. If she keeps her promise we'll have a way to return once we find and rescue Tayio."

Ashara was still staring at the spot where the figure had stood. "She was beautiful. I wonder what aid she'll give us. She said she'd help."

"She also said we'd find friends and enemies on the road," Yoros added. They looked at one another, and in their gazes they could each see the hope of the others that all their mysterious visitor had said would be true.

2

$\mathcal{A}$ day's ride ahead, another out-world group was already riding along the foothills. It had begun as a holiday and a quest for them. For Eilish and Trasso it was a holiday celebrating their marriage a little less than a year earlier, and for Kian Dae it was a quest.

Not that he himself minded; a cat, even an intelligent one, is not terribly interested in who his sire might have been. But asking that question had amused his human family for years. Now, with all well at Anskeep and Iroskeep, they were determined to follow any clues like a treasure hunt, the treasure being a final answer to the long-posed question.

They could afford to leave their homes for a while to play as they'd had little time to do in earlier years. Their ineffective ruler had died a year ago, replaced by his cousin and one who was distant kin to them as well. Huno ruled with solid competence. The spring had been a good one and the harvest was showing promise of being bountiful this year. Isha and Peschen had given them leave to spend a summer wandering, and in

Iroskeep, Trasso's father was only too happy to see his beloved son and new daughter-in-law enjoying themselves.

It was a merry party. They planned to be gone a moon or even two, so their families would not see them go alone. Instead Sirado, Eilish's brother and her lord's good friend, rode with them—a tall young man of twenty-two, with black hair and brown eyes, mounted on a solid bay gelding. Riding too were Dayshan, the middle-aged master-at-arms of Anskeep, and two younger men, servants from Trasso's home of Iroskeep, named Roshan and Hailin. Dayshan had weathered brown skin to match his medium-brown hair and eyes, and had more than once joked that he was born to be a master-at-arms since he came in camouflage. Of the servants, Roshan appeared a pale copy of Dayshan, while Hailin was more striking, with blond hair, pale blue eyes, and a fairer skin that, fortunately, still did not burn easily.

Kian Dae, Eilish's big cat (his name meaning "Great Hunter" in Khaddishar—something of a joke when he was a kitten, but nowadays accepted as one of the Universal Truths, not least by himself), rode in his usual flat-bottomed carrysack across Eilish's shoulders, being let down when he wished to hunt or trot along while the horses walked. There was, after all, no hurry. It was a pleasure excursion and all were taking pleasure in it.

They had gone southwest into the mountains behind Anskeep, there following narrow winding trails. They deferred to Kian Dae when the big tawny-furred, dark-brown-spotted cat seemed to have some idea of where he wanted to go.

Sirado had laughed at the cat's insistence on a previous twist and doubling-back on a new trail. "We chase our tails better than a kitten with a ball of wool. I believe we've traveled three sides of a square since yesterday and now we've doubled back on our tracks. We've ridden for three days and by now we must be almost home again."

There was amused agreement from everyone but Kian Dae, but the group continued to ride on even as they laughed. It was fun and an adventure and that was sufficient for them all.

It was close to dusk when Sirado finally halted. "Shall we make camp here?"

Eilish looked at the spot with disfavor. "No real shelter, although we can raise some, but there's no water. Let's ride on a while longer." Her brother looked at Trasso, who shrugged.

"She's right. The horses aren't tired yet and nor am I. Let's keep going and see if there's something better further on," Trasso said.

Sirado accepted that when no one argued. Dayshan would say quickly enough if he thought Trasso was wrong. The man had been made the keep's master-at-arms in place of his uncle almost a decade ago, and he knew his job.

Sirado surrendered. "All right. We'll ride little longer. It doesn't look as if it will rain, so after that we'll just take whatever shows itself if there's nothing better earlier."

Kian Dae had leaped from his carrysack and trotted ahead while they paused. Now he uttered a loud squawk and ran, bounding along the narrow hillside track at his best speed. Eilish, who had received an abrupt feeling of urgency from him, a need to be somewhere else as fast as possible, heeled her mount after him, calling anxiously. "Kian, Kian, wait. What is it?"

Trasso wasted no time. His mount was after hers in one leap while the others hastily followed. The big cat raced down the winding trail, and when he reached a small straight section of the path, he spun, leaping between boulders to one side and running onward. They followed, racing after him down a new trail. A thin thread of packed-down soil sloped away along the foothills of great mountains that towered above them, suddenly seeming to be much closer than they had been.

Dayshan pulled his mount to an abrupt halt and bellowed at them in his best master-at-arms voice. "Stop, hold up!" Even Kian Dae stopped and waited at the determination in that command.

Eilish turned her mount to look back. "What is it?"

"Look about you, lass."

She knew the old man. He would not make such a demand if there were nothing at which to look. She turned in the saddle, surveying all of the landscape she could see. Trasso and Sirado were doing the same thing. Her husband whistled softly on a long surprised note.

"I don't know where we are, but these aren't our mountains."

Eilish had seen that; now she struggled to discover why she believed it was so. Mountains were mountains, after all. Grass was—no, in this case it wasn't ordinary grass. Looking down, she noticed that it had an odd lavender tint over the green. She looked up. The sky had the same tint, more lilac than blue. The trees in the distance seemed green enough, however, and the small stream that trickled nearby appeared to be no more than water.

She dismounted and went toward it, but Kian Dae was there first. He lapped thirstily and she received a feeling of pleasure in the pure chill taste. Nor was there any fear in him, more a contentment that he'd led them somewhere they should be. She reached out to stroke a hand down his back.

"Very well, the water is good, and we're in no danger here—wherever 'here' is—but why did you run off like that?"

In return she received confusion. He wasn't sure. A sudden

compulsion to run had come upon him, a need to hurry down *this* road, a calling to be somewhere urgently—and here they were.

Under her tunic breast the prism she used to focus her abilities flared to rainbow life. Eilish lifted it out while Dayshan gave brisk instructions about finding wood and making a fire and camp.

The master-at-arms had already looked about them. Wherever they had arrived, this was a reasonable campsite. The trail curved away a little from a bulge in the rocks, but within those there was a large space. They'd be out of any wind there, the stream was close, there was a grassy area where they could picket the horses, and there was a patch of trees only a couple of hundred yards away. There might be dry wood there.

Eilish sank into contemplation and mental search, aided by the tear-shaped prism. That was odd; there was no feeling of warning that she could find, only a strange sense of welcome from the land around her. Not a welcome for her, instead it seemed to be directed toward Kian Dae. She probed gently and recognized that behind the welcome was a sort of recognition. Something in this land knew her cat, recognized him and welcomed his arrival. Now, *that* might explain why he'd been called.

She kept her voice down as she replaced the prism in her bodice. "I can't swear to it, but I believe something wanted us here."

"Where *is* here?" She looked at her brother, who'd asked that and grinned, making it appear cheerful.

"I have no idea. But I think that we aren't in our world any longer. I might believe that another country had grass of this color, but I think it unlikely that the sky changes color in other lands. No, when we followed Kian Dae between those boulders

I think we passed through a portal. The strange thing is that it let us pass so easily—" Her voice became thoughtful.

"Something called him to come quickly. The land recognizes and welcomes him. I think we are meant to be here, why I don't know. But I feel no evil, nor any ill will. Let's camp here tonight and in the morning we may be shown a path to take."

Trasso's gaze met that of his brother-in-law and they nodded. They were not comfortable about recent events; in fact, both were on edge. In a strange world there could be great dangers unrecognized, strangers who would rob, or rape, or murder. Beasts that were predators, with poisoned fangs, and a hunger for any fresh meat. Neither mentioned these dangers. They knew the possibilities, and it would do no good to scare themselves talking about it. They were in this place; better to eat, drink, rest while they could, and consider their options. When there was nothing they could do, it was best to behave calmly.

In the lee of the boulders Dayshan already had a small fire going in a fire pit with stones stacked higher around that to help hide the light from any who might be watching, so that they had makings of a comfortable camp. In short order a trail stew was bubbling in a pot over the fire, while sarren leaves in another pot made a hot sweet lemon-tasting draught that refreshed those who drank.

A commotion broke out in the small copse of trees and all of them jerked upright to listen. A brightly colored bird was scolding another. They flew at each other with flapping and squawks before one surrendered and flew off. Eilish looked after it.

"This land is not so different, they have birds, and," she added when an odd little furred animal with a short tail hopped out of a nearby crevice between boulders and leaped down the trail, "it looks as if they have rabbits."

Dayshan stared after it. "*That* was not a rabbit," he said firmly.

Eilish smiled. "Not in Khaddishar, but I suspect that it's what the people of this place call it—if there are people here—or anyway, I think they'll use some word in their tongue that means rabbit."

Dayshan nodded thoughtfully. "Yes, that may be so—if there are people here. Now, what do we do tomorrow?"

Sirado shrugged. "We follow Kian Dae; do we have a choice?" He stared around the circle of faces. The two younger servants kept silent. His sister broke the silence.

"I don't think we do. We're here for a purpose. When I open my mind I feel that the land welcomes Kian Dae, and is not hostile toward us," Eilish said slowly. "But we should still ride with great care and slowly. We have no need to hurry and it's better to be cautious."

Dayshan smiled approvingly. "Ah, as my uncle taught you. Few situations are improved by speed, many are better taken slowly so there's time to see ahead and consider what to do."

Eilish handed him a bowl of the stew and grinned, gray eyes amused. "Yes, Doshad taught us that, but you sound like a grandfather when you talk that way. You're forty, not eighty like Doshad."

Dayshan grinned companionably at her, his weather-tanned face crinkling in amusement. "I'm forty-four, twenty years older than you, my lass. I'm also Anskeep's master-at-arms, and your grandparents sent me to make sure you do nothing rash. I've seen some of what you three can do without looking ahead. It's put years on me. I could well be feeling eighty by the time this particular trip is over and we're home again—*if* the portal will open, *if* we can find it again, and *if* we haven't all been killed before that happens."

Trasso stood and bowed. "I could lay out your bedding for you, old man. Someone of your years might find it hard to bend over to do that. Allow me to bring your sarren, the priestesses say we should be kind to the elderly." He would have continued but for Dayshan's roar of mock rage.

"I'll give you elderly. I can ride you into the ground any day, my lad, and don't you forget it."

The Iroskeep servants looked horrified. Trasso observed this from the corner of his eye and hid a grin. They were young men from his keep and not used to a servant speaking that way, but Master-at-Arms Dayshan was a valued man and had license with Trasso's family. Besides which, his family had served Anskeep, the home of his wife's family, for generations, and Eilish and Sirado loved him as an uncle. If he had to take his two men aside and explain that, he would.

By now everyone was eating stew in silence for some time. Once he'd finished his meal, Sirado produced a small set of pipes and began to play very softly. He played another song, then another, ending with a slow, soft lullaby. Trasso stretched and yawned.

"I'm for bed after that. Who takes first guard?"

Dayshan listed the shifts. "Hailin can take first watch, then Roshan. I'll take third."

He caught Eilish's eye. "Tomorrow night you can take a turn but there's enough of us that we can sleep through on alternate nights."

She nodded, but fixed him with a look that said she'd take her turn and there was to be no undue pampering of the nobility. Dayshan turned his hands, palms out, and shrugged slightly at her. Then they both grinned. So he'd been caught trying. He'd try again—and probably fail again, they both knew. It was an old game.

The night was quiet, but at first light the birds started an argument at full volume. Everyone came awake, hearts racing, only to lie back and groan in disgust.

"This is supposed to be a break from waking early," Trasso complained. "If I wanted to get up at dawn I could have stayed home and listened to the men drill while old Esad yells at them."

Sirado peered at him from over the top of his bedding. "Why don't you move the drill area?"

"Because it's been right under the heir's window for generations and who am I to ruin a tradition," Trasso told him.

"You mean Esad won't let you?" Eilish laughed.

"No," he chuckled softly. "My father won't let me. He says he had to be woken up like that all the years he was heir and it never did him any harm." He looked at her hopefully. "You, though. My father would give us rooms in the other tower if you asked."

"Would he mind us breaking tradition and living there?"

"My father thinks you're the best thing to happen to the keep since my mother's old bite of a maid fell into the midden. If you asked he'd agree, and no, I don't think he'd really mind."

"Then I'll ask once we get home again. By the way, how was it that the maid fell into the midden?"

By now the others were listening. Trasso pursed up his lips. "I really couldn't say. But she was a talebearer and no one liked her. She was coin-hungry too. So it's possible someone took a purse, attached a very thin line to it, and laid it right there where she could see it when she came walking. She reached for it, the wind apparently caught it and it rolled toward the midden, she tried to catch it and tripped. I swear I had nothing to do with her tripping."

"But the coin, the line, and the timing may have?"

"Weeeeell." He chuckled. "I'd planned to twitch the coin

into the muck and watch her tear herself apart trying to decide if it was worth wading in to get it. Seeing her tripping and falling flat on her face into it was a bonus."

Everyone laughed. Dayshan guffawed. "I'd have given coins myself to see that happen to a few I've known."

Trasso stood and stretched. "It's about time we moved on, I think."

Sirado nodded, moving to saddle his solid bay gelding. "I hope Kian Dae knows where to go now."

The big cat, who'd been dozing by the fire, opened one eye and stared at him, before shutting it again. He knew where he should go; he was just making up his mind when to move. It was pleasant by the fire and the chill wasn't off the day yet. He sent that thought to Eilish, who scooped him up and placed him in his padded carrysack. The molded leather bottom provided a cup in which he could curl and it prevented his being squeezed. It was spaciously comfortable even over quite long journeys, as she knew.

"Then you can ride," she said quietly into one furry ear. "Just let me know if we need to move off the trail we'll be following."

She received a feeling of satisfaction in turn. The trail they were following would do for now.

It did so, for many miles and several days without signs of other travelers after that. On the third night an event occurred of which only Eilish had any inkling. She woke in the still time past moonhigh and lay listening. All about them the land was silent, yet she would have sworn she had felt a presence within the camp. She strained to listen and heard nothing. She lay back again while the feeling faded slowly. Roshan was on guard. He was a sensible, conscientious man. He'd be alert. Kian Dae would hear whatever Roshan did not, and he too had given no alarm.

She could neither see nor hear what watched her, since it had no intention of being discovered. But for long moments it stood, studying these visitors. Eilish, twenty-four, slight of body, sturdy of mind, dark brown hair in a single long plait as usual, and eyes that would be storm-gray if they were open. Her brother Sirado, twenty-two, heavier in build but still lean, with hair a shade darker and eyes that, while brown, had golden highlights from some angles.

Trasso, Eilish's husband, Sirado's best friend, twenty-six, solid of build and slightly less imaginative than his wife and friend. A practical man who thought things through, but who had a strong sense of humor—a trait they shared—and who'd been raised to responsibility. Trasso was also a fine swords-man and a good man to have at one's back.

Strange green-gold eyes refocused on the servants. Dayshan, the master-at-arms, was another good man at have at one's back. He was a fighter, late-middle-aged, careful, and very ex-perienced, not a man to rush in to anything recklessly. Roshan, who stood guard, was a paler copy of Dayshan, a man who was conscientious and completely practical, a loyal and honest servant. Not perfect; he liked women, and now and again—perhaps because he had no close family—he drank too much. In old age he could become a drunkard.

Hailin, an ambitious man who was unhappy with his menial position in life and wanted to have his own business where he could give the orders. He seemed innocent, his fair hair bleached in sunlight so that by the end of summer he was almost ash blond, and his light blue eyes showed up against the tanned brown of his face. But under that innocent look there was a driving ambition, and a seething resentment that others had the mind-gift that he lacked.

The mysterious figure stooped slowly, touching each of

the companions lightly on the forehead. Roshan, the first, saw nothing, heard nothing, and even the brush of fingers on his forehead was unnoticed. The intruder met the watchful eyes of the only one that might see it and touched again, smiling affectionately, saying nothing to Kian Dae, who remained motionless. Eilish, the last to receive the brush of fingers, stirred, half waking, turning in her bedding. The watcher shut down harder on the power that surrounded her, and Eilish slept again, while a tall, slender figure drifted away from the camp, clawed feet not quite touching the ground. In the darkness no one could see the smile that it wore, nor for some time would any know what it had wrought.

The next morning they moved on. To their right the mountains loomed against the sky while they rode the trail that traveled firmly along the upper foothills. Eilish was commenting on the trail as she and Trasso led out their group the morning after their visitation.

"I get the feeling that this track was originally made to stay away from the majority of travelers." She pointed downhill to where a line of brush marked the main road. "Look how this path keeps to the dips and lower sections. Most of the time someone on it up here still wouldn't be easily seen from down there."

Dayshan spoke from behind them. "It looks like an outlaw path, all right, although I think it was built on an original deer trail. Maybe they have a lot of bandits in this world?"

Trasso nodded. "Or wars, or raids, or even floods. Maybe it rains so much in winter that it's safer to ride above the plains."

"True, lad. I don't like the idea of our group being down on a road with a lot of travelers, all of who may be wanting to talk to us. We can't speak their language, they discover that, and we don't know how they feel about strangers who don't speak their tongue. We could be easily attacked, and how do we handle that—unable to ask for help, unable to explain to whoever up-holds the laws here that we did nothing. I say we stay on this upper trail and away from strangers as long as we can."

There were mutters of agreement from everyone. So far their holiday was proving to be more exciting than anticipated. But no one wanted it to become *too* much more so. Kian Dae yawned, curled comfortably in his carrysack. He felt a faint warning vibration within him. It wasn't much so far but it was growing. Soon something more would be required of him; he didn't know what, but to be ready when it came he should sleep. That way he'd be well rested.

The horses plodded on most of that day. Eilish called a sudden halt in the late afternoon when her prism flared to life. She flung up a hand in warning.

"Someone's coming up behind us on the trail. Off it, now, quickly. Into those trees."

They urged their mounts into the shelter of some trees and sat in taut silence. The sound of hoofbeats came faintly to their ears, the sound growing as two riders came into view around the bend. One—apparently human—was large, bulkily mus-cular, something that showed since he was bare-armed wearing only a sleeveless vest, hip-length and of some sort of fur. The other man was smaller, thinner of face and with a sly gaze. The men were talking while they rode and to the utter astonishment of Eilish and her companions what they said was intelligible. The large man was speaking.

". . . problems with Surah."

"Not again. Hells, Vani, don't they have anything better to do than start trouble with Shallahah?" The thin man was scornful.

The first man spoke again. "Maybe not, my dear Shaetyl. I was told in the city that Surah soldiers have been checking people on the main road. I deemed it prudent to use the upper trail."

"Ah, prudent."

The two men looked at each other and chuckled. "Aye, a man should be prudent when there's soldiers about. They can ask such awkward questions."

"Such as who are these people?" the large man asked.

"Exactly. It isn't as if I didn't pay for them. Slavery's legal in Shallahah and that's where they're going," the other added.

The man spoken to leered. "Maybe they think that since slavery isn't legal in Surah and the ones you have are mostly Surahans they should let them go."

His companion scowled. "I bought and paid for all of them in Surah—bar the woman—to be seven-year bond servants. They're legally slaves once I get them to Shallahah City. Anyway, they won't be running off. Once we got them out of Surah I chained them to the wagons. Those will drop down to the main road again behind us now that they're away from the two Lhandes. Once Kyeaan and Treyvan catch up with us by Jasta Pass we can have fun with the woman. It's well out of all of the Lhandes' territory and it'll be a long swing around the Peace Mountains past Kavarten and Ngahere to Shallahah City."

"How long will that be?"

"Another tenday at the rate they're traveling."

Their voices had become fainter as they passed, and with that last comment they rounded a bend in the trail and were gone.

Dayshan leaned to one side of his mount and spat vigorously. "Slavery!"

"Only in Shallahah, wherever that is. Surah doesn't approve," Sirado said.

"No, they just sell people into seven-year bondage. That doesn't sound to me to be much better," Dayshan offered tartly.

Eilish looked at them all. "Never mind slavery for the moment. Was there any of us who didn't understand every word those men said?" They stared at one another, reminded of their astonishment at the first words they overheard. Not at what was said to begin with, but that they understood it. Murmurs reached her. Everyone recognized that something strange had happened.

In his carrysack Kian Dae opened an eye again, and sent gently to Eilish. She received a blurred picture of their camp the night before, everyone asleep but Roshan, who was on guard. A tall, slender figure came walking silently past Roshan, who saw nothing. It stood looking them over, before touching each of them gently on the forehead, Eilish last, and, when she stirred at the touch, it slipped away beyond the boulders.

"Who was it?"

His next sending took her back to the time when she had fought for the life of her land against sorcery. Kian Dae had been there when she fought, injured in his attempt to help her. Someone had come and taken away his injuries and pain, allowed him a chance to fight on. Whoever had aided him then had had the same feeling, the same scent as their previous night's visitor.

Eilish sat her mount. Her thoughts were chaotic. Someone from here had been there—and here? Someone who seemed to have given all of them the ability to understand one of the languages here. Could this tie in with why Kian Dae was welcomed, why he appeared to be recognized by something here? But by what or whom? She spoke softly to everyone.

"Let's stop for the night and make a camp, now. The trees here should hide us from view. I have something that you all need to hear."

3

*T*wo wagons rolled slowly along the main road from Surah to Shallahah. Imprisoned in the first, Aycharna prayed to Pasht and despaired. It wasn't fair; she'd done nothing wrong. How could she be sold for a debt that her brother owed? Her father had told her once that the Lhandes didn't have slavery, but she'd been kidnapped in the Lhandes of Surah by this pair and hauled away. They'd given her a drink that made her feel faint and fuzzy, then shown some Pasht-cursed paper to a magistrate, who gave them a token and allowed them to take her. She'd been so confused and sick that she'd said nothing, made no protest aloud until it was too late. Now she was in road chains and traveling to Shallahah with slavers.

Her wide mouth curved in a wry twist as she pushed back short light brown hair. They didn't know as much about her as they thought. She'd been born in the area between the fringe of the Grass Sea and the Outlaw Coast. Most of the people there lived off the sea, but some had other, darker, ways of making a living. Her father had taught her a few tricks her brother didn't know about when he left home four years earlier—and since then she'd learned others. She removed the wire picklock from under her hair and started in on the locks again. She needed enough practice to be able to get them open quickly. Then, when the caravan of wagons, pack beasts, and people was where she felt it to be safest, she could make a run for it with real hope of escape.

She knew about Vani and Shaetyl, though. She'd heard the talk for years and seen some of those humans they held as slaves when they traveled through. Sometimes their caravan took the road past the Grass Sea and then people talked about them for weeks. Maybe that pair thought that people didn't know about them or their business. If so they were wrong. Gossip traveled and about Vani and Shaetyl it traveled on wings. She'd been very careful until they left to ride ahead.

"Woman, sit up and eat or go without."

Pasht curse the man, she found she was staring up in annoyance and controlled that. She nearly had the lock. But she mustn't get so involved again with what she did that she didn't see the overseer when he appeared. That was dangerous. Her father had always said, "One eye for the work, the other for danger."

"Here, take the bowl." Treyvan was in a hurry.

"Yes, lord." She lowered her hazel-eyed gaze and obediently accepted the wooden bowl of mush and ate it greedily, scraping up the last drop with her fingers. "Eat food when it's available, tomorrow it may not be" had been another of her father's sayings. She drank the fruit juice from the drinking bowl that was handed to her and prepared to walk all day again. Thus far no one had laid hands on her—good fortune that she was sure wouldn't last.

At least she wasn't too badly fed; the mush was bland but was filling enough, and the juice was a mixture of carris fruit and jaya. The combination in the right proportions wouldn't spoil for a tenday, even in the heat, and with a minor preservative spell added, it would stay good for twice that at need, even if it was diluted by half with water. On a diet of mush and juice even slaves who were made to walk all day would remain in reasonable health and not lose too much weight. And that was something that was necessary. No one would buy slaves that looked to be half dead—and it was wise not to look worthless; slavers had ways of dealing with those who had no value to them.

*I*n the trader's wagon a day's walk behind her, two friends who were also lovers and heart-sisters—and goddess-blessed in that bond—rode together ahead of their wagon and employees, chatting casually.

"It's been a good and profitable trip," Tiah commented.

"True, shaya," Kaitlen, her partner, agreed, calling her friend by the ancient word for those who were goddess-bonded. "And once we get back to Kavarten we can relax." She had used the Aradian name that actually meant heart-home, one of the countries of her felinoid people, where just under thirty years earlier the two had met and become heart-sisters, and where her partner's father still lived. "Is your father out on the road still?"

Anatiah, plump, with medium-brown hair and eyes, descended from human stock that had fled through a portal to this world, female, a trader in her own right and daughter of Master Trader Anamaskin, grinned. "Probably not by the time we get back. He was taking a caravan carrying wheat, woven fabric, and other trade goods along the back road that borders Ngahere and on past the Grass Sea. He plans to trade with the Hala'atha and return with furs and tanned leather, along with small items like buttons and toggles carved from bone and

antlers, they've become a middle-class fad this year in Shallahah City."

"A dangerous road to travel!" Kaitlen—one of the felinoid Aradian people—commented. "There has been talk of
larger groups of bandits on that road." Anatiah nodded.

"Maybe so, but he's hired extra guards and they'll stand
double watch all trip with never less than two at a time watching back-to-back. The nomads in the Grass Sea haven't recov-
ered their numbers yet from our king's punishment of them
twenty years ago. They're staying away from the road still, so
all Father has to worry about are the usual bandits."

"I like the *all.*"

Tiah laughed. "That's why he hired extra guards. I know
there are more bandits on that road, but he's a trader. Traders
go where the markets are, and the market is doing well in that
direction this season."

Kaitlen nodded. "Yes, because the bandits are worse."

Anatiah shrugged. "Of course. It's scarcity that makes
markets. But Father said he was probably going to join forces
with another trader he knows who was planning to go that
way. If he did they'll likely be too many for any bandits to take
on."

Kaitlen changed the subject. "Who's on the road ahead of
us? I saw their campsite last night when we pulled into the
roadside. Dirty pigs hadn't cleaned up their leavings."

Anatiah made a face. "Vani and Shaetyl's caravan of slaves."

"What? But I thought they'd been banned from Surah?"

"So did I. They must have greased the right palms."

Kaitlen looked thoughtful. "Or found a figurehead. Lhandes law allows that, doesn't it, Tiah?"

There might be only two Lhandes as yet, she thought, but
the earlier one of them, Surah by name, maintained the rule of

law. Small city-state or not, Duke Tassino believed that Lhandes, his in particular, should be properly governed and law-abiding.

Her heart-sister considered the question. "Yes. If all the proper papers are in place, if that banned pair aren't traveling with the caravan, and if the figurehead shows sufficient coin to indicate he can pay all bills and taxes before they depart. That's fairly rigorous, love."

"But probably worth it for that pair," her love said sourly. No Aradian approved of chattel slavery. The Aradian clans had practiced the taking of war slaves, but that had been generations ago and a slave of that kind had hope. Show his captors that he was valuable, settle in to be part of his new clan, perform usefully and well, and he'd have an excellent chance of freedom after a few years. After that he could either return to his clan or, if he was really valued where he was and if he wished to do so, stay with his new clan and settle down permanently.

"I really thought that a ban on them would stick after we proved to the Lhandes court that Vani had been buying up bond servants' bonds in Surah then taking them to Shallahah and reselling them as plain slaves. It cost them a big fine, with compensation to the slaves," Kaitlen added.

"I know. But the Lhandes law allows figureheads. Still . . ." Her tone became quietly thoughtful. "I wouldn't mind wagering that that precious pair aren't changing their ways. I'd love to get a look at the sale papers on the people they have with their caravan now."

Kaitlen nodded vigorously. "Why don't we close up the gap a little? I'm sure I could think up an excuse."

Tiah looked at her. "I'm quite sure you could, shaya. But I don't think the law would accept another fire breaking out accidentally in the same caravan. Not with us being right behind them the way we were last time and their figurehead—whoever he is—probably having been warned about us by Vani and Shaetyl."

"They'd still have to prove it." Kaitlen's grin showed her fighting fangs. "And if I'm right and some of those they'll have in chains will have got that way illegally, he'd be too busy explaining himself to a magistrate to complain about accidental fires."

"Maybe so."

Tiah was torn. She hated the system of slavery, having learned that attitude from her father, who despised it, and from long association with her heart-sister. She'd seen the abuses both in her own country of Shallahah and in the new city-states of the Lhandes, and was often saddened that Shallahah had accepted slavery ever since humans had first come to Aradia nine hundred years ago. The Aradians' slavery system allowed hope. The human system did not. Once a slave to humans you usually died in chains unless you had friends or family to buy you free. It was almost unheard of for a human slave to be voluntarily freed by an owner.

Rulers of the Lhandes—the city-states settled by disaffected nobles—allowed debt servitude for a specific time but not outright slavery. Tiah had an excellent imagination and could easily picture herself in chains. She could imagine the indignities, the brutality she'd face, and the compromises she'd have to make to survive. She shivered.

"It's worse for a woman too, usually," she said.

"They have a woman with them."

Tiah glared. "I didn't want to hear that. I suppose you picked up her scent. How do you know she's a slave?"

Kaitlen snorted. "Please, shaya. I'm an Aradian. My nose

works better than that thing you humans hang on your face to keep your eyes apart. And yes, I know she's a woman because when I checked that camp I picked up her scent. She was lying apart from the men and there were marks on the earth where her chains had dragged."

"Oh."

Kaitlen said nothing and allowed her heart-sister to think her thoughts undisturbed. This was how, three years ago, they'd come to do something about Vani and Shaetyl's system of making profits on slavery. Maybe they wouldn't have acted if it hadn't been that Vani and Shaetyl had pulled that trick on the sister of one of their own servants. Jessara had come to them in tears, her brother Jiro and her husband Gheevin backing her.

The three of them had sworn that while young Lilja had been foolish to get herself into a debt she could not repay, she was only under servant bond, and that for just a year to repay the debt. Nor would she ever have agreed to her removal from Surah, where some of the family had settled. Kaitlen and Anatiah had investigated with the help of friends, to find that the girl's bond had been resold to Vani and Shaetyl, who had forged an extension to it and resold Lilja in Shallahah as an outright slave. They'd sorted that out—with witnesses. The slaver duo blamed a former assistant—who had mysteriously disappeared—but the slavemasters had paid heavily for the whole business. She hoped that their figurehead didn't know about her and her shaya, or if he did, that he didn't know they were in the small caravan immediately behind him. If he knew that he'd be more cautious.

Something she hadn't told Tiah was that she was sure the woman planned escape. She'd scented the sweat of hard work, and the marks in the earth suggested some activity centered on the woman's ankle chains, probably the locks. Vani and Shaetyl wouldn't know about her ability to learn such things; they never hired Aradians. For one thing Aradians wouldn't have worked for them, and for another that pair were deeply prejudiced. She'd once heard them use the term "cats" about her kind, and sneer to their friends that a human was smarter than any animal.

She smiled at her partner. Thanks be to the goddess who'd blessed their bond. In their time they'd overcome both human and Aradian prejudice on their love. Most who knew they were shayana—heart-sisters and lovers as well—accepted that if Pasht, beloved goddess of both races, blessed them then it was all right. But even now there were some people who didn't feel that way. Vani and Shaetyl were two of them. It would be pleasant to tweak their tails.

In the slaver caravan ahead of Kait and Tiah, Aycharna was working on just that. She'd had the locks open once. Now she knew their wards it would be easier a second time, easier and quicker still the third time. She plodded along the road and kept her mouth shut and her head down. She knew who had her and knew too of their reputation. If she caused trouble before she was sure of escape she'd be made to regret it weeping. Vani and Shaetyl had a whispered reputation for what they did to tame any slaves who were difficult. She'd seen them look at her before they rode off and could guess what they had in mind once the wagons were far enough away from Surah. She had to escape before then.

In his seat the slaver figurehead, Kyeaan, scowled. Bad enough his father had lost most of his money in a foolish speculation, worse that when the man died Kyeaan had had to split what was left with three brothers. He was a gentleman, a son of minor nobility; he shouldn't have to take a job at all, let alone one as a figurehead for slave traders—and men at that who weren't even honest slavers. But all they'd wanted was a figurehead. He didn't have to do anything but bespeak magistrates and judges when it was necessary.

Aycharna stumbled a little and his attention went to her. Vani had warned him what would happen if he touched the woman, but she was a delectable piece. He'd admired the long free stride, the lustrous hazel eyes, and the short, shining hair. He'd allowed her a little more than the men. She'd been given warm water and soap to wash her hair. He'd made sure that her morning drinking bowl of fruit juice was full and of pure juice so she didn't go thirsty, and she'd been given an extra blanket. His gaze roamed over the sturdy shapely figure. She wasn't tall, but that was fine; he liked women to be shorter than he was.

If he was nice to her maybe she'd come to him voluntarily and keep her mouth shut to Vani and Shaetyl once they rejoined the caravan after the Jasta Pass. Then again, maybe she wouldn't, and if he went against them he'd lose this job. It was good as jobs went too; all he had to do was swear that these were his wagons, that these were his slaves, and that they were all legally so. In proof of that he had signed papers. He wasn't sure how legal those were, but they'd worked in Surah.

Vani and Shaetyl could have told him that while the papers on the men were, for once, mostly honest, the papers on the woman the figurehead lusted after were completely false. They'd been quietly forged on information from her brother one drunken night when he was complaining that she'd gone to Surah and left him to take care of the family business—that business consisting of removing anything valuable and portable from those incautious enough to allow it, although that was something he left unmentioned. Since Vani and Shaetyl actually had a fair idea of what his business might be, they anticipated no problems with the girl—or her family should they discover her fate. They wouldn't be likely to go near any court to make a complaint. It had been pure coincidence that they ran across the woman in Surah, but luck favored the ready and both men were always ready to make a profit.

That night while Aycharna worked on the locks again, Kyeaan came walking past her. He paused to look down.

"All right, girl?"

"Yes, master."

Master, he liked that. It sounded good from the men, better from this woman. A thought occurred to him. He was paid well enough for his work and he could perhaps afford a slave—this slave—once they were back in the city at Shallahah. He smiled down at her winningly. Aycharna thought his smile reminded her of a hungry kio—a dirty little scavenger.

"Well, if you have trouble with any of the men, sweetling, just tell me. I'll make sure no one bothers you."

She'd wager he would. She knew that look. He wanted her himself and that worried her. Vani and Shaetyl wouldn't like it, and if it happened and they found out about it they'd probably blame her. She gazed at him with a submissive look.

"Yes, master."

"Good girl. Don't worry about anything, I'll look after you. In fact," he said, glancing about to make sure everyone else was out of earshot, "I could look after you always. How would you like that?"

She'd rather eat sand and shit bricks, but she had to keep him sweet until she could get away from the slaver caravan. "Oh, master, that would be wonderful. You plan to buy me?" She pasted a worried look on her face. Better remind him before he thought to take his hopes somewhere with her tonight. "But will the other masters agree?"

Kyeaan puffed out his chest. "I'm their associate. I'm sure they'll agree if I wish it and at a reasonable price."

Stupid kio, Aycharna thought. If he believed that he'd believe anything. She'd met his masters and they wouldn't give a copper to starving children who were kin of theirs, let alone sell a valuable slave cut-price to a man who was merely their servant.

"If you think so, master, I'm sure it's true."

Kyeaan eyed her. There'd been doubt in her tone. Did she know something he didn't? he asked.

"Not to say 'know,' master. But I think they plan to keep me themselves. They said they would see me after the pass and that I'd probably be going with them after that."

Well, Vani had hinted that she would, and she could guess what they had in mind once they arrived. This kio would be nervous about crossing them no matter what his claims to be an associate were—as he should be. That pair didn't *have* associates who worked for them, only servants, and they could be very hard on those according to gossip. This fool would know those stories the same way she did.

Kyeaan did know, but he hadn't had a woman in three weeks and this one was a slave. She'd have to do anything he said or be punished. An idea struck him. Yes, anything at all, and he wasn't directly in charge of the slaves; Vani and Shaetyl's trusted slavemaster was. If the girl escaped it would almost certainly be Treyvan who was blamed.

If Kyeaan had her in his bed until they were almost at the pass, kept his activities from Treyvan, and at the last moment killed and buried her, no one would know what he'd done. They'd think she'd got away and maybe they'd hunt for her, post a reward in Shallahah, but no one would suspect him. If they did appear to be wondering about him he could always be indignant. The partners needed him to be the essential figurehead for their business. They wouldn't dare become too unpleasant in case he walked out on them. But he had to keep her thinking that whatever he did to her was with Vani and Shaetyl's permission. That way she'd cooperate without rousing the camp.

"I can talk to them, my sweet. I'm sure they'll agree. In fact I'll send a message to them tonight. I should hear back in another day, two at most, and after that we can talk, can't we?"

"Yes, master."

"Meanwhile you can sleep a bit further from the men. I don't want you at risk. Closer to me should make that sure, shouldn't it?"

"Yes, master."

Aycharna, watching him, could not read his thoughts—not entirely—but she could guess enough to be seriously scared. The stupid kio was going to risk it. Vani and Shaetyl would blame her. She'd heard enough about how they punished slaves to want to avoid their anger. Her mind was racing. If she slept farther from the men that would make an escape easier, but from the sound of it she had only one or two more nights of precarious safety before this scavenger came hunting her.

Kyeaan walked away, to be replaced very quietly by Treyvan. He leaned over her. "What was he saying, girl?"

"That I should sleep closer to his wagon, master. He was afraid some of the other slaves might try to rape me."

Treyvan snorted. "Of course, they'll drag twenty pounds of chain each over to you soundlessly along with the wagon they're attached to. They'll expect you to keep silent while they rape you, hope that I'll see and hear nothing, and believe that my kind and gentle employers won't punish them any-how if they achieve any of that."

She managed to look bewildered. "Master?"

He stared down at her, snorted again, and marched away. Aycharna hid a smile. With luck Treyvan would be so busy watching Kyeaan while Kyeaan watched for an opportunity to get at her that neither would be watching her. But it would have to be tonight even if this area was short of food and water that a woman on foot might find. If only she could unearth her papers at the same time. She knew they were in Kyeaan's wagon. She hadn't been shown them beyond the outer page and her brother's signature. But if she had them she could read well enough to puzzle out what they said. Once she read them she might find some loophole through which she could legally flee.

She should head back to Surah. In Shallahah she would probably be a slave no matter what the loopholes. Vani and Shaetyl could pay off someone to shut their eyes. Then they'd take out on her the loss of some of their profit before she was sold. If she was caught on the road by a Shallahan army pa-trol, she'd be returned to the slavers, and there were stretches of the road that were mostly desert; if she escaped there she could die before finding water. But if there was a possibility that her papers were false in some way, or if there was a loop-hole, she'd have a better chance of being heard in the Lhandes where she was a citizen—if she could return there.

She worked on the locks again that night. This wasn't a good place to run, but she had another idea. Guards and mas-ters often sat up quite late talking and drinking. If she got free the moment it was dark, she might be able to find her papers. She could conceal those; then if she escaped the next night she wouldn't have to waste time looking for them, she could just run. It still wouldn't be a good time, out in the middle of nowhere as they were, but it was better than the alternative. She curled around the locks and worked until, three candlemarks after dark, she heard footsteps coming in her direction.

"Are you awake, sweetling?" That was Kyeann's voice.

"*I'm* awake, sir. Can I do anything for you?" That was Treyvan, and she could have cheered. Kyeaan sounded grumpy.

"No, slavemaster. I was just checking that the girl is warm enough. Vani and Shaetyl asked me to take special care for her."

"Don't worry about that, sir. I'm keeping an eye on her. After all, the male slaves might fancy her, and we wouldn't want anything to happen like that, would we."

Kyeaan sounded slightly strangled. "No, no, we wouldn't. I'll leave it to you, slavemaster. I'm sure you have everything under control."

Treyvan sounded disconcertingly cheerful. "That I do, sir. You go to sleep and know that I'm always awake doing my job."

"Excellent," Kyeaan said sourly. "I commend you." To hell with going to his bed. He could use a drink, maybe several. Getting half drunk wasn't a woman, but it was better than nothing.

Treyvan watched him depart and smiled unpleasantly. His nominal superior was a skulking little kio and he'd have a word about him once the bosses met the caravan again. Kyeaan was here to be a figurehead and nothing more. Treyvan did the real work, and everyone knew it. He'd keep a closer eye on that fop from now on. He wondered briefly how the fool thought he'd keep any liaison with the woman quiet—then realized the idiot's possible plan. Treyvan had been a slavemaster for many years. Damn! Dead women told no tales, but if Kyeaan managed that the bosses would have *both* their heads.

He headed in the direction that Kyeaan had gone. He'd have to make sure the man never got anywhere near the woman from now on. He found his quarry drinking with the guards by their fire and settled in to watch his every movement. From now on the man wouldn't take a shit without Treyvan knowing.

Aycharna picked the last lock, laid the chains down silently, and drifted toward the back of Kyeaan's wagon. The road here ran through desert, and much as she'd like to run, it would be better to wait a night or two. Still, there were preparations she could make in advance. Once inside the wagon she lit a splinter of talis wood from his flint and steel by the candle. It would give just sufficient light, but unlike a candle it would release no scent. Nor if she had to leave hurriedly and Kyeaan lit his candle would he discover it to be still warm. She'd made a bundle of such splinters when they'd camped by a grove of the trees two nights ago and she'd found a dry branch. She carried them tied under her hair along with the picklock.

Now she had to pick the lock of his strongbox, and that took time, but the papers were there. What else would be useful or even lifesaving while she trudged back to Surah? She gathered up a candle end that still had the candlemarks scored into the wax and colored black. Twenty-four candlemarks—known often as 'marks—to the full day, with sixty candlemarkin—the name sometimes shortened to 'markin—to the candlemark. In her position a stub of candle could be very useful and maybe they wouldn't miss this one even if it was an end of one of the expensive candle clocks but she couldn't risk using it now.

She glanced out of the doorway at the stars. It looked to be between three and four candlemarks until dawn; that wasn't a lot of time. She remembered something else that she'd seen under the papers. She lifted them again to find a broken flint and steel. The flint had fallen out but the steel would work still;

all she had to do was find another flint, and along the road there was an outcropping of that here and there.

At the last candlemarkin she saw needles and thread in a dusty box in a corner by the bed and took one of the needles together with some lengths of the thread she unwound from the spools. She added those to the papers, steel, and candle end before dowsing her splinter, waited until her sight fully adjusted to the dark again, and slid silently from the wagon.

Back by her chains, she closed the manacles about her wrists and ankles and picked the locks to shut them once more. The dress they'd given her to wear was of shabby but thick material, and it was too large. Nothing she carried within the folds would show, but she dared not risk dropping her loot. That was the idea that had come to her when she saw the sewing box. Outside again the moonlight was enough to allow her to unpick some of the seams on her dress and sew the items inside, in places where, if Pasht Goddess was with her, no wandering hand would light on them.

The next day she was fortunate. Kyeaan had a bad hangover and spent most of his day sleeping in the wagon while they rolled along at walking pace. Treyvan kept an eye on him to be sure of that, something his quarry realized at sunhigh. Kyeaan moved to approach Aycharna when they rested briefly at that time but was foiled when the slavemaster headed his way the moment the figurehead moved toward her.

"Master Kyeaan, is there something you wish?"

"Just making sure all is well."

"It is, sir, believe me. I know my job. Any hint of trouble and you'll be the first to know." The look he received in return to that was murderous, but the slavemaster held his ground. He knew if there was a dispute about this who the bosses would back—and so did Kyeaan.

Aycharna kept her head well down and her face blank. Inside she was chuckling, but neither man must know that she'd heard what they said, let alone that she understood what was going on. Slaves who were too clever tended to have short life spans. But her escape would have to be tonight even if they were still in a desert area. It was becoming too dangerous for her to remain. She picked her sleeping spot very carefully that evening, right by a small patch of brush for which she had plans.

Right after she sat down, Kyeaan was again heading her way. Treyvan was on the other side of the wagon seeing to the feeding and watering of the male slaves, and he knew that nothing would happen in daylight anyway; there'd be too many eyes to see and mouths to talk.

"Fruit bread, girl?" Kyeaan was offering her a thick slice of the bread with berry spread, and she took it hastily, smiling up at him.

"That's very kind of you, master." Her look became almost adoring. "I'm so hungry and thirsty."

His chest expanded. "I can see to that." He strode to the large kettle and dipped out juice. He returned to offer the drinking bowl to her. "Drink up, girl, and I'll get you another."

She drank quickly and held out the empty pottery drinking bowl. The juice wasn't that bad; the mix and the preservative spell kept it from spoiling, but each day the taste became a little less sweet. He brought her a second bowlful and another slice of the fruit bread. Aycharna ate, drank, and smiled at the man until her face ached. She could take no food with her when she fled; this might be the last she ate for some time, and she'd best get all she could. In the end she had almost half a loaf of the fruit bread, most of a pot of berry spread, and four drinking bowls of the unwatered juice. She felt stuffed and bloated, but the feeling would wear off quickly enough and it should be sufficient to keep her going for a day or two.

Kyeaan beamed smugly. Food was a great tamer of slaves. Just look how the girl smiled at him. He leered back and Treyvan noticed both looks. Pasht's claws but the fool was still determined to have the girl. He'd have to stop that before it went any further. He grinned nastily to himself at an idea— Kyeaan had slept right through the midday halt—called the guard captain, and gave orders. That should do it. If that slinking little kio left his wagon after dark, the guards would challenge him and make it even clearer that they were watching him.

Kyeaan waited only until dusk. The girl was quite close and the brush near where she lay would make good cover for them. He emerged from the wagon to meet a suspicious guard.

"Sir?"

"It's Kyeaan."

"Yes, sir. I know."

He went to walk off and found himself followed. "What are you doing?"

"Orders, sir. Slavemaster Treyvan heard news from another caravan at our sunhigh halt, sir. There was a bandit attack on slavers a few days' walk down the road. I'm to make sure that any of our people moving around after dark come to no harm, sir."

"And if I want to take a piss are you going to hold it for me?"

"No, sir. But I'll be standing right there making sure no one sneaks up on you from behind with a sword, sir."

Kyeaan went to bed. That Pasht-cursed interfering bagir of a slavemaster thought he had him. He'd find out that he was wrong. Kyeaan would get a few good candlemarks' sleep, and in the 'marks after moonhigh, when the guards were less alert to movement within the camp, he'd slip out of the front of the wagon, where they wouldn't be expecting him.

Around the third candlemark from moonhigh he tried. There was a guard posted in a position to see the front of the wagon, and he too, while polite, was quite definite that Kyeaan wasn't going anywhere without the guard.

Kyeaan would have been wasting his time in any case, although he didn't know that. By the time the camp had settled and all but the current watch of guards were asleep—well before moonhigh—Aycharna had picked her locks again and was gone, trotting quietly into the moonlit dark. Behind her, threadbare blankets stuffed with brush lay curled in a reasonable imitation of someone sleeping. It would do, unless or until anyone tried to wake her, and if Pasht willed it that wouldn't be until dawn.

She didn't hurry—that was the way to wind yourself or tire early—but she kept moving steadily all night and into the dawn so long as nobody was in sight. She was very thirsty by that time, but she'd found no water. Ahead of her when it started to become lighter she saw wagons. By now Treyvan and Kyeaan would know she was missing. They'd also guess she'd be heading back to Surah, and if she slowed for a while they might miss her. She turned, trotted back to the last patch of heavy scrub, and vanished into it. There she found a comfortable spot to sit while she watched and listened.

*K*aitlen was riding ahead. They'd moved out early, so the light was still poor, but her sight was keen. She saw the retreating, vanishing figure and briefly showed her fangs. To Tiah she mind-sent.

That slaver caravan up ahead of us, I think they may have lost property. The girl must have walked all night.

Then someone will be after her. Is anyone in sight? Where is she?

There's no one in sight so far, and she's hiding in brush by the road just ahead. I feel a need to halt the wagon coming on, shaya.

There was the feel of a giggle. *Do that. Preferably by scrub so we'll have some shade, it's so hot today.* Kaitlen, ignoring the clouds and chill wind, rode ahead to the scrub, waving the wagon driver to turn in once they came level with her.

"Gheevin, I think one of the pack mules may be starting to go lame. We'll stop now while I look it over. I want all of you to enjoy your break over on the other side of the campsite. Well over. Just leave the mule and the supply wagon and its team on this side so my shaya and I have privacy."

The man to whom she spoke looked at her suspiciously but said nothing. The lean and balding Gheevin, his plump wife, Jessara, and her younger brother, Jiro, had worked for this pair for more than nine years, and he knew when to keep his mouth shut. They'd all three of them worked for her father before her, and the master trader was a canny man. His daughter followed in his footsteps. Gheevin wouldn't ask questions and waste time. He knew that if they needed to know, she'd tell them.

Kaitlen picked up a mule's hooves at random while Anatiah quietly unlocked the canvas cover at the back of the wagon before leaving it to consult with Kait over the mule's hoof. She had backed the wagon in which they usually carried their bedding, the heavier supplies and trade goods, right up to the scrub, and none of the servants in their group saw a slender figure slip out of the heavy brush and climb over the tailboard. Kaitlen, however, had no need to see that; her nose and ears told her when it happened.

She's safely inside the wagon, shaya, she sent.

Then we'll go back on the road.

Aloud, and for the record she said, "I don't see any problem, but we'll keep a watch on the beast. If he does begin to go lame we can spell him."

Down the road two riders emerged from the dust and the distance, one to either side of the road, their heads turning from side to side, watching constantly for a furtive movement. One was slightly ahead of the other. Kaitlen, noting his eager leaning forward in the saddle, made ready for their arrival.

4

*K*yeaan reached the traders first, as he'd planned. Treyvan would only put them off from giving any helpful reply. The man was positively crude. He smiled unctuously even while privately he found the sight of humans traveling with an Aradian distasteful. "Greetings, gracious lady. Would you have seen a lone woman on the road? She would be going toward Surah?"

"Your wife fled, has she?" Kaitlen asked cheerfully, guessing the slight foppish middle-aged man to be the slaver's figurehead. "No, honored sir, I've seen no one."

Kyeaan was offended by the suggestion that if he had a wife it was natural to leap to the conclusion that she'd have fled from him. "Certainly not. The woman is . . ."

Treyvan arrived, recognized the Aradian female at once, and broke in. "She's a thief. We hired her to cook for us and last night she stole coin and ran back to Surah."

Tiah, having heard their claims through Kaitlen's open mind-link, walked her mount to join them and looked inquiringly at Kaitlen. "Hunting a thief, so they say," she was informed tersely. Tiah smiled kindly at both men.

"It's a terrible thing to take someone in out of kindness and be repaid with ingratitude," she said. "If she was hired in Surah I imagine you'd have a contract for service? Or was she just some woman you picked up to work for you on the road?"

"Both," Treyvan said hastily, before Kyeaan could open his mouth. "We met her a couple of days out of Surah and she said she was going to stay with family in Shallahah and she could cook. We planned to have a service contract written and pay her once we reached Shallahah City." His smile became accusatory. "She cuddled up to Kyeaan here and found where we keep the strongbox, picked the lock and looted it. I'd say she has to be an experienced thief. No amateur could have opened that lock."

At least that was no more than the truth, he reflected. She'd opened the chain locks as easy as slipping in mud. After that she must have simply run for it. The coin was still where it should be no matter what he told this pair. Damned woman. Damn her brother too; he hadn't said anything about the girl being handy with a picklock.

Kait shrugged. "Why are you looking for her this close to your caravan? I imagine she'd have got a lot farther on a mule."

"She was on foot," Treyvan said before he thought.

From the back of the wagon Aycharna was alternately holding back giggles and squeals of outrage. She hadn't stolen even a copper! And as for cuddling up to that repulsive Kyeaan, it was he who'd been hunting her. But she had the feeling that these women had the measure of Treyvan and Kyeaan. She listened harder, her grin widening.

"And of course you plan to take her to the nearest Surah

magistrate when you catch her?" Kaitlen was asking, raising
a brow in question.

Treyvan's smile became lopsided. "Ah well, we have business in Shallahah City, we can't afford to turn back to Surah
and lose more than two tendays."

Kaitlen looked at the burly, balding slaver. "Then you'll
have to take the loss, won't you? According to Shallahan laws,
Surah citizens have the right to be tried for nonviolent crimes
in their own Lhandes if that is closer—and it is—unless you're
now claiming that she attacked and injured someone in this theft
that you say was committed by a rather unusual woman?"

"Unusual?" Kyeaan asked in confusion. Himself, he'd
thought the story was very believable. Especially when considering that Treyvan had invented it on the spur of the moment.

"Yes," Kaitlen said, her gaze fixed on him. "You meet a
woman walking along the road on her own and on foot. Apparently she isn't at all worried by the thought of bandits and
being murdered, or abducted and raped. If she's carrying food
or waterskins at all she can't carry enough on foot to make it
to the city, so for about half of her trip she's going to starve—if
she hasn't already died of thirst. You assume she'll make a good
cook on no evidence, ask her to join you—and she agrees, without service contract, to join an obvious slaver caravan? You
appear to have hired a madwoman."

Tiah looked at Kyeaan. "I don't know you, friend, but I
know Treyvan. He's experienced on the road and yet he too
seems to have accepted all this. He seems to have had no suspicion that the woman might be a decoy for bandits, no suspicion that there was something strange about her appearing on
the road alone without adequate supplies for her trip. What
does he know about her that you don't? Is he in league with

someone to cheat the owners out of their coin, using the woman for a scapegoat?"

Kyeaan opened his mouth, shut it again, and opened it a second time to reply, before finding that he couldn't think of anything convincing to say. Put that way, it *did* all sound very suspicious.

Treyvan snarled inwardly. Trust this pair to pick out all the weak spots in a good tale. Any more talking to them was only going to complicate matters. Best to cut line and just walk away. With an effort he prevented himself from frowning. Something had just occurred to him as they stood here: Why was the trader caravan halted here in the first place at all? His mind raced. It was still quite early in the morning and people on the road didn't often eat and drink at this time, and even if ordinary travelers did, few traders halted and drew off the road to do so. If they knew him and his business, then he also knew trader customs. If they were suspicious of his tale, he was becoming more suspicious of their own actions by the candle-markin.

Treyvan glanced casually across the flat area they'd used to pull off the road. Their wagon was settled right on the other side of the area, backed into horse-high scrub. Their people sat by a small fire drinking hot pata while they waited. All of their animals bar the wagon team and one mule were over with them. That was peculiar in itself, since he knew that those others of the women's group weren't merely servants, but old friends. Although now was not the time to say so, he thought.

He bowed politely. "Since you have not seen our thief, gracious ladies, we will not delay you any further. Please excuse my colleague and I." He swept Kyeaan off down the road past the traders and toward Surah before the fool could say something that this pair could fasten on to cause further embarrassment. They'd go on another couple of 'marks just to see if there was any sign of the damned girl. If not they'd have to return, catch up to their caravan, and think about what to do next.

Kaitlen nudged her pony, and it moved several paces down the road after them. Her ears fanned out, cupped in the slavers' direction. She heard the first questions and answers before they looked back to see her, lowered their voices, and increased their pace.

"Who are they?" Kyeaan asked again, once they were out of range of the traders' hearing.

"A couple of meddlers who know more than they're saying." Treyvan was terse. "Listen, did you check to see if the girl's bond papers were in the strongbox?"

Kyeaan gaped. "Why would I?"

"Because, you idiot, she could well have taken them. With those gone we don't have any evidence to reclaim her right now if someone like them takes her in and gets difficult about it with us." That was all Kaitlen heard, but the next few comments she could guess from their body language.

Kyeaan drew himself up. "How dare you call me an idiot. I wasn't the one she escaped from." He stabbed a finger at Treyvan. "You're the slavemaster. It's your job to make sure they don't escape."

"And it's your job to explain anything that needs explaining to a magistrate or judge, my lord figurehead. What do you intend to say to Vani and Shaetyl if we can't reclaim the girl because she took her papers when she fled and she's destroyed them?"

Kyeaan winced. No, his employers wouldn't be pleased if that had occurred, and they could always find another figurehead; an experienced slavemaster was harder to hire.

"So we have to find her."

"Aye, and make sure she keeps her mouth shut."

Kyeaan considered how good he'd been to the girl. The extra food, the drink he'd lavished on her, another blanket, kind words. Letting her sleep closer to his wagon for protection. He'd gone out of his way to help her and this was how he was repaid? By theft, ingratitude, making him look bad to his employers and imperiling his job?

"If we get her back she'll keep her mouth shut," he said softly, a thin note of savagery in his voice.

Treyvan glanced at him and said nothing. It was amusing how fast a man who claimed to be a nobleman and a gentleman descended into something else when he was personally affected. Not that he'd ever had any illusions about the nobility. People of their own rank might be able to trust them but, something of which Treyvan was well aware, so far as the nobility were concerned they owed nothing to those inferior in rank beyond the back of their hand for insolence. He grinned. This was one noble who'd find himself out of work once they reached the city and he could talk to his employers.

Behind them Kaitlen was leaning on the wagon side, talking to her heart-sister, but in reality they were talking for the benefit of the girl hidden in their supply wagon. There was something about the situation that urged them to intervene. They both of them felt as they had before—that the goddess was involved. If Pasht had something to do with this, they'd obey gladly.

"Would you hand her back?"

"Not to that pair. Never! I'd wager she isn't a slave legally anyway, I wish I could get a look at her slave papers. I only hope that she manages to keep out of the slavers' hands but I hate the thought of her being stranded out here alone on the road. We're five days out of Surah, how will she make it back there without food or a waterskin?"

"I don't think she'll survive trying, shaya. There are bandits on the road and if she takes to the upper trails there are other predators. It's been a lean winter and now that it's late spring a lot of them are looking to feed cubs. I wish she'd come to us, I'd have helped her. That pair are out of sight, maybe we should move on soon?"

Tiah sat silently, her hands occupied in rubbing oil into a bridle, but both were waiting. Their patience was rewarded. Kait was listening in link with her heart-sister, her keener hearing tuned for movement. There was a rustle in the wagon, the crunch of a footstep on the backboard, and the girl appeared, poised for flight into the brush, while her gaze flicked from one to the other.

Tiah grinned companionably. "Your abductors seem to have given up looking for you."

Aycharna winced, knowing Treyvan and Kyeaan. "Not for long. They'll come back when they think you're off-guard."

"We'll deal with that when or if we have to," Kait said. "It won't be the first time."

Tiah grinned. "No, I remember that time on the coast. We were met at the Hala'atha border by some officious little kio named S'Vraise who said that he and his friends were going to check our caravan and charge us a toll."

Aycharna was interested. "How many of them were there? Did they check your wagons?"

Kait spoke in a deadpan voice, although Aycharna noticed that her eyes were glinting with laughter. "Three and no they didn't check anything at all—they were too busy burying S'Vraise."

The ex-slave took a heartbeat or two to understand the

punch line and then burst into laughter, which turned abruptly to gasping sobs. Tiah stood, patted the girl on a heaving shoulder, and spoke gently.

"I know, it's been a strain but you're safe now. Sit down and try to relax. Would you like something to drink? We've hot pata, drager, good water, or we can even spare a glass of flame if you really need it. What do you say?"

"Drager would be pleasant. I thank you." She accepted the drinking bowl of the mildly alcoholic fruit juice that Kaitlen fetched her and sipped. None of the women said anything for some candlemarkins until Aycharna finished her drink and spoke cautiously.

"Did you mean what you said?"

"Yes, oh, all this is inconvenient for us, but Tiah and I don't like Vani and Shaetyl and we'd go a little out of our way for the chance of causing them trouble again. A couple of years ago they were making a habit of buying up bond-servant contracts in the Lhandes, taking the people to Shallahah City and selling them as real slaves. It wasn't legal, but it wasn't quite illegal either. Until they made the mistake of picking up one of Jessara's younger sisters." She pointed unobtrusively.

"That's Jessara over there with her husband and brother. They've worked for us for almost thirteen years and for my father before that. We got a copy made of Lilja's contract, tracked her down in the city, picked her up, and brought a complaint of forgery of a bond to the Shallahan courts. They released her from her bond, compensated her, fined Vani and Shaetyl, who also had to reimburse her owner, and we passed the official Shallahah judgment of bond forgery on to the Lhandes. Surah was annoyed enough about it to bar them from buying servant bonds in their Lhandes for five years."

Aycharna whistled softly. "That would have pleased them!"

"Oh, it did, they've stayed well away from us ever since. But we still hear about them now and again and neither of us likes what we hear. They're some of those who're prejudiced against Aradians—although in their case it's because the clans don't allow most forms of slavery and they can't make money from them. Now," she changed the subject firmly. "Did you steal from Treyvan and Kyeaan?"

"Sort of. I took the end of a candle clock, a broken flint and steel, a needle and a few lengths of thread, and my papers. I know the papers are wrong—they have to be—and I wanted to read them once it was light enough and I had time to puzzle out the words."

"Give them to Tiah," Kaitlen suggested. "She knows a lot about the laws in both places. Traders often have to and I leave that sort of thing mostly to her."

Tiah nodded and held out her hand. Aycharna turned her back, pulled the thread that opened the seam, and, turning around again, offered the sheets of folded, sealed paper.

Without compunction the woman broke the seal and scanned the contents swiftly. Then she looked up.

"Aycharna 'd Kadjo, huh? This says that you were taken for a bond servant to repay a debt owed to the courts by your brother, who is your legal guardian in Shallahah. Vani and Shaetyl were to return you to Shallahah and repay the debt to the court there, less the expenses of securing you, after which they'd have you under bond and they could sell that. These papers appear to be signed by your brother. Is that true?"

Aycharna tried to reply so fast that she could only splutter for a moment. Then the logjam cleared. "True? No, it tossing well isn't true. For one thing how could he be my guardian? My pa isn't dead yet. For another I've been living in Surah this two years past with my cousin. My brother knows all that, he wouldn't have signed that contract, my dad would skin him alive did he find out. We may not be much, but we don't sell family. An' to put a bleeking cap on it I'm not a minor who *needs* a guardian. I was eighteen last bornday."

"What is your brother's signature?" Kaitlen asked, looking at the paper.

"His name of course. Verrimini 's Kadjo."

"And he can write that?"

Aycharna drew herself up angrily. "My dad says knowing how to read and write is power and all his children can. Whenever he had enough money we got proper lessons." She flushed slightly. "I'm not so good on that script they use in Surah is all."

"But your brother can write his name in full?"

"I told you! Why do you keep asking?"

Wordlessly Tiah showed her the contract. The name was right, Verrimini 's Kadjo. But underneath that it was signed with a sprawling cross, the mark a man would make who couldn't write at all.

"That's a forgery."

"So I'd say."

"They can't *do* that!"

"They did it well enough to get you out of Surah legally. Maybe they greased the palm of a magistrate, but how did they keep you quiet?"

Aycharna grimaced. "They picked me up outside an inn when I was leaving. They grabbed me in the dark and pulled my head back by my hair, pinched my nose shut and poured something down my throat. They took me straight to the law after that. I could hear what was being said to the magistrate but I felt so awful I couldn't say anything. I was sick, giddy, and when I did try to talk I could only mumble."

Kaitlen nodded. "He was paid off, I'd say. But if he was

asked under priestess-laid truth-spell if you protested, he could honestly say that you'd never said a word against his decision." She considered the contract. "His name is clear enough. Low Court Magistrate Harko Valgon. I'll remember that. Sometime in the future we may meet him." Her smile showed all her fangs.

"What do you want to do, Aycharna?" Tiah looked at the girl. "It's a tenday more to Shallahah at our pace and a half-tenday back to Surah if you walk, but you aren't likely to make it there on your own. You can travel on with us if you wish."

"What if Vani and Shaetyl come hunting me?"

Kaitlen smiled. "We'll reason with them. I'm sure they'll listen."

In that moment there was something about her that abruptly reminded Aycharna that the Aradians were predators and even the king in Shallahah walked warily around the clans. She made up her mind on the spot. She believed these women were honest, and besides, if she got to the city she could seek out her father and have him and Verri come to court to forswear that contract. They could tell the court that it was a forgery. After that she'd enjoy watching the court ask questions of Vani and Shaetyl, that slimy little toad Kyeaan, and, she added to herself sarcastically, her dear, kind slavemaster, Treyvan.

"I'll come with you. I don't know what work I can do to help out but I'll be glad to do something."

"Agreed," Tiah said quietly. "Now, I think it's a good idea if you keep out of sight as much as possible. Once you get to the city I daresay your father can sort out the contract, but until then if you're stolen back, it may be hard for us to recover you or free you legally. That contract you have is probably one of three copies. They'll have left one in Surah, and they may have another in Shallahah City."

Aycharna had the sudden uncomfortable feeling of being enmeshed in a vast net. "What do I do?"

"Stay out of sight, be careful, and wait until we reach Shallahah. Where do you live?"

"I grew up along the border, between the Grass Sea and the coast. My mother was the daughter of a plainswoman taken captive. My father married her for love though."

The gaze of the women met. "So you know the plains?"

"A bit. I have cousins there. My mother sent them food after the great fires when the Grass Sea burned before I was born. Four or five times when I was small I spent a spring with them."

Tiah stood up. "Very well. You'll be traveling with us but we should change your clothes and your look as much as possible, that way if someone sees you from a distance you won't be so easily recognized. Nor if others see you with us can they pass on a good description to that pair chasing you. Come into the supply wagon and we'll see what we can find."

When they pulled back onto the road a candlemark later it would have been difficult for anyone who had not known Aycharna well to recognize her. Tiah had cut her hair even shorter and colored it to an almost black. It had been shaped to a cut more often worn by a male, and in place of her overlarge dress, the girl had donned tight-fitting trews, a loose shirt that tied at the wrists, and with a flamboyantly embroidered vest over that she looked nothing like herself. Her footwear would help, since she was now shod in boots a size too large over two pairs of knitted socks. That had altered her walk.

"A good job, shaya," Kaitlen assured Tiah after studying her friend's handiwork. She'd ridden a short distance down the road to look back while Aycharna walked around the wagon several times. "You humans can't be sure if she's male or female from a distance, and she no longer looks or walks like Aycharna."

The girl looked puzzled. "Your pardon if I speak rudely, but why us humans in particular?"

Tiah laughed. "You haven't known many Aradians, have you?" The girl shook her head. "No, well, Aradians can pick up a scent far better than we can. If the wind is blowing toward them they'd know if you are male or female from two or three hundred yards away."

"Do Vani and Shaetyl ever hire Aradians?"

Kaitlen snorted. "Aradians don't approve of their sort of slavery—or them. No, they don't have one working for them. And, so far as I know, none of my kind has ever been that desperate. It isn't Aradians working for them that we have to worry about. It's the travelers who may pass us on the road and talk to your hunters. But even after five or six years of friendship with their duke, Surah still doesn't attract many of my people." She chuckled. "And those who do visit are mostly from my own clan or the clans of friends. If I see any I'll ask for their silence about you—and receive it."

Aycharna's eyes rounded a little. "You're friendly with Duke Tassino?"

"Very long story," Tiah said. "We may tell it to you over dinner one night. Right now let's move on before someone comes to wonder why traders are wasting good traveling time."

*D*own the road toward Surah the two slavers were cursing. There was no sign of footprints anywhere off the road, although they'd ridden down both sides for more than a 'mark. It looked as if they'd definitely lost the girl, and their masters weren't going to be happy about it. Still less would they be pleased to hear who might have been involved in her loss. Treyvan was resigned to that for the moment.

"Look, we need to get back to our caravan. My head guard is efficient but limited. If he runs into any problem he can't solve with a fist or a sword then he's in trouble—and so are we. That pair and their wagon are going back to Shallahah City. Almost certainly they'll take the same road past Jasta Pass as we'd planned, so we'll have a tenday to think up some way to find out if they have the woman and to get her back again if they do."

"What if they don't?"

Treyvan shrugged. "Then knowing Vani and Shaetyl our pay will be docked of her price."

Kyeaan glared wordlessly. He needed his pay to keep up appearances once he was home. He couldn't afford to lose such an amount even if he had been considering buying her. Having a slave added consequence, having less cash and no slave wouldn't.

"If they're only half a day or so behind us one of us should go back after dark and watch them. See if there's any sign of her there."

Treyvan grinned unpleasantly. "Fine. You go. I know Kaitlen, and that damned cat has a nose on her that'd scent you a mile upwind. And if she does find you sneaking around their camp in the dark she'll kill you in a heartbeat and ask why you were there later."

"But—that'd be murder. They can't do that."

"Why not?" Treyvan asked reasonably. "All they'd have to say is that they walked into someone skulking around their wagon after moonhigh, whoever it was attacked them and they killed him in self-defense. They have powerful friends in both Shallahah and Surah. Their story would be accepted. Anyhow, if you want to take that chance I have no problem with it, just don't expect me to take the risk. There are other slaves to buy and I can always earn more coin. I have only one life."

Kyeaan thought about that while—almost two 'marks later—they rode back past Tiah and Kaitlen's wagon. Both women gave him polite waves and their employees stared at the slavers. Back at their own caravan he handed his mount's reins to a guard and climbed into his wagon to sit thinking, ignoring the rumbling of the wheels when it moved off. He came to the conclusion that he didn't wish to take the risk of raiding the trader camp any more than the slavemaster did. His face curdled into a furious scowl. It wasn't fair; how was it *his* fault that a slave had lock-picking skills and chose to employ them?

A sudden thought occurred, and he dived for the strongbox. When he came up empty-handed, his curses—learned since he'd joined Treyvan—would have pained his kin. That Pasht-cursed female *had* stolen her contract. He came to the conclusion that he should tell the slaver, despite what he knew wouldn't be well-received news.

He did so, and the slavemaster swore, still more colorfully and with a savage edge to his words. If that pair behind them had given the girl refuge, she'd have shown them the contract. They might recognize it was a forgery from what she could tell them. If so, then it wasn't a case of admitting the loss of a slave to Vani and Shaetyl. They had to get the girl back and shut her mouth, as well as the mouths of everyone who rode with Kaitlen and Anatiah.

"You were right," he told Kyeaan grimly. "We do have to find out if the girl's with them. Because if she is we'll have to do something before they can back her complaint in a court again."

"We?"

"Yes, *we,* you useless fop. If the girl goes to court to complain of a forged contract and illegal slavery, she'll name us both. It won't matter to me so far as reputation goes, I've been Vani and Shaetyl's slavemaster for twenty years and everyone knows it. But if your name is mentioned everyone will know the work you've been doing for Vani and Shaetyl too. Do you want that announced for a fact where everyone can hear it?"

Kyeaan paled. He emphatically didn't; his noble kin would never let him forget it. For the remainder of the day they walked together, before talking earnestly around their own campfire, well apart from the guards and slaves. The sole topic of conversation was how both could get out of this trouble. While they came to no conclusions, both were in remarkable unanimity for once that something must be done and that it was they who would have to do it.

*I*n their bed that night Tiah and Kaitlen lay together, also talking quietly.

"I feel that there may be some purpose in all of this," Tiah said softly.

"So do I." Kaitlen's voice was tarter. "And if 'someone' feels we need a little more purpose in our lives, I can guess who that someone is."

So could Tiah, and in another place, a goddess smiled affectionately. Her threads were coming together nicely.

5

Ashara had hunted higher into the hills several times during their travel. They had found the small hill deer to be delectable either roasted or in a stew, with a subtle, delicate flavor. Having spied on the road's traders and seen them eat both fish and birds, they had taken note of which and added these to their diet too. They ate well but they worried while they rode. Was Tayio still alive? Would they catch up with his captors in time to save him? Why had he been stolen anyway?

Kyrryl had considered all those questions from her niece and replied firmly. "Don't waste time asking. If Tayio was dead, I believe my prism would stop showing a direction." The opposite was true but she would not admit that to Ashara who adored the cub. "We may find him in time to save him from whatever they intend, we may not. How can we know? We don't know their purpose in stealing him until we find them. Although," her voice oozed suspicion, "I wonder if it isn't because he is so young that he can't control broadcasting his emotions. There's power in that, something they might want to use. But right now we're traveling in hope. If whoever it was who came to our fire that night spoke the truth, then there might be hope for Tayio."

Yoros nodded. "I believe it. Let's watch the people here where we can. We'll learn from their actions and listen to what they say among themselves. Maybe one of them saw something and will talk about it when one of us is listening. That too we can hope for."

After which suggestion the women made a game of sneaking against the wind toward any campfire that was seen and, so long as the group held none of the catlike people, listening to the chatter around it. In their own world they were used to the constant riding, fighting, and raiding that occurred. It was one of the reasons they'd been able to accept events; they were used to danger and while they still worried over dealing with the people here if or when they met them openly, they were also content to some extent to allow time to wait on events.

They made fair time even on the upper trails, since all were experienced travelers and had good mounts. Nor did they waste time on unnecessary stops, riding until dusk, and starting out again at first light. Such travel would have exhausted those not used to hard riding, but all three of them had ridden often for entire days and were hardened to the trail. The three were five days into their journey when Ashara came trotting back after a foray to listen at another campfire. Her eyes were wide with distress.

"They have slavery here."

Kyrryl looked up from the stew she was stirring. "What did you overhear?"

"There's four people at the campfire. Three brothers and the wife of one of them, going to a place called Surah. They have two pack mules and it sounds if they're going there to live with other family. Yesterday they moved up to the higher trail in case."

"In case of what?" Yoros questioned.

"On the road they saw a slaver caravan owned by people called Vani and Shaetyl. The people at the fire said they have a nasty reputation even for slavers. They said that their slaves are very badly treated, far worse than most."

Yoros looked worried. "I don't like the sound of that. Holding slaves is disgusting anyhow. Better to kill an enemy cleanly than make him a slave."

His gaze flickered over their group, considering. He and Kyrryl might not be so highly regarded. Surely slavers wouldn't be that interested in two people who were in their late thirties? But Ashara was seventeen, and a good-looking woman. On the other hand the three of them were trained warriors, well armed and on good, fit, well-fed mounts. Then again, their mounts, the pack pony, and their weapons might also be attractive as prizes to be taken.

"Did you get any idea of how many nonslaves there were in the slaver caravan?"

Ashara looked thoughtful. "Not really, but they did say that it wasn't a large group for Vani and Shaetyl. They seemed to think that usually their caravan has more people. If I had to guess I'd say, from the discussion, that maybe nine or ten in the group aren't slaves."

Kyrryl looked up from the stew. "Where are you going?"

"Back to keep listening, I thought I should let you know what I'd heard so far and tell you that I plan to return."

In the end she remained for several hours longer before she returned to tell her kin all she'd heard. Those to whom she'd listened had been gossiping late and usefully and she'd stowed everything that she'd heard in her memory. She came quietly out of the dark near to moonhigh, sat by the fire, and began her report.

"They seem to have come from a city called Shallahah. They're going to what sounds like two small countries—a sort of city-state—that they call Lhandes. The main one is Surah, it's been established for four generations. After that there's another one that's just started but is growing. That one's called Mirray and it isn't fully established yet. Apparently the king in Shallahah had some sort of argument with a powerful lord there about three or four years ago and he moved away to set up his own court and lands."

"The king agreed to the man leaving or he just left?" Yoros asked.

"I got the impression that it suited them both, but that it was more a case of jump or be pushed, than please may I leave?"

"Ah huh." Kyrryl was interested. "Did they mention why that may have been?"

"Something about trouble with nomadic clans on huge plains to the southeast of the city."

Yoros frowned. "Why would that make noblemen pack up to live a long way away?"

"Maybe the estates were nearest and the nomads kept attacking them?" Kyrryl offered.

Ashara broke in. "I don't know, that's just what they were saying. I can't swear to the information but from what I heard Shallahah sounds like a large, very long-established country with an all-powerful ruler. If the ruler gets angry enough at any of the great lords and they feel personally in danger one of them may pack up everything portable and go off to establish his own realm.

"Anyway, they went on to talk about the other people they'd seen on the road. There was that slaver caravan, but this was interesting, they were talking about a small trader caravan be-hind them. That's run by two women, one human, one who's one of those cat Aradians. They said that the women were shayana—whatever that means. But they implied it was some-thing really special, that it tied in to the goddess here and that a bond of that kind is rare. There was a real tone of awe when they spoke about that."

Kyrryl straightened. "A goddess! And a goddess—or a good imitation of one—appeared to us." She looked at her niece. "What else did you hear about these two women?"

"The people at the camp seemed to be saying that the women are generally liked and trusted. The ones I overheard know about them. One's called Anatiah, and the other one is Kaitlen. I don't know which is which, but one of them comes from a long line of traders and they have powerful friends in Surah and Shallahah. Then they laughed and said that the pair wouldn't be so welcome in the other Lhandes. No clear suggestions why, something about making some lord unpopu-lar with the king. But this is the good bit. They said that the women meddled in Vani and Shaetyl's affairs in Shallahah a few years ago and got the slavers heavily fined. The slavers don't like them at all and it's mutual. Apparently most Aradians don't approve of slavery."

Yoros spoke quietly. "There are pieces here, like a broken puzzle. There's a goddess who appears and gives us a gift of the language. There are these two women who are tied to her in some way and who dislike slavery. There are slavers who possibly could have been involved in Tayio's abduction, and then there's us. Traveling in search of something lost, given a gift and advice. What did she say that night?"

"You will find friends on the road as well as enemies," Kyrryl said thoughtfully. "It could be that these two women will aid us. It could be that the slavers are our enemies. But," she cautioned, "it would be wise not to jump to conclusions."

Yoros indicated his agreement. "In my experience, life is seldom what we expect it to be. Things happen that are the opposite of what we expect or hope that they'll be. We'll keep following Kyrryl's prism and be wary of others on the road until we know their involvement in any of this."

They slept well that night, with Ashara, Yoros, and Kyrryl splitting the watch among them. They ate before dawn and rode off along their trail the moment it was light enough to see. Toward evening they saw about two miles ahead of them another small group, a little downhill of them and just rounding the curve of the trail.

"They don't appear to be in any hurry," Yoros commented, straining to see. "I count six riders and they have pack ponies with them. Could they be traders too?"

Kyrryl shrugged. "They could be anything but slavers. None of them looks to be in chains. They all look to be adults from here. Do we catch them up or should we hold back?"

Ashara's eyes widened in distress when she thought about that. "We're all traveling the same way. If we stay behind them they'll slow us down. Couldn't we just ride past them, say something polite as we pass, and keep moving? We understand their language."

Yoros smiled at her. "We may understand it well enough, but do we speak it? None of us have tried to do that yet and we may have been only given the gift of understanding it. But you're right. If we stay behind them, then at their pace we could be slowed down by days. Let's carry on and make camp at our usual time. Then, if they don't break camp until later than we usually do, we can pass them while they are still camped, and we don't have to say anything to them. We could maybe nod and smile going by. With luck that should be enough to make us look harmless."

By dark there was no more than a mile between the groups. Both camped, lit small fires, and settled in.

*A*head of Kyrryl, Yoros, and Ashara, the six people who had settled into camp had been discussing the group that was hard on their heels. Sirado, Trasso, and Eilish weren't happy about it, but they hoped there was a simple solution. The three servants listened, but only Dayshan commented, and it was he who spoke first.

"They seem to be in a hurry."

Trasso nodded. "That could be all the better. They won't want to talk to us. I say sit tight in the morning; we can break camp after they've passed. Let them go ahead a mile or two before we follow."

Sirado grinned. "Yes, that way we have only to nod politely to them as they go by. No need to speak."

Comfortably curled in his carrysack, Kian Dae purred. Humans proposed, cats disposed.

*K*yrryl, her husband, and their niece rose well before dawn, and started out along the trail the moment it was light enough for their mounts to see the ground at their hooves. This section of the trail was so rough that in one place they had to dismount and lead their horses. It was half an hour before they reached the camp ahead.

The people in the camp were well awake but their camp was still set up. One man was baking something in a shallow pan over the fire, and two women were returning from the scrub to one side of the trail. Kyrryl slowed, nodded politely, and would have passed by but for two things. One was the large cat that came bouncing up to her mount, standing up against its shoulder to churr at her. She halted so that the animal would not be injured. The other thing was the embroidered design on the women's overtunics. She forgot courtesy then and stared, transfixed, ignoring the vocally indignant cat.

Almost two decades earlier, in her own world, her father's keep had guested a man from another country. Karoi had made friends with the young daughter of the keep and visited twice more in the next two years before dying in a shipwreck. He'd worn such embroidered tunics. One tunic, his favorite, had borne designs similar to those that these women wore. It was possible that was coincidence, but the design was intricate and the possibility that they could be some kin to her friend Karoi drew her. One of the women came laughing to reclaim the cat, and looked up at her.

"Your pardon, he is a cat and goes where he wills."

Kyrryl looked down. The embroidery could surely be no coincidence. They must be—they had to be—from Karoi's coastal country surely, but how? Her gaze flickered over the woman, seeing the slight figure, the long, single plait of dark brown hair that fell to her waist, and the quiet strength in the gray eyes. She'd be in her mid-twenties, Kyrryl estimated, and there was something about her that was likable, perhaps trustworthy?

Kyrryl stretched out a hand and, making an effort to change the language that had been placed within her mind, and in a phrase of the tongue that she had learned from Karoi, she said quietly, "Ishara na yllan?" It meant "Friend or foe?" But only one of his people would know that. If this woman did not understand the words, it could be she would only assume that Kyrryl and her companions were simply foreigners here. She

waited while the woman's eyes widened in surprise then narrowed in quick interest.

"Ishara—or at least half-friend to one who's from my own
world. How did you get here?" The woman's voice was soft.

Kyrryl swung down from her horse and stood holding his
reins. "Let's sit and talk, if you'll allow that? I think it's a
strange coincidence—if it is one—that we meet here. We may
be drawn together by some Power." The other woman nodded. Kyrryl signaled her group, and one by one they came forward, dismounted, and were introduced.

"I am Kyrryl, this is my husband Yoros, and our niece
Ashara. You are?"

"I am Eilish, this is my husband Trasso, and my younger
brother, Sirado. Our master-at-arms, Dayshan from Anskeep,
and our servants Hailin and Roshan from Iroskeep." Kian
Dae mewed and Eilish smiled. "And this is Kian Dae, a great
hunter."

Yoros nodded. "We're looking for a friend who was kidnapped," he told them briefly and said no more on the subject. He'd like to know more about these people before he told
them everything. "But how did you get here?"

Eilish began. "It feels foolish to admit it, but we're taking a
holiday from our keeps. Oh, we came on a quest too, but that's
nothing serious." The cat came and rubbed his jaw against her
shoulder where she sat and she hugged him.

"This is Kian Dae, the son of my brother Sirado's cat, Kian
Lai. He's almost eight now, and for years we've wondered with
whom his dam bred."

Yoros looked at the cat. "He's far larger than any cat I've
seen before and I've heard strange tales about some cats from
the bards."

Eilish nodded. "There is more besides his size and strength.

He has the ability to communicate mind-to-mind with me. And when, three years ago, a sorcerer attacked him as he protected me, someone only Kian could see healed him of his injuries. My husband and I married last year and we decided to ride into the hills with my brother and some of our people. We had no real plans, it was all lighthearted fun, a pleasant time with friends and family, but we spoke of being on a quest to discover Kian Dae's sire. It may be that someone heard and answered."

Kyrryl's gaze met that of Yoros and he spoke thoughtfully. "That's possible. Someone appeared to us not long after we arrived here. We thought she was a very powerful adept, or perhaps a goddess of this world. We're on a quest too, but on our quest hangs the life or death of a young one that we hold dear. The one who came to our camp said we'd meet friends as well as enemies on our road. Could you be the friends?"

Trasso leaned forward. "No unfriends to you at least. But whose life or death?"

Kyrryl took a deep breath, gambled, and began the fuller explanation of Tayio's disappearance.

"He's the tariling—the young one—of a race that share our lands. You may have heard of the Tarian? They are a feline people, intelligent, and they broadcast emotion. When happy and contented they can soothe grief or depression, and they can take pain from those who are hurt. Adults can close off their sending, but for a tariling, young and untrained, they broadcast all the time—unless they are asleep or unconscious. We believe that Tayio was stolen for some purpose. A youngling of his people would release a lot of power under the right circumstances."

"I saw a Tarian once, and I've heard stories," Trasso said softly. "His murder might release a lot of power?"

Kyrryl nodded. "That's our fear."

After her explanation they all talked, sharing events, some of their thoughts about what had happened, most of what they had learned thus far both from others and themselves, and what they intended to do or where they had planned to go next. At length they fell silent, each waiting for someone to speak. It was Kyrryl's niece who spoke first.

Ashara smiled at Sirado. "I think it would make sense for us to join forces. How do you say?"

His grin was companionable. "I agree. We rode out to please ourselves, and I'd enjoy going with you and helping however I can. I don't like people who kidnap and maybe intend to kill a young one. Even if the tariling isn't a human he's still innocent and intelligent."

Eilish nodded. "The question now is whether we should join you. I think it's a good idea myself. We'd add six swords to your group. Instead of three who are searching for something stolen and whom the thieves may meet with violence, there would be nine, and most of us experienced fighters. It gives us more options, we would be in less danger on the road, and we can still split into our two groups if we need to. The people you're following could suspect that you're after them, but they won't know us."

She turned to face Trasso, who nodded approval. Dayshan and the two servants from Iroskeep also indicated accord. Sirado had already spoken his agreement.

"It seems we agree. We are willing to ride with you, helping you if we can," Eilish said.

Kyrryl bowed from where she sat. "The goddess was right, we've found friends on the road and that's good. But she also implied we'd find enemies and I'm wondering now, are those enemies ahead of us? Are they the slavers we've heard about?"

Trasso considered that. "They may be. But something occurs

to me. The one who spoke to you said that you'd meet friends on the road. Have we been guided ever since we entered this world? I don't think our two groups met entirely by chance. And I don't think that we found ourselves here by accident. We've heard of slavers on the road, but what else have we heard?"

Yoros drew in a breath. "The two women who opposed the slavers! We've heard other travelers talking about them and saying they're on the lower road between us and the slavers."

"Isn't it possible that they're pieces in this game too? Should we meet them and see if they'll help? Maybe all this concerns them too?"

It was decided. They would return to the lower road, catch up with the traders ahead, and approach them cautiously in hopes that they would be the friends of whom the possible goddess had spoken. That day they rode hard, descending to the lower road to camp at night. As they lit their fire, they saw another fire in the distance. They hoped that those around it were the ones they wanted. If they were, then in the morning they would learn if the women would be their friends, and if they would aid those who came to ask them for help.

6

They kept a good guard over the camp that night. Well before first light, Dayshan, who had taken the last watch to be certain the group woke and rose in good time, gently nudged the servants with a foot.

"Wake up, lay out food and drink, then saddle the horses. It'll be a fine day and we can be on the road before dawn. It's a better road here than the upper trails, and if we ride at a walk the horses should not stumble even if it isn't completely light."

Sirado was woken by the bustle around the fire and rolled over in his bedding to glare at him. "Can't you sleep so you think no one else should either?"

"No," his master-at-arms retorted. "It's because it is good for the young to rise early and work. It teaches them to be as good as their elders at doing what needs to be done."

"I'd be better at doing anything if I had more sleep," Sirado grumbled. "This was supposed to be a trip to relax and enjoy the scenery."

"You'll enjoy it more awake."

Sirado yawned, stretched, and laughed. "That's probably

true. All right, I'm awake. Why don't you bother the others now?"

"Because," Dayshan said triumphantly, "*they're* all awake."

Ashara, who had dressed quickly and was drinking sarren by the fire, couldn't smother a giggle. Sirado gave her a mock glare. "You'll regret that when he starts waking *you* early."

"Maybe, but this morning I'm glad to be awake." She stood, and gestured to the lavender-grassed foothills and the mountains behind those that towered above them. "This is a beautiful land. I wouldn't want to live anywhere where there weren't any mountains."

Eilish nodded. "I feel the same way. The keep that was my home and the keep where I now live both lie on the border between flat land and foothills. Our mountains aren't so tall as these are but I feel safe with our mountains behind me. They feel like guards over our keeps and our people. Flat land grows crops to feed the belly; mountains feed the heart."

Trasso grinned. "They also rear fine sheep and tasty deer, both of which also fill the belly. Speaking of which, what have we to eat?"

"Cold roast fowl," Dayshan informed him. "It's left over from last night but none the worse for that. It will be light soon. If we eat quickly we can be on the road the moment that the horses can see their footing."

Kyrryl set an example by accepting her roast fowl and a drinking bowl of hot sarren from the kettle by the fire. The saddled horses stood hipshot, while Kian Dae padded over, demanded his breakfast, and retired with it to lie comfortably on his padded carrysack again. He'd hunt when there was time, but this morning he didn't think they'd wait for him—and a rushed hunt was no fun. Eilish laid down a small metal dish in front of him and poured water into that from her flask.

"It'll save you having to find a stream," she said aloud. In reply she received a picture of the big cat sneaking her flask for himself, removing the stopper and drinking. There was an underlying snicker.

"Humph. I see. What I don't give you'll take. Beware. I'm the one who has to carry you all day. I can miss the bumps in the trail or find them all until you're seasick."

A silent protest. She wouldn't do that to one who was her friend, would she?

"No, I suppose not." She leaned over and hugged him gently when his paw came up to pat her cheek. "You're a pest but I love you. Drink your water. We have to leave soon."

In that she was right, for they were back on the road again before it was completely light. But as Dayshan had thought, the main road here was smoother and the horses could plod along even in the semidark without stumbling.

Kyrryl counted them as they passed her. Nine people, one cat, and the three pack ponies. It was few enough to succeed in any serious endeavor, but somehow they must find Tayio, rescue him, and return with him to their own world. If only the women ahead could help, it might be possible. It was their world; they might know things that would give her a chance.

Eilish rode beside Trasso, Kian Dae comfortably curled in his carrysack on her shoulders. Despite his thirty-five pounds she was used to the weight and the sack's broad straps distributed it so that she felt he weighed less than he did.

Dayshan mounted first and still rode slightly ahead of them all. His mount, like those of Eilish and Trasso, was a dun with black mane and tail, and legs that were black to the knees and hocks. He found it amusing that Kyrryl and Yoros also rode dun mounts. Ashara's mare was a dark chestnut, while Sirado's mount was a plain lightish-colored bay. It made the whole group look remarkably uniform, he thought. But then it made sense. While bay or dun coats rarely took a high gloss, they did blend well into almost any scenery, being less noticeable. In addition he had found over the years that temperament tended to follow color. Duns in general were sensible, smart beasts, sure-footed and with good stamina.

He set the pace carefully. It would not do to exhaust the horses. He kept everyone moving at a steady walk, twice moving into a slow canter to stretch the horses' legs and when the road ran straight for a mile or more. At sunhigh he halted the sweating horses and their riders and gave quiet orders to Roshan and Hailin.

"Water the horses, give them a little grain, and let them rest a candlemark. Remove the saddles on all of them including the pack ponies, and rub them down before you resaddle them."

Roshan nodded. "What about our people, will you make the fire?"

"I see everything else is done. You take care of the beasts."

He waited until Roshan turned to the nearest horse, then looked around. It was clearly a campsite, being a half circle beaten out of the tall scrub that in some places lined the road. It was the height of a mounted man and would provide shelter, a windbreak from three directions, and some fuel for fires. Of course, it would also be cover for anyone sneaking up, but presumably if that worried any other traders they would halt in another spot or cut the scrub. He took a large handful of dry sticks from his saddlebag, arranged them within the circle of blackened stones, and started a fire with flint and steel.

He filled the kettle from his waterskin, added powdered sarren leaves, and put out bread and cheese from the packs. Then he strolled to the scrub to find more wood. It had been picked over well, but by thrusting deeper he found some dry wood, enough to permit the replacement of his kindling, and add sufficiently to the fire so that it would burn long enough to heat the kettle.

When he returned Ashara was questioning the halt. "I think we should have kept going. We must be catching them up. Now while we sit there they're getting farther ahead again."

Dayshan waited. Let the young lass's own family explain. She'd accept that better than being taught by a man she did not know.

Yoros looked at his niece. "The horses worked hard this morning," he said mildly.

"They aren't that tired. We could have kept going." Her tone was just that fraction contentious.

"Any creature works better for a rest now and again," Kyrryl told her quietly. "You know why we hurry, they don't. They are sweating, sweat itches and they are uncomfortable after a while. It is good for them to rest, cool down, and have the sweat rubbed from them, drink and relax for a little time. They will work better when we ride again." She looked up, holding the girl's gaze with her own. "They are servants, not slaves."

Ashara reddened. "I didn't mean . . ."

"No, I know. But it's sense, dearling, we rest a little now so that we'll all be fitter to keep going. Don't worry. Those ahead are traders. They'll move briskly, but I don't think they'll go faster than we can even with this break. If necessary we can ride on slowly after sundown. Last night was moonlight; from today's weather there will be a clear night again tonight. We'll catch them—if we want to."

"I thought we did?"

"Frankly I'd like to take a longer, closer look at them before

I go rushing up to make friends. But to do that, we need to be right behind them. That's why I want to catch up, not necessarily because I want to join them."

"Oh." Ashara nodded.

Dayshan smiled to himself. Good! It was always easier if people used common sense. He noticed that despite the urgency that must drive these others, the need to reclaim their lost one, they still accepted that their mounts should be decently treated, they used common sense—and they recognized his authority. Neither Kyrryl nor her husband had questioned his decision to rest briefly, and both had upheld that to their kinswoman.

When they moved off after sunhigh he quickened their pace. The horses could rest tonight, but today he too wanted to catch up with the traders before dark. In the daylight you could evaluate people better. This section of the road permitted them to canter more often, and he allowed that, keeping a watch to see if there was any sign of the traders ahead. There was not, and he swore silently. They too must not be wasting time. His group would have to push their mounts another day. He kept everyone moving and only halted them when there was little light left.

"Waste no time sitting up and talking," he said quietly to Eilish and Sirado. "We need to move out before first light if we want to catch these traders. They move faster than we'd expected. We'll have to do the same."

Both nodded agreement and when, after all had eaten and drunk, Sirado would have started a discussion, Kyrryl yawned widely.

"If we intend to catch up with the traders we'll have to start early again. I'm going to bed."

Yoros glanced at her, then at Dayshan, and a very faint

smile lit his eyes. "Yes, I must be growing old, but I find I'm tired. The sooner we sleep, the sooner we wake up and we can catch those ahead of us."

With minor grumbling Ashara accepted that there would be no sitting up that night. Roshan took first watch, and within a very short time everyone else was asleep, even Kian Dae, who had found the swifter pace of the day tiring despite being carried. However, it was he who woke soon after moonhigh, when he heard a tiny crunch of some rotten twig. No cat sleeps with more than one eye closed at a time. He came awake, listened, smelled the air, and slid out of his carrysack.

Eilish was on watch by then and he went to her, touching her with his nose and sending pictures while he did so. She dropped to one knee, receiving from him a mélange of scent, sight, and warning. Men came, sneaking up on the camp. Only eight that he could be sure of, but all carried the hunting scent— and more. To his friend he sent a wave of a smell compounded of unwashed bodies, old blood and sweat, and stale alcohol.

She nodded, sending in return the suggestion that he go elsewhere and keep out from underfoot. If a fight started in the dark he could take stragglers, but he shouldn't be where some night-blind human would fall over him. With that Kian Dae strongly agreed. He knew how limited humans were— unfortunately for them—and he'd be wary of blundering feet. A cat's tail was his dignity, and flattened paws hurt! Eilish grinned at the comment and went to wake Kyrryl. To her she whispered Kian Dae's information and her own deductions.

"Kian Dae says he believes there are eight of them, all adult men. From the smell I would believe them to be bandits."

From her sleeping rugs Ashara spoke softly but with conviction. "They're mad. Eight against nine, why would they risk that?"

Dayshan too spoke quietly. "Because, lass, they think they are not eight against nine. They see it as eight adult men attacking a camp that is asleep, unprepared, and which will panic. A camp containing only three or four men who can—or maybe even will—fight. The rest here are servants or women, and their sort often discounts them."

Ashara bit back a sudden desire to yell with laughter. Her aunt was a competent swordswoman and an excellent archer. She had trained all her life to be a fighter, while her uncle was a swordsman who could take on even the best of warriors. She'd watched Eilish's people with their master-at-arms and their servants too. Somehow she doubted that they were any less competent or that their servants would flee screaming into the night.

"The cat told you?" Ashara questioned.

Eilish nodded, the movement just visible in the moonlight. "He heard them, then he smelled them."

"What are they doing now?"

Eilish sent that to Kian Dae and received a picture of men spreading out into a semicircle as they approached, one at each end moving wider, out onto the road edge to make something closer to a complete circle.

She relayed this in a low voice. "I'd say they were expecting to stop any one of us who chooses to make a break for either end of the road. That would be an easier way to run. Probably they'll kill any fighters from behind when they're trying to pass—or so they think. Dayshan, you've had the most experience against bandits, what do you think we should do?"

Dayshan looked at Yoros and Kyrryl and, noting their agreement, spoke softly for a few sentences. Then, for a short time their camp was all quick, quiet movement before it stilled again. From the fringe of scrub eight bandits closed their circle around a sleeping camp. This was going to be easy. They'd been hunting toward Surah from Shallahah and seen the slaver caravan of Vani and Shaetyl on the road. It was well known that they'd buy slaves if they were out of the Lhandes and were offered good slaves at a low price.

The bandit leader licked his lips as he considered the group they'd seen. The oldest man looked hard and competent: he wouldn't be easy to take down. But he was only one. There were three other men, well dressed and probably reasonable swordsmen, but the rest were servants and women. None of those would fight—or would be any good at it if they tried.

He wasn't sure who the group was; they were well enough dressed, if the clothing looked a bit odd. Possibly they were traders, or perhaps minor nobility of some kind, from past the Grass Sea. In that case no one would come looking for any of them, and the slavers could be persuaded into paying better for any of this lot that was taken with that in mind.

They'd kill the men, let the male servants run if they had to lose anyone; they'd take the oldest woman for their amusement, sell the other two women undamaged—and the servants if they caught them. He should be very well paid for those they took. All of the women, even the one that must be middle-aged, were good-looking. Vani and Shaetyl would pay well enough for the group. He could get drunk for weeks and they'd have the oldest woman for the times they sobered up. There were all the horses and gear as well. Oh, yes, he'd do mightily well out of this night's work.

Kyrryl was listening carefully to the tiny sounds that told her the bandits were almost in position. She waited, judging her time.

The bandits fired the scrub at five points simultaneously

around the camp, then attacked with the loudest shouts they could manage. It would panic this bunch, they'd cut down the fighters and those they didn't want, and loot the camp. The fires would allow them to see all they required to accomplish that as well as frightening and confusing their victims. The packs on the pack ponies alone would be well worth investigation. It was unfortunate that they did not descend upon a sleeping and panicked-awake camp—unfortunate, that was, for the bandits.

Kyrryl cut down her man before he realized that the sleeping shapes around the fire had not stirred at the commotion. Ashara had strung her bow and was standing silently in the dark lower down on the other side of the road, where earlier she had moved to wait. The bandit, a dark shape creeping down the road toward the camp and silhouetted against the moonlight, never knew what hit him. Nor would he have appreciated the skill with which she shot. The arrow took him side to side through the throat. He died quickly and in silence.

Eilish had her sword waiting when her chosen target blundered into her. He wasn't so quiet in his permanent departure, but he went nonetheless. The bandit leader, realizing that somehow things had gone wrong, turned to run. He could always get another band to follow him; he couldn't get another life. Dayshan rose up. The leader had just enough time to understand he wouldn't have that either before he joined his men.

The whole event had been quite efficient, Dayshan considered when he checked the bodies a half candlemark later. No one on his side was injured, and from what Kian Dae could tell them none of the bandits had escaped, and the scrub fires had burned out quickly with no wind to fan them.

He corrected himself. Ashara had a sprained left wrist.

She'd run to her family in excitement, once this little engagement was over, tripped on a rut in the road, and fallen. But all in all they'd done very nicely. Nobles most of them might be, but they'd listened to him, behaved and fought very well, almost as well as real men-at-arms. Only Eilish and Sirado, who'd known him all their lives, guessed at his thoughts, and they were amused.

The bodies were removed from the camp to be stacked in a heap off the road away from the site. Sirado took on the unpleasant chore of checking them for coin or valuables. To aid him he had a small lantern and Kian Dae, who was interested. His haul was an old sword, two good knives—most of the bandits had carried clubs—a handful of coppers and several small items like flints and steels, and worthless jewelry of glass and tin.

Dayshan shrugged. "No wonder they attacked us. What we've got would be riches for that sort. And I wonder if they might not have been thinking about the caravan ahead."

Everyone looked at him. Kyrryl jumped to a conclusion and nodded. "The slaver caravan. You think that this Vani and Shaetyl might be prepared to buy slaves from bandits if they sell cheaply enough?"

"It's a possibility," Dayshan said cautiously. "But if it's so, then how far would they go to acquire slaves—or perhaps a strange beast they could sell for a good profit? And would they know if others were in that business?"

"We can ask them if we get the chance," Yoros suggested. "But I think right now we'd do well to get some sleep before we have to ride hard later on. That trader wagon is still ahead of us."

Sirado groaned. "I guess we can't sleep in. Oh, well. I chose to come on this trip, it's my own fault."

He laid out his sleeping rugs from the huddle into which they'd been kicked, and crawled into them. The others found their own bedding and followed suit, leaving Yoros to take the watch. To everyone's approval the remainder of the night was uneventful.

Dayshan woke them before dawn with hot sarren and a light meal. They saddled their mounts while the servants repacked the ponies' packs, and they were on the road again before it was full daylight. This time there was less talking. All were a little weary from the broken night, and none were happy about the bandits' possible intentions. It wasn't pleasant to think you might have been sold if the fight had gone the other way.

Kyrryl and Yoros had dropped back to talk together without being overheard. "We should never have let Ashara come with us."

Yoros sighed. "We had no way of knowing we'd pass through a portal, and you couldn't have stopped her easily, love. She's been in fights in our own lands, and she's seventeen. You were a year younger the first time you had to fight seriously. Would you have sat back and let someone else fight for you?"

She shook her head and he nodded. "Well then, at least she's with us, she doesn't face these things alone."

Ahead of them Ashara was thinking. This trip and the distress over Tayio were hard on her aunt and uncle; they weren't young anymore, and not getting a night's sleep always made them cross. They fussed over dangerous strangers, Ashara's being with them, and what her parents would say if they knew. She'd just have to watch out for her aunt and uncle. She didn't want them getting hurt. She'd look after them until they got home with Tayio. She rode on with a small smile of satisfaction at the thought.

*L*ess than half of a day's travel ahead, Kaitlen was speaking to her heart-sister. "Did you see the fire behind us last night? I'd say that it was at the last campsite we passed before we stopped."

"I saw it, shaya. That was quite a large fire, perhaps a company of soldiers is on the road."

"If I had to guess I'd think it was more likely to be bandits. It wasn't long after moonhigh, and that's when they like to attack. They probably set the brush on fire to have enough light to see who they were killing."

Aycharna hissed at them from behind the wagon curtain. "Or it could be someone looking for me. Someone sent by Treyvan and Kyeaan."

Privately Anatiah thought that unlikely; the fire had been too large. She received agreement from Kaitlen.

"Bandits are more probable," Kaitlen said aloud. "Treyvan and Kyeaan wouldn't need to attack a camp. They'd just lurk in the scrub and watch the camp until they were sure either you were there or you weren't."

They registered the relieved sigh from the girl and smiled at each other. *Actually that's true, shaya,* Tiah mind-sent. *When you think about it, it's more likely to have been bandits. But I would be happier to have Treyvan and Kyeaan farther in front of us. That way if they do think about sneaking back they'll have farther to come and they may change their minds. What say we slow down today? It doesn't have to be a great deal, just enough to put a better distance between their caravan and ours.*

Her shaya caught her gaze and nodded silently. After that

Tiah, who was currently driving the wagon while Gheevin, Jessara, and Jiro gathered firewood, unobtrusively slowed the horses. They also halted to eat and drink at sunhigh as well, conscious that this should give them a greater distance between their own wagon and the caravan of the slavers. Both felt more comfortable with that distance.

Ahead Vani and Shaetyl rode the high trail toward Jasta Pass, dreaming of the fun they'd have with the girl Treyvan kept for them, and of the profit they'd make on the latest caravan of slaves. Once they reached the pass they set up a small comfortable camp and waited. They were slavers and that was the way life was. They had no way of knowing that that was about to change.

On the main road Dayshan considered the sun and estimated times. If they moved just a little faster it was likely that they'd catch the traders before dark—if the others weren't moving faster still. Since Kaitlen and Tiah had agreed to slow down and had done so, he was taken by surprise—as much as Dayshan ever was—when his group rounded another bend and saw the caravan only half a mile ahead.

He reined back to Kyrryl and Eilish where they rode side by side talking. "Wagons ahead."

Both heads jerked up in surprise. "Already? Do you think it's the ones we want?" Kyrryl asked.

"From what Ashara reported overhearing earlier, I'd say it's them. Those travelers she listened to said that the trader caravan had the two owners, their three servants, a wagon, and a couple of pack mules. That's what's ahead of us. Of course, for all we know there are a dozen groups on the road that fit the description, but in case it is them, let's get ready and hope that they'll talk to us."

"Should we hurry?" Eilish was doubtful.

"The earlier we catch up to them the longer we'll have to watch them," Kyrryl said slowly. "The story we have to tell— if they'll listen—may be unbelievable, and they may not want to become involved even if they do believe us. We need time to decide if we want to risk talking to them, and then time to-gether to let them make their own judgments about us if we've decided to tell them our story. Yes, let's hurry, but not so much that we make them feel threatened."

They moved on briskly. Now and again they cantered briefly when the wagon ahead was around a bend out of sight. Once they were only a hundred yards back, Eilish and Kian Dae rode ahead. She slowed again some five horse lengths short of the wagon and on sudden impulse hailed it, while as she did so, Kian Dae sat up, peered over her shoulder, and rested a paw on her neck.

*T*he traders had been aware for some time that they were followed. They'd watched the group closing up behind them and registered that it did not appear to be hostile, or not openly so. However, it was wise to be wary on the road and the group following had nine people to their five. The women spared a moment to be grateful that the young lad, their jun-ior partner for the past four years, wasn't with them on this trip. He'd have assumed the worst and they'd have had to hold him back. However, in this case, everyone in their camp was a veteran and unlikely to act rashly.

The woman from the group behind moved forward while the shayana walked their horses from the far side of the wagon, each ready to draw a weapon at need as the stranger approached. Both noticed that the stranger wore unusual clothing; the tunic and pants were embroidered in unfamiliar patterns. Her bow, while normal enough as to type, seemed to be made from materials unlike those usually seen in either Shallahah or the Lhandes. They walked their mounts back toward her, coming to an abrupt halt, the attention of both women suddenly caught by the sight of the cat that craned over the stranger's shoulder.

To the trader women it looked like one of the tori, the small felines of the Toldin Mountains. Rare, precious, much valued by nobles for their eradication of vermin—and relentless in the tori's refusal to have anything to do with those who were cruel or who attempted to control the beasts. It said a considerable amount about this woman that the tori rode placidly in a carrysack at her shoulder and was clearly much attached to her. They glanced at each other, and it was the Aradian, direct as ever, who spoke the question in their minds.

7

*A*re you following us, or merely traveling more quickly?"
The woman grinned. "Both. It may be that we have
enemies in common, since, while we are not sure of it, we think
Vani and Shaetyl may have stolen someone very dear to our
friends."

The trader studied the stranger while she mind-sent to
her companion, *The enemy of my enemy is my friend—
perhaps—but I say we listen to them, shaya. There is no stink
of treachery from this one and if Vani and Shaetyl or any of
their wretched people are involved I would like to hear it.
Knowing any of their secrets could aid Aycharna and I think
Pasht wants that.*

Her shaya nodded to her and spoke to the waiting stranger.
"It's true we're not friends of that pair. But our camp's small
and you are dressed—oddly. Who are you and where do you
come from?"

"That's part of the story we'd like to tell you."

The Aradian nodded. "Call one more of your group to talk
with my heart-sister and I. Once we know your story we'll have

more idea of our common interests. We'll stop and make camp
in another candlemark. You may join us at the fire when we call
you once that's done. Until then we'd consider it a courtesy that
you stay behind us on the road."

The woman addressed bowed her head in acceptance. "My
name is Eilish. That is fair. We'll obey your request."

She turned her mount and rode to rejoin her friends and
family while the cat stared after the two females, human
and Aradian, sending to Eilish in his usual mixture of scents,
pictures, and emotions. She reached up to stroke him between
his ears.

"I know. You liked them. The truth is that I liked them myself. There's no feeling of falseness from them and anyone we
overheard talking speaks well of them when they were mentioned." He sent the sudden gust of surprise he'd smelled when
they saw him and she giggled. "Interesting. You should come
with us when we return. It smells as if they liked you and it
made them think the better of me that you were with us." She
felt his agreement and spoke of that first once she reached the
gathering of those who awaited her

"Sirado, Trasso, keep riding while I talk." With that she
turned her mount and nudged him back into a steady walk
after the traders. "Now, they said they'll met us once they've
stopped and made camp. They want us to hang back until then
and they'll talk to only two of us, me and someone else. I'd
suggest that Kyrryl come with me, if that's all right? Two
women to match two women, and I'll take Kian Dae with us
too. He says that they were very surprised to see him, but it
made their smell change. They approved of us more when they
saw he was there."

At that Kyrryl turned to look at the big cat riding comfortably in his carrysack. "I wonder," she said softly. "Now I really

do wonder! We have seen intelligent cat creatures here who speak and live like people the way the Tarian do." Her gaze met Eilish's. "Maybe there's more here than you think. You believed that you stumbled upon a portal, but a goddess or an adept visited your camp, and us too I believe, so that all of us were given the gift of speaking and understanding the language here." She took in a long slow breath. "I think your arrival was no accident, Eilish. I believe that you may find Kian Dae's sire came from this world and even that may have been no accident. I sense power moving here, power and purpose."

"Do you think it's dangerous?"

"In an unknown place there's always danger, but perhaps no more than we would face if we'd stumbled into another country we don't know." Her face twisted into a wry smile. "Tell me, Eilish: Have you found your own home to be always so very safe?"

Eilish's gaze met the gazes of her husband and brother. She could see them remembering things that had happened to them over the years. Her lips curved up into a broad grin and she laughed, with Sirado and Trasso echoing her amusement.

"On, no, by no means. So, will you ride to their camp with me?"

Kyrryl glanced around her watching family and gathered in their agreement. From the corner of her eye as they had ridden and talked she had also been observing the trader wagon. "I will. Look, they are slowing and drawing in to the roadside."

Yoros looked about him. "There's another level spot here across the road. Let's make camp there and we are within eyeshot of the traders but far enough from them that they don't feel threatened."

Trasso swung his horse over to the area Yoros had mentioned

and dismounted. "Dayshan, let Roshan and Hailin set up camp. They're to unsaddle the horses and pack ponies and care for them. If the women walk to their camp it'll look less intimidating. But . . ." He stood looking down the road to where the traders were lighting their fire. "I think the question is, should the women eat here now, or do they go to eat with the traders? It may be trader custom either way and it is on a rock of unknown customs we could founder."

Kyrryl shook her head. "We can discuss that with them."

With the fire lit the sarren kettle was soon bubbling away. They all took drinking bowls of the sweet lemon drink, and Yoros sighed, gulping a couple of mouthfuls. "That is better. I honestly was thirsty. You can say that to the traders to explain why we didn't wait to drink." He took the refilled drinking bowl his wife handed him. "Yes, go now, they look to be settled by their fires."

He watched while Kyrryl and Eilish walked down the road to where the two trader women sat waiting by a fire separate from that of their other companions, who were cooking something that smelled delicious in a large pot over the fire. Kian Dae bounded after the women as they walked, his tail aloft in a display of exuberance at being able to run again after a day in his carrysack. The breeze brought a gust of scent to his nose, and he reached out mentally to his friend. Eilish spoke softly to Kyrryl.

"They have just realized, I think, that Kian Dae is not from their world. He says they looked across the trail at him and there was great surprise in their smells."

"What told them that?"

"Something in his movements possibly, or maybe the cats here have six legs. I don't know but maybe that they'll tell us— among all the other things we would like to know."

She fell silent as they reached the fire. They halted a few paces short of it and Kyrryl bowed, keeping her speech slightly formal to indicate that they understood protocol. "Forgive us that we don't know your customs, we mean no discourtesy or disrespect. We beg your indulgence for those who come from far away. May we approach your fire?"

Tiah stood and bowed in return. "Be welcome at our fire, share food and drink with us. Sit and rest. May we know your names?"

They sat and looked at each other. Eilish broke the silence. "I am Eilish of Iroskeep, at our camp are my brother Sirado of Anskeep and my husband, Trasso. We have with us, Dayshan," she hoped that the tiny pause when she decided not to mention Dayshan's profession would not be noticed, "and our other servants, Roshan and Hailin. This is Kyrryl of Anskeep, with her are her husband Yoros, and his niece Ashara."

There was a reproving churr and a head was thrust against her shoulder. She smiled. "Here with me also is Kian Dae, son of Kian Lai of Anskeep." She stroked the cat between his ears. He turned to look at the traders, and a deep purr showed his approval of them and made everyone smile.

"He has a tail," Kaitlen said, staring at the flicking appendage that had earlier betrayed him. "The tori don't have tails like that."

"What sort of tails *do* they have?" Eilish asked with interest.

"They're short, the tail and fur curl like a puff of thistle seed. I've never seen a tori with a long tail. His ears are smaller too. The tori have ears like fans."

Kian Dae strolled over to her, his purr louder as he rubbed his head gently against her outstretched hand. He looked up and she exclaimed, "His eyes! They're amber-colored. The tori's eyes are green. What is he? He is no tori." She smiled as the big cat nibbled down her arm, then began licking her fur back into place. "He wants to be friends, and I won't refuse. But tell me." Her gaze met theirs. "Who are you, why are you on the road? Are you following us and what do you want, you and this not-tori?"

Kyrryl nodded. "It's a long story for my part so I'll speak first." She told of the stolen tariling, and the portal that they'd gone through without knowing it as they searched for him. Lastly she told of the shape that had come to their campfire in the night and offered a gift, and of what that gift had been. When she was done Kaitlen stood, and signaled one of her servants from the other fire. They brought filled plates of stew, which were passed to the four women along with drinking bowls of a hot brown drink.

"Tiwara stew and pata. Share food, drink, and fire while we consider your words." She waited until the bowls and drinking bowls were emptied. She refilled the drinking bowls and nodded to Eilish. "Your tale must be strange indeed if it's like the one we've just heard."

Eilish laughed. "No, it's less so. We too set out on a quest, but for amusement and to get out of our keeps after a long winter. We also hoped to solve a minor riddle that's puzzled us for years."

Her finger pointed to Kian Dae where he lay, belly happily exposed to the fire's warmth. "There's the author of our quest." All eyes turned to the cat, and he squawked smugly. "Yes. You started all this and what will be the end of it none of us knows, but it was this way." She turned to Kaitlen and Tiah and launched into her own story.

They listened, the only indication of more than ordinary interest coming when Eilish spoke of the feeling—and Kian

Dae's agreement—that someone of power had visited their camp too. And after that their discovery that they could also understand and speak a language from this world. Both traders sat up straighter and their gazes became intent.

"What can Kian Dae say about the one who was there?" Kaitlen asked. Eilish repeated his comments, and the traders looked at each other.

"Pasht," Tiah said softly but firmly. Kaitlen nodded.

"I agree. If she has a claw in this then these are sisters, and they're here for a purpose." She hissed, and a slender figure climbed slowly and unthreateningly from the supply wagon and joined them.

"Aycharna, these are friends. Tell them how you came here and from where, and anything else they want to know. I'll circle the camp in case anyone is about in the dark. I wouldn't want anyone from Vani and Shaetyl's caravan to see you or overhear what we're saying." She faded into the darkness as Aycharna explained why the slavers might want to find her.

When Kait returned, her heart-sister, Aycharna, and the two foreigners were drinking pata again. The cat was apparently sound asleep, but she noticed a sliver of amber showing under one eyelid. She grinned at him, showing her fangs. "I'm not fooled, little brother."

An eye opened completely and studied her before closing again. She gave the coughing chuckle of her kind. "You cats are not so different from the tori of the high hills. Your ears, eyes, and tail may not be alike, but I think in your hearts and minds you're close kin."

She sat by the fire, accepting pata from her shaya. "Now that we've exchanged tales and information, what do you think, my sister?"

Tiah looked around at them. "I think for once where there

has been mischief Vani, Shaetyl, and their employees have had no hand in it. Aycharna can give us times and the days of travel. I do not see how any of their caravan could have been involved." She reached out. "Kyrryl, show us the medallion you spoke about, the one that was lost by whoever stole Tayio. My heart-sister and I have traveled in several countries, and have friends in them. We might recognize something about this medallion that'll show us where to look for your lost one."

Kyrryl lifted the chain free of her clothing and unhooked the small medallion. She offered it in the palm of her hand, but it was neither Kaitlen nor Anatiah whose gasp broke the silence. Aycharna stared in horror at the swirl and spiral, black against silver.

"Kalthi! I saw a scroll once and it showed that symbol."

The shayana stared sharply at her. "That name is something I heard a long time ago in clan tales," Kaitlen said slowly. "They were demons raised by some madman, but what do you know about it?"

Aycharna winced. "The same tales as you, most likely. I have family in the Grass Sea and the stories I heard from them say that the Kalthi are wholly evil, and any time they've risen they've brought great sorrow."

"Why would they rise again now?" Kaitlen questioned.

"Because of the king's actions." There was a faint trace of defiance in the girl's voice. "Everyone knows that twenty years ago he broke the law of the plains when he deliberately set the Grass Sea on fire. Many clans died. There were others where only women and children survived and they had to join clans that had survived intact—losing their clan name forever."

"It *was* twenty years ago," Tiah said quietly, "and the people of the Grass Sea began it by murdering traders and looting their wagons. They were then foolish enough to wipe out a group sent with a treaty to the Hala'atha and led by the king's cousin—who was murdered. The tribes should have known that you touch those a ruler cares about at your peril."

"Yes," Aycharna said softly. "Very true, and your king should also have remembered that."

"Which means?" Kaitlen asked sharply.

"It is said the Kalthi arise only when there is a terrible need for vengeance."

Tiah's mind-voice came to her sister. *We heard at the time what a king's soldier said about their hunting of the plains people. My father said then that he feared what might come of it.*

He may have been right. Aloud she said to Aycharna, "We could argue that old business all night. There was injustice on both sides, but what's done is done. Let's decide what we can do to prevent matters being made much worse." And again silently to Tiah, *I feel Pasht's will in this. I think she expects us to do something. I won't risk our lives—or even too much trade if it can be avoided—but I think we should help if possible.*

Tiah's silent reply was a little reluctant, but she agreed.

Eilish nodded. "Where there is goodwill, difficulties may be overcome." She smiled. "Tell, me do you have maps?" Kait nodded. "Then may we see them?"

Tiah went for the large deerskin folder that held the precious items and laid one out on the ground. "Here, this is Shallahah and its capital."

"They both have the same name?"

Kait showed her fangs in a grin. "Tradition. The main city of any country or Lhandes bears the same name. Other, smaller towns or villages have their own names. If you refer to a country you just use the name alone. If you mean its capital, then you say—for instance—Shallahah City."

"What about the—Lann daze, did you say?"

"It's spelled L-h-a-n-d-e-s," Tiah informed her. "Surah, the first Lhandes, was founded about eighty years ago by the current duke's great-grandfather. He moved a long way from Shallahah with a couple of thousand people, and the capital city started from there. They have the city and a dozen small villages and maybe fifty miles square of land."

"How to they manage?" Kyrryl was interested.

"They're mostly self-sufficient. They trade luxuries for luxuries though, or items where they can be made more cheaply somewhere else. We often carry gems and jewelry settings, gems from Surah, and settings back. They have beaches where gems are found, but as yet they don't have jewelers who do the really fine work. And knitted goods too are a useful trade. A lot of women in the city knit and sell things like scarves, gloves, mittens, and tunics to a buyer. We take them in bulk to Surah and sell them there. They have fishing boats as well and trade dried fish with Shallahah for Sali-grain. That grows better in Shallahah and makes the finest flour for expensive cakes and pastries."

Both women listened and asked more questions, and in the end they talked far into the night. It was moonhigh before Kyrryl and Eilish returned to their camp, and they refused to talk further.

"Let be," Kyrryl told everyone wearily. "The news may not be good and we're exhausted. We've learned quite a lot about this area that may be useful and in the morning we'll tell you what was said. Then we can join the traders." There were exclamations. "Yes, they've agreed to help, and yes, they may know something that gives us a direction."

She plodded to her bedding, crawled in, and fell asleep the moment she relaxed. Eilish followed suit while Kian Dae, who had returned with them, snuggled into her stomach.

Dayshan had everyone up by first light. Both women ate and drank briskly, and talked still faster. By the time the traders were breaking camp, Dayshan was leading the group up the road to join them.

The trader servants eyed them. They felt that anything Kait and Tiah did was probably right, but this group looked strange, not like any they had ever met before, and they were wary. It was Tiah who spoke to them on the subject.

"These people will be joining us for a while. They are from far to the other side of the Grass Sea. We have decided to go some way along their road home as companions so that you three will continue on alone once we reach the Kavarten border. You will take the pack ponies and our goods to my father in Shallahah City. I'll give you a letter for him. Shirin should be there too by now and I'll give you another letter for him too."

Jessara grunted. She was a plump and active woman, dark of hair and eyes, sister to Jiro, who like her, was dark, and wife to Gheevin, whose hair, what there was of it, was almost blond. She had been with the sisters since they set up on their own and was comfortable with them.

"Humph, you two are up to something. Something to do with that girl that you've been hiding in the wagon, and this bunch who've joined us." She eyed them shrewdly.

The shayana exchanged grins. It was never much use trying to keep anything from Jessara. She saw all, remembered all, but very rarely told anything to anyone at all, and she would have decided that it was their business—up to now, when it had started to affect her. Kaitlen nodded.

"Yes, it's to do with the girl. She's from Shallahah but she moved to live with kin in Surah. Vani and Shaetyl pulled one of their bond-servant games on her and she escaped. The strangers' group is seeking someone stolen from them."

All three employees were listening closely. They knew it paid a trader to know what was going on along the road at any time. All the more so when strange things were happening.

"It *may* be." Kaitlen emphasized the second word heavily. "We cannot be sure, but it must be investigated, that the nomads in the Grass Sea are playing with something very dangerous, both to them and to Shallahah. We have no time to go to the city, no time to waste days getting in to talk at the palace and convincing them, and then still longer waiting for them to act. We are taking the girl who has cousins among the nomads, and the strangers who have weapons skill, Pasht's blessing, some power, and a lost one to recover, and we're going to do what can be done to prevent the storm that may be rising."

Jessara looked at them. "What can we do?"

"Take the trade goods we have and the letters we will write on to Shallahah. If we don't return Tiah's father will give you work, or you could remain with Shirin."

All three shook their heads at that. The boy had been a fourteen-year-old orphan when he joined them. Several years later he'd made money enough, because of unexpected luck, to buy a junior share in the business. They all liked him, but none of them wanted to work for the boy, fond though they were of him. Such reversals in position left all parties a little uncomfortable, which was why he was currently trading with two other employees of his own on the fringes of the Ngahere border.

"No, I thought not," Kait said. "Go to Tiah's father with the letters. He'll have work for you. For the meantime we'll all travel together, but you should ask the strangers no more than they offer to tell you. Treat the tori-like creature that travels with them with great respect. It's blessed by Pasht and holds her favor. Now, let's move, the sooner the trail is taken, the sooner the job is done."

They moved out, Jessara and her kin leading the pack ponies, and the shayana ahead of them all. Kyrryl's mingled group fell in behind the pack ponies. At night around the separate campfires they each discussed possibilities and what could be done.

Often they sang—the soft wandering chants of the Aradians, the plaintive ballads of Shallahah, songs Kyrryl and her group knew from their homes—and each learned from the other. It was Aycharna who sang one that all of the women liked and that became a favorite.

"This comes from the far side of the Grass Sea. My grandmother taught it to me when I was small. She said one who joined their clan from the wild lands on the other side of the plains taught it to them generations ago. There are deserts there, and pack creatures like dogs. There are wild horses too and her people sometimes went alone to capture and tame one. Particularly the women, since it was counted a warrior deed equal to the slaying of a predator."

She began to sing softly, a tune that wandered up and down within only a few notes, accompanying it with the rhythmic and metallic tapping of her eating knife against one of the pots.

On the fringes of the desert lies a land half green, half
    brown
Where the wild dun horses foal and graze.
They live in joyous freedom, never caring that their
    running
Lifts the dust to coat their hides in gray-brown haze.

Once while a child I'd seen that country and the horses
racing through it,
Oh that day I'd sworn that I'd sometime come back.
To take and tame a desert stallion, make him friend and
good companion,
'Til he bore me without protest as a comrade on his back.

I came back to that burned country, almost waterless and
starving,
But I stayed there 'til I knew well the herd and land,
I chose the mount I wanted as I watched him through my
days,
And then I named him for his color—Prince of Sand.

When the winter came upon me with deep snow and
freezing cold,
And the wolves were starving when that grew,
I made a second camp near water, 'neath an overhang
for shelter,
And the whole horse herd ignored me as someone
harmless that they knew.

Foaling time came on the land, so each mare sought out
a place,
Scraping snow away to find the cold-cured grass.
I saw a young dun mare choose her foaling place with
care—
Near my camp while I sat awaiting what would pass.

From out across the snow I heard the wolven call,
As the starving beasts came hunting in the cold.

But before the newborn stands the mare, and the pala are
   aware,
They must slay the dam before they have the foal.

Then I ran with branch aflame while the mare now
   slashed and lame,
Still stood staunch between her filly foal and death.
As I hurled the final coal, the rescued mare and foal
Both reached out to nose me gently as I held my panting
   breath.

Yes, I went into that country to tame and ride a desert
   stallion.
Came out leading filly foal and fang-scarred mare.
They're my friends now who love and trust me,
And if I had it yet to do, wolves again in mercy I would
   dare.

The land will share its treasure with those who learn
   to ask.
Friends will share a burden and aid a comrade's task.
The path was mine to choose—now a scarred mare shares
   the load,
And we're three friends together on a busy, joyous road.

While they traveled down the long road toward Jasta Pass
they sang that a lot. Kyrryl loved it; it had something of the
sound of other songs she'd heard in her world, although the
tune was different. Yet the song of a girl who had chosen a different road to the one she'd intended, and found that it suited
her better, was one that Kyrryl understood. Eilish simply liked
it for the horses.

It delighted Aycharna that her new friends liked the song and wanted to hear it often. It hinted that they might be also able to understand her plains-bred cousins and that perhaps with goodwill, and if the Kalthi *had* been called, some solution might be worked out to deal with them. The Kalthi were deadly, and while it was suggested in the stories that those who called them could order the demons to obey, it was also known that demons hungered . . . and that their hunger, once unleashed, could not always be controlled.

*T*he trader caravan moved briskly down the road. They reached Jasta Pass and camped while it was still light and only midafternoon. Treyvan and Kyeaan had arrived the night before, and, unknown to either group, the slavers were camped only a mile away in a slight dip. Treyvan went hunting both an indication from his employers of their presence, and something to eat. He found halpa—they were excellent roasted— but there were no obvious signals from Vani and Shaetyl.

"Where do you think they are?" Kyeaan asked.

Treyvan shrugged. "I have no idea, but they won't be far. Make the fire larger tonight. They'll see it and know where to come in the morning."

Later the next day Kyeaan realized it hadn't worked. He wanted to get on to Shallahah, collect his payment, and go home. That afternoon, bored with the camp, the guards, Treyvan, and the slaves, he went walking up the pass trail for a ways. He wandered through a fringe of trees and found himself at the edge of a small meadow of knee-high grass. On the far side of that, near a clump of brush, he saw something. He paused to look. Odd, something clothlike was fluttering in the breeze. He walked toward it through the grass, identifying what he was seeing with increasing incredulity. Then he spun on his heel and fled.

In his horror and panic he blundered down the slope, and arrived panting and wild-eyed not in his own camp but at the traders' circle just when they had settled around the fire. So panicked was he that he completely ignored the sight of Aycharna where she sat with Ashara. Kaitlen, recognizing both the man and his white-faced horror in a glance, caught him by the arm. Something very bad had happened and this one knew it. She wanted to know too—and right now. She shook him hard.

"What is it? What have you seen?"

He gasped for breath; then, still glaze-eyed with terror, he gabbled to them all.

8

We were expecting them. They're in pieces. Just torn into bits. Not only them, it's everything in their camp." He shuddered while his face went a greenish gray, and he vomited twice to one side before speaking again. "They're dead and spread all over their camp."

Kaitlen shook him again. "*Who* were you expecting, who's dead?" she snarled into his face.

He was startled into a coherent answer. "Vani and Shaetyl. We built a big fire last night. Treyvan said they'd be camped higher up the pass road so they could see our fire and know where to find us. But they didn't arrive. I went walking to get away from Treyvan for a while—the man is such a barbarian, no culture at all—and to see if I could find them. I only meant to go up the pass road a short way to look around. It was pleasant so I kept walking until I saw something moving and went to see what it was."

"And they were dead and torn to pieces," Tiah finished for him. "Why would that scare you so much? There are beasts in the Toldins. For all you know your esteemed masters ate something poisonous, died, and the animals found them after that."

He looked at her, a white rim showing around his eyes. "I don't have masters and you go and look, trader, then tell me that was animals. Let me go."

"To do what?"

He shivered. "To find my own camp, pack my things, and head for Shallahah City right now. I don't know what killed Vani and Shaetyl and I don't want to know. I'm not staying around in case it's still out there. Believe me, trader, I hold no grudges against you and even if I held a blood feud I still wouldn't stay around here."

He pulled free of her, glared around the circle of people gaping at him, and headed for the road. From there he could find his own camp and tell Treyvan what he'd seen. He knew the slavemaster: Treyvan would go looking for his employers' camp, and Kyeaan would take the opportunity that provided. He'd grab what coins the strongbox contained, and be gone long before Treyvan returned. He'd seen what he'd seen. Vani and Shaetyl wouldn't be back to accuse him of theft, and they owed him for this trip anyway.

He stumbled on down the slope, found the road and then his camp. He gave vague directions and a vivid description of the scene to a disbelieving slavemaster who set off at once to see for himself. Kyeaan never noticed that despite his directions being little more than a pointing finger and a mention of the time it had taken him, Treyvan seemed to know where he was going. The slavers' figurehead managed a faint smile when the man vanished up the road. He had his own mount with him on this trip; it would be the work of mere 'markin to roll up his possessions, saddle his horse, and break open the strongbox. The guards knew he was figurehead for their employers and they wouldn't interfere. They didn't, and very soon after his arrival at the slave camp Kyeaan was riding briskly out of it again on the road to the city. He'd find something else to do there, something a lot safer.

Trudging up the hill, Treyvan looked back, saw the rider, and snorted. Let him go. If his story was true then Treyvan would have the whole caravan as his own; that was worth far more than the fifty or so gold renis that the strongbox contained and that he guessed Kyeaan to have stolen. Neither Vani nor Shaetyl had family: they had no relatives to demand an accounting. If they were indeed dead, he'd take the whole caravan, wagons, slaves, beasts, and all, and be the owner. A bribe or two in the right places would ensure an unprotested change in the registered ownership.

After some searching he found the camp and, hard man though he was, even Treyvan was horrified. Not at the deaths—he'd seen death often enough in his trade—but he was no fool, and he'd had years of experience of bandit attacks and assassinations. This was much worse, and he shivered at the implications as he studied the devastation. Behind him he heard a soft rustling as feet brushed through the grass, and he spun, sword in hand.

*A*fter a quick discussion, Eilish, Kyrryl, Yoros, Aycharna, and the shayana, together with Kian Dae, who refused to be left behind, had come to see what they could find. The others of their group had remained to watch the road and guard their own camp. Kaitlen would be able to backtrack Kyeaan, she'd said to her friends, and she had. Now she held up a hand.

"Truce, slavemaster. Kyeaan blundered into our camp before he found you. We came to see the truth of his claims."

Treyvan looked at her and then at those who spread out behind her. Ignoring Aycharna—his employers were dead and it was unlikely he'd get the girl back without trouble—he spoke to them all. "It seems that he told the truth right enough, traders. See for yourselves. I'm leaving, I have business elsewhere."

Kaitlen studied the camp without moving from where she stood. The slavers had made a neat comfortable camp in the lee of several large trees with boulders and scrub mixed in about them. It formed a semicircle like a cup and had obviously been used to camp a number of times before. The two small tents were laid out, the mouth of each half facing the other. The fire between them had been lit inside a square dug deep from the turf with a wall of solid stones partially around that. The horses' saddles were upright to one side of the tent mouths, and the bridles were laid within the tents beside the sleeping pallets. There were no horses waiting, but all of them could see the deeply scored turf where hooves had churned and dug at the time that the beasts broke their hobbles and fled.

"Neat but not gaudy. They knew how to make a camp," Kyrryl commented.

"They would," Kaitlen said. "They get about, and slavers spend a lot of time on the road."

Yoros was considering the camp and its late occupants. "So they were experienced travelers. They would take all sensible precautions and very few risks?"

Tiah nodded, also looking at the evidence spread about them. "They were slavers, not fools. They'd been in the business most of their lives. They knew that very few people like slavers and others have outright grudges against them. They wouldn't take stupid chances. I'd wager that only the two of them and possibly Treyvan knew where they would be camped when they came here to wait for the caravan to arrive."

"And," Yoros said, still looking over the remains of the slavers, "this isn't exactly the sort of place you'd stumble upon by accident even if that man did. It's well away from the usual trail by the looks of it. It's hidden from view until you're almost on it. Why would anyone be blundering about in this direction, which leads to nothing? However, from here you can see all the way down the hillside if you move over here." He'd done so and now he pointed. They joined him.

"Look, you can see quite a length of the road from this point. You could see any campfire there after dark. I'd say that their slavemaster had a good idea of where they'd be and where he should camp. They'd have been waiting for a fire to show there and they'd normally have come down in the morning when he expected them."

"Except that they weren't able to go anywhere by the time he arrived," Kaitlen finished, adding thoughtfully, "Which, knowing where he's been camped, when, and how long it took him to get up here, tells us that he didn't kill them himself." She considered what remained of the slavers' bodies. "I'd say that he didn't have this done either. Treyvan wouldn't balk at a killing if it got him a good profit, let alone a whole slaver caravan, but no ordinary paid assassins did this."

As Kyeaan had told them, the slavers had been literally spread about their camp. They had been dismembered, heads torn off, limbs wrenched away from the torsos. The amount of blood suggested that almost none of the mutilation had occurred after they were dead. Something had seized them and ripped them apart while they still lived—although that condition wouldn't have continued for very long.

Kian Dae padded over to one of the pieces, sniffed gently, and sneezed. Eilish picked up his interest. The scent that lay about the camp and on the dismembered bodies was strange to him, like nothing he'd ever smelled before. It wasn't normal, not the smell of a warm-blooded animal nor even that of a snake or lizard. There was no scent of the sea similar to the sort a fish or sea mammal might have left either. There was acridity to it, a feel of air and darkness and of an almost insectlike scent. It had the smell of magic and power and nothing good. Eilish received his impressions and remained silent.

Tiah picked her way over to an arm, looking down at it. "No, look, there's no mark of any sword or tool, only these odd dents in the flesh on either side of the joints where they were torn. This was wrenched away by sheer strength. What could do that?"

Aycharna was a greenish gray. "Kalthi!"

Yoros spoke thoughtfully. "So, looking at what we have here, someone or perhaps several people came to the camp. They surprised two experienced slavers who'd always be on the alert for trouble. They then tore them apart without either running."

Kyrryl saw what he'd seen and nodded. "Yes, neither have any sign of damage to the heads. Whatever it was that killed them, one was held waiting while the other was slaughtered. Unless there were several people—or Kalthi—and this was done to both at once. But either way, it raises questions that I find alarming."

"Kalthi!" Aycharna said again.

Kyrryl turned to her. "I think it is time that we found out more about these Kalthi. Is this a way in which they kill? What do you know about them that makes you think this is their work?"

Aycharna sucked in a deep breath, and a little color came back to her face. "They're stories around the campfire, but not tales spun by the tellers. They're true warnings from the days before our people came to this world. It is said that when the portal opened and Pasht permitted us to pass into this world, the Kalthi appeared to balance that."

"Who tells the stories?"

"The wise ones of the clans and tribes who ride the Grass Sea. The stories they tell of the Kalthi warn and teach," Aycharna replied.

Yoros nodded. "And of what do they warn?"

"That one must not hold grudges. A grudge, held too long and too powerfully, may call the Kalthi, and once called they are not easily sent away. They live on killing, and while at first they may kill the enemy, after a while they become less focused and will turn to kill any they find."

Eilish touched her prism. Under her hand it was warm, and she knew that Aycharna believed what she was saying. That did not mean that it was the truth, only that the girl believed her own words.

"How do they say the Kalthi kill?" she asked.

The girl shivered. "This way," she said softly. "They say that the Kalthi can hypnotize, holding their victims in place to be killed. And when they kill they tear the victim limb from limb with the head last. The tales say that this is because they feed on the pain and terror, and best of all is for the victim to *see* himself torn to pieces, feel his agony and know that his own death is coming."

"The birds?" Eilish suddenly asked. "Where are the birds? These men have been dead some time but there are no scavengers. Why not?"

Aycharna had the same answer for that. "The birds will not come for days, not until the Kalthi are long gone and their emanations are dispersed."

Eilish nodded. She might have expected that answer. It might or might not be true, but right now the girl seemed to believe that these Kalthi of hers were responsible for anything bad that had happened anywhere. All right then, the other question.

"How do the Kalthi appear to the eye? Do they walk around like people or do they drift like mist on a mountainside?" Something in Kian Dae's sending to her suggested that. The scent seemed strange, as if it had floated down evenly—or been sprayed—over the camp.

Aycharna looked at her. "It's said they can be both. That sometimes they walk into a camp looking like ordinary travelers and they only reveal what they are when they start to kill those with whom they guest. At other times they're unseen until they become more solid and seize their victims. But I don't know the truth, only the tales, and those are very, very old." She bowed her head, shivering.

Her companions heard all this in grim silence. Aycharna's information—if the truth of it could be ascertained—could be useful in some way, perhaps even crucial in the recovery of Tayio, if the reason he'd been stolen had anything to do with these Kalthi. It seemed more likely the more they heard of the Kalthi, who, if they fed on pain and terror, would doubly enjoy the emotions of a tariling broadcasting with frantic power.

Kait straightened. "I suggest we clear this camp. I'd like to see if they had any slave bonds or contracts with them, and I see no reason to leave valuables for the birds."

They might, she thought, have need of any gold or items that they could find too. Gold bought information and assistance and she believed that the slavers had had no heirs to be cheated from their inheritance.

They checked the slavers' tents to find that the saddlebags of each man had held a substantial sum. Most was in the gold renis common to both Lhandes and Shallahah, but a little of the coin was in the silver ina and the copper itari. They took the expensive and good-quality weapons that they found as well, and the jewelry, of which both men had worn a fair supply; that was gaudy but reasonably valuable. With the scavenging done, Tiah took up a branch of scrub and began to push the limbs together in a heap.

"Better we bury these bits. Slavers or not, it isn't decent to leave them like this."

Yoros found the small camp shovel and began to dig. Kian Dae wandered about the area sniffing suspiciously while they lined the grave with the slavers' spare clothing taken from the tents. He smelled something more solid through the smell that misted over everything, and his squawk alerted Eilish, who walked over to look at his find.

"Everyone, look at this."

Lying by the tent mouth was something that looked like a tiny section of curved claw tip. Kian Dae sniffed at it again before wrinkling his nose and spitting vigorously. When she approached to stoop closer he pushed her back and she heeded his warning.

"I don't think we should touch it. Kian Dae seems to think it would be dangerous to handle. I'll mark it. If the scavengers feel the same way"—she received a clear message from the big cat that they would—"Kian Dae thinks they will, then we can leave it here for the road patrol to find, if we tell them about this."

Yoros walked a distance, came back with a cloth and a large flat rock, dropped the cloth on the claw, and then placed the rock on top of both. He returned to the men's grave, thrusting in the pieces of the bodies and covering them over with the folded tents. Then everyone but the cat combined to roll stones onto the raw earth. Two or three of them together strained to move the largest rocks that could be found, until a pile of them hid the raw earth and spread over the turf about it.

It was almost summer by now and there was ample food about for the beasts, so they were less likely to dig down and break into the grave, Tiah thought. She sent that opinion to Kaitlen.

So I think, shaya. But where do we go from here? To the city to report their deaths, to the plains to ask about the Kalthi, or do we say this is no business of ours and return to the road?

There's time to make that decision. Let's think about it first.

Yoros added a final boulder, picked up the shovel and the other items they were taking, and walked off downhill toward their own camp. Eilish followed with Kian Dae and Kyrryl while Aycharna trotted to catch up. Kaitlen and Tiah wandered more slowly after them.

Kaitlen was thinking about the missing horses. If someone had found them running loose and talked about it in the city, an investigation might be begun. There were a lot of horses in the city, and there was an excellent chance no one *would* recognize them, but making that assumption could be wrong—and dangerous. They'd been on their way to the city; it might be better to go there as planned, tell all of the events to her shaya's father, and, if he advised it, pass on the tale to the palace. They had friends there and the king would hear them if they asked for an audience. Clan wisdom said that it was always better to act than to react.

She waited until they were back in camp and all were sitting down, having told those who had remained behind of what they'd discovered at the slaver camp. Then she spoke softly.

"I don't know what you'll decide, but I've made a decision. The horses ran loose in their panic." She looked at Eilish. "Kian Dae tracked them partway down the hill, you said, and there was no sign that whatever killed Vani and Shaetyl caught the horses and killed them too?"

Eilish shook her head. "He said they were still running."

Kaitlen grunted. "Then there is this to consider. My heart-sister and I have seen the horses before. They're well-trained, beautiful, and quality animals. If they escaped, and it seems likely they did, someone will have found them, and if so they may take them on to the city, where they may be recognized sooner or later."

She explained her reasoning further while they sat and listened in silence. When she was done, Tiah nodded.

"Many don't like slavery, but if travelers are murdered on the road within the territories that Shallahah claims—and they claim to Jasta Pass—the authorities will want to know why and by whom. What you suggest hangs on several possibilities, but in the end it is at least possible someone will ask questions officially. We may be considered to have a grudge against Vani and Shaetyl. It's better and safer for us to tell what we found and ask for an investigation."

"I think our friends here shouldn't enter the city though," Kaitlen said firmly. "They may be asked who they are, and where they came from. What do they say then?"

"True, let us travel to my father's home outside the city. They can stay with him, while we go on to Shallahah to make our report." She looked around the circle of watching faces. "If you wait for us at the master trader's home, we can return and travel together after that—if you'd like our company."

Trasso smiled. "For myself I would." There were murmurs of agreement from everyone else. "But where do we look? The truth is that we've been jumping to a lot of conclusions. There's no real proof that the Kalthi are involved in Tayio's disappearance."

"Go into the Grass Sea, talk to my grandmother, Orla," Aycharna said. "Around our campfires she tells the ancient tales of the Kalthi, but she's a wise one and they don't tell everything they know. If she sees danger for the clans in what's going on, she can advise you."

Eilish nodded. "My brother, my husband, and I went on a lighthearted quest for amusement and to get away from our keep after a long winter inside walls. We've been trapped here and we have no other place to go and no reason to leave you. I think we should go and listen to Aycharna's grandmother. Where else can you look?" She stared at Yoros. "You think the Kalthi may be involved in Tayio's disappearance. If you do then wouldn't it be useful to learn as much about them as you can? And I am starting to believe too that there may have been a purpose in our arrival in this world, that we're here for a reason."

Around the campfire heads nodded one by one. They too felt that there was reason and purpose in their meeting. In the morning they moved on, heading around the Peace Mountains to the Kavarten border, where they separated.

Kaitlen and Anatiah paused long enough for Anatiah to write a note to her father; then they continued on to the city. The rest of the group made for Master Trader Anamaskin's home. There they were welcomed, housed, and entertained while Anamaskin read his daughter's letter and listened to their stories.

"It's ill-sounding," he said soberly once he had heard it all and had many of his questions answered as best they could. "I think it's a good idea to do two things. One is that I call in Hestrie, Kaitlen's brother and their clan's warlord. He's wise and experienced, and he knows something of the Grass Sea and the nomadic clans and tribes there. The other is that I think that Dharvath, the priestess of the clan's shrine, should return with him to hear what you say.

"I'll prepare saddlebags for you. On the plains it's best to travel as light as possible, but there are things you'd do well to have. It is wise, however, that you wait until my daughter and her shaya return from the city before you leave. They'll be able to tell us how this is being taken by the king's peacekeepers and what they may do about it."

They waited. Hestrie came in response to Anamaskin's message, and with him came his clan's priestess. Her black fur had turned almost completely to silver from age, but she rode a small sturdy mule that at her command sat down so that she could dismount more easily.

Anamaskin introduced her with some formality. "This is Dharvath, priestess of the clan shrine. I speak freely before her who is old in years and wisdom and filled with the light of Pasht."

Dharvath held up a large silver medallion. The face of it was etched with a figure so well drawn that it seemed to look at them out of the tiny gems that were the eyes. Kyrryl stared at it.

"That's your goddess?" she asked.

"That is Pasht."

Kyrryl wondered how to ask the next question, but Dharvath smiled. "You find it interesting that I look like my goddess," she said matter-of-factly. "I do, but here in this world we worship Pasht, humans and Aradians alike. It gives us unity; there have been dark times over our history when the two peoples have not always lived in peace. But Pasht is our lady, and even in time of greatest strife, that has rarely been questioned. Now, tell me your own story. What has been happening to you?"

Once again they talked until at last the priestess summed up what they knew.

"You," her claw-tipped finger indicated Yoros and Kyrryl, "had a young one of your friends stolen. You want to rescue him and return to your own world. You," her finger pointed at Eilish and Kian Dae, "quested originally for your own pleasure in the journey, but you seek out this one's sire and that searching has led you here. That portals were opened to you says to me that this is where you were meant to be.

"Portals do open now and again, perhaps once every few generations. Those on the other side enter sometimes when they do, usually in ones or twos but occasionally as a larger group, although that is rarer still. But for two such portals to open within days and within the same world, that is so rare I know of no record of such a previous event. It smells to me of the goddess and from your tales she has indeed had a claw in the business. I think you are all bound together in this, and not you only, but the shayana, and you." The priestess's claw tip pointed at Aycharna.

"Me, what'd I do?"

"You have knowledge that was or will be needed. Where Pasht shows a path will you refuse her will?"

Aycharna looked at Dharvath. "No," she said softly.

"Then I think it best that you prepare the way our trader friend has said. Be ready to ride the Grass Sea when the shayana return, and I shall ride with you. It is in my heart that Pasht shows me too a path to ride and I will not refuse. I have been hers all my life and I will not deny her now."

Kyrryl looked at the priestess, opened her mouth to ask for more information, and shut it again.

The priestess looked at her and smiled. "Good, then that is settled. We have only to wait for Kaitlen and Anatiah to return from the city and we can depart. I hope they don't keep us waiting. I feel a certain dangerous portent about events."

With that Kyrryl, Yoros, and their friends agreed. Kian Dae did not comment. Cats do not worry about the future; they live in the moment.

9

*I*n the city, Kaitlen and Anatiah were talking to an old friend. Neira was noble and kin to the king. She was in her sixties, had lived in the palace her whole life, and knew all the gossip of the city for the past three generations. She listened to the story of how Kyeaan had blundered into their camp babbling of death, of how they had gone to see what he was talking about, and what Kait and Tiah had found there.

"Vani and Shaetyl," she said, considering what she knew of them. "They took over from Vani's father and Shaetyl's uncle. Not the sort of background that usually breeds slavers either. The father and uncle came from ordinary lower-middle-class families. They had a little money, and once they were old enough, they began buying slaves. That generation was a byword for ruthlessness in their trade and the boys followed it.

"They make no show of wealth but I know the taxes they pay: these days they're rich. They own a second slaver caravan in charge of another figurehead, both own houses in the city, large houses and richly furnished. They each have more than twenty household slaves. They also have a large estate that they own jointly on the edge of the Shairne Desert. That too is worked by slaves and is of considerable value." She grinned at a thought.

"I hear they have no families now?" Kaitlen questioned.

"There may be a few remote third cousins. But the father and uncle died quite young. Not one ever asked why but I've always thought they were poisoned. Not necessarily by their heirs, but by someone."

"So Vani and Shaetyl took over their estates?"

"Yes, interestingly, it happened when they were visiting the caravan while it traveled on the road to Hala'atha regions past Ngahere. It was another year before the caravan returned, and Vani and Shaetyl simply reported to the officials that their kin had died—from bad fish they believed." She smiled. "It seems to have occurred to no one to ask how it was that that pair weren't killed by the fish too. But they'd already taken over all the property, there were no other heirs, they paid the inheritance taxes the moment they returned, and I suppose no one thought it worthwhile to question events any further. There may also have been a feeling even among the officials that two slavers dead was of no importance."

Tiah nodded. "In other words, there's no one left within either Vani's or Shaetyl's family with any grudge against them?"

"No. I would say that their deaths would have arisen from one of two reasons. The first, some slave they abused or illegally enslaved and who'd been subsequently freed or escaped and had the resources to pay for such a killing, hired it done. There were several freed slaves from your case against them three years ago."

"And the other," Kaitlen said slowly, "would be if they had simply got in the way of someone—or something—that swept them out of its path."

Neira eyed her and nodded. "Exactly. I don't like that second possibility, not at all! But it's true that these Kalthi the girl talked about are real. Odd stories have come out of the Grass Sea for generations and there are some records in the royal archives. If you'll wait, I'll get the key and we can look."

"For what?"

"A story I recall reading many years ago. I can't remember the details or who was involved, but I think I know during whose reign it happened. And," she paused significantly, "it involved people being dismembered by something that came out of the Grass Sea. Something that was said to have been called by the nomad tribes there."

Tiah stared. "Hold on. Aycharna gave us the impression that her people don't call the Kalthi on purpose. That done unconsciously if a large number of the nomads are badly enough upset by something, then the Kalthi come in response to the collective emotions."

Neira snorted. "Really! In that case why didn't the Kalthi appear twenty years ago when the king burned half the plains to punish them for plundering a royal caravan? No, I'm sure the event in the archives speaks of the massacre as being done by beings that were deliberately summoned."

"But if that's so," Kait said, "the same question applies: Why didn't they do it twenty years ago?"

"Let's go and see if we can find out," her shaya said. Neira nodded and led the way.

The palace archives were housed in a huge brick building that covered several acres. The archives held the documents of nine hundred years, ever since the kingdom was officially established, and five scribes worked full time copying documents to see that the oldest ones remained legible and available for reference, and anyone who could pay could obtain copies for their own records. The files were arranged by the reigns of Shallahah's rulers, and those sorted further into the years of that reign. Neira walked down the rows of neat shelving, muttering as she went.

"I know it was in the reign of Queen Meriah, daughter of Zosanna. Ah yes, here." She marked off a section of the files with a wave of her hand. "Start looking. It'll be in here somewhere and if I'm right again, it was toward the start of her reign."

It took all of a long and boring day, broken only by long drinks of water to get rid of the archive's dust, and light snacks to keep their stomachs from grumbling too loudly. In the late afternoon, after opening a large number of files that held interesting tales—but nothing to do with Kalthi—the file they were looking for was found, opened, and the story recognized by Kaitlen, with a yelp of delight. They read it together, and the three of them left looking very thoughtful.

"So Aycharna was right to some extent. We do have these things around, but only a handful and usually they don't kill like that," Kait said thoughtfully.

"No, but if they're 'excited,' as the archive put it, then they may attack one or two travelers." Tiah recited the remainder of that portion of the record. "'And if such an attack should occur, beware, for it may portend that the demon's kin are close to them, that the aether thins toward the opening of a portal whence may come others of their kind to ravage and slay.'" She shivered, and Neira looked at them.

"I don't like it either, so we do what we can. I can say that I know my cousin. If any of this is likely and you can prevent it, you won't have to worry about any losses you incur ignoring trade and running around after Kalthi. Now, come and eat, I'll find you a room and you can leave early."

• • •

*T*he shayana spent the night with Neira in her palace quarters. She provided breakfast at first light and saw them off.

"I know everything you know so far, my dears. If you fail I can tell my second cousin, the king, what you've told me. But I feel that it may be for you and these others to deal with the problem. I prayed in the shrine last night and I believe that I should say nothing about this business for a while. If you can, send me word of your progress. If you can't, then I'll wait a moon before I tell your story to my cousin—unless there's obvious Kalthi trouble before that."

"And he'll burn the other half of the plains," Tiah said softly, "and if the nomads can call the Kalthi that'll make certain that they do so again and again, so long so any are left alive who can call them."

Neira was firm. "I know, that's why I'll wait. But we can't risk the city and the people. Do what you can, but if you fail or fall you'll be avenged."

They hugged her, mounted their waiting horses, and headed for the road to Kavarten. Neira waved to them, then vanished inside the palace. A thought had come to her while she listened to their tale, something that would please the king. The treasury could always use more gold, and if Vani and Shaetyl had, as she believed, no heirs and they'd made no will, then court officials could claim all of their estates and houses in Shallahah.

She set the process in motion in the tax archives, then went to find the king's spymaster—a nondescript, bland-faced, and sensible man whom few people ever noticed. Varsheean listened to her story, called in Katchellin, his assistant—when he wasn't being a regular soldier elsewhere—and nodded to Neira, who repeated her tale. The men looked at her, then at each other.

"Not pleasant hearing. Tiah was right. If we burn the plains again and the nomad tribes out there *can* call these things, then we could be in deeper trouble than I like," Varsheean said at last.

Katchellin nodded. "But if they do plan to call them, and the archives are everything they say, then we're already in the cesspit. I have a suggestion." The other two waited.

"Neira is right. If we act too hastily we may ruin any chance the shayana and their allies have of solving the problem without war. But if they fail it will be our people who are attacked next. Therefore what we need is a barrier between the plains and Shallahah. Something that will give us time to be ready if there is an attack."

Varsheean grinned. "Yes, and I know a very convenient barrier to hand. Dasheri is out with troops on maneuvers near the Toldins. Chell, you'll ride out to take him orders from me. He's to move on to the Kavarten border and practice his maneuvers there. I'll ride for Kavarten and talk to Hestrie. He'll know all about this by now and I'll explain that with troops right on the border we can be there in a day to fight beside his clan if these Kalthi attack them. He's a realist and no fool, he'll see the logic."

Neira pursed her lips. "Yes, and if the Kalthi pass his clan and attack our people, we'll have the troops between them and the city. I approve."

Katchellin looked at her. "You said you'll be silent on this for a moon? Do you plan to tell the king before then?"

"No, not yet. We're doing all that's necessary, and he has other work. If the problem becomes more acute, or if it looks likely that the Kalthi will attack our lands, then we can tell him. Until that time comes, or the moon is over, I think it's best to act cautiously and say nothing."

Varsheean nodded. He had the power, within reason, to do whatever he pleased in such matters, and the king trusted his judgment. Katchellin would have the troops in place in three days; Varsheean would ride at once to talk to Hestrie, and, if the women had not yet left, he'd talk to them too. He knew Tiah and Kait personally and liked them. They had considerable wit and good sense.

Maybe if he reached them before they vanished into the Grass Sea he could also speak with these travelers who claimed to be from another world. It was quite possible that they were, he knew. There had been a number of such incursions over Shallahah's history. Even, he thought with a grin, by his own people who had poured out of a portal Pasht had opened for them nine hundred years earlier, as they ran for sanctuary with death and destruction on their heels.

Katchellin left, riding a two-horse relay. With luck and if neither of the beasts went lame, he'd be with Dasheri and his troops by nightfall. Two days forced march back and they'd be on the Kavarten border.

Varsheean was pleased to see scouts from Dasheri's troops when he arrived at the border three days later. He paused long enough to rest his horses, leave word for Katchellin and Dasheri, and eat a sunhigh snack while allowing his mount a brief rest. After that he was riding again, heading back to the master trader's compound to talk to the clan warlord whom he'd asked by messenger to be there.

He cantered in close to dusk to be met by Anamaskin himself, smiling broadly. "Good to see you, Varsheean. I have a room ready and Hestrie's here waiting to talk."

Varsheean sighed in relief. "And what of the shayana and their friends? Have they gone ahead?"

Anamaskin nodded. "Yesterday at first light. They left their pack ponies here, but the cat has gone with them, and I provided more weapons, waterskins, and dried food. The girl they rescued is guiding them to speak with the wise one of her mother's clan. Dharvath, priestess of Hestrie's clan, has ridden with them."

Varsheean's mouth dropped open at that. The Aradian in question was old beyond the usual length of her people's lives, and deeply beloved of the clan. It was startling to hear that she would risk her life riding into the Grass Sea—and an indication of just how seriously the old one took the events. The master trader continued.

"Once they've listened to the wisdom of the nomad wise one I don't know where they'll go or what they'll do. They said they'll try to get a message back to us if anyone is willing to bring it. What precautions have you taken so far?" Hestrie had emerged from the main house and was leaning against a post, listening closely.

"I had Katchellin ride to where one of my people is training troops by the Toldins, up toward Jasta Pass," Varsheean told them. "There are a hundred men and five officers on bandit patrol, led by Dasheri. The scouts for the troop were already here and checking along the border when I crossed. The troop will camp just on the Shallahan side of the border and train up and down it between Kavarten and Mersa Lake. If there's need and Hestrie permits, I can have them here in a day ready to fight beside the clan."

The Aradian uncoiled himself from his pose and nodded. "I permit." His fighting fangs showed in his smile. "I heard all that my sister and her shaya had to tell and like you, king's man, I don't like what I hear. Within the clan there are records of the Kalthi, known only to those in power."

He waved to the long bench before the house. "Let us sit and talk where none can overhear. I have information you must know."

"Have you told your sister and the others?"

"I have. That is why they rode out so quickly with their friends." He sat at one end of the bench, and the other two joined him. Hestrie's voice took on the slight singsong of a clan story-teller.

"Forty-seven generations ago when Valgara was warlady of our clan there was a drought on the plains. The records say that the wise ones from the plains gathered and said that to sur-vive, they needed to force our clans from their lands. They be-lieved they had no chance against us, but their wise ones said that a portal was about to open so they sent fighters to the por-tal, and when it did they had just enough time to go through, take prisoner one of those from the other side and return with him. It was said that the stranger's blood had greater power. They sacrificed him in a rite that called the Kalthi—who answered. Hundreds of us died before a priestess of Pasht succeeded in banishing them again."

Anamaskin's face twisted in fear and horror. "Pasht aid us! And my daughter and her shaya plan to fight them somehow? But why, Varsheean? It's a generation since the king punished the plains' tribes. Why are they calling the Kalthi to slaughter us now?"

Varsheean shrugged. "I have no idea."

Hestrie shook his head. "Nor I, but I think they'll call the Kalthi, and if the demons answer it'll be another massacre. I intend to call a council of my clan and our allies. If the Kalthi look likely to appear, we'll evacuate every clan anywhere near the plains' border. Your king made us promises of safety in the past. We'll send our nonfighters to him until the danger is

over. They can take tents and live on the coastal side of Shallahah. If the Kalthi attack Shallahah then my people can run for
safety along the coast past Ngahere to the Hala'atha. Once they
are away from here the fighters of the clans will ride against
the plains. If we die, we may still bring down our enemies, and
those who escape will raise the clan banners again."

"What about Tiah, Kait, and those who've gone with them?"

"If the Kalthi come against us, then we'll know they've
already fallen. I shall sing their names as I fight." His fangs
showed in full display. "For every enemy I kill I'll call a name
so the spirits of my sister and her shaya know themselves remembered and honored."

He fell silent with an air that indicated he'd said all that he
felt needed saying. Varsheean exchanged glances with Anamaskin.

"Then we wait upon events, master trader. If you have drager
the time will pass faster."

Wordlessly Anamaskin left to return with a large bottle
and drinking bowls. He shared the drink around and they sat
talking casually of other things, sipping and thinking of what
they'd heard. Where were their kin and their kin's friends
now, and would they succeed?

*D*eep in the Grass Sea Dharvath on her mule and Aycharna on a mount borrowed from Anamaskin led their
group. Eilish followed the old priestess, while Kian Dae trotted along on foot, taking a welcome rest from being in his carrysack. The wind blew softly from the north and the scent of
green grass was strong. Toward sunhigh Kian Dae abruptly
raised his nose, breathing in deeply. Overlaying the smell of
the long grass he could now smell horses, not their own but

others. He sent that to Eilish, who threw up her hand and called to those who rode with her.

"Kian Dae says there are horses up ahead. He can't smell people though. If there are any with them, it's likely to be only two or three."

"The tribe pasture their horses beyond the camps, sometimes as much as five miles away if they've been in that camp awhile," Aycharna said. "But the horses won't be alone. There'll be herds-boys and in this direction the beasts should be those of my mother's clan. Ride on slowly. Let me go farther out in front. They'll recognize my vest and hold off on shooting. At the least they'll want to find out who dares to ride the plains wearing a vest belonging to our tribe."

The garment of which she spoke was a round-necked, gaudily embroidered sleeveless tunic in black wool that fell to midthigh, and was split almost waist-high at both sides. She'd managed to find it among trade goods Tiah's father had in storage, and had hailed it with delight.

Aycharna cantered her mount a few paces until she headed the group; then she reined him in and moved on in the lead at a fast walk. The others fell in behind her, moving more slowly. Eilish stopped briefly to allow Kian Dae to jump from the grass to her saddlebow, then climb over her shoulder and into his carrysack, standing up in it, front paws on her shoulder as he watched.

His sharp ears caught the signal when Kaitlen turned to look down the line and warn them. "I heard a whistle, human not a bird. I'd say that one of the herds-boys has seen us. What do we do now?" This question to Aycharna.

"Stop and wait. I'll ride on a little farther. If it's just me, he isn't likely to panic and shoot. One of the other boys will ride for camp, the clan will send out scouts, and once they see who I am they'll approach. Follow my lead when they do."

They halted as she moved on. Then everyone sat quietly waiting. Tiah considered all that had happened since Aycharna had joined them and sent to Kait, *Wait, she says. Looking back, it seems to be almost all we do. Stop and wait for something else to happen.*

Kait showed her fangs in a smile. *Well, once we've waited things mostly *have* occurred, haven't they, heart-sister? I'm not sure that I want too many more like some of the events we've seen to keep happening. A quiet life for a trader is pleasant.*

Tiah looked at her and snickered. *Oh, yes? A quiet life! And when have we ever had that, shaya?*

Kaitlen considered. *True. I suppose that it's us. Some people attract trouble the way an overripe rock melon attracts the oswan. We seem to be two of them.*

And so far we've also escaped the trouble we've met.

Her shaya's mind-voice was sober. *May that continue, heart-sister. I have no wish to die young, and still less to see you dead.*

From within the shoulder-high grass a long rising whistle broke off on a series of questioning notes. Aycharna whistled something in reply, waving vigorously as two riders burst through the grass toward her. They stared, then advanced to pat her shoulders gently, one ending that with a long affectionate hug. Aycharna began to talk, leaning forward earnestly. The two young men listened, interrupting her now and again while looking over those who waited. Finally Aycharna pointed to the mule's rider and said something, and everyone could see the riders' sudden alertness. They nodded again, spoke, and Aycharna turned, beamed at Dharvath and all those with her, and called.

"Come ahead but move slowly and keep your hands from any weapons. The tribe will hear you. They offer guest-friendship until morning, and for Dharvath, the priestess of Pasht of whom they have heard, they offer honor and clan freedom so long as she wishes."

While they rode, members of the clan appeared silently from the grass, some afoot, others on horseback. They clasped Aycharna's hands and she dismounted to walk with them, laughing. They surrounded her, talking to her, and now and again one of them pulled her into a quick hug. All eyes widened, though, at the sight of Dharvath, and widened still further when Kian Dae craned to look back at them from over Eilish's shoulder. Those of the clan who saw him hissed softly, pointing him out to others. They knew of the tori from the high hills and their description, but none of the nomads had ever seen one. It was known that, like the dravencats of the Toldins, the beasts were greatly beloved of Pasht, and clever in their way. If one rode with this woman as a friend, then she too must not be insulted or harmed.

Kian Dae recognized admiration and awe when he saw them, and preened. Riding past, Dharvath made the blessing sign to many of the children. When she and her group halted at the edge of the camp and the clan's wise one approached, she signaled her mule to sit. She dismounted, and paused on the camp fringe before bowing slightly to the four quarters, speaking the formal blessing.

"Maiden, Mother, Warrior, Wise, bless the people of this clan and camp. Bless the beasts that they may be fruitful, bless the children that they may grow strong."

From the camp the clan's wise one walked forward chanting the ancient invocation to Pasht.

She is the morning dew, the light on the grass.
She is the sunset at night, and the shadows that pass.
She is the strength of the strong, the courage we seek.
She is the wisdom of age, and shield of the weak.
She is the laughter, tears, bright sun and the rain.
She is the grass, the trees, and the growing wild grain.
She is the heart of the mystery.

She bowed to the four quarters and then to Dharvath. "She sends a sister and I greet her who is come in honor. In Pasht's name enter our camp and be under her hand." She looked past the priestess and nodded, smiling, to Kaitlen and Anatiah. "I greet two also who once came to my people many years ago bringing a dead man for his death honor."

Anatiah started; then, studying the wise woman's face, she recognized the nomad wise one she and Kait had met more than half their lives ago.

"Orla?" she said uncertainly.

"Orla, child. Yes. It is pleasant to know that you remembered my name, since I have remembered you." She turned back to Dharvath. "Would you believe it, they were children, but they came bearing the body of a warrior of the plains who had died without death honor. They brought the body to my camp—riding boldly into the very camp of their enemies—and stayed with us under truce for one night. But that one," she pointed to Anatiah, "kissed an enemy farewell when they left, and I have never forgotten."

Dharvath smiled. "I know some of that tale from them. Once we've spoken of serious matters, lighten the talk by telling me the tale from your side. It is good to hear both halves of a story."

"I shall. Now, sit down. My people will tend your mounts

and we'll eat and talk. I know it will be no light matter that brings a clan priestess of the Moon Lady to the plains. You bring with you too one who has clan blood and clan right by the campfire, and she would not have guided you to us without weighty reasons."

Eilish accepted the slab of bread with roast meat balanced on it. The drinking bowl she was offered seemed to contain some sort of drink that was tart but not bitter. Kian Dae bounced around accepting meat where it was offered and purring when the children stroked him.

Orla smiled, watching him. "It speaks well of you that a tori travels at your side."

Dharvath shook her head. "Not a tori, but one who came through a portal Pasht opened, as did most of these. I believe she permitted them to pass, setting them in balance against a terrible danger that has been called." Her gaze met Orla's and she nodded once sharply in confirmation of the sudden horror in the wise woman's eyes.

Orla drew back. "On the plains? Who has done so?"

"A young one of their friends was taken, to sacrifice we think. They rode to find him. Others have joined them in this search and to prevent an evil Pasht rejects." Her face set in a frown.

"Once, long ago, our records tell, the plains sent the Kalthi against the clans. Many clan warriors died, but in the end many more were slain who had lived in the Grass Sea so that they were far weaker. I understand some of the reasons that your people may have done this again. But it is folly. The king in Shallahah will send men to burn the grass again, and this time he won't stop until the plains are destroyed."

Orla was silent, thinking. At last she raised her head. "If this has been done or planned, I don't know about it, but you're right. It is a folly that could lead to our destruction. Stay in our camp in honor and under truce. I shall ride with some of the tribe's warriors to ask questions of other wise ones whose camps are nearby."

She drew herself up, her words becoming formal again. "I reject such evil and such utter recklessness that may bring down every tribe or clan on the plains. I'll stand with you in this, my sister in Pasht, though I stand against all of the Grass Sea." She stood up.

"I'll waste no time. If this thing and the fools who plan it are to be discovered and stopped, it must be done quickly. I must make arrangements with other clans and those who can help me. I ride now. You rest here in safety and wait until I return with news."

Dharvath nodded. "We'll wait. Pasht grant we're wrong."

In return she received a half smile and a shrug. Orla feared that they were not, but she would have the truth of it from those she knew—or blood.

10

*N*ine other-worlders, two traders, a priestess of Pasht, and a cat rested as bidden. The clan erected spare tents to house them and provided extra bedding. The plains could be cold in the early hours of the morning.

Orla returned three days later drooping in her saddle. That was knowledge, Dharvath thought, as much as weariness. The kind of information you hadn't wanted to have or to hear. Her belief was confirmed once the wise one had received food, drink, and an hour's rest. Then she called the visitors and the clan elders together.

"The news isn't good," she said bluntly. "I must tell you of things that are not normally said, a Mystery, but one that's known to the wise of the tribes of the Grass Sea. Long ago we came through a portal into this world. It is said that with us came demons that by existing created a balance that allowed us to stay. The wise ones of our clans believe that this part of the tale is wrong, that the demons simply saw an opportunity and took it."

"The Kalthi?" Yoros asked softly.

"Indeed. It is also said that they come when there is a very powerful need for justice by a large number of people. This is false. The truth is that they come when someone calls them with a will to evil. As your friend discovered in your records." Her gaze turned to Tiah and Kaitlen. "They may be summoned by death, but the death rite that opens the portal must be the death of one who is from neither of our worlds. The sacrifice being different, their blood and death have the power to break open the portal where it would not normally be opened."

Dharvath nodded. "Even so." She smiled as the shayana turned indignant glares upon her. "As Orla says, this is a Mystery which is not normally discussed. But the priestesses of Pasht in Kavarten and Shallahah know the truth."

Yoros nodded. "What help can you give us to recover Tayio and will our few people be enough to stop demons who may come in their hundreds—or in even greater numbers?"

Orla looked at them. "I shall ride with you. Any calling of the Kalthi must be stopped. Our records show that they can only be called on certain nights of each year. It has been some time since the last suitable night, and since the Kalthi have not appeared it is clear that they have not yet been called. However, with the death of the two slavers, it is certain that someone does plan to open a portal. The intent is what is drawing those handful of Kalthi and making them mad for blood.

"If we can find who wants to do this and stop them before they can open the portal and call the demons on the next possible night, then we don't need more of us than there are. If the Kalthi attack Shallahah the king will fall upon us again, and this time he won't stop until all the plains' tribes are dead. To call the Kalthi is folly. Nor are they all-powerful. They can be defeated, although it would mean many thousands of deaths if they were

loosed against Shallahah or Kavarten when those lands were unprepared."

Kyrryl was looking thoughtful. "But someone has called
them. Maybe the reason does lie twenty years back. People can
hold a grudge that long. It could be that it's taken this long to
prepare, or that something has recently happened that made
the grudge much stronger."

Dharvath pursed her lips. "That is an interesting thought:
it makes sense to me. Orla, send word among the tribes and
clans of the Grass Sea and ask about anyone to whom this could
apply. Perhaps someone knows something and hasn't thought
to tell anyone about it."

"I'll do so, but it may take days and we can't wait to hear.
We need to ride now."

Trasso took Eilish's hand in his. "Where do we ride, wise
one?"

"I believe I know the direction, but Dharvath does not
ride with us. Her place is to return to her clan. Aycharna shall go
with her. She is no great rider and she could not keep up with
us." The girl glared, then dropped her gaze. "I speak truth,
child, and you know it," Orla told her. "Your part will be played,
do not fear, but not here and not now. Go with my Moon sister
and obey her, when the time is right you'll rejoin us."

Kian Dae approached to sit at her feet and looked up. "As
for you, small brother in fur. You too shall go with Dharvath.
We shall ride down the days and miles with little rest and such
riding is not for you. Go with my sister. Your friends will find
you when they have done their part in this."

Eilish gave a small protesting cry. What if something happened to either of them while they were apart? From the big
cat she received irritable agreement. He didn't approve of the
separation, but it was necessary. He had no intention of being

bumped and jostled for days in a carrysack until he was too stiff and sore to be of any use. He would go with the old woman and wait for his people to come back. Eilish accepted his decision. If he was determined, she could only agree.

Orla considered Kaitlen and Anatiah. "You also go with my Moon sister. I think your part is yet to be played. Return to your kin and tell them privately what has occurred. Await our return on the edge of the Grass Sea. If we succeed and I live, a messenger shall come to seek you out and tell you the results of our quest."

Kait snorted. "And if you don't succeed?"

"Then you'll know it without the need for a messenger," Orla said dryly. "If that happens do as you think best, but go as fast as you can to your king and tell him that a daughter of the plains died trying to save him, that not all of the people of the Grass Sea are evil."

Kyrryl shivered, her gaze going to Ashara. It had been a constant worry to her that her niece had been with her when she and Yoros came unwittingly through a portal. But Pasht had said that a portal should be opened for their return. They were not trapped; how then could she permit the girl to travel in search of demons and perhaps be killed? How could she go home to tell her beloved brother and sister-in-law that she had let Ashara ride with them here to her death? Ashara must wait here. She whispered her thoughts to her husband.

Yoros leaned over, and his hand closed on her wrist when he spoke softly so that only she could hear. "No."

"No?"

"No, my love. At home she's ridden as a warrior this past year. Shall we now say she's too young to fight?"

"It isn't that—"

"I know, but to forbid the girl to ride with us, to leave her like baggage with a people we don't know? That's an insult to her courage."

Kyrryl again felt a chill go through her. The gaze she turned on him was haunted. "Then she rides with us. But I believe that one of us who came through the portal won't live to ride back, and I fear it could be Ashara, Yoros."

"A foretelling?"

"I don't know, only that this is what I feel. It may be no more than my foolish fears, it may be the truth, I can't tell. But I believe it. Should we tell the others?"

He shook his head. "No. In a few days when we see if we are likely to find the enemy, then we might speak of it to Orla or one of our new friends—Trasso or Eilish maybe. Until then say nothing. To say it will weaken us with fears that may be unfounded."

Kyrryl nodded. Neither noticed that one had been watching them thoughtfully from under her brows while they talked. Kyrryl had no need to share her fears; there was one who already knew them, one who knew their worth—more than they did— but she too would say nothing, not yet.

*T*hey spent the night with the clan and rode out at first light. It may have been a gift of the goddess that all slept soundly and without dreams. Their path was to the south along the Kavarten border, and after that first few hours of riding when they broke out of the longer grass their speed increased to a steady canter. With their group came warriors of the clan driving almost all of the clan's saddled spare mounts.

They traveled using the beasts as relay, and after two days it seemed to them all that they'd ridden forever. Their world narrowed to the knee-high yellow and lavender grass that stretched as far as the eye could see. The endless lavender sky over them stretched to the horizon. To their right they could see the mountains growing closer, while beneath them their mounts held the slow rocking canter until they felt that they would sleep and slip from broad backs.

They alternated a walk with slow cantering. The ground was easy enough, but horses weary more quickly than experienced riders. A time came when all of the horses were slowed. Then, from out of the grass, clan warriors with different markings came, bringing fresh mounts. The group continued, their own horses running free with the extra mounts the way they had from the beginning so they should have familiar beasts to ride in any fight. Orla's warriors returned to their clan, driving their weary beasts back to their lands at a quiet walk.

Kyrryl reined her new mount over to Orla. "Are these people from one of the other clans you talked to?"

"They are. Their wise ones said that we should have help against the Kalthi and so they came with their spare mounts for us. But that's the most they're prepared to do so far."

"They won't fight the Kalthi?"

"Later perhaps, if the Kalthi come to the plains, but riding a long way to look for those who may have called the Kalthi? That is your task. I believe that this is why portals opened for you and will open again."

"Balance?" Kyrryl said softly. "And what else will provide it?"

Orla looked up, meeting her gaze. "That I think you have guessed, but leave it be. Everyone with us has made their choice. Free choice, free choosing, as is Pasht's law."

"How is it free choosing if they don't know?" She was thinking of the servants. They had no idea what they could face yet they followed their masters.

Orla smiled wryly. "We know this of life, none leave it

alive, but would you choose not to be born if you could choose?"

Kyrryl rode in silence, considering that, while they rocked on until dusk fell softly over them. They made camp and slept the sleep of the exhausted. When morning came they rode again, the mountains growing ever closer. Though a slow canter is an easy pace, after three days it was exhausting, even for those who had spent much of their lives in the saddle. Still, they were covering ground, and they all felt that they were nearing a goal.

Of the servants Kyrryl had considered, only Dayshan rode with full knowledge. Eilish, Sirado, or Trasso would as soon have considered flying as they would have considered keeping him in the dark about what they faced. Roshan rode placidly. If there was anything he should know, Dayshan or his master would tell him. Hailin rode placidly too—to all outward aspect. Yet within he seethed. He'd heard some of what was discussed and he wasn't at all sure he liked the prospects. But he'd also heard tell that in troubled times there could be golden opportunities for a man who kept his wits about him. He'd follow—for now, and in hopes that would hold true.

Twice more, horses were brought and they changed mounts, riding up the narrow strip of land between the seacoast and the foothills that led them east. The air was colder, and they were weary beyond telling. On the seventh night of their ride, they sat drooping by their campfire. Eilish leaned against her husband's shoulder. She missed Kian Dae but had accepted that he'd been right to remain with the old priestess and the freed slave. Still she said to her brother that she wondered how the cat was.

Sirado patted her hand when he offered her bread and cheese. "Don't worry, he'll be fine with Dharvath and Aycharna. They believe he's blessed by their goddess and the tribe will spoil him silly."

She smiled up at him as she accepted the food. "I do know that really, it's just that I'm so used to him being with me. But you're right and so was he. It was his choice to stay with them." She took the steaming drinking bowl he passed her, drank, and leaned against Trasso's shoulder, falling silent.

One of the horses stamped where it was hobbled. Clan warriors had taken back all but two mounts each for those who rode on down the land, one spare each, and their own mounts, with which they were familiar. They would use the clan's horses until such time as they thought they might have to fight. Then it would be good to have their familiar trained horses to ride. The three pack ponies Ashara, Roshan, and Hailin had led had also traveled with them. Anamaskin had seen to it that they were laden with suitable supplies, although those were now depleted.

On the other side of the fire sat Ashara, Kyrryl, and Yoros. They shared the meal without discussion, but the adults' gazes met at intervals.

Orla unobtrusively studied those with her about the fire. Particularly she watched the servants. Dayshan was a good man but he was in his mid-forties. Still, he was experienced in battle and riding, a man of steel and rawhide, and he kept up. She believed he would continue to do so. About the two younger servants she was not so sure. She found herself uncertain of the two men.

In the firelight she considered them. Roshan was in his early twenties, she judged. A solid young man, not clever but conscientious. He seemed to be a man you could set to a task and know it would be done whether it was overseen or not. He wasn't that bright, she thought, not a man from whom to expect clever ideas, but he was honest, hardworking, and sensible.

Hailin was perhaps five years older and there was something very faintly sly about him. He'd be the kind who lazed a little if he weren't watched. A picker-up of unwatched trifles too, she suspected. And, she summed him up to herself, the sort of man who believed that he was only looking after himself, that he wasn't doing anything very wrong. And in so thinking he fell into traps a more honest and less self-deceiving man would avoid. She'd seen his kind before in the tribes of the Grass Sea. Men like that weren't completely bad, but they could be as dangerous as if they had been. Yes, she would watch this one.

In neither of her last two appraisals was she entirely wrong. Roshan sat eating his meal in silence. He had nothing to say and he said it. Trasso was his master and it was for him to lead and Roshan to follow. Where they went and at what speed was none of Roshan's business. He knew Hailin despised him for that but he didn't much care. Hailin was a clever fellow, sometimes too clever, and he could go his own way.

Hailin ate his bread and cheese, drank a bowl of the odd hot drink the people of this land called pata, and thought busily while keeping his face bland. He'd been happy enough to ride out with Eilish and Trasso. He wasn't going to say no when they suggested that he be one of their group: the favor of the nobility could lead to better things. But he was coming to the belief that enough was enough. He was tired of chasing about, not knowing where he was going, and he was still less pleased to find he was doing it in company with Kyrryl and her kin. He'd known the woman for a woman of the power since the day they'd met; he thought the same was true of Eilish.

He sulked quietly. He'd hoped that coming on this stupid quest for a cat's sire would put him into the way of finding any small valuable something that had been left lying about. He could scoop that up and into his belt pouch, where later it would augment his savings. He'd expected that along the way they would visit other keeps in the hills. Maybe they would drop in on some of the larger garths. And in such places no one might notice if a trifle vanished, a coin here, a bit of broken jewelry there. One day he'd be out of the keep with savings enough to buy his own small business so that he could live well and with less work.

Instead of that, however, he'd been tricked into this place where he rode for days until the seat of his pants was worn thin. And what was worse, he did it in company of two women of his world he believed to be women of the power, and a very strange female. With his own ears he'd heard her admit she worshipped some heathen goddess. Really, he didn't care about that latter so much, it was the powers that he resented, just another thing that the rich or noble had and he didn't. He drifted briefly into a daydream where the powers were his and he used them to obtain riches and a title—before the sudden snap of a burning branch drew him back to everyday reality.

Hailin reminded himself that he should stay alert. There were always chances of improvement in wealth or position for a man who was ready to seize them. Right now he was in a strange land. He wasn't sure that he believed in all this talk of other worlds. Nobles talked such a lot at any time, and most of it was nonsense. But here he rode a fine young horse, a mare and a far better beast than his own aging gelding. If he could find a way to keep her and happen upon an item or two of real value once they got wherever it was that they were going, well, there'd be no reason he couldn't snap those up.

They rode on the next day but Orla halted them well short of dusk before she swung down from her mount and stretched wearily. "We are near the place I know from stories. I cannot swear that this is where you may find your missing one. What I do know is that the last time the Kalthi were called, it was here that they came."

"Leaving aside the Kalthi for this moment," Yoros said slowly, "how many people do we face? How many will be here?"

"That I can't say for certain." She shrugged at that. Who could ever be sure without seeing them? "But I *can* guess for you if you wish. There must be at least four people involved. For the most effective calling it takes four to call to the four winds, the four directions. Nor is this a thing likely to be approved by any-one of sense. No one in the clans and tribes I spoke to could tell me of anyone who was missing, anyone who held a grudge that festered into madness. For such a calling they would need to work in fours. And they can't be too many who are involved in this business or else once my question want around, someone would know or guess—and talk."

Dayshan looked at her. "So, four or possibly eight, but you think no more than that?" he asked.

"Yes."

"What about hangers-on? I mean, not everyone involved may be alone. They could have a wife, a brother, and a friend who isn't directly involved but who's come with them. If there are people like that and they stand aside we shouldn't harm them. They may have done little and know nothing of what was intended."

Orla shook her head. "I don't think there'll be any such people. It's barely possible but very unlikely. No one could be close to a calling without being aware of what was planned. Nor do I think those planning to call the Kalthi would bring friends or family as witnesses. If you ask for my own opinion, I'd say there are four and that they've come from a clan that sees nothing unusual in their absence since it is normal for them to be absent. Maybe they are hunters or raiders or maybe they often go to trade on the clan's behalf. It seems likely to me they have no close family and that their friends are those involved. But that's my belief and I could be wrong."

Her companions considered that and felt their spirits rise. There were ten of them, and against four, even if that four were engaged in black sorcery, they thought they'd have a chance. It was possible that none of the enemy were trained fighters, and one of their own group was a priestess; surely her goddess would favor her? Hailin's mind was on something else. He was considering all the chances of being killed or even hurt, and resolving once again to stay well away from any fight. Or as far away as he could later convince the survivors had been in everyone's interests.

Orla felt a sudden vibration in the air and knew that somewhere ahead the fools were laying out the limiting circles and wards to surround their calling the wickedness that was the Kalthi. The demons must be very carefully bound to their purpose, their wills weakened. It was that which took time. To open the portal took only one or two 'marks, less if the callers knew their business.

It would be best to say nothing of this to her companions just yet. Let them sleep, and in the morning she would lead them to the place. She only hoped that they'd succeed. Before she lay down to sleep, she prayed to Pasht that whatever happened to her, those who called would fail in their calling.

*F*ar to the northwest, two duos rode. One pair was Aycharna returning to Dharvath's clan—along with an irritable cat already missing his people. The other duo was Kaitlen and Anatiah, bound for their kin and later to the border where they would find soldiers—and good counsel, or so they hoped.

11

*K*aitlen and Anatiah were in conference with Hestrie and Anamaskin. "So Orla thinks she'll be killed stopping the Kalthi?"

"That was my impression," Kait said thoughtfully. "It might be that she hoped we would go to the king on our return but I wanted to talk to you two first. There's danger in forewarning the king. I don't want to see the Grass Sea burned again. The king did that a generation ago and it looks as if his actions then produced the hatred that's led to this Kalthi business. Then too, if he burns all the plains the clans will protest. Several of them border the Grass Sea and I for one wouldn't want to see it burn. There are dangers to the Aradian clans of Kavarten in such a firestorm."

Tiah nodded agreement. "And I think he forgets that the plains have an end. What about whoever lives on the far side of the Grass Sea? They may not be happy to find a firestorm approaching them."

Anamaskin pursed his lips. "Yes, indeed. The land does not stop where the plains do. As we traders know, beyond the plains lie mountains with fierce hill tribes who are mostly Aradian."

"And," Hestrie said softly, "we tend to stand by our people. If Aradian clans from the edge of the Grass Sea go to their cousins in the mountains to say that humans burned the plains and ruined the clan, then those who shelter them may feel that they too have a grudge. It is not impossible that they could do something about it."

Kait stared, her brow knitted. "You create a worrisome possibility with your 'if's. You mean that if the Kalthi attack Shallahah, the king almost certainly will burn the plains in retaliation. If he does, some of the plains clans will flee to kin in the far mountains to the northeast. If they complain to their kin, the mountain tribes may feel that they have a grievance against Shallahah and ride to war. Am I correct?"

Hestrie inclined his head silently, and they all stared at each other. At last Anamaskin spoke. "And if Aradian clans ride to war there is something else to consider. We humans have a bad habit of tarring everyone with the same brush. If humans are being attacked by Aradians, then there will always be some fool to say that they should attack an Aradian in turn—any Aradian. And who is closest to Shallahah but the clans in Kavarten?"

Their looks at each other were now appalled. Anamaskin nodded unhappily. "Yes, I think that we should say nothing of any of this to the king yet. If the wise one fails there will be time enough to tell him. But if Hestrie's 'if's occur, we could have a war between Aradians and humans, and such a war could destroy us all."

Their discussion continued for some time, since the four of them were desperate to find some solution that would not lead to the thing they feared. But in the end they found nothing.

• • •

When, a short distance ahead of her group, Orla had studied the site, they halted at her direction. In reply to questioning looks she explained her reasoning. "I know it's not quite dusk, but this is a good place to camp. The scrub is heavy enough to screen the firelight from anyone who may be camping lower down the slopes and who might otherwise see it from a long distance. We'll use dry wood and make a very small fire too, just enough to heat dinner."

Yoros nodded. "Is there any indication of who did use it last? I saw you looking," he added in explanation.

"Margarly's clan, I think. They're Aradian and a generation ago they used to ride this way to hunt shellfish on the coast. There are good beds of tuatua on the beach that way." She pointed south.

Ashara was interested. "You said that a generation ago they used to ride here? Why don't they come now? Are the shellfish growing fewer?"

Orla looked at her. "No, child. Margarly's clan died when fire came to the plains and none of her clan escaped."

"Oh." Ashara shuddered. "That must have been awful."

"It was," Orla replied. "Now, down that way"—she pointed—"Aratanga Pass is about a day's ride west."

Eilish was recalling the map she'd seen. "I see. So we've came over Jasta Pass, circled the Toldins, and come up around them to the place that you call the Outlaw Coast?"

"Yes. No ruler claims this strip. Now and again escaped slaves or bonded servants who have run from their bond settle here. Few live long lives; the land is free to take but not safe for those who don't have the numbers to hold it."

Most of those who listened to her nodded at that. A land

without an overlord usually was unsafe. To whom should settlers call for help if they were attacked, from whom should they ask justice? If there were no one, they would always be vulnerable to a stronger enemy.

They all woke early the next morning. It was as if something wanted them wakened and ready before even the first glimmers of light touched the sky. Once they'd eaten, cleaned camp, and saddled their own familiar mounts, they could see to where the sea glimmered in the distance. Above them sky lightened into its shade of lavender while the shadows slipped away. They left the spare mounts and the pack ponies tethered lightly to a long thin rope to eat grass.

Orla took her mount's reins. "I am not completely certain, but I believe that I know where these idiots who want to call the Kalthi are. If I'm right, they're half a day's ride from here, and their calling has just begun. To call the Kalthi and open a portal takes time. I think from what I sense now that they won't complete their calling until after sunhigh."

Kyrryl's head jerked up. "Orla! You should have told us."

Orla's voice held a sudden edge. "Why? I have said that it takes time to make the circle before they can open a portal for the Kalthi. They can't open the portal until sunhigh today and that's hours yet and we can reach them before it happens. Would you have ridden on all night in the dark, risked falls and broken bones, or injured mounts? The loss of any of us weakens our strength and we can't afford that. Would you blunder about in the dark, exhausting yourselves so that you can attack them a few hours earlier—and what would you do when you can see nothing?"

Yoros intervened. "You are right, wise one. A warrior chooses his ground and his time to be brought to battle. I think you know more about the Kalthi than you have said, though?"

Orla inclined her head. "I know a little more, yes. And I think that this is the time to share what I know. Let us ride while I talk." She swung onto her mount and led off. They followed, crowding their horses about her to listen.

"You have been told that the Kalthi can be called, and that they came with the humans who fled another world. What I haven't explained is the Kalthi, their calling, and the portal. Only a handful of them live in our world. Alone the few here can do little and haven't been seen by anyone in three generations. Their danger lies more in what they are. They can be used to anchor one end of a portal. If they are called to a suitable place and a portal is opened, then, we are told, many of their kind will pour in to attack who and where the openers of the portal direct them."

"How many?" Trasso asked.

"The last time it was hundreds," Orla said. "Many of the priestesses of Pasht combined when that happened, led by her Lahaya—her Sworn-Sword—and together they drove them back through the portal and closed it. It was hoped that they had expelled all of the Kalthi, but the Lahaya said she believed a few remained, and they could be an anchor for a portal again, through which their species could return if called. The shrine records I have seen were not so sure. But it now appears that she was right."

Sirado shrugged. "So we do it again and this time we do it right. I can't keep running here to someone else's world to chase away demons. I have my embroidery to do."

Scowls had been gathering on the faces about him while he spoke. With the last sentence they were dispelled by gusts of laughter. Sirado beamed. A good laugh made everyone feel better. If they had to fight, that was all to the good. It was something his grandfather had always told him. He caught the look of approval Dayshan tossed him and grinned back. If the master-at-arms approved, then he'd done the right thing.

Of them all Hailin, riding last in their line, continued to scowl unnoticed. Was there some way in which he could slip away, evade the coming fight? He'd stay alert for the chance in case, and if it appeared he'd be gone. He could always think up a good excuse for his disappearance—if anyone survived to hear it.

When the land leveled out, Orla had gradually increased her mount's speed. She heeled it into the familiar rocking canter after an hour's riding; and those behind her followed suit. After another hour she reined her sweating, leg-weary beast abruptly to one side and pulled it to a halt, to sit in silent meditation.

Kyrryl touched her prism. As well as being tuned to Tayio, it responded to the use of power in general and would indicate if evil was close. She concentrated, and the prism's light glowed red, a cluster of spots making a red glow moving on the prism's facets to show a direction, the distance indicated by the intensity of the spot of light. Whatever was happening was ahead of them, and she could also see—dimmed by the red glow—the light that was Tayio. His light was paling in fear and confusion. They must have him under some spell or other constraint, though; he wasn't mind-calling.

Orla's hand rose to point in the same direction. "There. They've begun. They'll open the portal in maybe a quarter candlemark."

"If there are only four of them," Kyrryl added quietly. "And if they haven't opened the portal yet, we may be in time to stop them and save Tayio. My prism says he's there."

Hailin, seeking some way to avoid a fight that looked imminent, looked at the ground beneath his mount. It was level enough, but it was still rough. A horse ridden carelessly at speed could stumble and throw him. And somehow he didn't think his companions would be riding slowly to attack what lay ahead.

He was right. Orla was explaining the lay of the land ahead. "Around this scrub there's a line of boulders and a rock ridge forming a long curve. The sea is just past that swell of land only a few hundred yards away. I sense those we seek. They've started opening the portal, and the Kalthi wait. I can feel their eagerness—and their hunger."

Ashara lifted her reins to signal her mount in the direction Orla had indicated. "Then what are we waiting for?"

Yoros reached out and caught her arm before she could move forward. "The right moment, my girl. Battle can always be joined, but a wise warrior waits for the right moment. We'd do better to surprise the enemy rather than to attack from the front while screaming challenges."

Halting her mount, Ashara flushed. Orla took the lead again. The wise one was chanting almost soundlessly, her hands weaving through a complicated pattern as her mount, the reins lying loose along its neck, followed a narrow thread of deer path. Her chanting rose and fell. The rest of the group crowded close, Hailin allowing his mount to slow still further until he was dropping back even from the tail end of those he followed. Orla finished chanting and turned.

"I've spelled our movements silent. We'll travel along the upper side of the ridge. If those who would call are where I believe them to be, then we shall pass them and attack from the pass end of the ridge, where they won't expect to see us. Keep silent. The spell is easier if it has only to muffle the sound of hooves or any normal noises a horse might make. Once we round the end of the ridge I'll stop again. Watch me and halt at once when I do."

They followed her in silence at a slow walk, always alert

for her sign. After ten 'markin she raised her hand in a signal to stop and they obeyed. She turned her mount, chanted briefly, so softly they could only see her lips move but heard nothing; then she spoke barely enough to be heard.

"I can't hold this spell once any one of them has seen us. I'll ride to one side holding the spell as long as I can. Like Kyrryl, I can sense only four men working the spell to open the portal. Yoros, you, Trasso, Sirado, and Dayshan attack our enemies. Kyrryl, rescue your lost one and stand ready to protect him if there are more here than we think, or if one of them breaks free to attack him. Roshan, you and Hailin wait at the outer edge of the fight ready to seize the reins of any horse if there's need for that. Eilish, you and Ashara stay mounted with your bows drawn. Spread out one to the north and the other to the south, and if any of our enemies break free and try to escape, kill them. Is everyone clear on what to do, or do any of you dispute my plan?"

Dayshan grinned cheerfully at her. "No, a nice simple scheme, lady. Easy to see you've led a war party before."

Orla blushed slightly. "I'm my clan's wise one. Now and again over the years I've had to be the clan's warlady. But if there's anything you'd like to add I'll listen."

"I'd say only one thing?" He received her nod of permission and smiled. His gaze touched each of them in turn. "The wise one has given us a sensible plan but few plans survive the first stroke of battle. Be ready to do whatever is needed, don't concentrate so hard on the enemy in front of you that you miss the one at your back. Try not to impede another comrade, but remember that the enemy is not cooperative, your plans are not theirs, and they won't always do what's expected." He fell silent and Orla bowed her head briefly.

"Pasht, Lady of the Moon, be with us, we go against evil in

your name." She nudged her mount to drift slightly uphill of them, and her hands began to weave the spell pattern again while Yoros, Trasso, Sirado, and Dayshan moved into a line and led out. They rounded the rocky ridge and passed a cluster of large boulders cemented together with earth. They could smell smoke now and hear a low chanting. Yoros was walking his mount slowly, keeping the beast's movements quiet to the best of his ability.

In heartbeats they would be in sight of those who would bring destruction to too many. He tightened his reins, and his well-trained mount tensed, ready to obey the command it sensed it was about to receive.

*A*t the back of a long lump of stone, Sepallo—once a loving husband and father named Kanin, who had taken another name, a Hala'atha word meaning "hatred"—was sorting his supplies. His mount waited, already saddled. He believed in always being ready in case events didn't go as he'd planned. Out of the stone's shelter and some hundred yards away as a crow flew, his four acolytes worked the rites of calling.

He called to them softly through the crack in the long stone. "Liano, Meloui, Leesak, Alenco, speed up the call. If the portal starts to open right on sunhigh it strengthens the spell."

He heard the chant quicken and smiled. Soon, very soon, he would have his revenge for the loss of his whole clan, and the death of the mate he'd adored along with the tiny daughter he'd barely had time to know. The king's men had come and burned the plains, and they and many others had died.

Sepallo smiled, slowly and viciously. He'd spent twenty years finding and training boys who'd lost everything. These four would do their work and the portal would open, the Kalthi would come and he'd send them against Shallahah and the king. Shallahah would pay over and over for the death of his beloved Yalana, his daughter, Gaisa, and his own ruin.

He reached up to run fingertips over his face. Thanks to his learning, few knew how he'd changed. Without it all would know how hideous he was; he'd been caught in the flames while he tried to reach his family, and his face had run like wax melting. His powers had saved his life, yet they could do nothing for his looks but hide them, and that only so long as he didn't touch skin to skin.

Twice, in the years that followed, he'd attempted to take a lover from the tribe. Each time she'd tried to flee in horror once she saw his face the way it really was. He'd killed them and disposed of the bodies. He couldn't risk that again with a free woman. A slave would have no choice, and Cleeono would give him several young and beautiful slaves if his plans went as hoped. His smile was a dreadful thing.

"Liano, Meloui, Leesak, Alenco, speak faster. Be ready to slay the sacrifice the moment the portal begins to open. Then start the chant to summon the Kalthi from the other side. They will flow through the portal once it's wide enough open and I'll bind them to their task."

He could feel their handful of exiled kin waiting eagerly on this side. He nodded to himself. They wanted to return to their own world. He might allow that—*if* they did their work well once the portal was opened, and *if* he could open the portal a second time to permit their departure.

Under the shield of his power that gave him a normal-seeming face, the ruined flesh twisted into a snarl of hatred. Shallahah would pay. He'd found a different chant for calling the Kalthi, the final portion of which could be hurried. The portal that opened would be smaller, its connection to this world slightly weaker, but that didn't matter. He had the sacrifice. His acolytes had done well there.

A flicker of cold warning ran down his spine and he stiffened. Someone came; he concentrated on the feeling. No, a number of them came, those who would prevent his vengeance if they could and there were more of them than his men could handle. Well, he'd planned for that too. He raised his voice a final time. As a precaution he'd accepted the four's blood-binding to him. They had assumed from what he'd said that it would do no more than give him the ability to protect them from the Kalthi should they attempt to turn on them once they were through the portal. He'd lied.

"Liano, Meloui, Leesak, Alenco, vazife muhakkak olm."

It took no more. They were bound to the opening of the portal. They must continue to chant, to fight against anyone who would prevent that. He could slip away and wait at a distance to see what happened. If his acolytes died, he could escape from pursuit, leave this empty land, gather other disciples and his patron and move against his enemies again. He chuckled softly. What? Did those who hunted him think that he had no other plan in place? He had more than one plan, he had followers to aid him, and he had Cleeono's father-in-law, Lord Varli, who hated Shallahah's king.

Outside the range of Orla's spell he heard the soft thud of approaching hooves and peered between one of the long stone's cracks. Now wasn't the time to take risks; there were ten of the enemy, and most bore weapons. His minions were bound to his will; they'd complete the calling or die, and he was best out of it now, before anyone realized he'd been here—or who he was. The tariling was exhausted and wouldn't survive another long, hard trip, but there were other possibilities.

He chanted a powerful spell of his own, cloaking it in a

secondary glamour and setting it to trigger when the time came. There! If his disciples failed he would have another hand to play—and the ante to open the game. He collected the coin and small valuables he had available, tucked them into a pouch at his waist, hitched the spare mounts behind his, and fled slowly and silently along the inner side of the ridge.

Yoros charged the moment he came into view of the four men who stood chanting in a circle seared into green turf. Within the circle a small bound tariling squealed recognition and struggled wildly. Behind Yoros, Trasso, Sirado, and Dayshan came riding, swords out and swinging at the four. They met Sepallo's disciples and rode over them slashing downward. The chant continued while they fought, the four callers ducking and evading the blows, now and again taking a strike on their dagger blades and deflecting the blow.

The space they had chosen was in a rough circle of waist-high unconnected stones, so Liano, Meloui, Leesak, and Alenco were able to use those to shelter themselves, continuing their chant. But they were unarmed except for their daggers, and such an uneven fight couldn't continue for long.

"Surrender!" Orla called from outside the circle of fighters. "Surrender and live."

Not that their lives would be long, she thought. The council of wise ones on the plains had agreed that anyone stupid enough to open a portal for the Kalthi should die—if there were believable witnesses to their folly. But they would live a little while longer if they surrendered, perhaps a moon or two, and life was usually sweet to the living. Not apparently to these four, she noted, since none even slowed to listen to her offer.

"Surrender, or be cut down."

Odd, it was as if they didn't hear her words. She murmured

a spell, allowed her eyes to slide into the unfocused look that would allow her to see otherness, and stared. Then she cursed. That one look had told her that these men were bound to their chant; they couldn't stop until either they were dead or the portal opened.

To the south Ashara had taken up her station, bow drawn. She had halted at the inner side of the end of the long rock ridge down which they had ridden to ambush the chanters. Eilish had gone the other way and was waiting in cover half a mile from where her husband and brother gave battle. She was a good and experienced archer.

Kyrryl hovered anxiously on the fringe of the battle. Tayio was bound against a slab of stone in the center of the circle, and the eight combatants swirled around him. There hadn't been a chance so far to free him. She had her knife ready to slash the ropes while her sword was out to defend herself or Tayio at need. Now and again she called an encouraging word to the frantic tariling. She could see a chain around his throat and guessed that it could be the reason why his mind-voice was silent.

Roshan was waiting, alert on his mount, watching in case anyone was unhorsed. If so he would catch the beast at once. This wasn't quite what Orla had intended. She'd assumed that the people involved in this would have mounts ready and try to flee and possibly be unhorsed in the melee; she hadn't known of Sepallo or his involvement until she saw the threads of power that bound his disciples—and his ability was sufficient to cloak him from her stare.

Farther along the ridge Hailin signaled his horse to back up very carefully. Only a step at a time, but after nine or ten such steps he was out of sight of his fellows. Then he turned his horse and rode quietly along the back of the ridge. He was sure he'd seen glimpses of a rider going the same way on the other side. And who could it be but someone more important than the men who died behind them?

Sepallo came around the end of the ridge and found he was face-to-face with Hailin, who held up his hand at once.

"I'm not looking for a fight, lord, just a word."

"And what word is that?"

"Well, it might be alms, or it could be the old saying that gold can strike a man blind. Have you heard that one?"

Sepallo hid his start of satisfaction. This man was one of those who'd hunted him, but whereas they seemed intent on keeping the portal closed, this one appeared to have other things on his mind. He nodded.

"Yes, a wise proverb. I have need of a blind man and I may have the gold to blur his sight. How much would it take?"

"A goodly sum, lord. Those with whom I travel wouldn't appreciate my blindness if they should find out about it."

Sepallo grinned, a smile that showed all his teeth like a cornered kio. "Oh, I may be able to offer such a sum." He reached to his belt, detached the purse containing two gold-link bracelets given him for expenses, and tossed it to Hailin. "Look at that and tell me how your sight feels."

Hailin accepted the bribe eagerly. He undid the cuff drawstring on one sleeve, and pushed the bracelets over his hand and partway up his arm before retying the cuff's drawstring and smiling.

He looked up. "It suffices, lord. I find I can see no one before me. I'll return and report that." Sepallo nodded and nudged his mount into a walk away from the sounds of fighting, cloaking his direction, while Hailin rode back slowly, planning his tale if he needed it.

In the circle of stone the last of Sepallo's men died still

trying to hold the chant. Kyrryl closed in on Tayio, freeing him from the chain about his throat and comforting him when his sending—the mental equivalent of screams—could now be heard. Eilish came riding back from the north, unstringing her bow as she rode.

Hailin had rejoined his fellow servant, his absence unnoticed, and was congratulating himself on his acumen. Everyone else thought that they'd killed all of the kidnappers, saved their lands, and avenged all injuries. Only he knew that someone had escaped—and that Hailin had received enough to shut his eyes to that escape to give him an improved future on his return.

It was Kyrryl who noticed that a member of their group had not yet rejoined them. "Ashara? Where's Ashara? Why isn't she here?"

Yoros looked about him. "Didn't she ride south to bar the escape of anyone who fled that way?"

"Who was left to flee?" Sirado asked.

Orla's lips set in anger at the question. "My fault. I had no time to tell you, but the men we fought were soul-bound. I traced threads from them to another in that direction." She indicated. "But he was cloaked and the threads snapped as soon as the men died and I lost the way."

Dayshan had turned and was striding through the jumble of rocks. From behind a clump of them he called out. "Here!" They joined him and he pointed down. "Their camp was here. They've left their bedding and saddlebags. See." He turned over bedding and they looked down. "They left their swords here too. They had horses hobbled in the lee of these rocks but they're gone. Look, here is where the beasts scratched themselves and left hair on the rough rock. They'd have had a mount apiece, I reckon."

Orla looked at the evidence for some time before she spoke bitterly. "There was a leader. He took their mounts and his own and escaped. And I don't think he went alone. He left the tariling because the poor little thing's exhausted and might die if it's dragged on another long ride. He has someone who will travel far better and make a fine sacrifice, one who will open a portal for the Kalthi. He has Ashara and if we don't find him in time she'll die to open the portal—and after her the plains and Shallahah will die too."

Tayio gave a small squeal then, and everyone turned to stare at him. His nose was rising in greeting to a figure wrapped in mist that stroked him gently. A voice like crystal chimes spoke, so softly it might not have been heard but for the power that edged every word.

"You can't follow a hard-riding trail with this one. The one who calls has taken another innocent, however, and that allows me to move further in the matter. Behold!" Her hands rose and about her glory shone rainbows and gold, bleeding into a silver arch. On the other side Kyrryl saw her home. Razaia and Chylo turned, jerking back from whatever it was that they saw on their side.

The figure turned to Kyrryl. "Your choice, your choosing, daughter of another world. Let the small one go home while you are free to follow your own trail."

Yoros walked forward and bowed. "We choose. Let him go through. We'll stay." He turned to Dayshan and Eilish. "You have no need to remain. This was never your trail and you have come far already."

Eilish looked at Trasso and her brother. The quick glance was enough to tell her their agreement in the decision.

"No, we couldn't leave Kian Dae, and we feel that it has become our quest too. We'll ride with you if you will have us?"

Yoros smiled. "If that is your wish. Nor could we find better companions." He addressed the figure. "Lady, you've heard our decisions. Send Tayio home and we'll remain to find our lost one—and the evil man who's taken her."

Orla walked forward and fell on one knee. "Bless us, Pasht. And if you have advice, I'll listen and remember."

A hand slid from the mist and became clear. The black fur shone with a crystalline power. "Daughter, ride with good heart. Courage shall lead the way; folly and greed shall weaken. One shall fall and two, and in that falling shall come triumph. Yet no future is set. Be strong to strengthen my words. Now, let the tariling return through the portal I have opened."

Her hand gestured and in response the arch blazed. From the other side came a wild feline call and the tariling answered, staggering forward. They heard his welcome, saw glimpses of Razaia and Chylo clutching him to their hearts while his sister danced around them. The silver light faded and was gone.

Pasht turned back to them. "The tariling is home. Make your decisions and make them well." The figure of the goddess faded.

Kyrryl spoke, her voice shaking with rage and with fear for her niece. "He's got Ashara. I'm getting her back. Who rides with me?"

She moved off, and wordlessly they heeled their mounts to walk behind her. Hailin came last. It was a reasonable idea to continue this quest—cautiously. He'd done very well out of it so far, and there might be more profit to come. He followed Kyrryl—but for reasons very different from those of his fellows.

12

Sepallo pushed the horses. He had no intention of following the usual trail back south and around the mountains along the Kavarten border. He could cross the Aratanga Pass only a few 'marks away and ride along the foothills to Mirray. Or he could go all the way up the coast, round the end of the Toldins, and continue through Surah. Mirray was only two days east from there, and he could find some way of keeping the girl quiet if he must.

He had three mounts for each of them and he had sufficient power to make the horses follow him without needing lead ropes. The woman too would make no trouble. He'd let her see his face and told her graphically of what he'd do if she wasted time. Her rape would be only the beginning.

Ashara had ridden in battle, and in rough lands. She was terrified, but not to witlessness as Sepallo believed. She had revived earlier than he'd known and had managed to remove a triangle of the decorative flat crystals from her saddle blanket. With no time to wash it, the blanket had been so dirty that she'd refolded it the last time she'd saddled her horse. The crystals had ended up under a layer of the blanket and Sepallo was unaware of their existence. Her horse walked beside her captor's, but he was riding a pace ahead and unless he glanced back at exactly the right time he'd see nothing. She'd use them cautiously and sparingly, but she could lay a trail for some time. The gods grant that her kin found it and followed.

In fact her kin were well behind her, milling in discussion with others in the group and growing desperate.

"How can we be sure where her kidnapper went?" Kyrryl asked, her face screwed up in distress. "From what I saw of trader maps, there's only one real trail."

Orla looked thoughtful. "Let me look at the men we killed and their clothing. Something may give us an idea." While the others watched, she examined the bodies more closely. After some time looking, muttering to herself, considering the face markings, and going back to check clothing, she looked up.

"These are all tribesmen." There was something in her voice that told them there was more. "I think I may have even seen the markings of one. If I'm right he came from a small tribe that was one of those that mostly died in the fires twenty years ago. Another clan took them in. The other men I don't know, but there's this."

She bent, and pulled aside the heavy tunic, then the under-shirt of the man she examined, and held up what was there. "This medallion is not plains work."

Yoros and Trasso bent to study the engraved silver disk while Dayshan leaned over their backs and looked carefully before he straightened up again. He grunted. "That's the sort of thing I've seen in our world. There it would be a lord's to-ken used to ask passage or perhaps to send with a message, the token showing from whom the message comes."

Yoros and Trasso looked up. "Yes," Trasso said thoughtfully.

"I've seen the tokens my father uses. That's exactly the sort of thing he gives out. They're small, unobtrusive, made only in tin so they have no value to thieves, and they have a couple of minor differences to our usual family crest but are like enough to it that a casual look seems to show only that. My father's men, though, all know what to look for."

He reached out and, with a jerk, snapped the light string on which that one hung. "This seems to show a flower and the mask of some sort of snarling animal rather like Kian Dae."

Orla took it from him and studied it closely. "A daska and a dravencat." She turned to see the questioning looks. "A daska blooms only on the edge of winter. A bloom of that kind is a statement that the lord survives in adversity. The dravencat mask says that he will fight for his own."

"And who wears such a badge?" Eilish asked.

Orla shrugged. "I know the symbols, I do not know the man."

"Then what we need to do is pack up our camp, spread out, and start looking for signs of six horses," Dayshan said firmly. "If we want to find the lass before this sorcerer does something to her, we have to be on his trail quickly. We have no time to sit around talking."

Kyrryl and Yoros eyed him gratefully. Sirado nodded. "That's sense to me."

Sirado looked up. "Why six horses?"

Dayshan counted on his fingers. "Your kin's mount, the sorcerer's horse, and didn't we find sign that these four men," his wave took in the sprawled bodies, "had horses. The beasts are gone and there's no sign they broke their hobbles and ran off in a panic. No, they were taken. And who else could have done that but the sorcerer? He's got three mounts he can ride relay, and force the lass to do the same."

Yoros nodded agreement. "Even if he doesn't push, with three mounts apiece he can ride longer without tiring them. He can stop for shorter times for them to graze. If none of them is working so hard they can get by on less grazing for a while. Even if he keeps to a steady walk he can outpace us if we hold to the same speed."

"So," Dayshan picked up the discussion. "What we need is to be on the trail—once we have some idea of what or where that might be. For now let's get packed."

That took only a short time. Then they were sitting their mounts gazing at each other in doubt and worry once more. It was the experienced master-at-arms who took the lead again.

"Is there another trail back the way we came? One that is likely to be overlooked by the usual travelers in that area?"

Orla pursed her lips. "There is one, a trail that runs through the upper foothills of the Toldins. It goes on to Kavarten. There is also the trail we used to get here, both run quite close together in some places."

"What of a trail south?"

"There's two. An upper trail and a lower one. Both run down the coast."

"No farther?" Dayshan was visualizing the maps the traders had shown him when he asked.

Orla looked doubtful. "There's Aratanga Pass just down the coast if he got around us. Apart from that he could go the length of the coast and into Surah from the other side."

Dayshan summed that up. "We have a number of possibilities. The sorcerer could have gone back the way we came by taking a less obvious trail. Or he could have swung back south by a higher trail, passed us, and gone on in that direction. If so then he has three trails he can take, and with a second pass to take him to occupied areas; he could go a very long way on paths where he's unlikely to be seen before he has to return to settled lands. The question now is, do we split up and scout each trail for signs of his passage?"

Yoros considered. "Ashara is a clever girl and has ridden a warrior trail before. She doesn't panic. If this sorcerer really has her and she is conscious with any mobility at all, she'll try to leave us signs."

Dayshan glanced up at the sky then at those who sat their mounts in a circle about him. "We need to make a decision, time's passing."

He looked at them and saw that the servants would say nothing. His own nobles were reluctant to speak in front of Ashara's kin. And her kin were afraid to make a choice in case it was the wrong one.

"Very well, we'll cover all possibilities. Who can track fairly well?" He considered the raised hands. "Yoros, you and Kyrryl take Orla. Orla knows where the southern trail runs. Follow it until nightfall. If you find no indications then double back on your tracks and return here. Those who go north will send someone back to leave signs if they find Ashara's trail. I presume you all know trail signs?"

He smiled at the chorus that assured him they did. "If one of you finds the trail, return here to leave signs to say so and indicate where."

He explained further, had them repeat it until he was certain all knew, then clapped his hands. "Let's move out. The sun waits in the sky for no one and we have a lost one to find."

"What about these, Dayshan?" Eilish looked down at the tumbled bodies. "There's their gear too. We could end up needing some of it if it's a long trail we take."

Dayshan nodded. "True, lass. Well, we'll leave Roshan and Hailin to clear up the bodies and their gear. They can take anything of value, hold back the pack ponies, and load anything we can use onto them." He turned to the two men. "Keep anything you think we could find of use. Wait here once you're done. Sooner or later someone from each group will return and depending on what is found, you'll know whom to follow." He looked at them. "Do you understand?"

Roshan nodded agreeably while Hailin also nodded, bland-faced but fuming quietly. He wasn't an idiot. What had been said would make sense and be understood by anyone but a complete fool and he didn't appreciate the suggestion. Master-at-arms Dayshan might be, but the man was nothing more than a puffed-up soldier, a common man of no particular education but pampered by Eilish and her kin. He drifted into a day-dream where he too was that highly esteemed and was abruptly dragged from it by Roshan's irritated question.

"Are you going to work, or are you going to sit on your horse looking at the mountains all day?" The words were tart, and Hailin hastened to dismount and help at once. He must do nothing suspicious until he was home again and could leave without suspicion. Besides, there could be other valuable pickings for him on the bodies. Men usually carried their valuables on them if there was danger.

"Why don't I sort out the bodies?" he offered to Roshan. "You could check their camp and see what should be kept? You're better at that than I am. I'll look over the area and see where we could put the bodies."

Roshan agreed, although he suspected Hailin was trying to shirk his share of the work. In that he was wrong. Hailin used his time alone to haul the bodies to a crevice he'd already noted that lay around the ridge end. With them and him out of sight he plundered all four bodies, checking hands, wrists, and necks for jewelry, seeking pouches and belt pockets. In a belt pocket of one of them, the man with the most expensive clothing, he found another medallion. It wasn't cheap plated silver. It was the same device as the others but larger, in gold, and the eyes in the dravencat mask were chips of some beautiful purple stone.

Hailin sat back on his heels and whistled very softly. "I dunno who you were, but that's worth serious coin."

He carefully tucked the medallion away, his mind racing while he worked to check the other bodies and roll them into the crevice. That stone was Zerrisss; he'd heard about it from one of the traders' people. It was a stone out of reach of all but very rich merchants or the nobility. A clear vivid purple was rare in any form, including dye, and in the gemstones its cost was prohibitive. Even those eye chips were worth a month's pay to an ordinary laboring man here.

He dumped the bodies and tossed rocks down over them until they vanished under the stones. Then he took up the small shovel he'd found in their camp and raked earth from the crevice edge over the stone. By the time Roshan joined him the bodies were decently buried.

"Did you find anything on them?"

Hailin shrugged. "Few silvers and coppers. Nothing much. Here's your share. Oh, and two of them had cheap silver rings in their belt pouches. Figured I should hold on to those to show Sirado."

"*Lord* Sirado. Why?"

Hailin showed him one of the rings. Roshan studied it with interest, then nodded, seeing what his fellow had seen. "Oh, right. The designs are the same. Sure the other two didn't have anything like that?"

"No, they didn't," Hailin said tersely.

Well, he thought. They hadn't. The medallion their possible

second-in-command had wasn't the same design as the rings, and Sirado and the others had already seen that device. A second one wouldn't tell them any more.

He stood and headed back to where his horse grazed. "If we have to wait I'm gonna be comfortable. We've done everything Lord Sirado said to do and I'm tired. I'm gonna cook something, have a drink, then catch a good, long sleep. It'll be nice to be able to rest for a while without someone yelling at me to do all the work."

Roshan stared suspiciously after him. He'd wager his next pay that Hailin had found something on the bodies that he wasn't sharing. He counted the coins he'd received, one silver and thirteen coppers. Not too bad, but if Hailin hadn't done better Roshan was the illegitimate son of Lord Peschen—and he wasn't.

O n the south trail, Yoros, Kyrryl, and Orla rode slowly, strung in a line that covered both trails for the moment while they were close together. On neither had they seen any sign of the passage of six horses, and by now it was well after sunhigh. Orla halted them.

"Wait here a moment. There's a stream ahead."

She cantered her mount forward, turned him, and walked along the stream bank. Her hands gestured, although they heard no sound, but she shook her head and returned.

"It's up to you if you want to continue northward," she said, looking at Yoros and Kyrryl. "But this stream is wide, shallow, and runs all the way down to the sea. If six horses had crossed over it anywhere at all, the hoofprints would show."

"Unless the sorcerer has hidden them with magic," Kyrryl pointed out.

Orla smiled at her. "Good thought. But I used power to

check. Not to cancel any spell, that takes a lot of energy, but just to see if there was one. There wasn't. If there isn't a spell and we can't see hoofprints . . . ?"

Yoros's head jerked up in understanding. "If there isn't a spell, we'd see them, but if we don't then they aren't there, so he didn't come this way."

He consulted quietly with Kyrryl. "We think we should ride both sides of the stream down to the sea then back up as high as possible. Just in case he took Ashara somewhere he could cross right away from the trail. If it was one of us being hunted that's what we'd do."

Orla nodded. "There's three of us. What say you and your wife ride both banks to the sea. I'll ride upward. If neither of us find anything we'll have to camp here for the night and return to the others in the morning. Maybe they'll have something, I always thought it more likely he'll make his escape down the Outlaw Coast."

They separated and rode at a steady walk, searching the stream banks while they rode. They found nothing, and it was full dark by the time they came together again. Yoros started a fire while Kyrryl, who had stopped briefly on the return trip to tickle a couple of the good mountain fish out of the stream, cleaned and spitted them. They ate in silence before crawling into their sleeping blankets, all but Orla who took first watch. She wanted to think about the device on the medallion. Something was nagging at her about that.

*T*o the south two groups of riders traveled the trails west, scanning the ground and vegetation. Eilish and Trasso had taken the lower trail and were finding the going easy but boring. The area between where the foothills evened out to the pebbled or sandy beaches of the coast was grassed in a short brownish lilac-colored grass that never seemed to grow more than ankle height. There were intermittent patches of a low scrub, rarely more than six or seven feet high with here and there a copse of scrubby trees.

Eilish stretched in the saddle and groaned. "This grass, it'll hide any smaller sign from view unless we ride right over it."

Trasso grinned at her. "I know, that's why I'm watching for hoof marks instead most of the time."

She looked at him. "What about the rest of the time?"

"Then I'm checking out bare patches of land. I never thought the girl was a fool. If she's conscious, has anything to drop, and is in a position to do that, surely she'll pick places where whatever she leaves can be seen?"

Eilish caught his glance and smiled at him. She knew he'd waited until she was starting to wonder about seeing nothing. This would give her something else on which to concentrate. She too had been looking at any bare patches along the trail edges, guessing that Ashara would leave something if she could. Sadly neither had seen anything thus far. They continued to ride slowly, staring at any muddy or bare spots on either side.

High above them Sirado and Dayshan had taken the upper, rougher track. Most of the time those below were out of their sight where trees and taller scrub flanked the high trail. Dayshan was lagging quietly. He suspected he was by far the more experienced tracker, and he had believed all along that this was the most likely road.

Above him in the trees brightly colored birds squawked angrily at them, and he smiled. Orla had said that they were heino, good eating, but they were thieves; they'd steal anything small and shiny. The trail had a few bare patches but so far there'd been no hoof marks he could see, so he was beginning to wonder if he'd been wrong about which way Ashara had been taken.

To one side, farther up the hill, he saw a dip where some of the grass had washed from the thin soil. A heino swooped, he saw the sun-bright flash in its claws, and, with a wordless shout, he seized his horseman's bow, strung it, and shot. He missed, but the shaft came close enough to scare the bird, screaming in fright and rage, into dropping its prize. Dayshan thrust his mount up the hillside to drop from the saddle and seize the crystal in turn.

Sirado came back calling eagerly. "What is it, did you see something or—I can't believe you'd be thinking of food?"

Sirado was craning his neck and Dayshan held out a hand to show his booty. "A crystal. I saw flash of it in the sun as the bird landed to pick it up. That's why I shot. If it had escaped with the thing we couldn't have been sure." He looked at Sirado, who'd spent quite a lot of their riding time chatting to the girl. "Look at it closely. Is that something of hers?"

The beam of relief was answer enough, but Sirado took the crystal gently, turning it over and pointing with a finger at the sparkling object. "Yes, it's hers. Look, it was pierced to be sewn to something, and not strung as a necklace. It's flat and the hole goes almost from edge to edge, not through the center thickness like an ordinary bead. That's so that it can be sewn flat to a saddle blanket. Hers was a gift and it had triangles of them on the upper side corners." He smiled briefly. "She was mad at herself for not thinking when she saddled her horse originally, a flashing saddle blanket isn't the sort of thing you take on a war trail. But it looks as if it'll come in useful now."

Dayshan nodded. "Right. So we know she was taken this way and we don't want to waste time. You take your spare mount and ride downhill as fast as you can without killing yourself. Tell Eilish to join me. Have Trasso ride west to the camp and send my fellow servants straight here along the lower road. They'll make faster time and we can keep a watch on it from above if we move to the upper trails. Either Hailin or Roshan may have to follow the other three a day or so depending on how far north they went."

"What'll you be doing?"

Dayshan's smile was grim. "I'll be following this sorcerer once you've gone down the hill and found your sister and Lord Trasso. The one we follow is a cunning man. He's been taking to the grass above the trail here whenever the usual trail is softer and might show hoof marks. The lass must have had the chance to drop a crystal in a patch where the grass was washed out in a small dip. It was just lucky we were here when the bird landed, I reckon. If we'd been even a few 'markin later that bird would have had the crystal away to its nest and we'd never have known.

"There's no time for talking. Take your mount and ride. We need to move along smartish or else we could be so far behind him the birds get the other crystals and we could lose the trail. Good fortune ride with you."

Dayshan watched Sirado's mount and the led beast plunge away, staying briefly on the upper trail to make time. "Hope he doesn't break his mount's legs either. That'd slow him badly even if it isn't going to grieve his family the same way," he muttered to himself before cheering himself up with the further consideration that Sirado was a sensible lad. He'd know better enough to bring help rather than trying to make an epic ride.

13

*E*ilish was the first to come trotting to meet him, with Trasso a close second. The girl was already calling.

"You've found something. Oh, please say you've found something."

Sirado grinned at her. "I've found something. Or, to be more exact, Dayshan found something." He held up a hand to stop further questions. "He found a crystal from her saddle blanket. It looks as if Ashara's alive and thinking. Trasso is to go back to the last camp to collect the others. Dayshan's following the trail up there." His wave took in the hillside above them.

"There's no need to hurry too much. He's the best tracker of all of us, I think, and we don't need to ruin the horses climbing hillsides at a gallop. He'll be following whatever trail he can find. We can just walk until we reach the upper trail and rejoin him."

It took only a 'mark before Eilish and Sirado had rejoined the master-at-arms. Her gaze met his when she halted her mount. "That was a very good job seeing what the bird had."

"Luck favors the ready, or so your granddad always says."

She grinned. Her grandfather did say that—and usually added the other old saying that "the harder I works, the luckier I gets."

She turned in the saddle to look far down the road below. If hard work could provide more luck for them she'd work very hard indeed. Ahead of her Dayshan returned to his trail.

"When would you reckon the others will find us?"

"That may depend on how far north they went. If it was more than a day's travel it could mean a couple of days before they come up with us. But that's all to the good so far as they are concerned. We'll be that much farther along and closer to Ashara if we can keep finding her markers. The sorcerer may have three horses each, but we have two and Orla may know a shortcut once we're sure which way he's traveling."

Dayshan turned and smiled at her. "I think he'll be moving too fast to have time to harm the lass. It's also likely from what I know of sacrifices that he needs her alive and undamaged." He saw her face brighten. "Good, stay optimistic. Your grandfather also says that a heavy load and a hard road are lighter with good heart."

Eilish looked down the coastal road on which they sat their mounts. "This road is fairly level, less rough, and we could ride faster. Why don't Trasso and I do that? If we ride hard for the remainder of the day, we can climb to the upper trail then and make camp ahead of you so that you can ride later into the day." Her eyes narrowed in thought.

"In fact I see no reason why some of us should not drop back to the lower road, ride hard for Aratanga Pass in the morning, and camp there. If we find sign that the sorcerer has gone over the pass, one of us can fetch Dayshan. If we find sign that he continued south, again we can fetch Dayshan." Her face twisted into feral anticipation. "And if we have passed him we can trap him between us."

Sirado grinned. "It sounds like a possible plan to me. Let's do it." He looked at his sister. "Race you down."

He spun his mount and heeled it into a sliding scramble. Eilish followed with a whoop and Dayshan grinned after them.

Sirado reached the lower road and he chuckled as he slowed. "Beat you down. That stopped you worrying, didn't it?"

"There's something to worry about, though. In my whole life I've never known the dangers we face here in this world."

"And you're so old, my little sister? What did you know of other worlds before we walked unwittingly into this one?"

"Somewhat." Her face became thoughtful. "For three years I was taught to use the small gifts of power that I have. Those who taught me have always known there were other worlds, and in some cases they have known a little about them."

Sirado looked at her half questioningly. She nodded slowly.

"Our world has rare portals that open and close. This world has them also, but from what Orla and the traders told me, they're slightly more common here. It may be that this world is a nexus in the web that binds us all." She seemed to shake off her thoughts with an almost physical effort. "But enough. Let us follow those ahead and we should hurry."

They moved steadily along the road, their spare horses trailing them obediently. Eilish hoped that Trasso would find the others quickly. It would be good if they could trap the sorcerer before he could reach more occupied lands—or find others to help in his plans.

A full day ahead of her Sepallo was still riding easily. With regular changes of mount for him and his captive and ample supplies to eat while they rode, he was making good time. He'd decided what to do and should be in Mirray in another tenday. He'd meet the other four of his disciples there. He'd summoned them by the power they'd given him over them, and they'd already be on their way. That they would obey him he knew. They too had kin and lovers to avenge and they could reach Mirray before he did.

He slipped into memory. He'd been young when his life was destroyed, only twenty-four. He was already married and he was deeply in love. More, Yalana, his beloved, had borne a babe who was the heart of them both. He'd loved, lived, and his life was perfect. Nothing would change—until the fire came. Until the men who set it came and found what the fires had left.

He'd been hunting a half day away when he saw the smoke rising. He'd returned as quickly as he could. He'd been struck down from behind when he rode up, come to and found his love dead, seen what they'd done to her while his baby daughter cried, tossed aside like garbage into the ruins of their plundered tent. The last man was still there, smiling down at him.

"If you escape the fires, plains filth, go and tell your kind this is what happens when you plunder a Shallahan caravan and murder the king's cousin." The laughter was coarse and knowing. "But I don't mind if you don't listen. The king will send us back and your women are a good afternoon's amusement. They fight so well and surrender so nicely. A pity we couldn't take that one with us for a bit more fun." He glanced at Sepallo's dead mate and the weakly crying Gaisa, laughed again, and rode to rejoin those who waited for him while the fires crept closer.

Sepallo stayed to do death honor to the one he'd loved

more than life. His head was swimming, but once that was done he took what food and intact waterskins he could find and ran, not knowing where, just away. He chose the wrong direction. The fires encircled him, although he escaped in the end—with a ruined face and Gaisa dead in his arms from breathing the smoke. After that he went a little mad perhaps, not that he cared.

He joined another clan and learned of the Kalthi from that clan's wise one, who was going senile and forgetting what was Mystery to be kept unspoken to those who weren't wise. He learned more from another wise one he took alone out on the plains and forced into speech. From him he found how to call the demons and what would buy their obedience. Soon, soon he'd have his revenge. No one would find him before he could accomplish the devastation that would ease his constant hatred; it might even salve a little of his grief.

Ashara flicked another crystal behind her to land on a patch of bare earth and prayed.

*T*rasso had not wasted time; still he only reached the boulders where Roshan and Hailin camped as the last light left the sky. The servants, not knowing who it was, had gone to ground in cover when he clattered up.

Roshan was first to recognize their master. "It's Lord Trasso." Hailin snorted silently. Damn, that meant they'd be in the saddle again at first light. This last day had been pleasant, once he'd plundered and buried the bodies. He'd slept most of the hours away, catching up on the sleep he'd missed on this wretched trip.

Trasso was unsaddling his mounts and rubbing them down while he talked. "And once it's light you're to go on along the coast road. One or another of us will find you but don't waste any time."

Roshan nodded while Hailin turned away ostensibly to stir the stew but in reality to keep the other two from seeing his deepening scowl. Hailin had expected a leisurely tour of hill keeps with willing maids and warm beds to sleep in. He'd expected good food, deference to a man from Iroskeep, and little work. Instead he'd been worked like a dog, run all over the miserable hills of some place he didn't know—and the food was terrible. There were no willing maids, no admiring younger serving men, and—he grinned suddenly in the growing dusk. This trip hadn't been *all* bad. Those gold-link bracelets and the medallion would allow him to buy a better business than he'd hoped. There could even be more plunder to be found. He stirred the stew harder while he dreamed.

The next morning his dreams evaporated quickly when cloudy skies turned to steady drizzle. He saddled wet mounts who were reluctant and uncooperative, was bidden a cheerful good morning by a fool noble who should have known better, and had to make everyone's breakfast. By the time he and Roshan were on the road he was holding the bitter conviction that the whole world was against him and always had been.

Trasso had left them the moment that he'd broken his fast and was moving far faster. His mounts were cantering when the spare horse he was leading abruptly pulled back, broke the lead rein, and came to a limping halt. Trasso said a number of things, reined back, and dismounted to examine at the beast. He saw at once that it had stepped in a rut and wrenched a foreleg. It wouldn't be going anywhere at speed for days if not weeks.

Swearing, he unsaddled the animal, removed its bridle,

and cached the gear wrapped in the blanket. He was just grateful that the animal wasn't ruined for good. It was a good horse, and had been loaned to him by one of the plains clans. It'd be a poor return for their generosity if it had been permanently damaged. As it was, with a bit of luck, it might drift toward its home.

The freed horse limped off the road and started to graze. There were streams in this area. It would manage, and he couldn't do anything more about it. Maybe he could ask Orla to let the clan know, or if they returned that way, he could pay for the horse? He changed mounts and took to the road again, still using words his old nurse would not have approved— although Eilish, Sirado, and Dayshan would have understood.

He found his quarries half a day's ride down the road, and the reunion was joyous, the more so when he shared his news.

"So what are the others doing?" Kyrryl asked. He explained that and Kyrryl smiled. "Good," she said. "Let's find them as quickly as possible. We're on the right trail, Tayio is rescued and all we have to do is catch up with Ashara. Once we do that we can take her back and all will be well."

Trasso opened his mouth to speak and shut up. He'd planned to point out the difficulties yet to come and the unlikelihood of it being that easy, but on second thought he decided it would be better to say nothing. Come to think of it, Kyrryl probably did know all that; she was just being hopeful, and who was he to take away hope.

Kyrryl had caught the look, however, and in abrupt anger she turned on Orla. "If your world is in such danger, why doesn't your goddess do more?"

"Because it is not her evil that strikes at us but the doing of our own kind," the wise one replied gently. "She can help us, but she may not intervene directly. Or so say the shrines. At some other time and place she may do so. Here and now it seems she will not."

"Why?"

Orla shrugged. "I'm a woman from the plains, not a learned high priestess at one of the great shrines. I can't answer you. I can only lay down my life if that is required."

Kyrryl met her gaze and bowed her head. "I spoke harshly and without justice. Forgive me?"

Orla had been waiting. "Yes, that I do, but there is still work to be done and no time to sit talking." She nudged her mount into a walk and then a canter. Kyrryl and Trasso followed her, Yoros behind them. The four of them swept down the road, caught up with Roshan and Hailin several hours later, and rode on until nightfall. They made a reluctant camp and were gone again at first light.

*A*head of them Dayshan was using language his mother wouldn't have liked either. He was worried that he'd lost the damned trail in the last three days since Trasso left. It had been a long time since he'd found a crystal. Perhaps the lass had run out of them or the sorcerer had seen what she was doing? Or maybe the eternally damned birds had stolen them? That gave him an idea. Maybe they had picked up a crystal, but how many? Two or more, or only one and the girl was spreading them out, afraid she'd run out before they got where they were going?

Once he got to camp and met up with the others he'd suggest that they ride well ahead on this trail and then backtrack toward him. Whoever found a crystal, the others leapfrog to him, and then they could do that again. It would bridge longer gaps more quickly and with so many of them they could ride back and forth to stay in touch.

He came disconsolately into camp that night with still no crystal to report but brightened, explaining his plan to the now reunited group.

Eilish patted his shoulder. "That should work and help us gain on the man. Good thinking."

"Only if we find crystals."

"We'll find them," Sirado assured him.

No one replied to that, all of them knowing that it wasn't a certainty but unwilling to say that aloud. At least they were all together again, and a hard road was always easier with good friends.

Yoros moved quietly over to where the pata kettle simmered. Despite the good news he felt the depression that was settling over them. The fear that they might still be too late, that Ashara would be sacrificed and the death of this world would begin. Under the edge of his tunic he held a small flask given him by Kaitlen before they'd parted company with the traders.

"When the road seems longest," she'd said to him. "When everyone feels that hope is fading. Dump this in the pata kettle. It's a distilled drink we call flame, and it's really potent. You'll sing half the night, sleep well, and rise with a lighter heart. If you're an hour later on the road it will be worth it."

He felt that the time of which she'd spoken had come. Unobtrusively he opened the flask and allowed half of the undiluted flame to pour into the kettle. It wasn't long before the effort on those who drank could be noticed.

Eilish picked up her eating knife and began to tap it against her bridle bit. The clear metallic sound fell into a pattern, and she began to sing softly. She sang an old bawdy song about a shopkeeper's daughter with a lover—who, unbeknown to her, was triplets. Trasso chuckled and joined in the chorus.

> *His loving is good and his loving is fine,*
> *But much more of his loving, I'll go out of my mind.*
> *I'm tired to my hair roots I can't love anymore,*
> *I've loved in the attic, on the bed, on the floor,*
> *I've loved while I eat and I drink from a cup—*
> *Now I'm taking up dancing where I can stand up!*

The song ended with laughter, and Sirado, with a wicked glint in his eye, began the next. Dayshan heard the opening line and fixed his lord with a glare.

> *Oh, the master-at-arms stuck up his head.*
> *An enemy archer just missed shooting him dead.*
> *"Go bring me that archer," he then said to me,*
> *So I hauled back the archer to my company.*
> *I stopped on the way and I punched in his head.*
> *"That's for bloody well missing, your target ain't dead!"*

Trasso and Eilish joined in the chorus and after a brief hesitation so did Roshan and Hailin who were familiar with the song. Yoros and Kyrryl were grinning as Sirado moved into the next verse with gusto.

> *Oh, the master-at-arms, the master-at-arms,*
> *For me he ain't got no, not no blooming charms.*
> *I don't want to join up with the artillery,*
> *Just want to stay making her ladyship's mill'nery.*
> *I like eating fish and steak with my peas,*
> *Like drinking hot rum when the weather's afreeze.*

But the master-at-arms he ain't none of these—
I don't like him!

Trasso laughed, and he then Eilish bawled out the next verses in turn, with the others gradually joining in the chorus as they learned it.

Oh, the master-at-arms was a prisoner escort,
A man's to be hung of the worst, thieving sort.
We marched out in the rain to the old hanging ground,
The wet prisoner complained he's hung over and bound.
Said our master-at-arms "You're lucky, at that.
"You're staying here, lad. We've got to march back."
Oh, the master-at-arms one day said to me,
I've heard the men talking behind cannon three.
Some of them said when I'm well cold and dead,
They'll come to my grave and piss over my head.
But I said to him, "Now, that I won't do—
I ain't standing for days in no bloody long queue!"

Dayshan was grinning. When Eilish stopped tapping her knife to the bit, he signaled her and started a song he'd heard from his uncle, who'd heard it from a sailor in another land's navy in the days when Doshad had followed Sirado's great-grandfather.

Oh, the navy was recruiting, working down the line,
They come to a country lad and he was looking fine.
The recruiter asked the boy, "Now can you swim and
*   float?"*
"Why?" said the puzzled lad. "Ain't you got no boat?"

It was almost moonhigh before the effect of the flame began to wear off. By then everyone was hoarse, and half asleep.
Yoros took the first guard once the others settled into their
bedding. He'd started this, so it was only fair that he should be
on first watch. Orla, who had not drunk more of the pata than
a single drinking bowl, relieved him with a smile two hours
later.

"That was flame, wasn't it?"

"How did you know?"

The woman looked at him wryly. "It'd be a fine thing if I
didn't at my age. Where did you get it?"

"Kaitlen." He repeated what the Aradian had said when
she gave it to him, and Orla nodded agreement.

"She was right. The sorcerer's well ahead. We don't know
where they're going. And with him alive there's mischief he can
plan. We could have to do everything over again. Rescue a sacrifice, kill the sorcerer's disciples, and stop him from opening a
portal and calling the Kalthi. Two steps forward, one back. We
needed the time to relax tonight, lad. You did the right thing."

"If anyone has a hangover in the morning I hope they'll
agree."

Orla grinned. "We'll be riding hard in the morning. I don't
think anyone will have the time or strength to complain. Now,
go and sleep."

He obeyed, leaving the wise one to watch the stars and
consider options. Some weren't to her liking, but she had her
eye on a possibility that might alter the worse for the better—
if she moved quickly enough when the time came. Meanwhile
she'd trust the goddess, those here—and whatever the traders
were doing now. A clever pair, those two, with friends in surprising places.

14

$\mathcal{K}$aitlen and Anatiah hadn't wasted time and, as Orla had recalled, they did have some surprising friends. They'd returned to Hestrie and Anamaskin first, telling them of events.

Anamaskin considered the tale. "So Orla believes that there is real danger. Danger so great that she is prepared to throw out the hatreds of a lifetime and cooperate with our clans and those of Shallahah. Moreover she has been able to convince other tribes and clans of the plains about this danger." He looked at Hestrie. "What do you think?"

"As you do, father of my sister's shaya. When enemies begin to act in your interests it is time to consider whether they may not know something you don't. It's clear that the plains' wise ones know of the Kalthi and believe that the danger of one of their people calling them is so great that old enmities must be put aside. More than that, they feel that the danger is so great they'll even cooperate with us. Tiah, tell me again what Orla said about the Kalthi and anything that you think when you remember her words."

Anatiah repeated the wise one's comments before adding,
"We can't ourselves evaluate the danger so clearly, but Dharvath also believes it to be really bad and she has had access in
other shrines to some of the ancient records on previous Kalthi
attacks. Orla believes that if the Kalthi attack Shallahah it'll
mean the destruction of all of the plains clans as the end result."

"In other words," Kait said quietly, "she believes that the
Kalthi will be sent to attack Shallahah and that in such an attack they will do so much damage and cause so many deaths
that the king will move against the Grass Sea in full force."

Hestrie nodded. "One final thing you haven't considered.
We don't know the sorcerer's race, and he could be Aradian. If
he is and humans from Shallahah discover that, it could stir up
people who'll say that one murderous Aradian is like another.
Kill them all."

Kaitlen gave a wordless growl of protest and Anamaskin
intervened. "This discussion is unprofitable. We don't know
who or what the sorcerer is, and while it's possible he's Aradian we don't know and it's just as likely that he could be
human. Now, Tiah, what do you know of Varsheean's plans
beyond having Dasheri's soldiers patrol the border?"

"Nothing."

"Helpful!"

She protested. "I can't tell you what he didn't tell me. But
we all know Varsheean. He won't be sitting cross-legged contemplating his navel."

"No, and for that reason I want you to be on the move too.
Go to him and suggest that he post people to wait—sensible
ones who will not under any circumstances act before they
think."

"Where?"

Anamaskin smiled grimly. "At Jasta Pass and at the far pass before Surah."

All turned to stare at him; then Hestrie nodded slowly. "Yes, yes I see.

*A*ll we know is that they are chasing those who abducted their tariling. If their leader discovers that he is sought he is more likely to have run for the outlaw lands."

"And from there he has only three ways to go if he doesn't double on his tracks and return to the plains," Anamaskin said.

"Three ways?" Kait could think of only two.

"The two passes, and also the coast does not stop after the second pass."

"I don't know the whole coast well," Hestrie said. "You mean there's a road beyond?"

"A passage across flat land anyhow, no actual road, but if one wants to then you can ride the length of the Outlaw Coast, round the far end of the Toldins, and return on their northern flanks along their foothills through Surah and down to Mirray. When I was young, together with a couple of other young fools both of whom are now dead, I rode that way once for the pleasure of exploration, the Lhandes of Mirray did not exist then, but Surah did."

"So it's possible. Should we ask Varsheean to post someone in Mirray?"

Anamaskin nodded thoughtfully. "Yes, to be on the safe side, ask Varsheean to see if the spies he undoubtedly has in Surah can watch for trouble coming around the end of the mountains."

"And if we do ask him, what is he to tell his watchers?"

Anamaskin considered. "Tell him this. He should set watchers at both passes, since the one who would call the Kalthi may try to escape through either pass with our friends in pursuit of him. If the watcher sees our friends he should approach them cautiously but openly, asking them for news and saying who he is and for whom he works."

Hestrie grinned, showing his fighting fangs. "You assume they'll speak freely to one they've never met who is sent by one they do not know? Have my sister or her shaya give a password to say so their friends will know we're behind this. Better yet, let the children go themselves."

Anatiah pursed her lips, thinking about that. Her gaze consulted Kait until both nodded. "Yes," Kait agreed. "It may be a good idea if we go that way. We could arrange a small caravan to lead to Surah. If we linger on the road we could be between the passes and in a position to be of assistance if it's needed."

"Go alone," Anamaskin said quietly. "Varsheean will see to it that you are passed from one lot of his spies to another."

"Our people won't ask questions if I tell them not to, and they won't talk in taverns. We don't want anything to look suspicious or have people we meet on the road asking questions. They will if it's just the two of us."

The master trader grunted. "Hurrmp, yes, possibly. All right. But only your own people. The ones you can trust. Who will you take?"

"We'll ask Jessara, her brother, and her husband. You know them. They know when to say nothing and stay low."

Anamaskin grinned slightly. Jessara, Jiro, and Gheevin had started with him slightly less than thirty years ago. They'd gone—with his blessing—to work for his daughter when she struck out with her shaya as independent traders. Jessara and Jiro were the children of an unlucky trader who'd never made enough to pass on to them an inheritance that would allow them to have their own caravan. Gheevin was the son of a small shopkeeper in Shallahah, but he was also the grandson of a trader, and that life had called him.

"Yes, you couldn't do better," he agreed. "But be careful. Say nothing to them until you're on the road. Then tell them no more than you feel they need to know and offer them the chance to return directly to me if they don't want to take the risks. I'm outfitting a caravan to go down the Ngahere-Shallahan border and along the coast into the Hala'atha territory this coming moon. They can join that and be gone several moons."

Tiah laughed. "You know them. How likely is that?"

"Not very," Anamaskin said wryly. "But they should have the offer. It's their decision how much they want to risk."

Kait stood and stretched slowly. "I'm for my bed. We'll ride for the city tomorrow. Jessara and the others should be at our depot there, and we can start sorting out a caravan and goods to trade in Surah. What if the sorcerer we hunt does double back and return to the plains?"

Hestrie also stood. "I'll have a clan watch set at the plains' fringe nearest us, sister. Orla sounds like a sensible and clever woman. If they return I think she will send word to us at once. But if we don't hear, still messengers shall go between you and I and Anamaskin so that you hear everything that we learn. Tell that to Varsheean as well."

They all sought their beds after that and slept. Kait and Tiah were first awake and lay talking before the smells of cooking food brought them out to eat with Hestrie and the master trader. By the ninth candlemark they were riding for Shallahah City at a pace that was sufficient to make excellent time without attracting too much notice. Six of Anamaskin's guards were riding with them on the excuse that they were taking a small but valuable pack of goods to the depot. In fact they were, since the master trader was too old a hand at intrigue to skimp on details.

With the guards riding two before and four behind them, the women rode in silence for some hours. They'd said all that was to be said, and the talk of the previous night and the early morning was weighing on them. If this business went as wrong as looked possible then they could find themselves embroiled in a war. And that war, although it might start as the city against the Grass Sea, could escalate into the Aradian clans against the humans. And that was something neither could endure. No matter what they had to do, such a thing must be prevented.

That night they took a room in a wayside inn and lit a fire. They had a bath and food sent up to their room and sat up talking until late over a series of maps that were well-drawn, recent copies from Anamaskin's collection of them. Kait was tracing the line of mountains and the passes with a grooming claw while Tiah leaned over her shoulder.

"We're working in the dark, shaya. But your father is right. Really, there are only four ways at most for our enemy to travel."

Tiah shook her head. "No, there are only three ways that immediately concern us. There are six ways in all." At her shaya's look of surprise she listed them.

"There are the three ways of concern to us. That the sorcerer may return to the plains to attack Shallahah or that he may flee through one of the passes and loop back to Shallahah. He may travel the length of the mountains and attack Surah, or he could take a ship from the Outlaw Coast and go anywhere, or he could cross the plains and the mountains beyond and go—anywhere. But if he does those last two we shall not know where he had gone or what he does there and it may not concern

us. If he attacks Surah, Tassino has good troops and will defend
the city strongly."

Kait looked down at the maps. "How soon do you think
that we should take to the road, shaya?"

"We have to reach the city, tell Jessara and the others what
we plan, arrange the caravan, and talk to Varsheean." She
was counting. "That's not going to be done in under another
four days no matter how we push. After that we have to travel
around the Peace Mountains and up toward Jasta Pass. Another
five days at wagon speed."

"We could push that."

"And be conspicuous. It's early summer, there is a steady
trickle of travelers and they all talk, love."

She raised her voice to the whining simper of a lower-
middle-class city woman of the gossiping sort. "We came
down the road to visit my sister in the city and those traders
passed us, you know, the shayana ones. Their pack beasts
were white with sweat and they seemed to be in such a hurry
you wouldn't believe. I kept wondering why all the way on
to the city. My Yamilee said that maybe they had some trade
they didn't want to miss, but our guard said that traders still
didn't usually abuse their animals like that. You know, it's
said that they were involved in that trouble with Surah three
years ago. You don't suppose something like that's happened
again, do you? It would be awful if Surah was starting something. I mean, they could."

She looked at Kait. "You know the rest. A day later the
whole city is buzzing with the suggestion that we're about to
be at war with Surah, Duke Tassino's spies will report that
to him, and the next thing is a diplomatic inquiry to the
king."

Kait threw up her hands. "I know. All right. So we can't

do anything that looks out of the ordinary. So how do we seek out Varsheean and talk to him without every gossip in the city commenting on that."

Tiah grinned. "Please, you've known him how long? He'll be looking for us. We just put up at the Happy Oswan and leave the window ajar once we blow out the lantern. Someone will come calling."

"Then they'd better say who it is before they climb in," Kait said grimly. "Until this mess is resolved I'm taking no chances. Speaking of which, shaya, think of a way to take extra horses. Just in case we have to let the caravan go on to Surah while we go elsewhere. I have a feeling that an extra pair of mounts could be very useful."

"That's easy. When we're talking to Varsheean I'll ask him to have them available for us." She looked at her heart-sister. "Bed, beloved. It grows late and we start early." She washed, slipped into bed, and reached for Kait once her shaya joined her.

"One thing about this: Danger always makes me feel that I should use every opportunity." She gave a mock growl. "Come here, beloved, this could be our last chance."

Kait obeyed, laughing. "And if you're saying that every night for tendays until this is over we're going to be completely exhausted when it is—even if we've done little else."

"But happy?"

"Very happy!"

They reached the city two days later to find the depot busy and their three employees waiting at the inn where they normally stayed. Kait saw to the stabling of their mounts, the delivery of the pack Anamaskin had sent with them, and arranging and paying for their room at the Happy Oswan. Tiah had gone with Jessara to purchase food for the caravan while Jiro and

Gheevin, lists in hands, had gone to pick up trade merchandise for the trip.

It took all of that day, something both the women had foreseen, and it was after dark before they returned to the inn to eat in their rooms with minor tasks still to accomplish. Both were tired and grubby and exasperated with the slowness forced on them lest they become too conspicuous. Kait was complaining softly as they entered their room.

"I just want to groom my fur and eat, heart-sister. I feel filthy and I'm starving. And if we have to wait for Varsheean to turn up I could bite him instead of the roast you ordered."

A voice spoke softly. "Fortunate, then, that you don't have to wait. Keep the lantern low and when your food comes take it at the door so the servant doesn't see anything."

They turned swiftly, both with knives flickering into their hands, to find the king's spymaster slipping silently into the room behind them. Kait relaxed a little and grinned at him while Tiah swore a string of the more descriptive phrases she'd learned from Kait over the years. Ending with—

"And damn me for a striped tori with blunted claws, we could both be killed one day soon if we're slowing up that badly. One of us should have heard you sneaking along behind us."

Varsheean grinned. "You're right. Maybe you should be taking refresher courses with Hestrie, but just now I don't have time to admire your cursing, or to sit around discussing how age has slowed you both." His grin widened at Kait's mock snarl.

Tiah's gaze sharpened on him suddenly, seeing that beneath the usual banter Varsheean was serious. She sent that to Kait and they both sat on the edge of their bed, leaving the only stool for their visitor. They waited, their faces sober again, as he seated himself. A servant arrived with food and drink, which was taken from him at the door before he could enter. They shared that among the three of them, the women taking turns as they brought Varsheean up to date with their own events.

Varsheean listened, interrupting suddenly with, "Pasht's claws. That fits with something I've been told."

"What?"

"Later, finish your tale."

They did so, falling silent once it was done and watching him, knowing that he would not have called on them without a good reason.

"Yes," he said, to those watching eyes, knowing the women to be trustworthy and loyal to Shallahah. "We may have Lhandes trouble again too, and no, not from Duke Tassino. This time it may be Mirray and its cursed duke. How much do you know of why Cleeono packed and fled Shallahah three years ago?"

Tiah considered. The gossip of the time had been that the duke had done something to annoy the king and was to have been heavily fined. That, in her opinion, wasn't sufficient to explain why a duke would abruptly pack up everything that he owned that was portable and go live fifteen days' travel away— abandoning his lands to the king to gift to someone else.

The other, more knowledgeable gossip she'd heard from friends closer to seats of power had suggested that the king had discovered some dark activities of his cousin-by-marriage. And the duke had hastily removed himself in one piece—before he could be divided into two pieces via the royal headsman.

She said this to Varsheean, who nodded slowly. "Yes, in essence that's closer to correct. Briefly, the king was called secretly to the bedside of a dying woman, the lady Sionath, who was his cousin and whom Lord Cleeono wed nearly thirty

years ago. She claimed to have found out only a short time earlier that her husband had been involved with Rhanwyn, the
king's sister, in the original conspiracy to murder her cousin.
She said that she had hesitated but in the end cousinly loyalty
had decided her to speak."

Kait and Tiah looked at each other. Rhanwyn's conspiracy,
a dangerous plan to murder her royal brother and seize the
throne of Shallahah, had been foiled by those loyal to the king.
Some of those involved were exiled, others beheaded or otherwise executed. Rhanwyn had escaped by being accidentally
killed in the attempt, but her followers had paid heavily.

"How did she find out?"

"She said that his latest mistress died in childbirth and
confessed to her as she lay dying. I would say from what I know
of everyone involved that Sionath had probably been in the
original conspiracy with Cleeono—who wasn't suspected at
the time. After all, why would he have boasted of it to a rela-
tively new mistress when the conspiracy with Rhanwyn was a
generation ago?"

"I can see a number of possibilities in that tangle, few of
which add up to treason," Tiah said quietly, looking at
Varsheean.

"Quite so, until the king made inquiries and found it to be
the truth," Varsheean said tartly. "The king was always fond of
Sionath, Cleeono is the father of her children, and the whole
business *was* a long time ago. Rather than have the man executed he gave him the option of quietly going into exile. Cleeono
took that offer with surprising alacrity. You've have thought he
was guilty of something and afraid the extent of what that was
would come out."

"Ahhhh," Tiah said.

"Ah indeed. Cleeono took up land on this side of Surah,

settled down there, and has been making a nice little Lhandes.
He's been trading with Surah, breeding some excellent desert-
hardy horses, and producing some very fine mountain sheep
fleeces. I've never trusted the man," he went on thoughtfully.
"And I trusted him a lot less after I heard that. So I ran one
of my men into Mirray with him when he went. I primed him
with good excuses as to why he was happy to be out of Shallahah, and recently he's become the man the duke often employs
for minor deeds of the darker sort . . . on which he doesn't
want to have too much light cast."

Kait chuckled, the soft growling laughter of an Aradian.
"I see, so Duke Cleeono thinks he has a man conveniently
prepared to do his ducal bidding in committing petty
crimes—which the man is and does, if you don't count that
he also reports everything to you."

"Exactly!"

Tiah's eyes narrowed suspiciously. "So just what has he reported to you, Varsheean?"

"You do know that Cleeono married again almost the moment that he'd declared Mirray an independent Lhandes—
nearly two years ago? The happy wife was a widow and is a
nasty piece of work in her late twenties, the youngest daughter
of old Lord Varli—and the apple of his eye. However, gossip
has it that Kadia poisoned her first husband and her servants
hate her. My man overheard her and Cleeono talking a couple
of tendays ago. The duke was assuring her that their 'royal'
plans were moving forward very well."

Tiah looked at him. "It could have been harmless."

"It could, my dear. But right after that I stopped hearing
from my spy. He's a very reliable man who's worked for me for
years. If he's gone silent there's a strong chance that it's the silence of the grave and if so, I'd find his death a bit—suspicious."

He leaned forward to look at her. "Put everything together and I don't like the sounds of any of it. That was before I heard your tale. Now I can add that I don't like the idea of these Kalthi."

"Yes," Kait said slowly.

Tiah shrugged and became practical. "So you aren't here to wish us goddess speed on the Surah road. We didn't think so. What do you want us to do?"

"Find a reason to go to Mirray. I'm not asking you to spy; for one thing you aren't trained, and for another you're known to be solidly loyal to the king. No one is going to talk to you about any treason they may be planning and if they think you're suspicious you'll be found dead in a ditch with the whole Lhandes swearing innocence.

"No, I want you in a position to bring word to me if events boil over. Or possibly to be there to help those who are chasing that madman who wants to call demons—if he ends up in Surah or Mirray before they catch up to him." Varsheean's face twisted in a scowl of outraged frustration.

"The man must be completely crazy. I don't care what ills he thinks he's suffered or what real grief he's had. Apart from anything else, do they think they can keep a plan like that completely quiet?"

"Apparently." Kait's tone was acid.

Tiah snarled angrily as she thought of other aspects. "Then anyone who thinks that is deluded."

There was a long, thoughtful silence before Varsheean spoke. "I don't like any of this at all. When you were here in the city last I had a word with Katchellin. He passed word to Dasheri to take troops to maneuver along the Kavarten-Shallahan border, and they've been there for most of a tenday with Captain Itharo Geytha's-kin riding out to take command." Kait nodded, the surname was the sort used by the Hala'atha, and if the man had risen to be a captain he was ferociously loyal to Shallahah—and extremely competent.

"I'll be writing letters about this most of the night," Varsheean continued. "I want you to take letters to Captains Itharo, Dasheri, and Katchellin. Discuss this business with them, but then I'd like you to go on to Surah as fast as you can without rousing suspicion. Speak privately to your friends there, but be careful how much you tell them."

"Then we go on to Mirray I suppose?"

"Yes, pick a number of small, low-weight valuable goods from the city that you can return with to Mirray. Something that you can sell there with the excuse that they don't sell so well in Surah. I want you to trade, gossip your heads off, look as innocent and harmless as you possibly can, and wait for some of my men to contact you."

"And when they do?"

Varsheean's face set. "Then do what your consciences advise, remembering what you read in the ancient court records here of how the Kalthi act."

Both were still wordlessly considering that when he let himself out of the room. Nor did they speak to each other again before they slept.

15

Next day Kait and Tiah argued over possible trade goods. Kait solved the problem of what they might take to trade in Mirray by cutting the discussion short.

"Why don't we talk to Amaya once we reach Surah? If her friends who comb the beaches for gems have found some of good quality we could take those on to Mirray."

Tiah looked at her shaya. "Heart-sister, there are times when I find in you great intelligence. That's a brilliant idea. Cleeono is still establishing his court, I have a good pack of last summer's furs we can take, and we can add jewelry settings without the gems. We go straight to Amaya when we arrive, buy anything suitable she and her friends can produce. Then have the gems we buy put into the settings to take back through Mirray."

They worked until dusk before returning to the inn, but the hard work had been worth it. The mules, the essential lead mule in particular, were ready, their employees had packed the trade goods selected, and Ruwaen the jeweler had been able to supply twenty lots of complete jewelry settings. They waited only for Varsheean's letters. A tap came at the window a few 'markin after they had lit the lantern. Tiah opened the window while Kait stood ready in case. But it was Varsheean who hauled himself nimbly over the sill from the woodshed roof.

"Well met, ladies."

Kait reached for the stool and thrust it toward him. "Sit down and we'll talk first for a moment."

He obeyed, smiling, as Kait listed their readiness to leave in the morning, and some of their plans, adjustable as always. Once she was done, Varsheean looked up and produced two packets of letters.

"Here are the messages I want you to give to various people along your route. This lot is for Itharo, Katchellin, and Dasheri." He passed Kait a moderately thick package. "The other ones," he passed over several small thin missives that looked to be single sheets of light paper, folded and sealed, "are to be given to those who will identify themselves to you in Surah and Mirray." He lowered his voice and gave explicit and careful directions on those who might be expected to approach the traders.

"Don't make any huge fuss hiding these. If a spy from either Lhandes reads them then all he'll find is a letter to someone's aunt moaning on about life in general and theirs in particular, complaining about recent weather and her husband's or her aching joints. *My* spies can decode them but no one who doesn't know the system is likely to be able to do that. And yes, the people they're supposedly written by do exist."

Tiah looked interested. "There're times when a trader could use a good code."

"You'll already know this kind. It's based on a combination of allusions and substitutions. If I write that our mutual aunt is developing a cold, it may mean that war is looking likely. Or if I ask if he remembers the old well, it may mean that a message is waiting for him hidden in a hole in boulders in a certain place."

Tiah and Kait looked at each other and grinned. They had used such a system in the past. It was one of the best, since it was impossible to break effectively—unless you could persuade someone who knew all the allusions to talk.

"You could communicate with us the same way?" Kait suggested. "We have enough background in common to make it possible if there's an emergency."

Varsheean nodded. "I thought of that, since you may be going into danger. With my man possibly dead in Mirray you can't take chances of anyone opening a letter from you with what could be vital information." He produced a sheet of blank paper, a traveling pen, and an inkpot and wrote while they waited patiently. "Both of you read this, please. Memorize it, and once you're certain you know all the words, burn it." A look told the women that it was a list of substitutions.

Kait giggled. "'For Aunt Koloh read Shallahah,'" she quoted.

"Quite so, and if you see anyone else's communications, don't jump to conclusions. The list is different for most groups, even for each person in some places. I and a couple of others who shall be nameless are the only ones to have all of these lists." He stood up. "Don't forget to burn that. Now, I'll leave you to sleep. You'll have a busy day tomorrow. I'll see myself out."

He opened the window, rolled neatly over the sill and down to the roof of the woodshed, and dropped lightly to the ground below. Tiah shut the window, turned down the latch, pulled the heavy drape across, and nodded toward the bed.

"He's right. We'll be on the road early and I'd like a good

night's sleep first." She yawned widely. "I wonder where Orla and the others are tonight?"

Orla and the others were camped. From the trail sign it looked as if Ashara and her captor were a little less than a day's ride in front of them. They'd gained slightly more than half a day since they'd begun doing what Dayshan suggested. With all of their number together again in the general vicinity they could ride back and forth to stay in touch with each group.

They had refined on that too after further discussion, with one of their number riding farther ahead still to find a good campsite and make camp. Often it was dark when the others arrived, but they would know they were still on the trail, and would have a fire and hot food and drink without wasting time that they could spend seeking trail sign.

Kyrryl stretched out her hands to the flames. "That's so good." She looked up at Yoros when he stooped to hand her a drinking bowl of hot pata. "We're making up time on them, aren't we?"

"We are, beloved. But it may now be time to do as Trasso has just suggested and send riders ahead again to the farther pass. Aratanga Pass is behind us. Our quarry has continued all the way up the coast before rounding the mountains. From the map it looks as if he'll meet no one to ask questions until he reaches Surah."

Orla nodded thoughtfully. Within the Grass Sea, tribes could be at war with no warning, just an attack out of the grass. They had rigid codes that covered warfare, but there was always someone who could find a loophole. And the wise one of any tribe should be paranoid, constantly wary, and the more she knew of those with power, the better for her people. She considered her own experiences in light of what could be going on in Shallahah and the Lhandes and spoke slowly, thinking as she talked.

"Word does come to the plains—of rulers and their quarrels," she said.

They looked at her. "And that word is?" Eilish questioned.

"That the king in Shallahah had a dangerous falling-out with a duke who was married to one of the king's kin. The duke packed up everything he could take and moved far away to take up new land near the Lhandes of Surah. It is also rumored that duke was furious about having to leave."

Trasso, knowing the ways of intrigue, grasped the possibilities. "You think that this duke could be behind the sorcerer?"

"It's possible. A duke would have the wealth, and he'd have men to obey his commands." Her gaze met theirs as she scanned their faces. "Wouldn't it be a fine revenge for him if demons attacked Shallahah and murdered the king who had him exiled—and all of the court who stood by and allowed it?"

"Yes," Eilish said softly. "It would. We need to catch up with Ashara."

"We must follow faster on her trail," Trasso said.

Dayshan grunted. "In the morning I'll ride a day forward. Once there I'll start back looking for dropped crystals. Two of you can ride with me. If I find a crystal I'll send someone back to tell you. I'll ride on farther again and make a cold camp while the other one makes camp for you. If I find another crystal you'll have a place to go at once when you ride on the next day, and then we can do it all over again."

Orla was calculating. "If things go well for us we might

catch up with the man before we reach the end of the mountains and ride into Surah."

Kyrryl and Yoros looked at each other, and their smiles were unpleasantly similar. "I do hope so," she said softly. "There are a number of things I'd really like to discuss with this sorcerer."

On a tiring horse eight candlemarks ahead of her, the man she hoped to kill was considering his options. The horses were holding up reasonably well, and unless something unfortunate happened they'd last long enough for him to reach the far end of the mountains and the Lhandes of Surah and Mirray. The girl he held captive was—if not resigned to her fate—at least riding as she was told and not trying to escape.

His smile to himself was sad where none could see it. She'd doubtless feared rape after his earlier threats and was only happy to discover he'd done nothing so far. The truth was that he'd never desired any woman but his Yalana. This child was safe enough—from that anyhow. His mind wandered to another child, his own little one: Gaisa. She'd have been wed by now with children of her own if the king had not burned the plains for a crime he and his had never committed.

The king, he mused, a man who broke plains law and set fires deliberately. No plains clan would have forgiven one of their people who did such a thing. Why then had this ruler assumed they would do so with an out-plains man? In the plains tribes a fire-setter died horribly; this king should die the moment it could be arranged. Sepallo would have vengeance, and the spirits of Yalana and Gaisa and those of his friends who had died would sleep in peace at last, to await his own coming.

His mount stumbled, ending his reverie. He halted the

horses and gazed about him. This would make a good enough site to camp. There was a large boulder embedded in the hillside with brush growing to one side. He'd hobble the horses here where there was a patch of grass above the deer trail and make a fire in the boulder's lee. He dismounted to begin the familiar routine, making signs to his captive that she should do the same.

Ashara obeyed, her gaze flickering all over the site while she worked. There, a patch of bare earth just ahead along the deer trail they were following. She used her saddle for a pillow and arranged the blanket about her carefully so her captor should not see the line of crystals still sewn around one corner. She would have those off it and tucked into her clothing once it was dark.

Using her teeth, she managed to pull free more of the crystals before sleeping that night. Next morning she saddled the horses when her captor signaled her to do so, doused the fire, and covered the ashes before packing up both lots of the bedding. Sepallo mounted and led them west for another day's riding. The trail here was very narrow, and without turning he could not see what she was doing. She dropped a crystal into the bare patch of soil beneath her mount when they passed over it . . . and prayed.

*T*iah and Kait were on the road to the Lhandes by first light. Jessara, Jiro, and Gheevin rode behind them, leading in turn the short string of pack mules. Tiah had carefully picked out larger beasts from their stables, trail-broken and very fit. They'd just come in from a trip down the Ngahere border, and while they'd been well fed on that run, they'd also been worked hard. They were in condition to be pushed a little. Not so much that passersby would notice, but enough to make better time than usual. The string leader was the largest of the pack mules, an aggressive beast that liked to travel and didn't like strangers. He was an excellent choice; in the past, would-be mule thieves had deeply regretted meeting him.

"Did Varsheean say where we would meet Itharo and the soldiers?"

Kait nodded. "They're on the Kavarten border, but just about the time we reach there they should have arrived at the camp a day's travel past your father's warehouses, I'd expect them to be camped at the border by that small stream that runs down to Mersa Lake."

Tiah visualized the map. "Good. We should be there to see him by tomorrow night."

After a day's steady travel with little time for rest, they were there to meet whoever appeared, and it was Captain Itharo, a happy-faced man of medium height and something of a dandy in his tailored uniform, who came quickly to meet them. "Well met, ladies. I believe you may have letters for me and for those with me?"

Kait grinned cheerfully at the captain. They'd met him in the trouble with Surah five years ago, and she liked him—the human was almost as good at scouting as she was. Tiah produced the packet Varsheean gave her.

"Here, and I've dangerous possibilities to tell you about that we couldn't write. It should not be overheard by anyone but you, Chell—and Dasheri if you trust him."

Itharo pursed his lips. "Tell me and Chell first. If I think Dasheri should know about anything I'll tell him later. My men are camped a mile ahead. Make your camp a few hundred yards from ours. You'll know the right place when we get there. Our tent is pitched about twenty feet from a short line of thick brush. Wait until dusk. I'll call the guards to the front to speak to them about keeping watch; then you can walk to my tent and enter from the back. I'll loosen the ropes there. Once you're inside we can talk while we all four eat. I'll have guards out at a distance so that no one approaches us."

"It sounds good to me," Kait agreed.

The way minor plans often do, this one worked. At the eighth candlemark past noon, Tiah and Kait rolled under the back of the tent and straightened up to be greeted by Katchellin.

"Good, I presume no one noticed you since the guards aren't shouting challenges. Sit on my bedding, here's food and pata. Itharo will be back in a moment." The women sat and accepted the drinking bowls. Katchellin placed two plates of stew between them and grinned. "Itharo told you you'd be arriving. I'd say that it was nice to see you again if I didn't think it's a bad omen."

Tiah nodded with her mouth full. She swallowed and grinned wryly. "I'm afraid it may be. Have you read the letters yet?" He nodded. "Then you know most of the facts so far. What we can add is a few suggestions, and a conclusion that could be jumped to here and there."

Katchellin sighed. "As usual. Well, at least we're all used to that. I've taken decisive action on the basis of more flimsy notions than we heard about in the letters. If you can add anything to those we'll be grateful."

Captain Itharo entered in time to hear the last comments and nodded in turn. "That's very true." He took the plate and drinking bowl handed to him and sat. "Now, talk softly. It's unlikely that anyone sneaking about could get close enough to hear that I have visitors let alone what we're saying, but I'd like to keep even that information a secret."

Tiah and Kait talked while Itharo and Katchellin listened

intently. At last Katchellin got up to pour them more pata as he and his captain considered all they'd heard. Katchellin sighed when they finished speaking.

"It's a nasty tale, Cleeono's a fool and that wife of his is a kio," he said, and Kait laughed.

"Please! You insult kios. They're only vicious small scavengers. She isn't that small..." Everyone grinned at that. Cleeono's young wife was a buxom woman of the top-heavy sort that the duke was known to prefer.

"She's vicious at any time—ask her previous husband," Tiah commented. "Since we started wondering about her and Cleeono I asked around our trader contacts in the city and no one had a good word to say for her. Some of them had words to say, certainly, but they weren't good."

Itharo considered what she'd said. "Her reputation is known but she's like that openly. Myself, I'd be expecting someone who was keeping a lower profile."

"Or," Tiah added, "the same lady could be involved after all and relying on her openness not to be suspected."

Itharo changed the subject. "Leave just before first light if you can. I'll be moving my men out after you and we'll be only a candlemark or so behind your caravan the whole way to Jasta Pass. After that I plan to detach a scouting party, ostensibly to check out the foothills above the road and west for some distance. Chell will lead that group with ten men. It should ensure your safety for several days and explain why you're hurrying. Naturally you won't want the rough and licentious soldiery to catch up with you."

Both women grinned at him. "That sounds an excellent plan," Tiah said more soberly. "And after that?"

"After that I rather think that someone else may contact you. Someone traveling the same road."

"Ah." Tiah might have guessed. Varsheean wasn't taking chances on them being attacked on the road. Not that one man would be of great help, but he could take word of what had happened to—"I see. Chell and his men will be following us still. Just farther back."

"Precisely. We don't want his men—or any other travelers—speculating on why he's following traders, so it needs to be clear that he isn't. But he'll be a day behind you the whole way to Surah. If anyone asks, he's patrolling for bandits."

Kait and Tiah looked at each other and laughed. That story would do nicely. Everyone still remembered the troubles of five years earlier when the so-called bandit raids on many trader caravans had turned out to be a political intrigue—but most people still didn't know that. A patrol from Shallahah checking the length of the road for lurking bandits would make sense to travelers, and it would please almost all of them too.

The women talked a little longer, then sneaked back to their own camp and turned in. When the first streaks of faint lavender light began to brighten the sky, they were already starting off slowly but steadily down the rutted road to the Lhandes. The soldiers followed them a candlemark later with Dasheri in the lead. Katchellin, quietly riding with his captain in the middle of the group, rode a very good horse. If he needed to talk to the women ahead of them again he could catch up to them quite easily.

16

Two sets of riders fled along the Outlaw Coast. Sepallo hurried, but not unduly. No one followed, of that he was sure. He'd been careful and cunning. The traitor who'd let him past for a pair of worthless bracelets—what need would he have of such trinkets very soon—had not seen which way he'd gone. Even if the man went back on his payment, those who might follow would not know which trail to take. Yet he didn't want to waste time; he needed to be in Mirray for noon on midsummer's day, the day of greatest power, the long day.

With none to see, his eyes filled with tears as he rode. It had been on a midsummer day that he'd married before his clan on the wide plains of sweet-smelling grass.

He began to talk to Ashara. In a conversational voice he explained his plans. This foreign woman didn't understand what he said; she couldn't know. But it pleased him to be able to explain his reasons for what he'd do to Shallahah. He also mentioned where his plans would come to fruition. Two candlemarks later he moved ahead of her, feeling temporarily purged.

Ashara, her mount walking carefully along a bad section of the trail, was able to slide another crystal from her belt pocket. She'd tucked some into her shirt cuffs, others into her boots. If he found one cache he might not look for more. The sorcerer had checked her possessions only cursorily immediately after he took her. Was he too confident or just uncaring? She didn't know.

He'd looked for weapons and taken her sword, her eating knife, her flint and steel, but he'd only glanced at her body and not looked through her clothing. He'd apparently assumed that anything worth taking away from her would be obvious. She hid a rueful grin; if only he hadn't been right so far as weapons were concerned.

And she'd understood every word the sorcerer had said to her. She felt a surge of unwilling pity. It must have been terrible for him on that day. Yet it had been awful too for those people in the king's caravan that the plains clans had murdered and looted. He had given her one piece of information in his ramblings. She'd try to leave that behind at each site from now on. She too had looked with interest at the trader maps.

She flicked the crystal—a small, glittering arc in the sunshine—into a patch of earth, hoping desperately that there would be sufficient baubles to last out the journey.

*B*ehind them Kyrryl was looking at the tracks she'd found, and smiling. It was a dangerous expression, bearing the same relation to a grin as the snarl of a wolf. Yoros looked at Dayshan and nodded.

"Yes, we're making up time on him."

The master-at-arms bent over the tracks and looked grim. "We are, mostly because he isn't pushing his mounts. I'd say he thinks that no one is following and he doesn't want to tire the horses or risk them coming up lame." He bent further to lift the crystal from its fragrant bed. "And the lass is still leaving signs for us. I wish we could let her know we're closing on them."

Kyrryl looked wistfully at the crystal. "So do I, but I did have an idea. We've been looking over campsites but not tracking much outside the actual site when we find it, so as not to waste time. How much privacy does he give her, I wonder?"

Dayshan swore angrily as he understood. "I'm an old fool. I never thought of that. I thought that he'd watch the campsite to ensure she left no marks. If he allows her to go behind a bush when they stop then she could leave us more than crystals. Does she know trail sign?"

Kyrryl nodded and Dayshan grunted thoughtfully. "Yoros, after me I'd say you're the best tracker and you know the lass. If we identify a site they've used, you stay there and search for anything more she may have left. The rest of us will continue to leapfrog and you'll catch us up each time once you're done."

"We should be near a campsite in a couple more candle-marks," Yoros offered. "I'll ride ahead and start there—if I can find it."

Eilish nodded agreement, She wished this were over, with Ashara back safe with her kin and all of them home. She worried all the time about what would happen if they couldn't return. What ever had possessed them to think of this quest? She missed Kian Dae too and really hoped that he was safe in Dharvath's shrine.

Their group split to continue the hunt, leaving Roshan and Hailin to follow along the upper track with the spare mounts.

*I*n the shrine of Dharvath's clan, Kian Dae slept on a small cot near the old priestess. Aycharna slept soundly in a larger bed in the next room, but the cat only drowsed. Something was calling him, something or someone who had the feel of the one who once had aided him in battle, and now he was needed in turn. He woke into full alertness when Dharvath whispered in her sleep—and he understood the words.

"Yes, if it be thy will. All three of us then?" There was a pause before she spoke again in question. "And the direction we take?" In her sleep she nodded acceptance, smiled, and relaxed back into quieter slumber. Kian Dae lay awake longer. The feel of the visitor had faded but it had touched him, leaving something different behind. His mind felt clearer, thoughts fitting better into words rather than the usual emotions, pictures, sensations.

Out on the road to the Lhandes, Katchellin had padded silently into their tent for a secret conference with Kait and Tiah. "One of Varsheean's men brought me word from Mirray on his way to the city to tell Varsheean, and no, it's no real news as yet. Varsheean has all his men sieving court and street gossip for any solid indication of Cleeono's plans. All they can really tell him is that there seems to be a remarkable amount of confidence among the Mirrayan court that they'll have their rights back sometime soon."

"How soon is soon?" Kait showed her fangs in an irritable smile.

"One of the men overheard a discussion mentioning that Lord Gelani—one of Cleeono's closest cronies—has purchased a piece of coastal land in Shallahah. It could be nothing, but Gelani was involved with Cleeono and the king would have made a fatal appointment for him as well if he hadn't chosen to leave. Gelani isn't going back . . ." He paused and said the next seven words with heavy significance. "Not so long as the king lives!"

Kait looked puzzled. "But why would he buy land? Even if he thinks that the king is going to be killed, wouldn't Cleeono give him land if they return and Cleeono becomes the ruler?"

Katchellin was watching Tiah.

She bit her lower lip, considering that information, putting it together with possible assumptions. "Yes," she said slowly. "Yes, so if Gelani has purchased Shallahah land, he probably expects to be able to take possession of it at some point. Of course, he could be buying it to provide for a family member still in Shallahah. What do you know about Gelani? I'm not familiar with him but is he a greedy man, a miser? The sort who always has something tucked away in case of unexpected calamity?"

Katchellin nodded. "He's the sort to have money tucked away, and he believes in taking precautions."

"Then his purchase may say something to us," Tiah said thoughtfully. A trader learned how people thought, and Tiah was the daughter of a master trader and third-generation trader. "If I was Varsheean I'd do two things. I'd check to see if Gelani may be assisting a family member, and I'd get a copy of the bill of sale, it may tell you something."

"I'll suggest he has that done," Katchellin said. "My thanks for your assistance." He dropped to roll under the edge of the tent back and paused, looking up at the women. "I can tell you one thing, if this conspiracy succeeds and the king dies I'll make it my mission to kill every damned noble involved. He's a good man as well as a good ruler."

When he vanished under the tent edge Kait stared after him. There'd been a startling amount of rage in that judgment. She believed he'd do it, but there was something more personal behind his decision, not just the outrage of a man who served a man he approved.

She turned to Tiah. "What was that about?"

"A long story."

Kait laughed softly. "Then come to bed with me, heart-sister, and tell it to me. I do enjoy a good bedtime tale."

They crawled into bed and Tiah hugged her shaya close. "I won't make too long a story of it but I heard it from Itharo two years ago. Katchellin was orphaned when he was seven. His father was a soldier who was killed in a skirmish with bandits. His mother went back to live with her kin, then died of summer sickness a year later. By rights her husband left a soldier's pension to her but her elder brother managed to have her sign it away. When she died he put Chell to work, long hours and little food. On top of that Chell's older cousins beat him up whenever they felt like it."

"He'd have fought back."

"He did, which made them worse. One day when Chell was ten the king—still the prince then—was riding through the city and caught it happening in an alleyway near the uncle's business. The cousin was twice Chell's size, half his age again, and starved as he was Chell was still holding his own. The prince stepped in, found out what was going on, and got the pension back. Then he arranged for Chell to board with a retired soldier who'd known Chell's father. Chell grew up, joined the army—although I know he has a sideline spying for Varsheean as well as being Itharo's second-in-command—and he's never forgotten how the king saved him."

Kait's voice was drowsy. "I do like loyalty."

"So does the king," Tiah agreed. She cuddled down in the warm bedding. While she drifted into sleep she was thinking of Katchellin's oath. She'd pity those nobles if the king died, but if it did happen, she thought she'd be helping Chell herself, she and her heart-sister.

The next day they were on the road again. Close to dusk their plodding caravan was jolted out of any complacency. Kait and Tiah had lagged a little, talking about Katchellin's news and discussing their own speculations. One of the beasts, Kotu, the leader of the pack-mule string, fit and less heavily loaded than his brethren, had forged slightly ahead. Jiro had half turned in a quick movement to push the beast back in line when an arrow from roadside cover took him in the shoulder. He screamed in pain and fell. His kinsman leaped their mounts forward to cover him when six figures burst from the roadside brush.

Kait heeled her mount into a flying rush to cut them off from retreat. In her opinion the only good bandit was a dead one, and she'd like to do her share in seeing that they ended that way. This lot must be desperate. Six against five wasn't very good odds for bandits. Tiah was half a stride behind her, sword already swinging. Their voices soared up, blending in a cry that told their servants they were coming—while it warned the attackers that they should run.

To her mild surprise none of the bandits turned to flee. Her blade lashed around and down—to be parried in turn. Her sword point circled, feinting, while the other hand went smoothly to her belt. Her fingers gripped the hilt of one of her short, beautifully balanced throwing knives, slotted almost invisibly into the belt. She flicked backhanded across her body and the bandit fell, the hilt jutting from his throat.

Kait had ridden a man down, her mount trampling him enthusiastically under its hooves as he writhed screaming. He grasped its leg, trying to roll himself away from the stamping agony. For his pains a hoof slammed into the front of his skull.

There was a sound like a rock melon being hit with an ax and the yells stopped abruptly. Kait had no time for his troubles. She was fencing with another man, one who had had some training in fighting from the ground against a mounted opponent.

"Pasht!" Her sword struck home and the man reeled away to crumple motionless on the road.

In the center of the travel-rutted road, Jessara had dismounted to tend her husband while her brother stood guard over them. He'd managed to slice one bandit across the forearm, but a second was closing in.

The string of seven mules milled nearby, torn between fear at the noise of the fight, and roused to anger or fear by the scent of blood that surrounded them. Kotu, the lightly loaded mule, was string leader, a jack mule with an uncertain temper and a deep dislike for anyone unknown to him. The injured bandit seized him by the halter and attempted to pull him off the road so that his companion could reach the traders. Kotu stretched his neck and took the bandit firmly by the arm. The jack's teeth were large and yellow but his victim had almost no time to notice that before they were sunk almost to the bone in his wounded arm.

His agonized screams attracted unwanted notice. Given a choice, the bandit would rather Gheevin ignored him. Gheevin felt otherwise, and the angry mule found himself holding a dead man. He spat out the arm and looked around hopefully to see whom he could bite or kick next. There were only two men remaining who were not his people. One was running down the road with Tiah riding in pursuit, and Kait had just cut down the other man. Tiah, dealing with the last bandit, had no desire to make this a long chase. Her hand went to her belt and a second throwing knife took her quarry neatly at the base of his skull. Silence descended on the road.

Kait came trotting back to where Jiro lay gasping. "How bad is it?"

Jessara looked up from her position beside her husband. "It could be a lot worse. The arrow needs to come out, though, and he won't be fit for much for a few weeks after that."

Tiah returned, slotting her knife back into her belt and swearing. "Shaya, there's something strange about these bandits."

"I know, six to five aren't the usual bandit odds, they like two to one or better. Did any of them survive?"

Tiah went to check and returned. "One of them, not that he'll be around for long I think. He's the one Kotu got and Gheevin finished. They both thought he was dead but he isn't— yet. He's dying but he's delirious. If he was paid to keep quiet he may talk. I'm just not sure that anything he says will be much use."

"Jessara, Gheevin. Move Jiro off the road, set up camp here, and boil two lots of water," Kait ordered. "Get the hashas juice from the medicine pouch and dose him. It'll take time for that to work and for the water to boil. Let's go and talk to that mule fodder."

Leaving their employees to do as directed, the women returned to the bandit and looked down at him as he lay sprawled, half on one side. Blood where he'd been cut and bitten soaked his sleeve, and the stab wound Gheevin had inflicted near his spine was oozing blood. He stared up, but it was clear it was not the women that he saw.

"Stupid man, stupid fool. Never said."

Tiah squatted beside him. Kait leaned past her and quietly removed the bandit's sword and eating knife. She lightly ran her hands over his clothing. She found no other weapons, but she'd be watching him.

"Stupid," the bandit raved. "Din' tell us. I was asked last moment to make six, better odds."

"Who asked you?"

"Man inna tavern. Had five men, friends. Didn't tell me."

"Who didn't tell you?" Tiah asked softly. Her hand went out to stroke his hair. "Just lie quiet and it'll be better soon. Who didn't tell you?"

The answer she received startled them both considerably. "Treyvan."

"Vani and Shaetyl's Treyvan? Why did he pay you to kill two women?" She kept her voice low and soothing.

"Din' tell us fighters, jus' two dumb women. Said he owed them a grudge anyway, but he was paid too. Cheated me."

"Yes, the women were fighters and you were cheated. Treyvan cheated you. Why did he want you to kill them?"

"Said some noble. Sent men and needed another. They was nosing about. Talkin' to the wrong people. Warning to them. Cheated me!" The last words were a muted gasp of outrage. Bandits weren't supposed to be cheated, they were supposed to do the cheating—and the killing. His chest heaved up in a final shuddering breath and collapsed. It didn't rise again. Kait and Tiah stood and gazed at each other over the body.

"Get that written down, shaya, Varsheean will want to hear it."

"So will Katchellin, and he'll be here tonight once he sees that we've camped early," Tiah agreed. She produced a small sheaf of paper and a short quill, opened the tiny brass inkpot she carried when traveling, and wrote quickly before waving the paper in the air to dry the ink.

"Now, let's see what we can do for Jiro, and after that we can think about all of this."

Tending Jiro wasn't pleasant, but it was nothing they were unable to handle. They weren't experts, but they'd learned the basics of caring for common injuries and illnesses. The arrow shaft was carefully snapped below the vanes, the protruding point broken off on the other side of the victim's shoulder, and the plain shaft withdrawn. Jiro was unconscious from the hashas and never moved.

Kait sat back on her heels. "Clean it through." She watched her shaya do so and nodded as she inspected the swab that had been doused with flame and pulled through the wound channel on a length of wire.

"There doesn't seem to be anything carried into the wound. I think that if Pasht is with us he'll be fine. There's no damage to the tendons. But he isn't going to be of any use for a couple of tendays."

"There's the foothills shrine. We could leave him there."

"We could be gone a lot longer, heart-sister. Jessara and Gheevin won't be pleased about it and neither Jiro nor the shrine would be happy to have him stay up to two moons. No, I have a better thought. Didn't Itharo have supply wagons with him?"

Tiah smiled at her. "Good idea. Katchellin's likely to come up with us tonight. We can ask for the loan of a couple of his men to take Jiro back to Itharo's camp in a litter. He's returning to the city any day now while Chell continues to follow us. I can write a letter to go with Jiro to our trade compound."

With that settled, Jiro groaning his way back to consciousness, and the second lot of water boiling for pata, they put the attack aside for the moment to eat. Jessara was worried about her brother.

"We have a friend coming up the road behind us," Tiah said quietly. "We'll wait here, and when he arrives we'll ask for Jiro to be taken back to the city. Don't worry, he can stay in our compound, Shirin will be back by now, and he'll make sure that Jiro is properly tended."

They ate and drank in silence until the shayana retired early to their tent. Tiah brought out the sheet of paper on which she'd written the dying bandit's ramblings, holding it to the lamp so that she could see. Then she studied the words, repeating them aloud as Kait listened intently.

"Said some noble. Sent men and needed another. They was nosing about. Talkin' to the wrong people. Warning to them." She looked up at her heart-sister. "Do you get from that, my shaya, that it was we who were talking to the wrong people, and that our deaths were to be a warning to those undesirables to whom we talked?"

"Yes, but why Treyvan—if that's who's meant? He isn't noble?"

"No, but he does have something of a name for being able to find what a noble might want. He sells slaves in a lot of places and I've heard he brings other items if asked," Tiah said slowly. "I think he'd be only too happy to arrange our deaths to pay us for that court case, he just wouldn't lay out good coin on it himself."

"So some noble who didn't like who we were talking to . . ."

"No," Tiah interrupted. "I think it's more the other way around. And the only people we've been talking to who might attract that sort of attention have been Varsheean or Itharo and Katchellin."

"Varsheean took great care that no one saw him with us at the inn," Kait commented.

"The same with the other two when we met them on the road. But I don't think it could have been them. There hasn't been time for anyone who might have seen us with them to talk about it, and whoever heard that to find Treyvan. But if someone saw Varsheean meet us that first night in Shallahah they've had a half tenday to find someone willing to get rid of us for a price."

"And that's another thing," Kait said, suddenly remembering her thought earlier. "Did you notice that these were better fighters than the usual bandits? Not good enough to be ex-soldiers, but maybe part-trained by a nobleman's master-at-arms?"

"I wondered about that at the first crossing of swords," Tiah confirmed. "Men-at-arms aren't unlikely, and he did say that there was some lord involved. Maybe the other five were lord's men?"

Tiah stood up and put aside her drinking bowl of pata, which had gone cold as they talked. "Let's check again on Jiro. He may need more hashas juice. That's a clean, simple wound, but I know from experience that won't make it hurt any the less."

They walked back to see to their wounded man, and if the expression on each face was grimmer than usual, that was only to be expected. No one liked bandits, and traders loathed them. It was satisfying that they'd killed six between them. Gheevin had collected the weapons and other loot from the bodies and dumped them well back into roadside brush for the scavengers.

"Anatiah?" She waited. The use of her full name was a signal that it was official.

"I stripped the bandits of weapons and anything in their belt pouches, and look." He held out cupped hands and opened them to show the gleam of gold. "Each of them had renis. What bandit carries so much gold?"

17

$\mathcal{K}$ait took a step forward, "Did you count how many coins from each? Did they all have the same amount?"

"I did, and no, they didn't. The one who talked to you had five gold while all the others had eight. That's two moons' pay for an honest man."

Kait nodded to him, mind-sending to her shaya, *Or perhaps what was left of ten renis after they'd waited a while in the city for their sixth man to join them? He only received half of that, the other half they received was for what—or who—they knew that he didn't. Either way that's a lot of money, heartsister. Someone really did want us gone.*

Aloud she said to Gheevin, "The weapons go into trade goods. If there is anything from the clothing you want, take it. The coin and jewelry is to be divided into six shares, Jiro gets two because he was injured and everyone else receives one share each."

Gheevin and Jessara both beamed. Just the amount of renis found would double their pay for this trip.

Kait grinned back, guessing their thoughts. "Was there any interesting jewelry?"

"Only this?" He turned to call, "Jessara, bring that token we found on the one we thought might be their leader."

His wife trotted up and proffered a small silver-plated item the size of a coin depending from a long, fine chain. All of them looked at it.

"A daska and a dravencat," Kait said, considering the emblems. "Do we have any idea whose arms they are?"

Tiah shook her head slowly. "It's vaguely familiar to me but I can't place it. It's not symbols of one of the great lords' houses, I don't think. I'm not sure, but it could be a cadet branch from somewhere the far side of Shallahah. I can tell you one thing though, it doesn't come from Surah."

"That's a relief."

Not from Surah meant that Duke Tassino probably wasn't involved. Their trade was less likely to be disrupted by squabbling between countries, and their friends in Surah weren't going to be in any immediate danger. It also meant that if they absolutely had to they could talk to Tassino about some of this.

Tiah took the small medallion and swung it on the chain. "I'll hang on to this, Gheevin. Count it as part of my share. Was there anything else? Did any of the others have the same sort of item?"

"No, we searched them again to be sure after Jessara found that one, but there was nothing."

"All right. Unsaddle the mules and give Kotu a piece of bread and a good brushing. He fought well for us today."

Gheevin grinned, remembering. "That he did. Don't worry, I'll see he gets his reward. It was a good day's work you did when you bought him from that idiot who ill-treated him."

Kait laughed. "Well, you have to admit he had cause. I saw those teeth marks the seller was wearing and they'd have hurt."

Gheevin snorted. "People who can't handle mules shouldn't own them. Kotu's fine if he's respected." Kait motioned to the waiting mules, and he nodded, heading over to begin work.

Tiah was turning the medallion over and over in her hands before she glanced up at the sky. "It'll be full dark in another two 'marks. Let's get the camp set up and wait. If you see Chell don't signal him, he'll know there's been some sort of trouble with us not being a full day's ride down the road anyhow."

"Why not? Oh, you think someone among his soldiers is a traitor and might talk?"

"Not really, Itharo will have picked the men carefully, but you know what my father always says."

Together they chorused, "The best way of getting out of trouble is not to get into it in the first place."

"Exactly. No, I don't think Chell's got a traitor with him. What I do think is that a soldier might not think harm to take coin just to chatter to the payer about minor events on the road. Or he could get drunk and talk. I don't want there to be any apparent connection between Chell and us, not the smallest hint of a connection. It may come to where we have to meet him openly, but until then, I don't want any gossip that can be reported."

"Makes sense. On another topic, shaya, do we need a replacement for Jiro? Or can we manage without him?" As they talked they were erecting their own tent, laying out their bedding from one of the mules, and, with that task completed, walking into the roadside brush to find dry firewood.

Tiah picked up a handful of sticks and groaned. "Oh stars! Yes, that could be a problem, but not a bad one really, we *could* manage shorthanded if we have to?"

"It might not be a problem anyway," Kait said thought-fully. "Don't you remember saying to me earlier that Shirin would be back at the compound with his people by now?"

"Yes. I don't want him out here, he'll be tired from his trip but I suppose he could send us Farni. He lives in Surah and he'd be taking temporary work to get home anyway."

Kait shook her head firmly. "No, I'd rather do without that man. I don't like him, I don't want him traveling with us for days, and I certainly don't want him snooping around either our caravan or our people."

Tiah raised an inquiring eyebrow. "Why?"

"I can't say, heart-sister. All I can tell you is that I don't trust the man. I don't believe he has any loyalties. I saw him for the tenday after Shirin hired him and before they left for the border. I think he's one of those people who works for money—from anyone."

"You don't think he's mixed up in this somehow, do you?" Tiah asked despairingly. "You know, shaya, I'm starting to be-come paranoid. I keep wondering if everyone we meet may not be involved somehow."

Kait chuckled. "No, I don't think we have to worry about that. But I'd wager someone besides us is paying him. He had eyes everywhere as soon as he was in the compound."

"Oh, another trader?"

"I'd say so, and I'd planned to mention it to Shirin once we met up again. But do we want even another trader getting long reports about everything any of us have said or done?"

"No, we do not." Tiah was clear on that. "All right, we man-age without a replacement." She considered that. "We could stay a bit closer to Chell and his soldiers too, if we're careful not to let them wonder about it."

Kait added a small chunk of rotten wood to her gleanings

and headed back to where the fire was dancing nicely around the pata kettle. They ate, talked casually, and, once it became fully dark, checked Jiro's bandages again. Kait held the lantern closer.

"The bleeding's stopped. I won't disturb the final layer in case I start it again," Tiah said to Jessara. "Give him another half dose of the hashas juice after moonhigh."

And to the others, "We stand double watch tonight. Just in case that lot who attacked us isn't the only one around."

Kait moaned. Double watch meant two by two, which in turn meant that no one would be getting more than a half night's sleep. That would be complicated by the fact that Chell would most likely be slipping in to see them. Although—if they managed that the right way they could stand their watch and still talk to him without anyone seeing. She sent a quick burst of mental pictures to her shaya, and received agreement.

"We'll take first watch in another candlemark." She was counting. "It'll be ninth 'mark after noon by then. We'll stand watch until two after moonhigh. Give Jiro the hashas juice when you start your watch and we can give him another half dose before we have to move him in the morning. Finish the pata, bank the fire, and get to your bedding. We're going to be working longer hours from here on."

Knowing the truth of that, no one lingered. In much less than a candlemark the camp was silent, the three employees asleep in their tent while Kait silently prowled the perimeter. Tiah sat near their tent, which had been set up at a reasonable distance from the other. Her gaze was carefully averted from the glow of the fire during the time that she waited. Kait drifted back a half candlemark later, a dark figure following her silently. It circled their tent, entered, and lay flat on the bedding. If any of their employees woke they would see only Kait and Tiah standing watch by the tent, talking idly—in tones too low for the words to be distinguished—between walking rounds of the camp perimeter.

"You camped early, the road bears the marks of fighting—yes, I saw the blood—and you're standing double watch," the figure observed in a low voice that would not carry to those in the second tent. "Just what trouble have you two been finding now?"

When they told him, their visitor swore. "What were the arms on this medallion you found? A daska and a dravencat?" He dug into his memory and snarled softly as it came to him. "Well, well, this goes deeper than we thought it might. Those are the arms for old Lord Varli, Cleeono's father-in-law. But why would he be having traders murdered on the road?"

"As we think the bandit said," Kait pointed out. "Because someone saw us talking to someone and assumed either that we were involved and dangerous, or that we could learn too much and talk in turn. But I don't like any of this, Chell."

"And you think I do?" was the retort. "Look, Itharo is only a couple of days back toward the city. I'll break up our lot and four of them can take your man back to Itharo. I'll send a letter with them to make sure different men take him on to the city. Dasheri can lead them. He's no fool, he'll make sure no one gossips. I'll go on for a couple of candlemarks ahead of you but I'll make the excuse that because of the bandits I want the road scouted both ways." His grin showed in the moonlight.

"I'll slow us each afternoon so that once we camp we're only an hour apart. I'll stay in touch and if there's any trouble, send Jessara to me. If you can't do that, detach the mule string and send them running my way. Any genuine bandits will either stop fighting you and chase them or, if they don't, you'll know they have another agenda."

"In which case we do what?"

"Make a *very* determined effort to get Jessara clear and to stay alive," Chell muttered. "Itharo and I would be seriously annoyed if anything happened to you two. So would your father and brother—and I don't want them blaming me for it. I'm going back to my camp. Stay where you are in the morning; I'll move out early. I know we all know each other, but play it as if we don't. Just in case anyone's watching from a distance."

Both women nodded, and he rolled from the tent opening, moving into the brush without sound. Tiah glanced up at the sky. Pasht but she was tired, and this business was becoming more confusing by the 'markin. She set off to walk the camp bounds while Kait circled in the opposite direction. They kept moving until it was near the time the watch would change. Then they met and spoke together before waking Gheevin.

Katchellin was there in the morning, asking officious questions, going to look over the bodies, listening to a tale of bandits and injury and shouting orders. He gave no indication he had ever met any of them before, and if his men knew differently— and some did—they were careful to follow his lead. He openly borrowed paper, quill, and Tiah's small traveling inkpot while Jiro was dosed again, and wrote a letter to send back with the wounded man and the four soldiers transporting him. Jiro's bundle of personal possessions was placed beside him on the litter while he was tucked into his own bedding. Katchellin looked over his arrangements and nodded politely to the traders, speaking quite loudly and very clearly.

"I can't remain with you. My orders are to patrol this section of the road in case of bandits, but since it seems that there definitely are bandits, I'll patrol farther down the road. My orders give me discretion as to distance. There was word that several small caravans would be leaving Mirray shortly. I'll patrol toward Mirray just in case. I have no wish to be rude, but we don't need to have civilians underfoot. However, I'll make no objection if you wish to stay within a reasonable distance of our camp."

Tiah bowed ceremoniously. "All gratitude to you, Captain, for your kindness to our employee. And yes, we would indeed welcome your camp's proximity while you travel in the same direction."

Katchellin drew himself up. "Ah, well, only my duty."

"A duty well done. I shall be sure to see that your superiors hear of it on our return to the city," Tiah assured him, keeping her face straight as the group split, a drowsing Jiro being borne off to the northwest in the litter, while Katchellin and his six men rode briskly west. Tiah turned to look at the camp and those who'd remained.

"All right. Time we were moving on too. I don't want them getting too far ahead of us in case there's more of those Pasht-cursed bandits about." Her voice too was loud and clear, and she made no sign when Kait mind-sent.

Chell was right. There is someone watching. I saw a flash of glass in the scrub on that rise.

Far-seer, you think?

I suspect so, another pointer to the nobility. But what member of the nobility would be out here spying on traders? That's someone who's been given the far-seer and orders to watch us.

Tiah was exasperated. *What *is* all this, shaya? What do they think that Varsheean told us—or we told Varsheean—and how do they think that spying on us and sending men to murder us will help their plans? We know nothing, we're doing nothing much, and all they're doing in turn is to tell us that something's going on.*

Kait sent amusement. *It is said that only the guilty flee when no one pursues. And thus do evil plots come to nothing,* she added sententiously.

Very proper, Tiah returned. *But I'd like to know about these plots myself. I'm becoming very curious—as well as confused.*

As am I, heart-sister. Let us see if we can find answers in Mirray. Since many of the conspirators seem to be there, perhaps we'll discover something there too.

Probably more people wanting to murder us, Tiah sent glumly. *I wonder when we became so unpopular?*

In reply she received a chuckle and pictures of Kait being stalked by a shadowy figure. Kait slunk around a corner and took the stalker by the throat once he too rounded the bend and came within her reach. Tiah grinned. Yes, their bandit had talked even if he hadn't known much. If they could lay hands on a conspirator in Mirray it was possible he'd know more—and could talk more informatively. If that were so they'd both be very pleased to listen. It was becoming irritating to feel themselves in the middle of vast events without the faintest idea of how or why. She'd welcome a little enlightenment.

A bit of that came while they rode alone behind their employees and the pack-mule string.

"Do you think Varli married his daughter to Cleeono to bind him into the conspiracy? Or did he only join after she married the duke and was all this Cleeono's idea?" Kait asked.

"I have no idea. I didn't even remember that those were his arms until Chell said so," Tiah replied. "I knew they were familiar; I'd seen those once or twice before, but that was all.

I can remember my father talking about the family once with a trader who knows them. From everything I can recall about Varli's family he has a fairly large estate on the far side of Shallahah but his land backs onto the desert so it isn't as valuable as it seems. There's plenty of land, yes, but it's not very fertile. His isn't an old family in the direct line either, it's a cadet branch of the—" Her voice trailed away abruptly and she froze.

"A cadet branch?" Kait prompted.

The reply came slowly. "A cadet branch of the royal house. I don't remember all the details. I may never have heard them. But about four generations ago Varli's great-grandfather married the youngest daughter of the then king. He already had a title, some kind of minor nobility that was quite long-standing, so the match wasn't completely unsuitable. The king gave him that land by the desert and the family have lived there in obscurity ever since."

"Are they wealthy?"

"Comfortable, I think, not rich. But they aren't fashionable, don't bother with court, and it's one of Father's friends who usually does that circuit to trade."

"But they are of royal descent and legitimate descent at that," Kait commented. "And maybe it's recently occurred to them that it would be nice to be a bit closer to the throne. We've been assuming that most of what's been going on is unrelated. Maybe it isn't. Maybe it's part of the same plot and we all have different ends and loops of the tangle."

"That's possible, and I think we should mention it to Chell the moment we have the chance."

Their discussion of the ramifications of Varli, Treyvan, Varsheean, the king, Varli's daughter, and the kidnapping of the tariling lasted until they camped. When there was no sign of Katchellin that night, Tiah fretted.

"We need to tell him about this. Varsheean should know."

"He probably does, dear heart."

"I know, but in case he doesn't."

Kait shrugged. "He'll be here when he can be. Right now, though, we need to wake the others and get some sleep."

With that done they were able to crawl into their bedding. They were too tired to talk further, but Tiah's last angry thought was that too many of the nobility were selfish arrogant fools. Shallahah had a good king, Cleeono wouldn't be a better one under any circumstances, and all Varli and that pack of half-wits would accomplish was to kill a number of people and to cause the loss of their heads for everyone involved in this plot. Dimly she felt Kait's agreement before sleep drowned them both.

*K*atchellin arrived secretly the following night. Kait nudged her the moment he appeared. "Tell him about Varli?" she hissed.

Tiah could almost see Chell's ears prick up at the name. "Varli, what do you know about him?"

"Very little." She repeated almost everything she'd managed to remember, holding the one item for the last.

Because of his background Chell had the occasional gap in his knowledge of noble families. And that bit about Varli's house was something many people wouldn't know or might not recall anyway. During her ride she'd finally pinned down the memory of where she'd learned it. It was something her father had spoken about. Not to her, but to his friend who traded that circuit, while Tiah was within hearing and before she and Kait struck out as traders on their own. That made it more than eighteen years ago, but she'd always been interested in talk about the nobility and how best to sell to them.

She fell silent after telling him all but that final memory, and Katchellin looked at her. "There's something else, isn't there?"

She nodded. "It may be nothing or it may be the motive behind a lot of this." She explained the origins of Varli's house, and Chell whistled very softly.

"I didn't know, and it's possible that Varsheean and the others don't remember either. I'd say it wasn't a bad motive. The throne's changed hands a number of times over the centuries, and not always within the direct bloodline either. The king's great-grandfather had been called Ishika Ruthless—in some quarters. When he was twenty-one he took the throne in a coup from his half-uncle. He got away with it and his line's ruled now for four generations. So Varli's daughter is in direct descent from him as is the king."

"And the king still has a number of cousins who are closer to him in blood," Tiah commented.

Katchellin looked at her. "Does he? And who are they? Women, and most of them either too old, too young, or sworn to a shrine."

"He has cubs," Kait put in quietly.

"Oh, yes, indeed he has." There was a taint of sarcasm overlying the agreement. "Fine children too. Just consider them, how old they are, and who their dam is."

The women glanced at each other, knowing the point he made. The king had only been wed two and half years and his children were eighteen-month-old twin girls and a babe in arms. His princess was from one of the tribes beyond the Grass Sea—tribes considered by her adopted people to consist solely of barbarians—and, while most people liked her, the nobles of Shallahah would never consent to her direct rule. Nor would they be happy with her as regent for more than fifteen years.

"No," Tiah agreed. "They'd want one of their own to take

the crown, or be regent if not outright ruler, and there are several powerful nobles suitable."

The mischief—as they all knew—lay in the word "several."

Katchellin was muttering to himself. Tiah nudged him and his words became more audible.

"So the king dies in an attack by sorcery from the plains. Maybe a number of major nobles and many of the women of his house are killed too. The surviving nobles would howl for a war leader. They'd want an adult male to take the throne immediately, someone to give any necessary orders and strike at the plains tribes and clans to avenge their dead. Things were very touchy with some of the clans beyond the Grass Sea when our current king came to power. That was why his father chose him to be the heir. Varli wouldn't expect to take the throne; he's too old and he's never had the name of a warrior."

"No," Tiah almost whispered. "But Cleeono is wed to a daughter of the blood of Ishika Ruthless—and Cleeono was one of those who rode to punish the plains clans twenty years ago. It could be argued that he knows the plains, the clans there, and has proven his ability to deal with them once. If he already has heirs he would do well as a compromise."

"And he does," Katchellin snarled softly. "Twins run in Ishika's line and Cleeono's new lady bore him twins, a boy and a girl."

Both women stared at him. "When?" Kait asked. "I never even heard she was bearing."

"And isn't that something to note?" Katchellin said. "It's usual to announce such a thing the moment the healers are certain. She isn't some shopkeeper's wife and no one would be interested. This is the duchess of Mirray we're talking about. But they kept it quiet right until she was almost due. Varsheean got word to me yesterday that she'd borne a son and daughter. I couldn't come last night after that. I was sitting in my tent writing everything I'd learned so far from you and elsewhere and all the possible conclusions I'd drawn." He heaved a dramatic sigh.

"And I suppose I'll be doing the same thing about this conversation the rest of tonight."

Kait grinned cheerfully. "You thrive on it, Chell. But you still haven't said. How long ago did she have her twins?"

He sobered. "Three tendays ago."

"After which everything started happening," Kait commented. "But there wouldn't have been time."

"No." Tiah glanced at Katchellin. "Not if they'd waited to start a conspiracy until the twins arrived. But they'd have known she was bearing eight moons ago. Besides which they could count on a period of internal running in circles in Shallahah if the king and some of the great lords were killed. Count back, shaya. It's only been a couple of tendays since someone kidnapped that tariling. The sorcerer probably knew when the portal would open. The shrines often do if they're close to where it will happen. I'd make a guess that the portal opened on the far side of the plains where his old clan lived, and that he knew it would. Maybe he's been planning all of this for years— which would give him time to find willing conspirators."

Katchellin nodded slowly. "Something for everyone. The sorcerer gets his revenge on the king who burned the plains. Cleeono and Varli get ultimate power. Their hangers-on get the promise of being back in Shallahah, richer, and perhaps of a higher rank—since if a lot of court nobles have been killed then their estates and titles are available. Varli's daughter is queen and the mother of the new royal line, and Treyvan—"

"Probably gets his throat cut," Kait broke in cynically. "As will any other minor players in this little drama. The whole thing is not to have people guess that who was responsible for the death of the king—and probably hundreds of other innocent people, many of whom could be friends and relations of Cleeono's people in Mirray."

"Agreed. The trick is to appear as saviors," Katchellin summed up. "So we have two chances. We need to stop the sacrifice, or keep the portal from being opened. But if we fail in both hopes, we need to have reliable witnesses to what happened, who was responsible, and if possible we need some sort of solid proof of who ordered this."

"And if we fail and the sacrifice is made," Tiah continued. "If the portal is opened and the Kalthi come through when called. We need to have the king prepared to hide while his soldiers protect the city. He'd be the one the Kalthi attack first, him and his kin."

Katchellin looked at her in silence for a moment before he spoke. "And you both know the king. He won't do that," he said, his tone resigned. "He isn't a coward, he won't permit himself to be seen that way, and yes, Varsheean could make him understand the danger to Shallahah if he's murdered, but I'm telling you. He still won't hide."

Kait half fisted her hands and flexed her fighting claws between her knuckles. "Then we have only to see that there's no sacrifice," she said. "Or that it's the right one. I wonder what would happen if I tossed the sorcerer through instead of the sacrifice when he opens his portal? Orla said the sacrifice needed to be someone from another world."

Katchellin snickered. "I don't know what that'd do, but as you say, it could be fascinating to see. Maybe the Kalthi would all turn blue and drop dead."

Kait's laugh blended with his amusement. "Maybe the sorcerer would too. I think it's an experiment I'd enjoy trying."

Tiah looked at them. "It may be one that we have to make in the end," she said soberly. "But before we can do anything like that we may need to speak to friends in Surah, find the sorcerer, find where he plans to set up his portal—if that's in Mirray—and send word of all this to Varsheean. He may be able to help. I hope he can, because unless we know more I'm scared for us all."

18

Kian Dae was bored. Traveling was usually tiring, jolting, or interesting. Here he was quite simply bored, and that showed no sign of changing in the near future. Over his head they were talking again.

"Do you think that she was right?"

"Child, the Moon Lady speaks only truth. She showed me this place and said it was there we should go. I am hers, I obey."

Aycharna grinned. "It's a lot more comfortable than my last journey."

"The clan has a care for my old bones."

"And a care for bandits."

Dharvath peered from the horse litter and smiled at the ten heavily armed and alert Aradian warriors who surrounded it. "Yes, indeed. We travel in style and comfort."

"But not quickly."

"There was no demand that we be swift, only that we be there."

"Where is there? You never said."

"I'll know when we arrive." Her tone was of one content to do a superior's bidding.

Aycharna subsided into the cushioned comfort while Kian Dae curled up more firmly, laid his tail over his nose, and relaxed under Dharvath's stroking hand. Of course, travel wasn't entirely bad when you had regular meals and got the amount of attention he received. These odd people seemed to honor a cat just as they should. He missed his humans, though, and he only hoped that they were moving toward them the way she had said. No doubt they'd be pleased to see him. His people always were.

A day's ride short of the Surahan border Sepallo was becoming weary. The constant riding, watching over his captive, holding the spare mounts to following the ridden beasts, all that was exhausting over the long days and nights. He was relentless in his purpose, but no matter how determined the mind, in time the body wears out. He was nearing Surah too. He'd have to ride through both Lhandes, and nothing must look suspicious. He regarded Ashara darkly. She'd escape if she could, scream for help if she had the chance. There must be some way he could safely silence her and which wouldn't drain more of his energy in new spells.

Sepallo brooded until a thought came to him. Hashas tea! If he fed that to her just before they reached Surah City, claimed she was mind-damaged and that he as a relative was taking her back to other kin in Mirray, and if they rode through the night? That might well serve. He had none of the herb, but he had coin still, he could bind and hide the woman, go into the city and buy the hashas, then return for her. Yes indeed, that plan should work and she'd suffer no injury. She would even have a respite from the fears she undoubtedly suffered. He was being kind rather than cruel and his Yalana would have approved. He rode on with a lighter heart.

Ashara shivered. She'd seen how he was slumped deep in thought. She'd also seen that he had come to a conclusion and thought that it probably meant something bad for her. Tonight she must somehow leave word for those she hoped had followed her. She prayed harder and, watching her captor, cautiously tossed out another crystal.

*T*hree candlemarks behind her, a circle of her friends and kin gathered around a map laid out on the ground. Dayshan and Yoros talked quietly with Kyrryl, Eilish, Trasso, Sirado, and Orla. Dayshan was looking worried.

"I think she may be running out of the crystals. I've noticed that they're farther apart."

Kyrryl was counting. "Not yet. But she has to have some idea by now that he's going all of the way down the coast and then around the end of the mountains. Orla, did she ever see this map that you recall?"

"She did. I remember her commenting."

"Then if she can remember what she saw she should know the trail he's taking."

Sirado looked up from studying the map. "There's one thing that worries me." Their attention focused on him. "Look, it's all right for him if he's going to Surah. What if it's Mirray he wants?"

Everyone looked blank for a moment until Eilish gave a small cry. "Of course, how does he get her through Surah without her yelling for help. Even if she's permitted him to think she doesn't understand or speak the language here, a scream can talk in any language."

Orla shrugged. "Not necessarily. He has only to say she's his daughter and mad. Few will interfere with a man's family affairs. If she demanded aid in Pasht's name then they might, but would she know to do so?" She watched as one by one they shook their heads. "No, I feared not." She looked down at the map, then up again at the faces that surrounded it.

"There is something you are not considering. How far behind him are we now? It seems likely that it's only hours."

"Less than half a day I would say, lady." Yoros nodded.

"Then let us ride harder still. If we can be almost on his heels when he enters Surah people who see him pass may recall him more easily. If we have a good tale to explain why we're after them, then people will talk to us. What money is available?"

Yoros cursed. "Not much, and what we have isn't from here."

"No matter, the money changers in Surah will weigh and trade it as metal of whatever kind. If any official questions you, keep to your tale that you are from one of the tribes to the far side of the Grass Sea, here to see the wonders of civilization."

Sirado contrived to look offended. "Are you saying that we look like barbarians?"

"You don't look like people we know," Orla said dryly. "That will do."

"Won't they question the story if we say we're from far away but speak your language?" Kyrryl questioned.

"No, they'll just applaud your taste in learning it from the traders who visit you. Look wide-eyed at the wonders of their city. If anyone talks to you, admire the buildings, talk about how well paved the streets are, and comment on how their shops hold marvelous things. Be awestruck and deferential. It's a good story, it means that everyone will make allowances for any minor errors you make." She thought a moment. "And we can use that to ask about Ashara."

"How?" Dayshan was interested.

"You tell them that she's one of your tribe, that she ran away from her husband with a traveling trickster and you want her back. Say that she stole coin and jewelry from several people before she fled. That you believe it was under his influence. That way if we do catch up to her in Surah, and can make a noise about it, the peacekeepers will haul us all in. I can call for a priestess of Pasht, talk to her privately, and we may be able to get your kinswoman back without difficulty once there's her testimony that she's been abducted."

"What will they do to the sorcerer if you tell someone what he plans?" Eilish asked. "Will they imprison him?"

"That depends on him." Orla shrugged. "I can't speak for what he'll do. He's mad."

Dayshan stood and stretched. "We're losing time. I say we leapfrog again. One thing, milady Orla: Have you any idea what the trails are like at the Surahan border? It occurs to me that the higher trail may have to drop down to cross the border. If that's so it might be possible for two of us to ride fast for the border now and make up some of the time that will take him."

Orla considered. "Yes, one to find out, one to ride back. But better four of us, three to ride on into Surah, one to change the coin, two to follow, one to return for the others."

Yoros spoke up. "Kyrryl and I will be those who follow. Best you are our money changer, Orla. You could also tell our tale there and perhaps rouse some assistance. You'll know what to say and you can claim you met us and wanted to help."

Her eyes twinkled. "You do not know the clans of the

plains. We are seldom helpful save in the matter of relieving those who travel of the weight of their goods."

Yoros was abruptly exasperated. "Say whatever seems best. We have no time to waste in this. Eilish, you ride light. Will you come with us three and return once we know if they have already crossed the border?"

"Willingly."

He too stood and turned toward the saddled horses. "Then I say we go now, without delay. We may have to make temporary camp for the night, but if we ride now we may be at the border by sunhigh tomorrow."

He mounted his horse and Kyrryl joined him on her own beast, while Orla and Eilish looked at them. Eilish nodded.

"It makes sense." Both stepped into their saddles and rode forward. Eilish looked down at her brother and husband. "I'll return tomorrow. Keep following Ashara's crystals. If her captor turns off somewhere we need to have an idea of what he does."

She put her horse in motion after the other three, who were already moving down the trail. Yoros heeled his mount for a little more speed. After too many days it was exhilarating to think that in another day or two he could have his niece back with them. Farazyn and Vershai would never forgive him if he let something happen to their daughter. And after he got Ashara back he'd never leave home again.

He glanced sideways at Orla. This world was interesting, they'd made friends, but he missed his home, his kin, and the familiar land over which he usually rode. He held back a sigh. Everything that had happened appeared to be for a good purpose, with this sorcerer to blame for most of the bad events. He only wished that next time there was a need it would be someone else chosen—and none of his kin either.

Orla rode quietly, thinking. Last night the crystal whisper had awakened her. She'd listened. None of this evil was of the Lady's doing, but she knew best how to stitch ripped events together again until what had been wrong was made right. A wise one of the plains was no less hers because they used different forms of worship and built no permanent shrines. What the Lady required, those who were sworn to her would do.

Back at the tail of those who followed, Hailin was hopeful. He'd listened while his betters talked, said nothing, but learned much. They were only a day or two away from a city. They hoped to catch up to the sorcerer there, but what if Hailin could somehow deflect them? He'd have to let the man know how he'd helped, of course, but then he might be grateful. Hailin smiled at the thought of just *how* grateful the sorcerer might be. He and his servants seemed to have gold and jewels enough; a few more for the services Hailin could render would be nothing. He smiled more widely to himself, not noticing the eyes that watched his self-satisfaction—and wondered.

Roshan said nothing, but he was considering his fellow servant's smirk, and disliking the look of it. He didn't trust Hailin as far as he could have thrown him one-handed against a high wind, and if he was so happy it must be about something to his own benefit. Hailin was money-hungry and never happy for others. Roshan, less quick thinking and more stolid then his fellow servant, still decided to watch the fellow. You couldn't trust him where something for nothing was concerned.

On the Shallahah-Lhandes road Kait and Tiah jogged along ahead of their employees and the pack-mule string. They'd be making camp once they saw a suitable place to halt their caravan. It had been a half tenday since the bandit attack, and messages by fast courier had come and gone from Varsheean. The threads were slowly coming together.

They were moving faster toward Mirray. They must get through the new Lhandes of Mirray as fast as they possibly could, sell their merchandise in Surah, then return to Mirray. It would take fast work and hard riding over a tenday, but Varsheean wanted to know any gossip they might pick up. Kait turned her mount off the road.

"Here's a good spot, shaya. It's no distance to the stream for water, there's dry wood, and shelter. Our tent goes here." She pointed. "Their tent can go there."

Tiah grinned approval at her. The tents would be a useful distance apart, enough for Chell to come and go without attracting Jessara or Gheevin's notice. She would be interested to see his latest message from Varsheean. The last message said that the spymaster felt that it was time that his king knew some of what was going on.

They made a comfortable camp, hung the pata kettle over the fire, and tucked the stewpot into the red-hot coals to one side. Jessara and Gheevin unsaddled the mules and rubbed them down carefully before hobbling them and returning to eat by the fire.

"Usual system," Kait said. "My shaya and I will take watch until two 'marks past moonhigh. Then I'll call you. Sleep sound until them." She watched as they headed for their tent before turning to Tiah. "Loosen the back of the tent. If there's real news Chell may come early while there's still some light and if so it'll be safer for him to come under the back where they can't see him."

Tiah wandered into their tent to do that and was just raising the back when a whisper came.

"Tiah?"

"Chell? We though you might be early if there was any major news. Come under, quickly." His familiar figure rolled under the tent edge and into a sitting position to grin at her.

"I did and there is. Where's Kait?"

"Around and about." Her leaner shape joined them, shadowing the tent mouth. "I'll listen from here and keep watch."

Katchellin took a breath and began. "Varsheean got word to me only an hour ago. I'll read what he says; then we can talk." He removed from the breast of his tunic two thin sheets of paper, folded and sealed but with the seal now broken. He unfolded them and began to read in low tones.

" 'I have told the king of all I know in this matter believing it to be the right time. He has given me free rein, saying that he trusts me to work in his interest and knowing that Katchellin would never do otherwise also.'" In the growing dusk the women could still see Chell redden a little with pride as he said those last words.

" 'Blank warrants follow you signed by the king's hand. Thus says the king! If there is clear proof that men have conspired to regicide and murder. If they have conspired to the destruction of the lives and property of those in Shallahah and in a Lhandes that is not their own. Then shall such warrants be executed and those who have conspired shall be returned to me, the king, for judgment, and for death if the charges be proven. Yet if this is not possible but you have proof you believe to be convincing, and the danger is great, at need shall you execute those responsible by proxy in my place, and at your hands shall it be deemed proper. I shall trust your own judgment in this, and at need you may speak of what is known to my good friend and fellow ruler, Duke Tassino of Surah.

And should such conspirators be citizen of his Lhandes of Surah, then the judgment and Justice shall be in his hands.'"

Katchellin looked up from the papers. "In other words, we have almost unlimited power to do whatever we think is right and best at the time, including killing the sorcerer, Duke Cleeono, and his kin and court and telling the whole story to Tassino."

"And the king can then second-guess it all," Kait said dryly.

"Why?"

"He does say twice that we have to have proof. What proof do you think we're going to get?"

Katchellin grunted. It might have been in acknowledgment, or in sardonic amusement. "Yes, I suppose he does, but you could hardly expect him to say in writing that we can kill anyone we like in someone else's Lhandes on the remote possibility they've done something he wouldn't approve. We make the judgment that there's sufficient proof then stand by it if there's trouble. If there isn't enough proof he can deny what we've done . . . and us." He grinned at them. "If we kill the right people no one will be around to complain anyhow."

Kait rolled her eyes. "Great. That's your solution, is it? Have a massacre. Not that it matters. I'd say that if we do catch up to this sorcerer, well, the last we heard he had a stolen creature from another world, and plans to use it as a sacrifice to open a portal for the Kalthi, surely that will be enough for us to damn him. If we do get out hands on him either he knows what he's doing and he'll talk thinking to save his life or he's crazy and will probably talk anyway wanting to explain how right he is about what he'd planned to do. And if Cleeono and his family really are behind this I can't imagine that they won't be on the spot watching when the portal opens and the Kalthi arrive, to make sure that their interests are served."

"I'm sure the Kalthi will serve their own interests."

"You know what I mean. Cleeono's interests. And if he and his family and court are there and we prevent the portal being opened, or if it does and the Kalthi don't eat the lot of them, we'll still be waiting to grab Cleeono—with the king's warrant in writing."

"I can't help but wonder about Cleeono," Tiah commented. "He hasn't the reputation of being a stupid man. But first he may have been involved in a plot to assassinate the king, now this. What does he think he's doing?"

Katchellin shrugged. "Who knows. Maybe someone, his wife, or Lord Varli, is influencing him. Or greed and ambition have overcome common sense. If you look at what's happened we've been lucky. The Kalthi portal could have been opened without warning and the first we knew about that would have been a horde of demons overrunning Shallahah."

"Orla thinks they might overrun wherever they are when they came through first," Kait said dryly.

"And then move on. So either way they're a danger." Tiah looked at her. "I'm not enthusiastic about the Kalthi being here under any circumstances." Since Kait agreed she made no reply to that.

Tiah spoke again thoughtfully. "I think we get Tassino's warrant as well if we can, and maybe a few of his men for backup. I do think that we should tell him about this, and ask for help. You know he thinks he owes Kait and me for what we did a few years back. And I hardly think he'll like the idea of a mad sorcerer opening a portal to call Kalthi into Mirray with the chance they'll attack his Lhandes next door too."

Katchellin looked at Kait. "Yes, we do have access to him," she confirmed. "Yes he will listen to us, yes, he'll probably help, and no, he isn't likely to be happy at all about that last bit. Does that answer all the questions you were going to ask?"

"Yes."

"Then I suggest you get some sleep. It wouldn't be a bad idea if we moved faster from now on." He nodded, slid back under the tent edge, and disappeared into the growing darkness, leaving the shayana to eat then start their watch.

*T*hey traveled more quickly the next four days—not at a much greater speed, but by breaking camp earlier and not halting until the edge of darkness. Either Kait or Tiah would ride ahead and choose the campsite, gather wood, and start a fire; by doing this they were moving more quickly, but it was tiring for all concerned. Tiah, however, had become worried about the time they were taking, and Katchellin agreed, so they continued with the system. A day short of Mirray he slid under the back of the tent after dark with news that startled the women.

"I've gotten a letter by courier from Varsheean. It seems he too has a feeling that events may be coming to a head and he wants to be in the right place before then." He stared at the paper. "You may not believe this, but he's gone over Jasta Pass to the coast, and intends to take ship to Surah. From there some of his people will have arranged guards and he'll be going on to Mirray on the main Lhandes road."

Tiah gaped. "He gets seasick," she said flatly.

"I know." Katchellin looked at them. "He really does, so take it as a measure of how seriously he takes this, that he'd go by ship all the way down the coast."

Kait was thinking about that. "Chell's right. Look at the

result. From Shallahah to Mirray by the road, even on horse-back with no delays, is ten or thirteen days' riding. A ship wait-ing on the coast on the other side of the pass at this season will catch the winds for another month. They switch between southwest and southeast but a ship can tack on them. They'll have to be careful on that coast. They need to stand well out, and getting into Surah can be tricky, but it's still a faster trip. We have another day to Mirray, two after that to Surah, a day's trading there, and two days back. And that's before we can even be in a position to start asking around in another five days." She looked at Katchellin. "When would he have caught the ship?"

"If there were no delays after he wrote this, it would take him two days to be over the pass and down on the coast by fast relay. If the ship was waiting he'll be sailing tomorrow morning."

"And at this season with the winds, he could make it from there to Surah in three days. So if we aren't delayed we may meet him there. Do you know where he's likely to be, Chell?"

Katchellin grinned. "He'll probably be at the Inn of the Dravencat."

Tiah groaned. "I see."

Kait looked at her. "You see what, shaya?"

"Years ago my father recommended that inn to us if we ever went to Surah to trade." She made an exasperated sound in the back of her throat. "He just never mentioned that it was a hotbed of spies. I should have known. That's why Varsheean was pleased to find us there five years ago when we had all that business with the bandits who weren't bandits."

Katchellin nodded. "I'd think so. We've used that inn be-fore. I suspect Tassino knows all about it by now, but he'd leave it alone on the principle that it's better to know where your enemy is than have to hunt for him. And it doesn't necessarily label you spies if you use the place. Other traders use it, and ordinary travelers too."

Kait looked at Tiah. "We could drop Jessara and Gheevin in Surah, though. Leave most of the mules with them to trade what they carry, sell the spare mules at Surah, all but Kotu and his pack, and ride to Mirray again. That could cut a day off the round trip for us?"

Tiah nodded. It would, and the more she heard the more she was afraid that time was running out. She'd quietly interrogated Orla for everything the woman could tell her about the Kalthi, and she'll suggested to her father that he go back to the palace archives and glean any information from them on anything that could be done to protect people from the Kalthi. If there was anything that might save lives, he would pass it on to Neira, who'd pass it on to the king. Even so, if the Kalthi were called successfully a lot of people were probably going to die.

Most of a day later she was still thinking about that when the Mirrayan guards checked them through the opening where the city gate would be—once they had that as well as walls around the city that were more than a bare shoulder height. Her gaze was busy as they passed through the growing number of buildings, through the streets that were being paved, and the shops, ranging from open-fronted roofless stalls to recently built better quality shops, clearly owned by well-to-do merchants, displaying expensive merchandise, a guard at the door. Every time she came through here it was larger and busier, dirtier and noisier.

It was near dark when she halted the small caravan. "We'll stay here but I want us on the road before first light." She waited for Jessara and Gheevin to say something, but both eyed her and merely nodded.

"All right, make camp."

The night was warm enough but too short, she thought when they started out the next morning. Only streaks of lights were visible as yet and she really missed her warm bedding. Oh, well. If they pushed their travel again today they'd be in Surah by late tonight. They could go straight to the inn and take a room, and she could have a hot bath and fall into bed with her shaya. Chell had said that he too would be moving faster; he should be only a 'mark in time behind them. Please Pasht that the inn had enough hot water and not too many other guests. She was very happy to discover on arrival that her prayers seemed to have been answered on both points.

Kait came in from the inn's stables. "No sign of anyone we know, heart-sister. Two trader caravans left yesterday to return to Shallahah, so the inn's only half full. They'll have a bath sent up for you in a half 'mark, food at any moment. I've arranged for Jessara and Gheevin to have our usual place at the market and paid for a room for them for a week. I've told them we'll be staying the night but taking Kotu and leaving for Mirray again about sunhigh."

"Ahhhh, you mean I can sleep in?"

Kait laughed affectionately. "I know what you mean. This whole trip it's been as if we're wading through high water. We keep trying to make up time and never seem to catch up to events. Don't worry, things will work out—at least I hope that they will."

Tiah hugged her silently. Kait was a fatalist in some ways. She did her best and left it at that. Tiah was more of a worrier. She would have worried her way to bed and lain sleepless through the night but for Kait. She'd seen to it that the food was hot, plentiful, and mostly Tiah's favorite dishes. The bath was hotter and the massage she gave her heart-sister after that was relaxing—the loving that followed still more so. Despite her tendency to worry, Tiah had little energy left. She slept worry-free and dreamlessly all night in the bed at the inn.

*A*s she slept Sepallo departed Surah with Ashara swaying vacant-eyed on her mount. He'd judged the dosage very well, he thought. She'd been reluctant to drink her tea but he'd been adamant, kind but firm. She'd obeyed him as she must. He'd been fortunate; in the brief stop he'd made just inside the Surah border, to buy more provisions for the road, he'd met a small, fat, garrulous, and well-intentioned fool.

"I'm going to the far side of the Surah Lhandes myself, sir. I live near the road to Mirray and you and your afflicted daughter are welcome to ride with me if it would please you. I can tell you I've lived here all my life and I know every shortcut if I do say so myself. I can get through the streets faster than anyone I know. Yes, you're most welcome to ride along with me. The company of an intelligent man is always welcome."

He continued to chatter while they rode, and Sepallo made no objection. The man seemed to know many in the city and be on good terms with everyone. It made Sepallo and his captive less conspicuous, and it seemed to be true enough that their companion knew all the shortcuts. They neatly by-passed crowded streets, blocked alleyways, and city quarters that might be dangerous to unwary travelers.

Sepallo bit back a disdainful snort at the constant talking. The man was a chattering idiot, but useful enough, Sepallo mused. That was what men of his kind were for, to be of use to others who were more intelligent. In much less time than he'd expected they were on the far side of Surah City and their guide was biding them an effusive farewell.

"I must leave you here, sir. My wife will be expecting me

and one can't disappoint a lady." He guffawed. "Not if you want to stay in her good graces you can't. It's been a pleasant ride, in excellent company. Maybe I'll see you if you pass through Surah again, sir? I shall hope for it."

He rode his mount around a corner, dismounted and dived through a shop, out the other side, and grabbed a waiting man.

"Tell Duke Cleeono that his man's on the way. He's got a young woman with him, drugged I'd say. But that's none of our business, just tell the duke."

He grinned in the direction in which the sorcerer and his captive had gone. The fool had taken him at face value, which just showed what happened to men who thought themselves superior. They were usually wrong. The short fat man made a very good living taking messages, passing on information or gathering it—from a number of people, all of whom liked to know of odd events, and from the odder people who might be involved in them. He liked being paid for his work, and being paid more than once for the same information was excellent business.

He'd wager that man and his supposed daughter fitted the bill very profitably. He'd wander back through a few Surahan inns and listen for talk that could be related to them. And if anyone wanted to know where a man like his recent companion had gone, Jazvendra was the man to tell them—if the price offered was right. He didn't much care who did what, or to whom, so long as it wasn't him. A possible kidnapping wasn't particularly exciting. In his time he'd seen much darker doings.

*L*ater the same night, Orla and her weary group arrived in Surah heading for Mirray, when they found the single word Ashara had left. Their spirits rose, knowing finally that they were on the right track. They had no idea that their trader friends were in Surah until Kait, Tiah, and Katchellin and his men were about to depart. They all met in the inn's courtyard at sunhigh when a lanky man sidled up to Katchellin under cover of the commotion.

"Someone wants ter meet yer," he hissed.

Katchellin looked, recognized the one who accosted him as one of Varsheean's men, and nodded.

"Where?" he asked in a low voice. A jerk of the head indicated an empty stable at the end of the row. They moved down the line of horses and entered the stable, Katchellin watching to make sure no one approached.

"Talk."

"Varsheean sent word we were to watch for anything odd. Don't know if this is, but you know Jazvendra?" Katchellin nodded emphatically. He certainly did know the slimy little two-faced toad. Jazvendra and his habit of selling information he'd gleaned—and he gleaned very well—had ruined at least one spying operation of Varsheean's in the past.

"What's he got to do with anything?"

"He's selling. Says a man rode through last night heading for Mirray. Jazvendra was told by Cleeono to make sure the man got through Surah City quickly and without problems. This man had a woman with him who looked to be drugged. Jazvendra will sell you a description of them both if you're interested. He also says he thinks he knows where they're headed."

Katchellin made an instant decision. "Tell him to meet us on the road out of Surah. Just before the guard post there's an inn. He'll know it. Tell him I'll meet him there as soon as I can and if his information's good then he'll be very well paid.

Go and do that now, then find me and let me know if he agrees. I'll be on the road heading in that direction in a candlemark." He eyed Varsheean's man.

"Don't scare him or I'll have your hide, but I want him watched. He isn't to go anywhere that you don't know. Just in case he changes his mind about this sale I want to be able to pick him up any time I need to. If you're afraid you're really going to lose him, grab him."

"The duke won't like me grabbing one of his citizens."

Katchellin smiled unpleasantly. "Those I'm with are about to have a brief word with the duke. He's an old friend of theirs. I'll tell him if you have to grab Jazvendra that it was on my orders. Go. Now!" He returned briskly to the courtyard, looked around to make sure none of the inn staff were in the immediate vicinity, and took Tiah by one arm, speaking softly but clearly enough to be heard.

"Never mind the reunion. I gather that these people are the ones looking for someone they've lost. I have possible news of the kidnapper."

There was instant silence, and Katchellin began to talk.

19

M ove over this way," Katchellin said softly. "That way we're out of the path of those coming and going. Now, Kait you move back: you can hear from a distance. Tiah, watch for anyone trying to overhear me. You others, this isn't a street play and we don't want a crowd scene, pick who listens and who passes it on. I don't want more than three or four around me."

That produced Orla, Yoros and Kyrryl, and Eilish. Kait was mind-sending to Tiah, who lounged by the stable's main door. The others spread about the courtyard, seeing to it that no one approached the small group where Katchellin talked quickly. Once he was interrupted, when Orla explained who Ashara was and how the sorcerer had her rather than the tariling he'd originally stolen. When he was finished he looked at them.

"Tell the others of your group what I've said. I don't have time to, I'll be going to that inn at once or I won't be in time, and Jazvendra is the nervous sort." He grinned savagely. "He should be, mind you. He sells everything that he knows to so many different factions around here that it's a miracle he hasn't been murdered by now, and he knows it. But knowing it makes him very jumpy and he won't wait beyond the hour I sent word that it would take me to be there."

Yoros raised an eyebrow. "You have a watch on him?"

"I do, but he's as slippery as an eel. He knows every alley and shortcut in Surah and I don't want to take the risk of losing him. You people sort out your mounts, pay your bill, and follow me. Kait and Tiah will be along later. They have someone else to talk to."

The two women had gone into the stable, emerging with Kotu on a lead rope, and their horses. Kait swung up onto her mount and started him and the mule out of the courtyard. Tiah stayed a moment.

"We may be delayed with Tassino, I don't know. But we'll either pick you up on the road or meet you in Mirray. We had plans to get raw gems and have them set in Surah but there isn't going to be time for any of that. We can meet our young friend who sells them, though, and bring them on to Mirray unset. Just in case we need entry to the court."

"I know, in this business it's all hurry up and wait."

"That's often so but it may not be that way this time." She looked at him. "I think that the sorcerer could mean to call the Kalthi earlier than planned. It's high summer in a few days, and it's a time of power from now on."

Katchellin laid a hand on her arm. "Do what you can. That's all any of us can do. But I think the opposite: I believe that we may have to wait for a half tenday while the noble we know makes his arrangements and surely the actual day of high summer would be the best time? And besides, his sort don't like to be hurried, they like time to consider—and to gloat about what they'll do when their plans all work out."

Tiah nodded slowly as she thought about that. "You could be right, Chell. But I don't think we'll waste any time just in case. Have one of your people watch for our arrival in Mirray if we don't catch up to you on the road. I'd rather not tell everyone our business by leaving word with the guards at the border."

"I will, and you keep an eye out for Varsheean. By my calculations he should be landing in Surah in a day or so. If you're still here you may meet him."

"Oh joy. You know, that man gets us into some real situations."

Katchellin laughed. "Me too, but when you think about it, I'd rather know what's going on and be in the thick of it and you have to give him that. Around him you're involved."

Tiah's gaze met his and they silently acknowledged the truth in his words. Certainly in this case, the woman thought. Not to know could mean demons falling on them—and on their kin and friends—to devour them without warning. As it was, her father knew everything they did, or almost so. He'd try to see to it that everyone they cared about was safe.

She swung onto her mount and sent him after Kait and Kotu. Gheevin and Jessara were down at the market selling by now. They would be there for a tenday before they started home with another trader caravan that was leaving then. By the time they left Surah it should all be over in Mirray. And if it wasn't, well, there was probably not much anyone could do. She'd sent a message to Amaya the gemcomber to meet them at the palace gate. Right now she and Kait would have to talk to Duke Tassino and hope he'd listen—and not make a bad situation worse by acting too openly or in force.

They reached the palace, were admitted, and were given private audience with Tassino. It took almost three candlemarks, but that was par for the course. At least it didn't cost them coin, Kait thought.

"What?" Surah's ruler, Duke Tassino, was a short, stocky young man who was usually sensible. But it seemed that the news that demons could be called through a portal on his border any day now wasn't something he felt called to be sensible about.

Tiah was waving her hands at him. "Please, Duke, hush. We don't want panic. It may take some days before anything happens. If we can make preparations in secret to prevent this it would be safer for all concerned."

Tassino simmered down slightly and nodded. "I put my brother-in-law in charge of my army, as you know. I'll have him called."

Both women nodded at that. They did know Kerrith tae Halkier. Some five years earlier he'd helped them foil an attempt to take over Surah's throne. Kerrith was intelligent— and his wife, Tassino's half-sister Triana, was even more so.

"Ask the lady Triana to come with him, Your Grace," Tiah suggested. Tassino considered that, grinned, and gave orders. They waited in the small private audience room until the doors opened to admit Kerrith and Triana.

"Lord Duke?" Kerrith was formal.

"Brother?" His wife, the duke's half-sister, was less so.

"Sit down, both of you. Our friends here bring us some very disturbing news. To begin with, does the word 'Kalthi' mean anything to you?"

Triana blanched. "The archives. When your great-grand-father left Shallahah he had many of the archives copied to bring with him."

Tassino nodded. He'd vaguely known about that. His great-grandfather had been a cousin of the then king. They'd conspired in a coup to bring down the prince's half-uncle, who was a corrupt and vicious man. But the new king, while he was fond of his cousin, also felt that he'd be fonder if there was some distance between them. There'd been a lot of gossip about it at the time, but the truth was that Tassino's great-grandfather had departed by mutual agreement and with assistance—at least, that had been the official version in the archives.

Tassino, who'd also heard the family version, smiled wryly to himself. The assistance would have been very pointed if his ancestor had attempted to remain, but as it was he'd done well. He'd carved out a kingdom of his own a very long way from Shallahah, settled in, and been happy and secure in his new lands. The business with Faaleno could have been very disruptive both to the Lhandes of Surah and to the duke personally. Thanks in good part to these two trader women—and to the honor and loyalty of his half-sister and her husband—he'd stayed alive and on his throne.

Triana was remembering other things. "It was while I was young. I often hid away from those who bullied or toadied to me. I read alone for candlemarks in the archives. They never thought to look for me there and I enjoyed reading about our ancestors."

"And they spoke of these Kalthi?"

Triana nodded. "They are demons of a sort. Not the kind that some of the peasants fear. They are not smoke or mist: they are real and solid. If a portal is opened with some sort of sacrifice and a calling then they will come through and do the caller's biding."

Tiah spoke. "For a very short time, perhaps. But once they're here they don't go back willingly. Thanks to a friend we've read the archives in Shallahah."

Tassino picked up her explanation at once. "You mean that

once they are here they cannot be normally sent back, and while they may obey their original orders initially, they do not remain obedient for long?"

"Yes." Kait's answer to that was brief.

The duke nodded. "Tell these here," he ordered. "And quickly, because if what you say proves to be correct we may not have much time."

Kait took up the story while they listened. Once she was done there was a brief silence. Tassino looked at Triana and her husband.

"Maneuvers, don't you think? Down by the borders?"

Triana shook her head. "Too obvious. Cleeono isn't a fool but that wife of his is a real viper. If we suddenly move a hundred soldiers down to their border Kadia will force this sorcerer to wait until we go home again. Then either she'll see to it that the portal opens elsewhere, or she'll sit waiting long enough for us to forget and relax, then she'll have him move." Her smile to her half-brother was reassuring.

"Maneuvers by all means, it's a good idea, but not where it will frighten them into changing their plans. Send the soldiers out into the foothills and announce that they're practicing war games and some secret display to celebrate the ten-year anniversary of your accession to the throne. Cleeono will hear about that, but all it's likely to do is give him the idea of doing something similar."

Tassino grinned at her. "Thanks be to Pasht that you're my sister. You have some excellent ideas. I wouldn't like if you were Cleeono's kin."

Triana shuddered affectedly. "Please, brother. The thought makes me nauseous."

Kait chuckled. "It'd make him feel a lot sicker, I'd wager. You'd have poisoned him a long time ago if you were. But your plan sounds like a good idea to me too. We could add to it, though."

She settled down to discuss other schemes while three nobles and her shaya listened intently. Tassino knew how much they'd done to help save his Lhandes from civil war and to foil Faaleno's attempt on the throne five years ago. Since then he'd heard hints here and there that they had friends, contacts and debtors who owed them. They appeared to be no more than traders but Triana talked to them as friends and his half-sister was shrewd.

At length, he leaned back. "Very well. I think that's as flexible as we can be in our plans without making so many we lose track of what it is that we intend to do. Go and talk to Amaya. Leave the rest of the plans here to the three of us and know you'll have friends at your back."

When Tassino called, one of the scribes appeared. He handed the duke a scroll, bowed, and departed, shutting the door firmly behind him.

"Take this," Tassino said, handing it to Kait. "It's a warrant to execute my justice on anyone found to be threatening the lives of my people. I can't give you the authority to act within Cleeono's borders, but I can give it to you covering my Lhandes and any land that isn't directly claimed and marked that lies between us."

Triana gave a small ladylike snort. "And the dead do so little complaining. If you have to act drastically and without much proof against that pack of kios, just be sure they end up dead. We'll all sleep easier for that, including your king."

Kait grinned at this realistic view of life, bowed politely, and left with her heart-sister. Once at the royal stables, they reclaimed their mounts and Kotu and headed to find Amaya. The young girl they'd first met, who gemcombed the Surahan beaches, was growing. She was acquiring an education and had quietly chosen to become an agent for many of the younger children who combed the pebble beaches of Surah in search of valuable gems. She'd received the traders' message a tenday ago and had bought judiciously. She waited, and with her, they were pleased to note, came two hired and bonded guards.

"I've a good selection. Mostly the larger gaudier stones you asked but also some of the smaller matched pairs for earrings or to set off a pendant." She moved to a niche in the palace wall and emptied the pouch that had hung around her neck. Tiah chose quickly.

"These of the larger stones, these of the smaller. What price?"

They haggled amiably and briefly before Amaya smiled. "That's fair enough. I gather you're in a hurry and that there may be danger. Is there anything I can do to help?"

Kait looked at the girl they'd known for six years and of whom they were both very fond. "No, but go to ground in a couple of days. Stay inside with your mother, make sure your house has all of the doors and windows heavily barred, and that you have enough food and drink and other supplies for several tendays. Don't go out unless you must, say you are ill, say you are observing some shrine penance. Say anything, but don't start a panic, and don't relax too soon and go outside."

Amaya's gaze met hers. "It's that serious?"

"Life and death, dearling."

"Then I'll do as you say. Ride safely, I'll hope to hear the tale when you return."

"If we return from Mirray," Tiah said, her mouth suddenly set in a hard line, "everyone will probably have heard the tale already." She folded the stones they'd purchased into a cloth and tucked it into her clothing. "Be well, Amaya. Pasht's claws be your protection."

They left the girl looking after them, her face blank while she thought furiously. She'd known them more than a third of her life and she owed them a lot. Besides that she loved them both. They were going to Mirray, and from what they'd said they'd be in great danger there—and she'd heard some odd tales about Cleeono of late. Amaya had contacts of her own these days. She set off to have words with one or two. If those to whom she owed so much were going into danger, maybe she could help.

*E*arly the next morning the ship on which Varsheean was a passenger was just dropping anchor off the coast of Surah. He intended to be in the city within the hour and would first seek out a few of his men. In the event he didn't have to do any looking. Tarryen tae Halkier, Kerrith's son who was also the duke's heir presumptive, was on the landing pier with a small detachment of palace guards. Varsheean recognized him.

"Orders to escort you to the palace at once, sir."

Varsheean blinked once. He was spymaster for Shallahah's king. He knew it, Duke Tassino knew it, and he knew the duke knew. But it wasn't etiquette to admit to knowing it, and still less so to demand Varsheean's presence in the palace. It meant either that Duke Tassino thought he had something of great importance to impart to the opposition—and could be wrong—or that he really did, and wasn't.

He went quietly. Better to make no fuss that would get his face remembered. Tarryen had been an unlicked cub who'd thought himself a soldier five or so years back. Now he *was* a soldier, and the improvement showed in his bearing and the snap with which his men obeyed.

"Can you suggest why the duke should wish to see me?" He kept his voice low.

Tarryen did the same with his single-word reply. "Kalthi."

"Ah." That explained it, leaving another mystery. He'd given the shayana and Katchellin permission to talk to the duke at need. He hadn't expected the duke to understand the dangers so well that he'd throw etiquette to the wind and openly send for Varsheean. That second mystery was dispelled as soon as he was closeted with the duke and his half-sister.

Triana leaned forward, speaking the moment the door was shut on them. "We know who you are and we know what you do, but this isn't the time to bother about it. Kaitlen and Anatiah were here yesterday to explain what they believe Cleeono has planned." She reached for a stack of scrolls and placed them on the table.

"When I was a girl I read the archive copies we have here that were brought from Shallahah palace when Surah was founded. They list two attacks by Kalthi in the past. The first scroll is very old and not particularly informative. The second was from less than three hundred years ago and graphically details the attack of the time. It lists the dead, the property damage, and the almost eight years it took to clean up and rebuild after the last of them had been killed. It explains how hard they are to kill, some possible preventive measures against their attacks, and their preferred victims. It also explains some of the ways in which they kill—and can be killed."

Varsheean took a deep but unobtrusive breath. Interesting! The Surahan archives apparently had better records in this area than he'd found in Shallahah's palace. But then copies sometimes were of better quality if they'd been made before the originals succumbed to vermin or damp. All right, he didn't have to explain anything or give any warnings. Now they needed soldiers for a frontal attack if required, and men who could act with cunning and stealth. He opened his mouth and was overridden by the duke.

"After discussion with the traders and my sister and her husband we have sent out a century of soldiers under Kerrith's command. Ostensibly they are practicing war games and a display intended for my next coronation anniversary. In reality they are traveling through the Toldin foothills, circling Mirray to the east and approaching that Lhandes from the desert side. We know Cleeono had an estate there on the desert fringe to the north of the city—before he moved to a more fertile part of Mirray—and we think that if he plans to use any place in Mirray then there is the most likely. The traders know where Kerrith will be waiting to meet them and they have a warrant signed by me allowing them to call on him at need."

Triana took up the flow. "They also have warrants from my brother for Cleeono's execution along with anyone else with him who is deemed to be guilty of capital offenses. That's if Duke Cleeono should be discovered outside the boundaries of his own Lhandes and shown by at least two reliable witnesses to have been responsible for the opening of a portal and the introduction of the Kalthi."

Varsheean blinked again. Pasht's claws! The duke of Surah and his kin hadn't been timid in their decisions. They'd listened, decided, and acted boldly in a matter of hours. If one of their people tried to kill Cleeono and was taken alive with a warrant like that on him, it would be civil war between the two Lhandes. He considered consequences. Of course, Tassino knew that. Clearly he'd thought that the other option—of the Kalthi descending on Surah's helpless people—was worse, and Varsheean didn't know that he'd disagree. Tassino and Triana had acted as royalty and he could do no less. He made up his mind and stood.

"Your Grace," he said, bowing with the full obeisance due a king. "Command me."

Triana smiled at him. "Sit down and let's sort out what each of us knows. Firstly the sorcerer." She recounted all that Orla and her group had told Kait and Tiah. "He and his captive passed through the Surah road gate the night before last." She moved on to tell what the traders had done, and knew or guessed. "They have one of your men with them." Varsheean didn't ask how the lady Triana knew about Katchellin; he was afraid he could guess. It seemed that he had few secrets left here. Once this business was resolved he'd have to find new spies to keep an eye on Surah.

Tassino took up the story after that. "We've sent Kerrith and soldiers. I've also sent a five-patrol in street garb to follow the traders once they enter Mirray City. They're men who have served me in various ways. They won't betray themselves as soldiers and they knew what the women look like. They are men who served under Tarryen when Faaleno attacked the palace."

He grinned at Varsheean. "I daresay too you know about a gemcombers' agent named Amaya. My people tell me that she provided uncut gems for the traders yesterday and thereafter she had several of her people follow them toward Mirray."

Varsheean nodded. He knew about Amaya. She was around fifteen but he also knew that she had some interesting friends and contacts and that a number of the street children and younger gemcombers answered to her.

Tassino poured drinking bowls of spiced pata and offered them to his half-sister and guest. "It would seem that many travelers are converging on Mirray for good reasons, and now you've come. What's your own purpose, spymaster?"

Varsheean swallowed half the bowlful of hot spicy liquid and looked up. "To help in any way I can. To prevent a sorcerer from destroying our people, yours or mine, and to bring him to open justice in the king's or your courts if that is possible."

"And if it is not?"

Varsheean's normal expression of vague amiability changed to the aspect of a starving and rabid dog. For the first time both the duke and his half-sister saw the real man within the plump, nondescript veneer.

"Then I'll kill the sons of kios myself if it's necessary to stop that portal being opened." His grin was hard. "That's if the plains' wise one doesn't get to the sorcerer first. I gather from what I've learned that the plains clans and tribes and their priestesses aren't any happier than we are about this business of his attempting to call the Kalthi. They see clearly that if the Kalthi attack Shallahah and succeed in killing the king, at some point Shallahah will recover enough to turn on the plains to burn them to nothing and kill everyone there. If the sorcerer fails and thinks to escape back to the Grass Sea, he'll find he has another thought coming."

"Good." Tassino stretched. "Then it only remains to let you go on your way and wish you goddess's fortune and speed. It seems to me that almost any way in which you succeed in your plans is to our advantage."

Varsheean stood. "Thank you, Your Grace, and milady. One thing, I arrived by ship." He paused and Tassino nodded.

"You'll find two men outside. They have horses for you and a warrant. You may commandeer any beast at need. They'll accompany you to ensure your safety in that event."

Varsheean hid a wry smile and left to find his horse—and his guards. He was on the road in a candlemarkin, past the city portal in a 'mark, and moving on down the road to Mirray at a slow gallop. A canter would allow his mount to continue longer but Varsheean was no longer sure that he had the time to spare. He did have allies, and that was one advantage. If only he also had current intelligence from his spies. He *really* wanted to know what Cleeono was doing.

He'd have been pleased if he could have overheard his enemy. Cleeono was stamping and swearing at a vague-looking man who seemed oblivious of the odium being heaped on his head. He waited until the tirade had ceased and spoke blandly. He was being well paid to deliver a message. That was what he intended to do, and the duke could choke on it.

"The one who sent me said that he waits at your estate as requested. He does not have the one originally sought, but he has another who will serve the purpose. He will wait for you to join him at sunhigh the day after tomorrow. If you are not there, he will begin the rite and hope you can be present in time to impress your own additional orders if any."

He bowed, turned on his heel, and departed. Cleeono stared after him, shaking his head like a fly-badgered halpa. Damn sorcerer. Didn't the man understand that he did his work at his duke's desire, how and where his duke ordered?

Sepallo would have disputed that—if he'd bothered to listen. He had his own agenda and the grief of years to avenge. It took time to make the required preparations. The best time to open a portal was when the sun was slipping from the highest point in the sky. That was the day after high summer and right after sunhigh on that day, but a day—or even two—early would do, and it was going to do so, if he could arrange that.

If he could hold the portal open from then until moonhigh that night he could have thousands of the Kalthi enter this world. They would cover the king and all his lands. No one in

Shallahah would survive, not in the day or night and all the times in between. It was a pity that he must use the woman, but he had no one else suitable, and it was her own people who had stolen back his other sacrifice. She was what he had.

O n the road just short of the Mirrayan city gates a cat hissed softly to himself. He was tired of traveling. The horse litter was comfortable enough, the attention he received was very agreeable, and the food was both good and ample, but he missed his humans more each day. The old one who was in some way one of his kind grew weak. He could smell that, but there was no smell of pain, only of acceptance coupled with a sort of odd happiness.

There was another who came after dark when all others in the camp slept. Only he knew that, and that she talked to him, impressing on him in vivid pictures and with the soft crystal sounds of her voice what was needed from him. Kian Dae listened to the growing hubbub as they entered Mirray City and waited.

T hat day, the fifteenth of middle summer, the Inn of the Dravencat was filled to capacity, to the hand-rubbing delight of the proprietor. Sepallo had bypassed it with his captive. Almost no one else did. Orla and her group had arrived first, the nine of them with sufficient mounts to all but fill the stables. The proprietor took one look at the number of horses and sent his son to the nearest inn, a street away and fortunately run by a kinsman.

"Tell your uncle that I look likely to be filled in both stables and rooms tonight. Ask him if I should have more guests arrive, will he house them and stable their mounts for ten percent to me for my commission."

His brother was more than willing, which was useful, since Kait, Tiah, and Katchellin were the next to arrive, followed almost at once by Duke Tassino's men. The proprietor rubbed his hands again and managed to house them all, although some of the horses had to be stabled at his brother's inn.

He found it annoying that think as he might he was unable to find rooms for the man with two apparent bodyguards who arrived after that, nor for the three young people who came in a candlemark later. They were housed at his brother's inn, and the proprietor was able to console himself that at least he'd receive a ten-percent commission on everything they spent there.

The lord Kerrith tae Halkier spent a chilly night on the desert fringe surrounded by his century, so that while he may have been less comfortable he certainly felt safe. Dharvath, Aycharna, and Kian Dae would have found themselves in a third inn had it not been for the big cat. Once within range of his human, he knew it and called. Eilish, who'd been chatting idly to husband and brother over dinner in Sirado's room, shot upright.

"Kian Dae's here!"

When she fled the room the men were still asking questions. She sped down the stairs, and into the courtyard. Cat and woman met in a whirl of fur and hair and loud joyful sounds while the men, who had followed Eilish at similar speed, beamed at Dharvath when they saw her.

"We weren't expecting you to be in Mirray," Trasso said softly. "Is there a reason for this?"

"Indeed. First let us see if the innkeeper can find us room to stay, then we can eat, rest, and talk. I must confess that I'm weary to my bones." She turned to the Aradian warriors with her. "Please, find yourselves a suitable inn, I think that there is no room here."

The proprietor, arriving at that moment, confirmed her

belief. "I'm very sorry, sirs. But the lady speaks the truth. My own inn is full to the rafters, as is my brother's inn in the next street. You could try the Inn of Many Delights two streets over. They make a specialty of rock melon and other fruit dishes and they charge high because of it. But you'd be very comfortable there if price is not too great an object."

The warriors rode away while Eilish was assuring Kian Dae that he would sleep on her bed as usual. While they talked, Yoros was thinking. The priestess was old, and he could see her exhaustion. It would be unfair to send her off with Aycharna seeking another inn. Besides, he'd like to know what had brought them to Mirray when that had never been the plan. He looked around the stables near where they stood and spoke to her decisively.

"Roshan and Hailin have a room in the inn here. They can sleep in the hayloft while you and Aycharna have their room. We should have you with us so that we can talk more easily."

Kait and Tiah found that while they had a room, and stabling for their own mounts, there was no room for Kotu. At length a small loose box was found for him with a friend of the innkeeper's who, while not in the business, was not averse to earning coin.

"It's a pity about his pack," Kait muttered as they settled the beast with clean straw, a filled water bucket, and a hay net.

"I know." Tiah sighed at the lost profit. "But maybe once this is over we'll be able to get the gems set and sell the jewelry around the Surahan court. It looks likely we'll have no time to do that before we find this sorcerer."

They checked that Kotu was happy enough, warned their benefactor's ostler not to enter or touch the mule—the beast's food and water could be replenished from over the door—and left to meet their friends.

It took time to settle everyone. And more time and talk again when Varsheean arrived, marched upstairs, and announced himself to the traders and Katchellin. Nor, despite the considerable amount of experience embodied in the crowd finally gathered in an upstairs room, did any of them know they were overheard, and Varsheean would have been mortified had he realized.

Amaya had sent her best, two thieves and an assassin-in-training, none of whom looked to be any more than the innocent children of trader-class families. If they were seen on the inn's roof they could pass it off as a childish game. They were unseen, however, and a small hand drill provided a way to slip a window latch. With the shutter very slightly ajar, voices came to them, if not loudly, then still clearly enough for most of the discussion to be overheard.

The room in which Dharvath and the others met was hot and crowded. Small enough too, Tiah thought with an inward grin, that anyone contemplating swinging a small feline would have laid out everyone here at the first swing. And if the growing sounds of chatter didn't die down a little, she'd be wishing she had that feline and could do so. She was a trader, and she didn't *like* small, overcrowded, overheated rooms.

"Quiet!" Dharvath commanded. "Let us choose one to speak for each group, then let them speak in turn. You speak first," she said, looking at Kyrryl, "then we'll hear Eilish, then the traders, then this one," pointing at Varsheean. "This is no time to chatter. Be clear and quick in your tale. Once all have spoken we shall ask questions in turn again. Now, speak." She looked at Orla and waited.

Kyrryl began. There was silence as she explained how they'd come here.

Kyrryl finished with information that made those who

hadn't heard it sit up. "Ashara was able to leave us two words. I found them written into the earth outside the campsite just before they entered Surah."

Dharvath nodded. "And the words were?"

"'Mirray,' 'duke.'"

"And you understood from that?"

"That the sorcerer was taking her to Mirray and the duke there was involved."

"Good. Now, Eilish or Sirado may have something to tell us perhaps?"

Eilish intervened. "There is no need for me or my kin or Dayshan to speak. We were there with our friends and we saw nothing they didn't."

Dharvath nodded, signaling to Kaitlen, who told what else she knew.

Varsheean pursed his lips. "I have no more to add save that the duke gave me warrants of his own against Duke Cleeono. But I think now, milady, it is time we heard your tale. I don't think you came on a long weary road for your own amusement."

Dharvath smiled at him. "No, but why I did come I'm unable to say for sure. I only know that Pasht came to me in the early 'marks of a night, bidding me rise and ride, taking with me Kian Dae—and Aycharna if I wished. I am her priestess. I obeyed."

Varsheean nodded. "Then we are all here in Mirray to prevent what the sorcerer would do. Cleeono is not of such importance. I have been receiving information during my ride from Surah. He has an estate on the northern side of the city on the desert fringe. It is most likely that it's there his sorcerer will attempt to open the portal."

Orla cleared her throat gently, waiting until the others

turned to listen. "The best time for opening the portal would be at just past sunhigh the day after tomorrow. If he can keep the portal open from then until moonhigh he'll overwhelm Shallahah with the numbers of Kalthi who will gain entrance."

"If we kill the sorcerer he won't be opening any portals," Katchellin growled.

"And if he does open the portal we still have a brief time, perhaps a handful of 'markin, to shut it again before his call brings them," Orla added.

"How do we do that?"

The plains wise one looked at them, her face abruptly blank. "I do not know. There was nothing in our tales to tell me." Her voice was bitter. "Those who might have known died twenty years ago when the king fired the plains. If Shallahah dies now it's on his head. I've done all that I can, told you all that I know. I can do no more."

There was a long silence before Dharvath wavered to her feet. "I know. If we reach the sorcerer and kill him before he opens the portal that is well. If not, then I know how to close it."

"How?" It was Eilish who asked.

Dharvath looked at her gently. "I am forbidden to say." She remained adamant on the points, both that she could do so if it were necessary, and that she could not speak of her method. With that they had to be content, seeking their rooms to sleep as she ordered.

20

They rose and ate early. Varsheean had returned to sleep in his own inn but was with them almost as soon as they arrived at the stables.

"We should ride separately," he said while they saddled their mounts. "It'd look suspicious to have so many of us traveling together, the more so since we'll be riding north across country. Have the servants stay behind today; we don't need them."

Dayshan glared at the spymaster, to receive a look from Sirado, who whispered, "You're master-at-arms, not a servant." Dayshan's face cleared as he moved to join Sirado, Trasso, and Eilish.

Roshan looked at his master. "Where you go, I go, my lord, unless you forbid me."

Sirado hesitated. "If you wish, follow us once you have saddled your horse, but go and eat first. I know you haven't had breakfast yet."

Roshan, who'd been serving food to Sirado, Trasso, and Eilish, then packing food for them to take before helping to saddle

their mounts, and would have eaten later, nodded gratefully.
"I'll do that, lord, I'll catch up with you in a 'mark or two."

Kian Dae had gone with Aycharna back to the room she
was sharing with Dharvath. She could be private there and
the cat could sleep without the swaying that had marked the
horse litter. Roshan went back inside, followed by Hailin, who
nudged him.

"I'm going out for the day since I'm allowed to stay here.
I'll be back before sunset."

Roshan grunted acceptance. He did not see his fellow servant hire a mount from the livery two streets away and ride in
the same direction as the others. He would have wondered,
had he seen that, why Hailin would hire a mount when he had
a good beast of his own.

If he'd been asked—and answered truthfully—Hailin
would have said that he had no wish for anyone who knew
him to find his mount sweating and lathered on their return.
If he was to see what they did and where they went he'd be
covering more ground.

*D*harvath had spoken privately and formally to Aycharna
before she departed with Varsheean. "Kinswoman of Orla,
I lay a task upon you."

The woman bowed her head. She'd known, she thought,
that she'd been permitted to come for reasons other than her
initial involvement. Now, finally, she would learn why.

The old priestess smiled. "No, it is neither difficult nor will
it be ill done. But I would have you enter Eilish's room while
she is gone and note where she keeps the travel pouch for Kian
Dae. I cannot speak to her of this. She is not of our people nor
does she worship Pasht and that is who has commanded me.
But tomorrow we ride out at first light."

"He won't be hurt?" Aycharna asked. "Eilish would never forgive me. And I—I find I have grown fond of him."

"He will not be harmed, I swear it. That is not his purpose."

"Then I am willing to aid in whatever way you ask, wise one."

Dharvath smiled and sent the girl for hot, spiced pata and some of the small yemas-fruit bread rolls. To herself she mused on people. They heard what they wanted to hear, all of them, even the most sensible and cautious. But that was well. She too had a part to play in this, and what that was none must know until the time came for her to act.

And in order to accomplish her share she would have to escape the attentions of her clan warriors. Her arrival would be conspicuous if she appeared with a contingent of armed Aradians grouped about her in close formation. With that in mind she gave further instructions to Aycharna on her return, before composing herself to rest for the day. She would spend a portion of the evening in Mirray's shrine communing with her goddess. Tomorrow would bring effort enough.

*I*t brought more initial problems than she suspected. Kait knew her own breed—and she knew Dharvath, who had been the clan's priestess for a very long time. The old one was stubborn, and she hadn't liked the suggestion that she should not be involved with their apprehension of Cleeono and the probable execution of the sorcerer. To make sure that the honored one stayed out of trouble, Kait had quietly vanished into the stable and seen to it that Dharvath wouldn't be riding her mule today.

By way of further insurance she spoke quietly to the clan warriors. Then she returned to spend time with her shaya, smiling smugly. The priestess wouldn't be hiring any other mount for herself either. So far as the warriors knew she had no coin of her own. It was they who paid. Kait chuckled silently. Dharvath might be angry with her, but better that than Kait having to explain to her clan how an elderly female, valued beyond even her warlord brother, had been harmed. If they needed her to shut the portal, she could always be summoned.

After that the two women headed for a jeweler with the settings of gold or silver and the gemstones purchased from Amaya. The stones they'd taken were of the sort that could be polished into berry-cut form swiftly. They would then be flat on the bottom and domed on the tops, suitable for immediate setting, particularly into bracelets and collar-necklaces. If anyone asked what the traders were doing in Mirray, they had believable answers to that question and expensive merchandise to sell the nobles if they needed to request access to the court.

O utside the city those who hunted the sorcerer spread out to circle the more populous area. Mirray was almost without settlers so far in the north and in some of the northeastern areas near the Shairne Desert. That may have been why Cleeono had taken land there for an estate, Varsheean thought as he rode in silence with his guards. He suspected that the duke had unsavory habits that he practiced on his own distant estate well away from prying eyes—or his wife, who usually stayed year-round in the palace.

Varsheean had brought more detailed maps of his own with him. He had directed this search and would be mildly surprised if it didn't succeed. He believed that the duke would have the sorcerer and the sacrifice at Cleeono's estate, and he was also convinced that the duke would attend the calling. He smiled unpleasantly. He had directed the others to circle, sent them around the fringe of Mirray to come up on the estate from the far side and at a distance. It should take them several candlemarks to reach the same cover as that brush copse in which the three of them waited.

He and the two guards had ridden hard and fast directly to the site from where he wanted to watch, and now he lurked silently. Yes, he'd been right. There was no sign of the duke or the sacrifice, but there was a man obviously in charge—a tall, lean man wearing the garb of a wise one of the plains and directing four younger men while they brought wood for two fires. There was a breeze blowing toward him and, from the cover of thick brush near the line of trees where they worked, Varsheean could hear what they said.

"Two fires, here and here." He tossed down a branch in each place. "Then two more, here and here. The heart of each is to be the jars Tahari is bringing in the cart."

"They'll burn, wise one?"

"Their contents will, yes, and for many hours when we fire them just before sunhigh. Once the fires in them sink low, more of the fire-maker can be tossed in wineskins into the fire. The duke has provided me with a large stock of filled wineskins for that purpose."

"And the sacrifice, wise one, she is secure?"

"The duke has her safe. She'll be brought to this site when she's needed."

Varsheean exchanged looks with the guards. That was useful. Two clear unambiguous statements in the presence of witnesses that the duke knew what was going on here and was involved. This information would be sufficiently damning in case they had to execute the duke themselves—and later defend that action. They watched for another candlemark as the large, squat jars were brought and placed carefully in position with wood stacked about them. The sorcerer was chanting, drawing lines and adding herbs, powders, and branches from several varieties of trees and shrubs.

Varsheean felt a chill down his spine. This fool, this incredible idiot, would call demons over which he believed he had complete control. Varsheean had talked to the high priestess at the Mersa Lake shrine before he took ship. He'd approached her with proof that he was the king's man, with all the authority that gave him, and she'd been able to search the shrine records, which were more comprehensive than those at the palace. He'd been fairly frank on what he believed to be planned. She'd had the shrine's records brought to her, studied them, steepled her fingers, and considered him thoughtfully over them.

"Whoever is involved in this is a half-wit," she said trenchantly. "To begin with, he apparently believes that a portal can be opened, the Kalthi called, and they can be loosed in our world. In all that he is, unfortunately, quite correct. He then seems to think that he can order the Kalthi to attack whomever he wants to be rid of no matter how far from the portal, and the demons will obey. In that he is wrong, quite wrong!"

"Can you explain further?"

"Yes." She stared at him sternly. "It is very simple. The Kalthi are not genuine demons as we think of them. They're dwellers in another world who live very long lives and breed seldom. They'll lay waste to whatever land they find themselves in and to the largest centers of population within that land. This nitwit believes that in the past those who called the Kalthi gave them orders that were obeyed. He—or whoever told him that—is wrong. It was simpler than that. They called the Kalthi near where those they wished to destroy were living, the Kalthi came, were told to kill the enemy, and merely attacked the nearest city. Which—and I emphasize this, king's man—by a coincidence happened to be the one the caller wished destroyed."

Varsheean kept his face blank by a massive effort of will. Inside he was torn by the conflicting desires to dance with delight and wince with horror. Shallahah looked likely to be safe from attack. But he had kin living in Surah, and in both Surah and Mirray he had a number of friends and men who answered to his orders. He could see what had happened all those years ago. The Kalthi had been called to enter an area containing only small, scattered clans or tribes. Naturally they had gone to the nearest large concentration of people—in Shallahah City. The sorcerer who'd sent them had commanded them to do so, however, and believed—and probably passed on that belief—that they'd obeyed the order of the one who called them.

Cleeono, if he was truly involved in this madness, was assuming—because his tame sorcerer honestly believed—that the Kalthi could be called and ordered to obey. They could then be sent hundreds of miles to Shallahah to destroy the king, court, and probably most of the soldiers, who'd die trying to protect the city. It wasn't that Cleeono was an idiot, as they'd wondered, it was that he'd made the mistake of believing his sorcerer was right in everything he told the duke—and since the sorcerer honestly believed what he was saying, Cleeono had believed too.

What would happen instead was that the demons would destroy Mirray City. Unslaked—and ineffectively opposed—they might then move on to Surah and leave only devastation and the corpses of those who hadn't had time to run. They might then, and only then, travel to his home in Shallahah City. Hmmmm, that raised other questions.

"Lady, do we know how far the Kalthi will travel once

they have destroyed all within their immediate vicinity? Do they live long in our lands, can they survive and breed here?"

The high priestess of the Mersa Lake shrine smiled grimly. "The records knew, thus I know. The Kalthi do not travel far nor do they live long and they do not breed. Our lands are not fit for them. They died, why precisely we do not know, but they do not live far beyond a half tenday once they have entered our lands. We have a few here sometimes, but as we of the shrine know, there's a very small portal that opens irregularly from their world now and again and permits a handful of them to pass into our world. I heard about Vani and Shaetyl. The Kalthi that killed them are already long dead by now."

She looked at Varsheean. "There's a lot of misinformation around about the Kalthi. Once you have this business under control I must see that accurate copies are made from our records here, and distributed to other shrines and to wise ones. The Kalthi are always a nuisance, but with this nitwit's plans they could escalate into a real plague."

"How fast can they move?"

"Very fast, but not necessarily far. That's a different thing. The records say that they can move more quickly than can humans or Aradians, hence one Kalthi can slay several, sometimes many people before it's killed in turn. But they don't travel far in distance once they've found suitable prey. They kill everyone near them before they move on. And last time they didn't travel more than a day or two's travel from their place of arrival. Evacuation proved to be a part solution."

Varsheean considered. That could mean that Surah was safe, but not that anyone's safety there was guaranteed. What it did mean was that if the Kalthi descended on Mirray, and if Tassino evacuated his population with orders to take food and bedding and move into the mountains and scatter, then they'd possibly be safe—or safer, and in a half tenday the Kalthi should all be dead.

"Do the Kalthi destroy buildings, eat animals, and human food?"

The high priestess eyed him. "No, our records say that the destruction of buildings appeared incidental. They damaged them in an effort to reach people hiding inside. They did kill animals, dogs that attacked them, and as they began to die, they killed horses, mules, and donkeys to eat. It was clear that these were not their preferred food. Nor did they touch our ordinary food like bread, fruit, or grain at all."

It looked likely that the most probable area to be devastated was the Lhandes of Mirray, whose duke intended to call the horror. The biter well bitten—if only the likelihood was not that so many innocents would die along with their duke. He rose, bowed, and uttered formal thanks. "This information is of great value, lady."

"I give thanks to Pasht if that is so. I ask in her name, king's man, that if some fool plans to open a portal and call in Kalthi you slay him before he can do so."

Varsheean nodded. "If it is within my power, lady, this I intend to do." He rode from the shrine deep in thought. He couldn't spend time traveling overland to Surah. He must take a ship and before that he must talk to the king, obtain warrants both to send to Katchellin and to take with himself to Surah. All these things he had successfully done—while picking up the news that Lord Varli had vanished from his estate. Varsheean sighed. He could guess where the lord was going. At least he'd have all the conspirators in one place.

He came back to watching the scene before him. He'd been right in so many of his fears. The sorcerer was placing the finishing touches on his site. Varsheean had all the information he required; his guards were witnesses to the fact that Cleeono was involved. Varsheean must now decide how best to make use of all the amateurs who wanted to help. He sighed. Amateurs, they were so enthusiastic and usually so useless. However, circumstances sometimes changed without warning. He'd permit them to come here. He could find something for them to do to help him and if there was nothing vital, he could always create some goal at which they could be directed.

He studied the sorcerer. There were a lot of guards around him, but maybe . . . He looked at possible cover. If they could inch closer he might be able to risk an attack. A dead sorcerer would stop this madness in its tracks. The sorcerer said something to a guard and turned to walk away. The guards fell in around him; one brought a horse, and the sorcerer mounted, riding away. Varsheean cursed and hissed at the guards, sliding silently backward and regaining his own mount.

He rode hastily around the area of scrub he'd used as cover, but peer as he might there was no sign of the wretched man and his guards. They couldn't have gone to the manor house; if they had he'd moved fast enough to have seen them entering. No, they must have gone in another direction, and it was the sorcerer who was key. Without him dead, arresting Cleeono wouldn't be that useful. There was always some ambitious, power-hungry noble who would believe anything a sorcerer told him.

He muttered and changed direction. Shortly thereafter, some two miles from the edge of Cleeono's estate, he intercepted the amateurs when they moved in.

"The sorcerer was there, but he's surrounded by guards and before I could take a chance and kill him, he went somewhere else and we couldn't move fast enough to see where. He has set up the site and plans to begin the rite at sunhigh the day after tomorrow as Orla thought."

He described the path to the site that had the best cover, and the site itself. "The sorcerer also said clearly that Cleeono is involved in providing items to help open the portal, and that he's holding the sacrifice to produce at the right time." He nodded to his two guards. "These men both witnessed what was said by the sorcerer of Cleeono's involvement." The guards in turn indicated that they had, and Varsheean smiled.

"I suggest that we scatter and return to our inns again. We know where to come when the time is right. We can hope that the duke will attend, and that we can frustrate the portal's being opened."

He started for the city and in ones and twos his companions fell in to ride behind him. Varsheean was well satisfied with his day. If only tomorrow and the day after when the portal would be opened went as well as today, he could return to his king with word that the crisis was over. Although he remembered other times when such hopes had gone astray.

He arrived back at the inn, ate and drank with some of his companions, then closeted himself alone in his small room to go over contingency plans. It was always well to remember the ancient saying—that few plans survived first contact with the enemy. Cleeono was dangerous and the sorcerer was witless. Varsheean knew from experience that that didn't mean that quite by accident he couldn't do something devastatingly effective and completely unexpected.

The next day by his orders they remained indoors at their inns. Only Kait and Tiah rode out to collect the first half-dozen settings now inlaid with the berry-cut gems. These they took to Mirray palace in the late afternoon. They paid bribes to enter and only after the coin had changed hands did they receive the news.

The guard was smug. "Hard luck, ladies. Court's mostly empty."

"But the duke? We have finely set jewelry from Shallahah for both men and women of your court. We hoped to see Duke Cleeono, the duchess Kadia, and her father, Lord Varli?"

"Yeah, duke's usually here around midsummer but I guess he's decided otherwise this year. They've all gone off to his estates in the country."

"Even the old lord?"

"Yeah."

Tiah's face fell noticeably. "When did they go? Would it be worth our while following them?" Another coin changed hands and the guard shook his head.

"Nope, look, I tell you true. The duke and that wife a his have been so ill-tempered of late I wouldn't hope to sell them nothing. They left only a 'mark ago with the old lord grumping and complaining about having to have someone or another in his traveling coach with him. Dunno who, but he was real put out. I'd wait until they come back to court. Some a the other lords 'n' ladies went with them."

"Do you expect them to return soon?"

"Dunno. I did hear it depends on somethin' they got planned. If it all works out they'll be back in a half tenday. If not, well, it may be some time. I ain't been told."

Tiah smiled. "You've been so kind and helpful. Please, allow me." She pressed a third coin on him unobtrusively and swept her shaya off to their inn at speed, where they reported the conversation to Varsheean, who smiled approvingly.

"Good. Then it looks like it'll be tomorrow. We leave the moment there is any light in the sky. I may have missed the man before, but I know exactly where he'll be this time, and everyone there should be distracted by what he's doing. That'll give us a chance to kill him and end this."

At first light next morning all but Dharvath, Aycharna, and Kian Dae rode out. Roshan rode meekly behind Dayshan. Varsheean preceded them with his guards, with whom he had come to an agreement.

"Duke Tassino said you were to guard me. If the portal is opened, you'll fail. Therefore to obey your orders you need to obey me so I can prevent the portal's opening."

He'd taken the precaution of explaining to them during the ride to Cleeono's estate the previous day some of what was going on and the terrible danger in which Surah stood if the sorcerer's plans succeeded. The guards wanted to obey their duke, whom they respected; they also loved their Lhandes and their friends and family there and were horrified by Cleeono's plans. Given the right rationale they'd decided they could obey their duke *and* Varsheean.

"I plan to use you for messengers to those who help us. Some, like the traders, you know already; the others you've seen. I have discussed with them some of the possibilities, so if you go to them with my orders there'll be no trouble. By being my battlefield messengers we may be able to prevent the portal from being opened. Will you do as I ask?"

The guards looked at each other, then back at the spymaster, and nodded slowly. One of them spoke.

"We've discussed it, sir. We reckon you have the right of it. If we obey you, we obey our duke and save our people too." His solid face lightened into humor for a moment. "An' we also reckon that if we fail we won't be left alive to be punished. Our duke understands battlefield luck. If we succeed he'll forgive us."

"Good."

He produced a map he'd made of the estate and its approaches, the patches of cover where he wanted his companions to hide, and the roads and paths to and within it.

"This is where the others will be." He pointed them out.
"Lady Kyrryl and Lord Yoros here. The lady Eilish, the lords
Sirado and Trasso with their master-at-arms and their servant,
Roshan, will be there. The traders will be here."

There would be others as well who intended to be present
at the struggle, but Varsheean had no knowledge of that so
far. He was hoping to make a quick attack once the sorcerer
appeared with his captive—and have a fast end to the problem. It should be possible to sweep up the three nobles too if
the goddess smiled on him.

"Go to these places now and check that those I've named are
in place. Tell them that we attack either when the sorcerer
appears, or once there is any indication that the portal is mani-
festing. Everyone should be focused on the sorcerer or the portal. *Do not be seen!*" The guards retired silently, to return in an
hour with the assurance that everyone was hidden and ready.

*I*n another small patch of cover there were those who also
waited: three older street children sent by Amaya, who
loved Kait and Tiah. Two of the three were very good thieves,
and the third was an even better assassin-in-training.

And in another copse there were five men in street garb,
with wide-ranging orders from their duke in Surah and who
were determined to carry them out.

*C*losing on the estate too were Aycharna herself, and Dharvath on Kotu, with Kian Dae riding comfortably in the
travel pouch Aycharna had stolen from Eilish's room. Dharvath

smiled slightly as she rode. It hadn't been easy but she'd managed everything she'd planned. Not the least was losing the clan warriors and obtaining a mount once she had discovered that someone had seen to it that her own mule couldn't be used. Tiah had mentioned where their pack mule was stabled. Ordinary ostlers might not easily handle Kotu or enter his stall, but Dharvath was a priestess of Pasht; to her all beasts were kindred and even Kotu was no exception.

The old priestess had spent the evening in Mirray's shrine. Those there were not used to seeing Aradians, but they could not deny a priestess of Pasht. Dharvath had been admitted to the inner sanctuary and left alone. There she had talked, listened, and been comforted. Now she led her tiny group toward the site of the portal, praying while she rode.

A third group rode toward the estate, tracking the hoofprints of Dharvath's mount. They rode in silence, determined to find their charge and protect her. Dharvath had not left her clan warriors quite so far behind as she believed.

*B*eyond the cover where Kyrryl and Yoros lurked, Hailin waited, carefully dressed in drab clothing that blended into the landscape. He'd followed them yesterday and seen where to go, returning before them to have it appear he'd done no more than laze away the day while they were gone. He'd done well out of the situation thus far and if luck was with him he hoped to do better still. People would die today; he'd pluck the feathers they died with and he'd bought a fair-sized pouch in the market to hold his spoils. Few people went empty-handed anywhere, even into a battle. If Hailin were seen his master would not be happy about it, but with the plunder he'd gained so far that didn't matter. If he was discharged he could merely leave his employment earlier and start the business he planned.

Hailin, self-involved as always, had never really listened to the talk about the sorcerer or his plans. He believed vaguely that this was some foolish squabble between two small countries in which his master had allowed himself to become involved. One of them had hired a sorcerer who intended to kill a king. Hailin wasn't a king, and with luck no one here would be interested in someone wearing the livery of neither country, he thought. He settled himself—buzzardlike—to wait for the fight to begin.

And half a candlemark away Kerrith led his century toward the estate from the empty lands of the northeast. He knew from his own scouts that the portion of the land there was uninhabited save by the occasional shepherds, whose presence would be signaled by their herd beasts. Nor—he hoped fervently—would anyone else think to approach from this direction. He sent his scouts farther out to make certain he wasn't surprised if anyone did appear, and slowed his own advance. He'd attack when the situation required and when everyone else was occupied.

*A*bout to arrive on stage there were also Duke Cleeono, his wife, Kadia, and his father-in-law, Varli, who'd managed to slip away from Shallahah City, and circle the Shairne Desert by the coast road to arrive at his daughter's door a day earlier. This was the culmination of his own plans, and he didn't intend to miss any of the action. He believed that no one in Shallahah had any idea that he was elsewhere but at his estates, and he congratulated himself on his cunning.

Besides which, now would be an excellent time to be away from Shallahah. He'd given strict orders to a few of his people—the ones he could halfway trust—but things could go wrong and he had no desire to be a meal for some misguided Kalthi. Lord Varli shrugged. Some of those who lived on his lands could die, but if so the survivors would breed replacements—and be more inclined to obey him in future. As for his kin, his wife was a boring old termagant, his mistress had become overly rapacious of late, and he'd miss neither if events fell out that way. It was his own precious skin that he fully intended to keep in one unblemished piece.

Sepallo waited a mile away in a barn that was commonly used to store hay. Something had warned him that he was being watched, and he'd learned to listen to such warnings. He'd also changed his robe to the nondescript tunic and trousers usually worn by a farmworker. At last, when he felt the time was right, he called the two guards who were waiting with him and rode toward Cleeono's estate. There he joined his four acolytes at the site where they and he would open the portal. He made sure that he appeared apart from them, though, looking like an idler who was simply enjoying the free spectacle. One of his robed disciples was nearer the main house on the path to the clearing and called back to his master at a half candlemark short of sunhigh.

"Wise one, they are coming with the sacrifice."

In his concealment Varsheean tensed. As soon as they could identify the sorcerer, or when the duke came in sight and once the rite was begun, he and his companions would pounce. They would arrest the sorcerer and his acolytes if possible, kill them if not. They would arrest Cleeono and his wife, free the girl, and dismantle the preparations for the portal.

Cleeono, like the sorcerer, was rather more careful of his own skin than the spymaster had foreseen. That was reinforced by the determination of his wife and father-in-law to stay in one piece as well. The duke was certainly arriving with the sacrifice but he was also arriving with fifty men-at-arms, almost all of his personal force. They were marching a short distance behind the three nobles, intending to appear a part of the ceremony but be available if anything went wrong with the rite of calling.

And Varsheean could not see Sepallo in his different clothing until the sorcerer took an active part in the rite. The sorcerer lit the fires, stationed his four subordinates, placed Ashara at the center of the paved square, and signaled decisively. His men began the long complex interweaving harmonies that would open the portal to death and destruction for Shallahah's king and Sepallo's long-desired vengeance. Under his robe the sorcerer's hand closed on a medallion. This one did not show a daska and a dravencat mask; instead, the names of his dead wife and child had been engraved deep into the surface. He'd call in their names.

The duke stepped to the edge of the clearing, his wife to one side of him and his father-in-law on the left hand. Varsheean tensed to attack when fifty armed men in Mirrayan uniform tramped into the clearing, ranged themselves about it, and stood at ease. The first stirring showed in the air between the fires and the portal began to firm above the fires, livid blue-gray ripples of light extending downward as the lower section too began to solidify.

Varsheean started. They had to ignore the duke's men and attack now, else the portal would open and the sorcerer would begin his calling. His side had only a dozen people, but he couldn't hesitate. They were all fighters and they knew why they were here and what could befall them. For the lives of thousands and to obey his king's command it was necessary to sacrifice his friends.

He nodded to his guards. "Start shooting—carefully. I want one of the duke's soldiers down for each shaft. Once you've used all your arrows, attack with swords."

He watched as the first shaft was drawn, loosed, and hissed down. A man-at-arms in the rear line of Cleeono's guards fell silently to the dusty grass.

Nexus! Catalyst!
All concerned were here as the heart of power
bloomed in the first blood shed.

Varsheean's men were old hands and sensible. They were shooting at the back of the men-at-arms and shooting for silent kills. It didn't last. A man-at-arms moved and the third shaft sliced down, taking him through the back of his shoulder instead of his heart. He screamed in pain, half turned, saw the bodies of comrades behind him, and shouted a warning.

The scream then the shout alerted everyone. From two other positions arrows began to rain down. Varsheean cursed in a shaking voice as he realized that a part of the initial rite had set wards about the square in which the fires had been lit. No missile would pass them and they could probably keep out a lot of people too. He ran forward shouting, to be intercepted by the duke's men who charged to surround their masters and the square. Within the shelter of men and wards the acolytes chanted on.

Kait and Tiah came running with Katchellin, Kyrryl, and Yoros. Roshan followed, knife in hand. Bewildered by the chaos, and unsure who to attack, he stayed behind Eilish and watched warily about him. Orla entered the fray behind them. Eilish ran forward with husband and brother beside her, Roshan in her wake, followed by five men with swords and a way of fighting reminiscent of trained soldiers. It seemed that this situation should be covered by their duke's orders.

Dharvath considered the growing melee from her shrub then sidled Kotu around it and approached from behind the southern fire. Aycharna, bearing Kian Dae's carrysack, walked beside them. Dharvath was casting power over them with all her skill, and when they were within a hundred paces of the fires she halted the mule.

"Give me the cat's pouch."

"What are you going to do, wise one?"

"No more than I must." She looked at her companion. "Child, you heard me say that if the portal is open only I know how to close it. If I had many priestesses with me, all women of Pasht's power, then we could do it the way these fools have opened it. With a chant bleeding power into the weaving. Here I am alone. I could not tell the priestesses of Mirray shrine what we feared and ask for their help. I spoke to them, and they were polite enough but I saw that they wouldn't follow me because I'm Aradian and they're humans. Therefore I do what must be done."

She touched Aycharna's forehead, bleeding power through her fingers. "Wait. If you are attacked, defend yourself. Otherwise wait for a friend to come. I lay this upon you: You shall not enter this fight. It is for you to watch and bear witness to events."

She lowered her hand, watching Aycharna's eyes intently, then nodded. Yes, that had been sufficient. The woman would hide as ordered. With luck she would live and return to her kin. Dharvath smiled a little. Orla had denied it but she too knew what needed to be done to shut a portal once the Kalthi had answered—and it was looking more and more likely that they would receive the call. Let Orla receive her kinswoman at Dharvath's hands and know that not all that came from Kavarten and Shallahah was evil or foolishness.

She nudged Kotu forward at a steady walk, and he obeyed. The scent of blood and steel, hatred, pain, and rage was in his nostrils so that they flared, sucking them in. There was a fight and he was being offered a part in it. The big jack mule walked forward eagerly.

Varsheean and his companions were being driven back. With less than twenty against fifty they couldn't gain the paved square between the fires. Sepallo watched his portal firming into existence. Ashara writhed at his feet, trying to free herself without his notice, but she was tied too tightly.

Amaya's three hovered around the battle's edge, picking off a man here and there, never letting themselves be confronted directly. They were thieves and an assassin, not soldiers.

Ten Aradian warriors, having lost sight of their priestess but now aware of the fight, hurled themselves into the thick of it. Cleeono's men-at-arms gave back briefly, but some of his servants had been summoned and arrived before the line could be breached. The whole area was a mass of struggling, yelling fighters as almost a hundred battled, one side to gain the square and close the portal, the other side to prevent it.

His men had no idea of what he'd planned. They'd have been horrified to learn. But then the duke was aware of the sentimentality of ordinary folk—Kadia had pointed that out to him a number of times in case he was not. And he had seen to it that his soldiers and servants knew only that he planned a great event in favor of the people of Mirray, something the Shallahan king would prevent if he could.

From a distance Kerrith's scouts heard and saw. They came back at speed and Kerrith gave orders.

LYN McCONCHIE

"Surround the whole battle. Move inward, killing anyone in the duke's livery. Watch behind you in case he has rein-forcements. Try to keep the duke and his kin alive but I'll pun-ish no one who can show that he acted to save his life." There was a faint snort from his sergeant.

"You won't have to. Cleeono won't fight. He's too fond of his own skin. So is Lord Varli, and while I've always heard the duchess has a poisonous tongue, I've never heard that she can kill a man with it."

Kerrith laughed. "Likely, but we're soldiers; we expect the unexpected. Move out!" A century of Surah's best soldiers fol-lowed his command.

But within the fires' square the portal had begun to open. Varsheean screamed in rage and fear and attacked desperately. He was still unable to break through the line of Cleeono's guards when the chant changed from the opening invocation to a compelling call.

Sepallo raised Ashara to her feet, his mad exultation at the success he anticipated giving him a giant's strength. In 'markin the Kalthi would answer, they would pour from the portal to obey his orders, they would kill Shallahah's king, destroy the city then all the surrounding lands and the people within them. He would be revenged for the death of all he had loved. After that he didn't care; he'd be free to go to Yalana and Gaisa.

Hailin too was busy, though not at fighting; there was no profit in that. He'd worked his way unnoticed into the depths of a large shrub at the edge of the fires' square and darted halfway out now and again to drag a body into his cover. He'd been right: Even with battle brewing men often had some-thing of value about them. He'd found rings, bracelets, religious medallions, and coins. He'd sorted his loot, placing it as he went into a pouch about his neck. Once his prey had a pouch filled with the small gold coins they used here, he stuffed that hastily into a sleeve and tightened the cuff drawstring. The coppers he left in a heap under the bush. He could always return for those if there was time and the chance.

He smirked to himself. So far he'd gleaned sufficient loot to set himself up to be a major merchant. He didn't have a sword, so, perhaps because of that, no one in this fight seemed to even have noticed him. He did see Dharvath and the cat approaching, and he snorted. Stupid old woman—and he'd always disliked the animal too. They looked to be ignoring him, and he returned the favor.

Sepallo threw back his head and screamed a mad ululation of ecstasy when the first Kalthi came in sight beyond the portal. It was answering his call as he'd demanded. Once it passed the portal he would kill the woman, bind the portal open and the Kalthi to his will in her blood and flesh. His scream temporarily overcame the sounds of battle. Varsheean's side recognized the danger and fought harder. Cleeono's side did not know, but responded. These foreigners weren't going to spoil their duke's plans.

And on the edge of the fires' square, a very old Aradian priestess, a bad-tempered jack mule, and a cat passed Sepallo's wards that guarded the square. Hailin, with the medallion Sepallo had given to his chief disciple in the pouch about his neck, saw another man fall: Cleeono's master-at-arms, a man who carried his accumulated salary on hands and wrists. Hailin hesitated, before, overcome by the sight of the gold and gemstone-decorated rings and bracelets, he slid into the square—passed in by the medallion—and seized the body. He was stripping the jewels from it when the first Kalthi stepped into the portal opening behind him.

It bellowed, and all fighters close enough to see it clearly froze. The thing was huge, with fangs that dripped acid saliva, and with four claw-tipped arms that opened and shut hungrily. Behind it crowded a hundred more ready to enter. The duke's men disengaged from the fight with almost supernatural speed. They dived through the press of their attackers and bolted, yelling in terrified horror. Behind them they left their duke and his family unguarded.

Eilish too had passed the ward. It had not been created to keep out people from another world, and she leaped through without even realizing its existence. Roshan was at her shoulder when he caught his foot on an uneven stone. In his forward stumble he knocked Sepallo sideways. The sorcerer lost his grip on Ashara and she fell, rolling as fast as she could away from her captor to one side below the edge of the portal. Sepallo yelled in mindless fury at the loss of his required sacrifice and followed.

Roshan staggered, flailing his arms and fighting for balance. Dharvath nudged Kotu forward to the very edge of the portal and dismounted, reaching over her shoulder to haul Kian Dae from his pouch. He hissed, ears flat to his head, while Roshan flailed, falling across the portal's threshold. The cat recognized his time. The nearest Kalthi stretched out an arm to cross through, touched fur—and a paw sank claws to the bone in a Kalthi's arm. It howled—a sound that was echoed by Sepallo as the Kalthi reached across, seizing him in rage at the sudden agony. The calling had not been completed and nothing bound it even temporarily. Small pieces of sorcerer rained down on the ground.

Power arced, discharging from the portal through the dead sorcerer who had called it into being. Portal power meeting and piercing three beings that stood within its reach. An Aradian who was a willing sacrifice, a servant; a man of neither the Aradian nor the Kalthi worlds, and a cat; born of the blood of two worlds. Power roared through them. Roshan crumpled silently, sucked into the closing portal. He was dead from the arcing power before he landed on Kalthi soil—Eilish's cry of horror and despair his requiem.

Dharvath crumpled slowly to the ground. Her lips curved in a smile. Before her the portal was shutting. She watched the power circle, turning back on itself. It faded and was gone. The danger was ended. Her lands, her clan, her friends, all were safe. Her eyes closed.

Kotu looked around for someone to kick. It seemed that none of those nearby wished to try conclusions with him, and his rider had dismounted, leaving his reins hooked to his saddle. That meant that he was free to look for food or anything else he wished. He ambled past the fires and toward the nearest patch of clean grass, where he encountered Hailin. The man was standing where the mule wanted to be, and he kicked. Not one of his hardest kicks but enough to bounce Hailin off another fighter—who whirled and struck. Hailin was lucky: the blow, taken hastily with the flat of his opponent's sword, merely knocked him out. He sprawled to the ground, there to be found later and removed, still unconscious, to where Eilish tended Dayshan's badly slashed arm, the slow tears sliding down her cheeks while she mourned the death of a good man.

Kian Dae stood in the square, spat, swore, licked Kalthi blood from his claws—and spat vigorously again in disgust at the taste. He'd taught that thing a lesson; whatever it was wouldn't be grabbing at a cat again in a hurry. He got his paw cleaned to his satisfaction and stalked off in search of Eilish. He'd smelled her scent just a few 'markin ago.

*K*errith tae Halkier and his century had continued to fight despite odd sounds and flares of light. They could not see what was happening by the square, and they had work to do. The duke's men seemed to have collapsed abruptly and were fleeing, and that was excellent. Kerrith opened his line and let them go, before he formally arrested the duke, the duke's wife, and Lord Varli and ordered them bound. Then he went to see what was going on where a small knot of people knelt by the body of an old Aradian.

Aycharna had reached Dharvath first. She cradled the body and wept. Kyrryl approached and Aycharna looked up at her.

"She knew all along. She had to die to earth the power and shut the portal if the Kalthi came. She made me stay back, she said I had to watch and bear witness."

Kait, who'd joined them, looked down at the body and nodded. "Her health was failing. She wouldn't have seen another year's beginning. It was her choice, to die well in Pasht's name or to die slowly."

Orla limped up and knelt to lay a hand on Dharvath's body. "Pasht, let her pass freely through your gate. It is done, the portal the sorcerer would have opened is shut, this one paid the price, a willing sacrifice according to thy law, and all portals are open to her."

Dharvath's body thinned to mist and was gone. The plains' wise one stood, her voice ringing out. "So it is ended. Let us now return home, pausing only to drink to friendship and punish the lesser fools who have survived what they caused." She strode toward her horse. Varsheean laughed shortly and followed, pausing only to address Kerrith.

"Orla's right. I have warrants from Surah and Shallahah to back your own orders. Tell the duke's men on his estate to burn the bodies of those who fell from among his men-at-arms and servants. Have your men take up our own fallen for burial honors. Bring that idiot and his kin, and we'll ride back to Mirray. Your duke can have all three of these for judgment. But I'm for home. My king would like to hear of events as soon as possible, and I'd like to be there to tell him."

Silently those still standing gathered their horses, mounted, and followed him. Kait unobtrusively scooped up a bulging pouch of jewelry and coins from near the side of one of the fires, now going out. There was no need to waste what someone else had dropped. She and her heart-sister could always use it, and she didn't see why it should be left for the burial detail—who'd probably be mostly from Mirray anyhow.

She joined Tiah, riding side by side with her shaya. Kyrryl, Ashara, and Yoros trotted by, smiling. Everything lost was found, and they were going home.

AFTERMATH

*B*efore they rode west the two groups from another world, and a number of their friends and helpers, escorted the prisoners to Surah, where Duke Tassino's court judged those whose desire for a throne would have brought death to most of their own people—and many others.

Cleeono was angrily defiant when arraigned. "I was tricked. Sepallo told me that he could control the things, they'd kill in Shallahah and nowhere else." He looked at the court slyly. "You're all from the Lhandes of Surah, you don't love the Shallahan king. You'd have done the same if you'd had the chance."

Truthfully, they might perhaps have done so if the right opportunity had presented itself, Varsheean reflected, and if the result would have been less bloody. But now, before them, they had an excellent example of just how badly things could go wrong—and if the chance did come their way in future they might look twice at it.

Cleeono had been a curious mixture of clever and credulous throughout this lethal business. He'd assumed, schemed, and plotted, and not once had he bothered to check what he was being told—because it was what he wanted to hear. The result would have been that he'd have seen most of his people slaughtered, and possibly a large number of the people in Surah massacred too. That had been made very clear by a number of witnesses, and the Surahan judges and Duke Tassino weren't impressed.

"Send for the lady Kadia, wife to Cleeono." Tassino leaned forward. "Sufficient proof has been brought to show that she too was implicated in these events."

Cleeono snarled up at the duke. "Implicated? Without her nagging at me day and night, telling me what her father said, how important I could become, I'd never have been involved. It was her idea. She was the one who had most to do with the sorcerer."

"We'll hear from her when she gets here. Until then we will hear from witnesses against your father-in-law, and you will be silent."

His father-in-law was also intransigent. "You can't do anything to me. I'm Lord Varli. I'm a noble of Shallahah. I can only be tried in a court of the nobles of my own people." He continued to protest and complain of injustice while the court conferred.

Varsheean produced the warrants he and Katchellin had been given, and spoke clearly to both court and defendant. "My king has given the ducal court of Surah full rights in this matter. I hold also a warrant giving me the right to execute Shallahan justice against any citizen—including nobles—of that country at my own discretion. I am satisfied that the testimony of the witnesses and the proof presented verifies that this man—Lord Varli—conspired to have our king murdered in order to place his son-in-law on the throne with his daughter as queen. The law in Shallahah demands that would-be regicides be branded, blinded, and then burned alive. How says the court of Surah?"

The court said "guilty," and added that in Surah the duke practiced merciful hanging. Lord Varli shut up abruptly. A quick hanging was infinitely to be preferred to the terms of execution in Varsheean's warrant. Proceedings were interrupted by the arrival of the guards sent to bring Lady Kadia.

"Lord Duke." Guard Sergeant Giarne was annoyed. Someone in his detachment had been careless, and when he found out who that had been, they'd pay. "Lady Kadia . . ." He broke off what he'd been about to say. The duke wasn't a man to blame the messenger who came with bad news, but Giarne wasn't certain how to comment honestly without offense. No one who'd known the lady had liked her and a bare statement of the sort he'd like to use wouldn't sound well in a court. He bit back "the cowardly bitch has offed herself," and substituted a more neutral statement. "My Lord Duke, the lady Kadia cannot be brought to court."

Tassino nodded to him. "And why is that, Guard Sergeant Giarne?"

The guard sergeant sounded terminally exasperated. "She's dead, my lord. Somehow, someone smuggled poison to her."

Tassino considered that. His guards were good men, loyal and sensible; they'd have kept possible conspirators away from the lady. Giarne too was a careful man and he'd have taken no chances with a possible regicide. A thought occurred to him and he asked, "Where was she being held?"

"In her own rooms, my lord duke."

The duke sighed. "Where she probably already kept poison in case anything went wrong—or perhaps for her enemies. Not the fault of you or your men, Guard Sergeant."

Giarne took a relieved breath, and the duke grinned at him before turning back to consider another problem with Varsheean and his judges.

"All right, what about Mirray? Who rules there now? The royal children are only babies, their nobles are tainted with treason, and someone has to run the damned place for the next twenty years."

Varsheean grinned cheerfully. "Maybe you should give the job to Triana and Kerrith, my lord duke. They could be regents and from what I've seen of your sister she'd do an excellent job."

Tassino was still seriously considering that when his visitors left Surah.

*T*hey made camp early that night, feeling that they were able to relax at last. They ate slowly, talking, arguing over small portions of the events of which they'd been a part, commenting on some of the people involved, mourning Dharvath, and hours went by while they gossiped about what might happen later in Surah and Shallahah. Soon they would not be together, but while they were they'd enjoy their companionship, and the warmth of being the friends that they'd become. Eilish, Sirado, and Trasso were also mourning the death of Roshan. Even Hailin appeared to have been subdued by the death of his fellow servant, Sirado thought. The man wasn't quite so self-involved so he'd believed him to be.

It was well after moonrise, as they sat or sprawled around the small fire, that Sirado took up the small stringed instrument he'd borrowed from Kait.

"I have made a song, a small song of no great value, yet perhaps you would care to hear it?"

Many voices assured him that they would.

"I call it 'The Questing Road.'" He began to play softly, and then he sang.

Long the road and dark the way,
Under a foreign sun.
Hard the way and cruel the fight,
Before our Quest was done.

But friends we found along the way,
To keep our spirits bright,
Those in another land were still—
Companions in the Light.

It matters not the shape or breed,
The color or the kind,
What counts is that 'gainst dark they stood,
With us in heart and mind.

As one we fought, together stood,
'Til Right and Light both shone.
Now home we take the path again,
From quests that we have won.

The friends we found along quest's road,
Live on within our minds,
Reminding us of this one truth—
Shape or color, pawed or hoofed,
Our hearts make us one kind.

He ended with a long, soft, lingering chord before setting the instrument aside. In silence all went to their tasks before seeking their bedding. Sirado's "small song of no great value" had spoken for them all. There was no more that needed to be said that night.

After they broke camp the next morning, Kait and Tiah rode silently for the first few miles. They had loved Dharvath; now they must return to tell Kait's clan that their old, and much loved, priestess would not return to them and how she had died. The shayana had mourned the old woman in the shrine at Surah and prayed before the altar. Yet now their road lay homeward, and without volition their spirits began to rise.

Varsheean and Katchellin had left on the ship. The spy-master needed to be home to report to his king, and he'd have work for Katchellin once that was done. Orla stayed with the remainder of the riders while they traveled along the foothills toward the place where the plains' wise one had said that they would find their departure. They halted where she ordered, and Orla moved to stand before them.

"Pasht, Lady." Her hands rose. "Those to whom you prom-ised a gate home are come. Let you give them leave to depart." There was a shadow, a glint, and out of nothing handfuls of green gems poured about Ashara's feet. She gathered them up laughing, hearing a voice speak softly.

"Go in peace, go in friendship with gifts to share among you. There can be no return, but know that you and your deeds shall be remembered."

The air broke open like curtains drawing apart, and beyond they could see familiar mountains, the silver glimmering of a far river. Home! Ashara was first through with a whoop. Yoros fol-lowed, while Kyrryl hung back to smile at those who remained.

"I'll remember you all too. I'll have the gems made into jewelry we'll wear and that will be a treasure for our house. Ashara will write the tale of these days here for us and for her parents to hold in our keep's muniments room forever. We knew there were other worlds. I never knew that I would find friends there." She turned and raised her hand in farewell as she crossed. The gate closed behind her.

Orla reached for the reins of her mount. "Another day's riding and there'll be fewer of us again." She reached out to stroke Kian Dae's head. "I'll be sorry to see you go, little brother." He purred approval. That was the way it should be. Who wouldn't miss a cat?

When Eilish and her group halted at dusk the next day, the portal opened for them. Orla had barely reined her mount when it appeared glowing softly in the air. She turned to bow to them.

"This time the portal opens for me. The Lady is gracious and Aycharna and I will take the short road back to the plains. You can find your own way through it to your home once we are gone. Ride safely, friends."

She nodded to her kinswoman, lifted her reins, and rode into the gate with Aycharna behind her. They were gone and the gate flickered in invitation.

Eilish sighed, looking at it. "Kyrryl and her friends got their tariling and Ashara back. We went hunting Kian Dae's sire and never found him. We'll mourn the good man we lost and we'll have to tell the keep how he died and while he had no close kin he did help to support two elderly second cousins and we should recompense them. This was meant to be a quest for fun, not a struggle between life and death." She looked at Kait and Tiah. "We've been good friends too, but we'll never see you again. Somehow I feel that we only lost without any gain in all this."

The voice that unexpectedly answered was crystal made into words. "Not so, my daughter. Some things I can give you. Before you stands Kian Dae's sire."

Eilish gasped. From the air a shape materialized. A great cat stood there, blocky of body but still with a shape that promised speed and agility as well as power. His coat was a rich gold and his eyes shone the same green gold of the Aradians she had met. At first glance he was no more than brute strength and speed, but in his eyes as he raised his head to study her she saw intelligence. He walked toward her, reared back on his hind legs, and reached to lick Kian Dae's face. He purred thunderously, receiving a quieter echo of his own greeting in turn from Kian Dae.

"Behold, Swift Slayer, a dravencat of the high hills," the crystal voice introduced them to him. "Against the powers of darkness his kind have defenses. It may not harm them in memory of an ancient time when they stood against such powers and a great lady of their kind died to hold open the portal."

Eilish looked at Swift Slayer, who, if she'd been on foot, would have stood more than waist high on her, remembered Kian Dae's dam, an ordinary-sized cat, and shook her head.

"That isn't possible."

The laugh was the whisper of cascading crystal. "All things are possible where the power works, daughter. I called my child when I saw what might come from many choices, and your brother's cat came to him as was required to create a balance. From them they bred by power one who was a bridge to save your people and mine. Now, for the one you lost, I make recompense, since it was for my world that he died. Go in peace knowing the truth, be blessed all the days of your lives, and may your days be long in your own lands."

She gestured, and two handfuls of bright stones poured from nowhere into Kian Dae's carrysack. He squawked a mock protest, and even Pasht laughed.

The gate opened wider in invitation, and Hailin, who was

nearest, rode through quickly, furtively patting his draw-stringed sleeves. He might have lost the pouch with most of his ill-gotten gains, but, he smiled to himself, he hadn't come out of this completely empty-handed. He had the medallion, the sorcerer's bracelets, and he'd stuffed a small pouch containing a generous handful of gold coins into his sleeve toward the end of the fight. That wasn't the fortune he'd lost, but it'd buy him a prosperous small business all the same.

Sirado followed him, with Trasso, and Eilish bearing Kian Dae in his carrysack. They halted on the other side to look back and wave. They had just time to see the traders' hands raised in reply and hear voices calling farewell before the gate was gone.

Tiah looked at her heart-sister. "Let's go home, love. I haven't had a long hot bath for tendays, and I'd really like to stop riding and rest for a while."

Kait looked at where her goddess and the dravencat had stood. *"I'd* like a quieter life, shaya, but from everything that's happened to us so far, I fear that's something that we won't be getting any time soon."

She grinned to herself, sending a picture to Tiah. Nonetheless they'd acquired something they'd both find useful. She had a large pouch of valuables that had seemed to belong to no one once the fight was over—and that would provide more generous savings for their old age. She'd also remember that they owed slavemaster Treyvan something for his aid to Cleeono against them. One day she hoped that they might have a chance to repay him for Jiro's shoulder.

Tiah giggled, leaning over to take her hand as they rode. They'd lost nothing, found something—and, more important, they were going home.

ABOUT THE AUTHOR

LYN MCCONCHIE has written a number of novels. Her collaborations with Andre Norton include *The Duke's Ballad*, *The Key of the Keplian*, and *Silver May Tarnish*, all Witch World novels. Their *Beast Master's Ark* earned McConchie one of her three New Zealand's Sir Julius Vogel Awards for Best Science Fiction or Fantasy Novel; that novel was followed by *Beast Master's Circus* and *Beast Master's Quest*.

She also has written a Western novel, *South of Rio Chama*, and nonfiction, including *Farming Daze*. Her children's books, notably her Troll series, are set in her native New Zealand.

The Questing Road is her first solo fantasy novel. She lives in New Zealand, where she writes and runs a farm.